DEVOTION'S COVENANT

THE NEW PROTECTORATE: BOOK FOUR

ABIGAIL KELLY

AUTHOR'S NOTE

Devotion's Covenant is a standalone novel within the wider *New Protectorate Series* and can be read as such. However, it does contain some spoilers for other books in the series, so I recommend reading *Consort's Glory, Burden's Bonds, Strike,* and *Vital* if you'd like to avoid them. A full character directory can be found at abigailkkelly.com. Content warnings can also be found there, as well as in the backmatter of this book, alongside a glossary.

~Abigail

FULL SERIES LIST

The United Territories and Allies

ESTABLISHED 1917

The United Territories and Allies
Current borders (2044) established
in the 1917 Peace Charter.

Member territories share a common
currency and many laws, but
maintain individual sovereignty. Each
territory holds representation in the
UTA Congress and Court, found in
the United Neutral Zone.

CURRENT EVENTS

A REPORT ON THE CURRENT EVENTS OF THE UNITED
TERRITORIES AND ALLIES FROM 2044 TO PRESENT:

NOTHING HAS BEEN QUITE THE SAME SINCE THEODORE
Solbourne, sovereign ruler of the Elvish Protectorate, shocked the
world with his surprise marriage to Margot Goode, a witch and
granddaughter of the formidable Sophie Goode. They were wed
in St. Emaine's cathedral less than a year after his older sister's
abdication — another unprecedented event. The first union of an
elf to a non-elf in three generations, the young couple came
together under dire circumstances but have proven themselves to
be a force for change.

Since their groundbreaking marriage, the sovereign's cousin,
Camille Dia Solbourne, mated Viktor Hamilton, alpha of a
wealthy shifter pack previously located in San Francisco. The
sovereign couple gave their blessing to the new mating, and the
pack has since moved to the Shifter Alliance and brought the
Solbourne connection with them. Rumors continue to swirl
around a possible trade agreement between the EVP and the
Alliance — a sign of friendship from the historically isolated elves,

who have only just lifted their ban on taking mates outside of their community.

When Dr. Atria Le Roy revealed her and Dr. Ruby Goode's groundbreaking work on magical energy generation, Margot and Theodore made yet another shocking announcement: they would fully fund the research and development for the prototype m-generator in San Francisco. Dr. Le Roy, a witch and former priestess previously unknown to the public, is strongly suspected to be mated to the orcish Patrol Captain Kazimier Rione, who is rumored to be head of intelligence for the entire territory. Her and Dr. Goode's work was highly classified, and there have been unconfirmed reports that bad actors attempted to get their hands on the technology prior to its reveal to the world. This is substantiated by the mysterious disappearance of Dr. Goode, a cousin of Margot Goode.

In happier news, werewolves received formal recognition in the UTA Congress, sponsored by the Elvish Protectorate's representative, former sovereign Delilah Solbourne, nearly two centuries after their creation by Dr. Wyeth at the height of the war. A recent exhibition at the Fairmont Museum of Art became a sensation when it revealed the previously shrouded identity of the world's first were: Josephine Wyeth Beornson, the world famous illustrator and daughter of the doctor himself. The push to give weres legal recognition in tandem with the exhibition have thrown were issues into the spotlight. It's revived interest in solving the mystery of who, exactly, is ultimately responsible for their creation.

It appears that the UTA is changing rapidly, and while new alliances and unions are being made, hidden dangers and old pains are being dragged to the surface. Discontent simmers amongst the old guard even as hopes for a better, more connected future flourish elsewhere.

Since the end of the Great War, the one hundred years of violence that nearly tore the continent apart, the UTA has enjoyed a tense peace... but that could change in an instant.

CHAPTER ONE

MAY 2048 - SAN FRANCISCO, THE ELVISH
PROTECTORATE

IT WAS NOT THE FIRST TIME PETRA ZASKODNA SAT
across from a murderer. It would not be the last.

The bar wasn't filthy, not like many of the establishments
she'd frequented since she was a little girl clinging to her father's
coattails, but it had the patina of grime that came from something
other than spilled beer and sweat. It was the sticky residue of the
wretched.

No matter how well she played her role, Petra knew she would
always find her kin in the wretched.

There was something comforting about being unseen
amongst the dregs of the world. While she couldn't exactly say she
missed it, Petra liked the honesty of the people who spent their
time in bars like The Broken Tooth. Even when they lied, it was
the honest sort: mumbled assurances that they had cut back on
their drinking, outrage at being called out for cheating at poker, a
cheerful assurance that they'd have the money soon, definitely,
don't worry.

Everyone in the bar knew the secret language of those lies, so really, they weren't lies at all. Petra had learned that language early.

But in her new life, the stakes were a lot higher than a simple poker game in the back of a dive bar, or even a dispute over a botched blood delivery between two upstart vampire families.

In her world, the lies she told would get her killed. Eventually. *Not tonight.*

Tonight, she relaxed in a dark corner booth Rasmus, the half-feral were who organized this meeting, had reserved for her. She pretended to nurse a glass of cheap red wine. A blues song buzzed through ancient speakers over her head and across the room. A cracked screen showed an endless loop of arena fights.

Petra canted her head to one side, scrutinizing the screen. The spray of cracks was definitely the result of a preternaturally strong fist. Or perhaps a head.

There hadn't been any fights yet, but she'd only been waiting for ten minutes. There was still plenty of time for one of the temperamental weres to start a brawl. The bar was their territory, but the other factions who called the underbelly of San Francisco home were always testing boundaries, jockeying for a better place in the hierarchy. That tension made the air endlessly combustible. Fights were inevitable and — mostly — harmless.

Her parents had lived that way. They died that way, too.

Petra ran her thumb over the thick stem of her wine glass, her gaze on the door. The bar wasn't particularly crowded and she wouldn't be familiar with the man she'd come to meet, but she couldn't help but be on alert. Demons weren't common in the city, so she figured she'd be able to spot him.

But that wasn't the only reason she scanned the bar again and again. Even with her glamour in place, she worried someone would recognize her at any moment.

When she usurped the position of San Francisco's High Priestess, she didn't anticipate the level of notoriety it would come with. She hadn't thought that far ahead. Seeing as she so rarely ventured off of cathedral grounds, it wasn't normally an issue, but when she set up a meeting with one of the most dangerous men in the entire United Territories and Allies...

The knot of unease tightened in her belly. It'd been there ever since she stepped foot in the bar and had only gotten worse as she sat waiting for a monster to show his face.

Your glamour is perfect, she assured herself for the hundredth time. It was the one thing her arrant father, unable to use magic himself, had made sure she knew how to do. He'd paid the old witch in the apartment above them to tutor her every Sunday.

"You can never have too many disguises," he'd told her with a pat to her head before he sent her upstairs.

Petra had taken that bit of advice to heart. She'd welded it to her very soul, crafting armor layer by layer, mask by mask, until she knew she could survive anything — even a meeting with Shade.

Her glamour was more meticulously crafted than the average. Most were a simple smoke screen, a shifting, unfocused image of a face, but that in itself tended to attract attention in the same way a balaclava did. No, a much more effective but infinitely more magically difficult method was to create an illusion of a completely different face.

The woman sitting in the corner booth was not Petra Zaskodna, but a cute brunette with a snubbed nose, pale skin, and dark eyes. She wore Petra's clothes, but not her robes of office. No one would think to connect the esteemed High Priestess with a beaten leather jacket, slim-fitted jeans, and sturdy snakeskin boots.

And yet...

Petra licked her lips, tasting the ghost of wine there, and casually turned her head to take in the other side of the bar. The hair rose on the back of her neck.

She was being watched.

Considering she'd spent the last three years under near-constant, hidden surveillance, she knew the feeling well.

Her heart beat a quicker rhythm, but she was careful not to

breathe too quickly or change her expression as she observed the patrons of the bar weaving around tables. She'd been busy watching the entrance, thinking that Shade would waltz in at any moment, so she hadn't done more than give the back of the bar a cursory look when she arrived.

Now she peered closer, into the smoky shadows that nearly obscured a beaten up pool table. A single light shaded by dusty stained glass hung over the table. Its glow barely penetrated the gloom in that far corner and, as she watched, it flickered, as if it struggled against the shadows.

It hadn't been that dark when she arrived.

She remembered seeing a few men gathered around, drunkenly arguing over what counted as hustling when she took her seat. The light was brighter then, and the glow of a branded neon sign had illuminated the far wall. At some point in the ten minutes she'd been there, it had been extinguished.

Petra's gaze flickered across the bar again, searching for vaguely familiar faces.

The men were gone. No one sat at the high tables closest to the pool table's dim alcove.

Petra's fingers curled reflexively around the stem of her wine glass. The knot of unease hardened into a stone, a heaviness in the pit of her stomach, as the sensation of being watched hardened into the certainty that she was being hunted.

She knew that feeling well, too.

Carefully — oh-so-carefully — Petra turned her attention back to the alcove. It didn't matter how hard she strained to see into the shadows. She couldn't make out anything beyond the center of the pool table, lit with jaundiced light.

It flickered once. Twice.

It went out.

Fight or flight instincts surged. The sound of the drunken crowd, the tinny blues music, the clank of glasses on the tables — all of it was muffled as every survival instinct strained to find the predator in the dark.

A pair of amber eyes flickered into being, twin flames struck into existence in the time between heartbeats. They peered back at her.

Petra didn't jump. Not exactly. Rather, she stiffened all at once, each muscle seizing until she was completely frozen there in the tacky booth, her fingers locked around her wine glass.

She couldn't look away. She knew those were eyes, but she struggled to accept it. In the darkness, they appeared to glow with an unnatural light — liquid metal heated to such a degree that they had their own luminescence. A light that was both beautiful and a warning not to touch.

The smoky air forced Petra to blink. When she opened her eyes again, not even a second later, the neon sign glowed faintly on the alcove's wall once more. It cast the alcove, and the man lounging in the far corner, into shades of candied violet.

The faintest rim of golden light from the rest of the bar kissed tousled curls, broad shoulders, and spread legs. It gilded his horns, too, just enough to see their wicked shape in the dark. They arched back, slightly to the side of his brow and curled, almost completely, until the sharp tips brushed his hair.

One hand held a whiskey glass to his lips. The other lifted, two fingers curling, to beckon her into the dark.

"Are you sure?" Rasmus had asked her again when she'd arrived at the bar. The man didn't owe her anything, but he tried to look out for her in his own gruff way. *"You know how dangerous that demon is, right?"*

Yes, she knew. Even though she'd been more or less out of the criminal world since it made her an orphan, she knew people.

And every one of those people feared Shade.

Petra forced her fingers to relax, to let go of the wine glass. They cramped. The rest of her did, too, as she consciously tried to ease the tension in her shoulders, her thighs, even in her face.

You're dealing with bigger predators than him, she thought, flattening her palms on the tabletop. *Buck up, buttercup.*

She stood up and shimmied, as gracefully as she could, out of the booth. Each step felt heavier than the last, but she worked hard to keep her expression neutral, her gait even, as she rounded an empty table. Her gaze remained locked on the demon, who casually sipped from his glass. There was barely enough light to see his face, but she got the sense that he was smiling.

Everything in her, every lesson she'd learned on the streets and animal instinct, balked as she crossed into that alcove.

But Petra didn't stop. She kept walking, measured and steady, around the abandoned pool table, toward him.

He'd commandeered the only table in the alcove — a small, square thing barely big enough for a couple of drinks. It was framed by two chairs on either side, turned to face the pool table but angled just enough so one could have a conversation with the person in the opposite seat.

Petra eyed the set-up, assessing possible escape routes and the distance between the chairs. Perhaps he'd chosen the chairs for the same reason she'd requested a booth from Rasmus: when dealing with a predator, it was always best practice to keep one's back to a wall.

Unfortunately, *she'd* chosen the booth because it was private but also easily viewable by the rest of the bar. *His* choice was tucked completely out of sight. If no one wandered by — and she doubted they would — then they might as well have been in their own private room.

Cold sweat dewed on the back of her neck, beneath her fall of glamoured hair. *Shit.*

The demon dwarfed both the seat and the table. Even his glass looked small in his clawed hand. He wasn't even in his shadow form and she was certain he could kill her with one strike. She got the peculiar sense that she was seeing an illusion, and that the *real* demon was bigger, more monstrous than the man before her. All that wild energy was compressed, a spring ready to release at any moment and reveal the true face of the monster.

That was a good thing, she reassured herself as she sat in the empty chair. Petra needed someone deadly. The gods knew her enemies were.

The demon rested his drink on his thigh. The large ice cube in the center clinked against the glass as he assessed her with those amber-on-black eyes.

This close, she could just make out the general shape of his features. They were even, symmetrical. High cheekbones and proud brow. His skin was pale in the faint light of the neon sign and his smile...

His smile was a thing of nightmares.

It unspooled slowly, like the drawing of a blade across a whetstone. She swore she could hear it, that distinctive *shwick* of metal on stone — a promise of pain in a sound, a *look*.

The tip of his tongue danced along the edge of a sharp incisor. He said nothing, but something in the way the dark fringe of his lashes lowered over those horrible eyes made her hackles rise.

Normal people felt the impulse to fill the quiet. They hated the sound of their own thoughts. When faced with someone like Shade, they probably felt compelled to say *something*, anything at all, to fill the silence and assure themselves that he was actually like them. If they said something, he'd reply. That meant they didn't need to be so scared, right? It was the impulse of the sheep assuring itself that the disguised wolf couldn't be a wolf, no matter how odd its wool looked.

But Petra knew the game. She didn't say a word.

After a full minute had passed, the demon's smile widened into a grin. The sight of it was made all the more unsettling by the fact that he had a beauty mark above his lip. She wasn't sure why it bothered her, only that it did.

Looking at her in a way that could only be interpreted as taking her measure, he said, "You left your drink."

Her muscles coiled again. Shade's voice was not the cold, flat thing she expected. It was a deep, unabashed southern *drawl*.

"I'll get another," she lied.

Her stomach dropped at the sight of his widening grin. She'd always thought that the phrase *the cat that got the cream* was an exaggeration for run of the mill smugness, but looking at *that* smile...

The demon set the glass on the table between them. "How about we share?"

Petra didn't spare the drink a glance. "No, thank you."

He settled back in his seat, broad shoulders rounding in a careless slouch as his legs spread. They were long enough that the one closest to her nearly brushed her knee. Petra didn't give in to the impulse to move away, but she wanted to.

"Why not?"

"I don't drink hard liquor."

"Why?"

Because it's dangerous to get drunk around a predator. Because I can't afford to walk back into the temple even a little buzzed. Because if my parents hadn't ended up shot, they would have died in a bar, bottles in hand.

"Because I don't like the taste."

The demon said nothing. He pinched the tip of his tongue between his teeth and watched her, his big body as still as a corpse.

At length, he asked, "And what's your name, pretty thing?"

"Didn't Rasmus tell you?"

"Rasmus tells me a lot of things. I'd be stupid to believe even a fraction of them."

That, she had to admit, was wise. Rasmus Adams was a good man — deep, *deep* down — but he was only trustworthy if you squinted. Or if you planned on giving him something he wanted. In her case, she was desperate enough to do a bit of squinting as well as giving him what he wanted.

Or rather, *who* he wanted.

"My name's Zenna," she told him, shoulders relaxed and tone *just* the right amount of nervous.

Shade picked up the drink again. Speaking against the rim, he murmured, "And what do you need from me, pretty Zenna?"

"I need information on someone. The kind you could only

get if you... say, hypothetically, broke into their suite and hacked their computers." She sucked in a deep breath as discreetly as she could. "Could you do that?"

He swallowed a sip and set the glass back down, closer to her side of the table than before. "Is that all? I'm a little insulted. You called for a racehorse when it sounds like an ass would suffice."

"An ass wouldn't qualify for this race, I promise," she replied.

"And why's that?"

"Because the man I need information on is..." Petra paused, trying to think of a way to describe him that encompassed just how dangerous he could be. "...influential. Incredibly influential. And paranoid. If I could pay someone like Rasmus to do it, I would, but I don't think they'd take the job — or live to collect."

Shade tipped his head against the grimy wall. His throat was a beautiful arch. A perfect ridgeline of muscle and bone stretching out from the black collar of his dress shirt. His lips pursed. "Mm, sounds very dramatic. Did you take acting classes when you were a kid? Bet you made a real cute Dorothy or some shit."

Petra breathed through her nose twice, fighting the urge to show him her teeth. "It's the truth."

"Now, why should I believe that?"

"What?"

In slow, languid movements, the demon rose from his seat to tower over her. For the first time since she spotted him, she noticed that he wore a black on black suit, neatly tailored and minimalist. It seemed at odds with the mop of curls on his head and yet also perfectly *him*.

When he stepped away from his chair, Petra's middle tightened, preparing her to stand up as well, to stop him from leaving until he heard her offer. Her desperation was almost tangible, oozing out of her pores like stale sweat.

Before she could launch herself out of her chair, he stepped up to her knees and casually pushed them to one side with the back of his hand.

Petra watched, bewildered, as he hiked up his slacks and

dropped into a crouch before her. At last they were at eye level —
and far, far too close.

The air between them wavered, just for a moment, as her
magic crackled to life in response to the threat. Petra clutched the
tacky armrests of the chair. *Rein it in!*

Being a luminist, a witch with the ability to manipulate light,
was all well and good until one lost their temper. Then things
tended to catch fire. Normally, she kept fantastic control on her
magic and tried to lean on that rigid self-discipline as she grappled
with her emotions.

She failed, though. She could tell by the way his eyebrows rose
and that smile made another appearance.

Reaching across her body to snag the glass from the table, he
sighed, "Now... I'll be the first to say there's nothing wrong with
lyin'. I love to lie. I try to do it every day." He swirled his drink
with one hand while the other found a home on the armrest just
behind hers, overlapping their limbs until he'd made a cage out of
his body.

"But the thing is, Zenna, when it comes to clients, I don't like
liars. There's only ever room for one of those in any relationship, I
reckon, and since I'm the more skilled party here..." He tipped the
glass toward her. "Why don't you drink hard liquor?"

He's fucking with me, she realized. The thought scalded her.
He *had* been fucking with her, probably from the very first word
out of his mouth.

If her spine got any stiffer, she worried the entire column
would shatter. Speaking through her teeth, all pretense stripped
away, she answered, "Lots of reasons. Most pertinent being that I
can't risk it."

He took a deliberate sip. His eyes never left hers as he collected
a drop from the rim with the tip of his tongue. "Does this look
spiked to you?"

"Why would you spike a potential client's drink?" Petra tried
to rein in her tartness, but it was hard when she needed this so
desperately and he was just... *provoking* her. There wasn't any

damn time for games. "I'm not worried about you drugging me. I can't afford to have my senses dulled."

"I don't have any plans to hurt you." Those glowing eyes went heavy-lidded. "Yet."

Petra's temper got the better of her at last. Leaning closer, until they were almost nose to nose, she whispered, "Believe it or not, demon, you *aren't* the boogeyman I'm afraid of."

She didn't expect him to move away, but she also didn't anticipate he'd tilt his head to one side and suck in a deep, noisy breath. As he did it, movement drew her eye over his shoulder — to the writhing shadows that blanketed the pool table and floor all around him.

"Now *that,*" he murmured on his exhale, "is the truth. Stupid of you, but honest."

CHAPTER TWO

Petra eased back. It meant he won, but she didn't care. She wasn't scared of Shade, not really, but she also didn't have any particular desire to die by shadow strangulation that night, either. "What? Did you *smell* it on me?"

"No, I just like the way you smell." Before she could dwell too deeply on that, he asked, "What's your name?"

Her mouth went dry. It was useless to lie again, seeing as he somehow knew she'd given him a fake one, but that didn't mean she had to give him an answer. "I'd rather keep that to myself. You don't need it to take the job."

"Need it? 'Course not." Shade's attention drifted over her face, down her throat, to examine her jacket and plain blue shirt underneath. "I don't *need* anything. I don't need this job. I don't need this whiskey. I don't need your name. I don't need to see your real face." His gaze traveled back up to fix her with a look so flat, so bland, it managed to unsettle her more than that violent smile. "But I want it."

"And I want a man of reasonable skill and a healthy disregard for danger to help me before someone puts a bolt in the back of my head," she shot back.

Shade had the gall to *roll his eyes.*

Petra dearly wanted to smash the whiskey glass against one of his horns, but managed to restrain herself. Speaking tightly, she asked, "Do you want the job or not?"

He shrugged. "Y'can't afford me."

"You don't know that."

It was a smirk that played around the corners of his mouth then. "I do."

"How?" she demanded. "You can't just look at a person and know—"

A claw hooked in the fabric of her shirt, just beneath the collar. Before she could think to fight him, he'd tugged until her ear was level with his lips and she could feel the stale air of the bar against the sweaty skin between her breasts. Her gold necklace, the one she'd been too stupid to take off, dangled between them. She could smell his breath, the tang of whiskey and something uniquely him. He didn't wear cologne. His scent was subtle, raw. Oddly compelling.

His lips didn't quite touch the shell of her ear, but she could feel them moving against flyaway strands of her hair when he whispered, "Not even San Francisco's High Priestess makes enough to afford me."

A wave of nausea nearly made her sway in her seat. *How does he know?* She'd fucked up somewhere, somehow. "I don't know what you're talking about. I have an inheritance. A very, very large inheritance. I haven't touched a dime. I swear I can pay you whatever you charge me." Backed into a corner, she couldn't help but let a bit of her real desperation into her voice when she added, "You can have all of it."

He didn't move. For a long time, his only reply was another deep breath and slow exhale.

"You're scared."

"Yes."

There was no use in denying it. She'd been scared since the day she received the ashes in the mail: a neat little box with a plastic lining and a flimsy plastic plaque glued on the lid.

Maximilian Dooraker, High Priest of Glory's Temple. Death in dutiful service. - 1856-2044

She wasn't sure what tipped her off, but something in his demeanor changed. Shade eased back, but he didn't give her space. Instead, he gripped her jaw with one large, clawed hand and turned her head to better peer into her face.

She jolted at the contact, her skin burning with a sudden defensive flush. The air shimmered again, more violently this time, as her magic screamed outward from the core of her being to press against the surface of skin — begging for release.

"There she is," he whispered, apparently untroubled by the way the air between them had heated to an almost unbearable degree. She could see him a little better, lit as he was by her own burgeoning glow. Too bad it made him *more* intimidating, not less.

Shade rubbed his thumb against her jaw as if he wanted to test the texture of her skin, or perhaps in fascination with the way it cast its own weak light. "The goddess's own flesh," he said, lips curled in that mocking smile. "Isn't that what they say in those press releases? *The rising star of Glory's Temple.* San Francisco's personal sunshine. And yet here she is, practically in the lap of a *demon.* How very scandalous of you, High Priestess. You shouldn't be here. Don't you know what kind of monsters play in the dark?"

Petra's breath sawed in and out of her chest. Despair crashed into anger and then mortification. The urge to cry humiliated her almost as much as his mockery.

She didn't care what Shade or anyone else thought of her. She didn't even care about whatever bullshit fluff the Temple's overzealous PR department put out about her.

All she came for, all she had existed for since the day she received those ashes in the mail was the truth. And she was wasting what little time she had left to get it on a man who had never intended to help her in the first place.

Cautiousness burned away. She slapped his wrist with the back of her hand, dislodging his grip on her jaw. "Let me go."

"No."

Petra kept her hands away from the wooden chair, afraid she might accidentally ignite it, but she felt no such compunction in regards to Shade's suit.

He let her grab his lapel, playful interest glittering in his lambent eyes. It smoldered under her palm. When thin tendrils of smoke began to mix with the clouds of cigarette smoke in the air, she bit out, "Let me *go.*"

"Are you going to burn me alive, little goddess?"

"Yes. If I have to." Petra tugged him close to whisper in a clipped, flat voice, "It's not like I haven't done it before."

It had been a long time, but she knew how to defend herself. Pushed to it, Petra could be a monster all on her own.

She was quickly learning that Shade didn't disguise his thoughts behind a mask. His expressions were mercurial, the variations of his smile endless. When he looked at her then, it was with a grin that was positively *wolfish.* "It won't look very good to your adoring worshippers to see their favorite priestess running away from the scene of a crime, would it?"

"They wouldn't know it was me."

"They wouldn't?" He lifted his glass to his lips again and took a long sip. "You're awfully recognizable."

"No, I'm not—" The words died on her tongue.

There, hanging on either side of their faces, was her curtain of blonde hair.

Petra released him with a hard shove, but he didn't do more than a slight rocking back on his haunches. His laughter grated against her pride like broken glass.

She hadn't even felt the glamour's release. Too late she recalled the way he'd rubbed her skin — no doubt wiping away the carefully concealed, skin-tone sigilwork she'd painted there to anchor the spell.

Petra stood quickly enough to send her chair back into the wall with a dull *thunk*.

A burning desire to say something, anything, to wipe that smug look off of his pretty face ate away at her gut, but she'd already wasted too much time and effort on him.

Casting the demon a scathing look, she made to step around him, toward the small door that led to the staff area.

Except she couldn't move.

Shadows coiled around her legs, holding fast, as Shade took a leisurely stroll around her. He leaned against the pool table, drink in hand, and gave her another knife-like grin.

"Tell me your name."

Already caught and too angry to care, Petra blazed bright in the artificial darkness he'd summoned. *"Fuck you."*

He clicked his tongue. "Stubborn. I like that. Can cause some trouble, though. I like that, too."

She wanted to hit him. She wanted to hit him and hit him and hit him until she couldn't lift her arm anymore. "If you were never going to take the job, then why are you even here? Why are you doing this?"

"I never said I wasn't gonna take the job," he replied, "only that you can't afford my fee. Even if you think you can, I don't want your money."

All at once, the wildfire inside her went up in smoke. "What do you want?"

"Tell me why you're so scared and maybe I'll share."

The urge to hit him came back with a vengeance. Speaking through her teeth, she explained the situation a bit like she was speaking to an unruly five year old. "The man I need information on is powerful within the Gloriae."

He almost looked disappointed. "So you're worried about losing your cushy job."

That almost startled a laugh out of her. *Worried about my job?* Gods, she never even wanted it in the first place. The only reason she joined the Temple was because of Max and the only reason she became San Francisco's High Priestess was to discover what happened to him.

Despite what everyone around her thought, Petra Zaskodna wasn't ambitious. She was a survivor so exhausted by treading water she'd resigned herself to drowning. A rat who'd chosen to get on a sinking ship.

All at once, the fight bled out of her. Petra closed her eyes, her glow dimming until it vanished completely, like a candle snuffed by the darkness that held her. "Can you do it or not?"

He frowned, eyes narrowing. "'Course I can." The bastard didn't even give her time to feel relief before he added, "But I want something more valuable than money in return."

Dread trickled, drop by drop, into her veins. "What?"

The demon swirled his drink, mostly melted ice now. All the while, she could feel his shadows creeping up her legs, the ghost of a touch, until they'd wrapped around her waist. She forced herself to keep still, not to panic at the feeling of delicate constriction. "I've heard rumors that you have connections to a certain Sovereign's Consort."

She didn't need to think about it. "Absolutely not."

"You don't even know what I want from her," he protested without heat, as if he *knew* she'd react vehemently and thought it was awfully funny.

"I don't care what it is, you aren't getting to Margot or the sovereign through me."

She might've been a liar. She might have conned her way into being San Francisco's High Priestess. She might have forged a relationship with Margot Goode on a pretense, to dig for information on the Elvish Protectorate's involvement in Max's death.

But she was damn loyal to the people who earned it.

Margot considered her a friend. They were both new to the city, and though they were witches with vastly different backgrounds, there was a connection between them that had blossomed into a friendship. Constrained by her quest and the lies it forced her to tell, Petra hadn't been able to give that relationship the amount of herself it deserved, but that didn't mean she would throw Margot under the bus.

Shade rolled his eyes again. "I don't want her liver. I just want access to the m-generator." He paused. "Or its blueprints. Either one."

Petra only vaguely understood what he was talking about. A week or so prior, the media had been set aflame by the news that there'd been a breakthrough in the field of m-energy — the study of magic and its use as a clean energy source.

People had been trying to figure out a way to capture magic from the atmosphere for at least a thousand years, so it was big news when an unknown witch announced that she and her research partner — another Goode, *surprise, surprise* — had solved the problem with a state-of-the-art generator.

There'd been some hubbub about the EVP volunteering to completely fund the first prototype right there in San Francisco, as it was a city that had historically suffered due to the destructive nature of atmospheric magic. At that point, Petra had stopped paying attention.

Even so, she knew enough to understand that there was no way on Burden's green Earth she would be able to get Shade anywhere *near* that prototype.

"I can't do that," she sighed, more exhausted with every second that passed. "I really can't. Even if I would *ever* put Margot in the same room as you, it still wouldn't work. That generator will be the single most intensely guarded thing on the entire continent."

Although Margot might be a close second. She shuddered to imagine what the sovereign would do if he found out she'd allowed a man like Shade anywhere near her. She had a teeny-tiny soft spot for elves, but that didn't mean she was stupid. The sovereign could pop her head off her shoulders as easily as a kid's fist crushes a to-go yogurt.

Shade made a sucking sound with his teeth. "Ah, it was worth a try. Good thing I want something else, then."

Pushing back on the pool table, he stood up straight and closed the distance between them. Shadows crawled up his legs, too, but they didn't stop at his waist. Instead, the tendrils slithered up his arms and around his chest to consume his whole body up to the neck. There they stayed, moving restlessly along the base of his throat, as if they had a mind of their own.

"Tell me your name." This time there was no playful note in his drawl.

"Why? You know it."

He blinked slowly, once, but his expression didn't change. He was very still. "I want you to give it to me."

She could only stare at him. This meant something. The entire conversation had been an assessment of her, and now she felt like she was being tested on a subject she didn't even know if she'd studied.

"Petra," she rasped, at a loss. "My name is Petra."

And there was that slow, violent smile again. Her heart beat faster at the sight of it. She couldn't tell if her body wanted her to run away from it or, for reasons she couldn't possibly comprehend, run *toward* it.

The shadows curled around her right hand. She watched, disconcerted, as they lifted it up just in time to accept his nearly empty drink.

Using two fingers, Shade guided the glass to her mouth. It rested there, cool and wet from his lips, when he murmured, "There's a good girl. Now drink."

For the life of her, Petra couldn't understand why she did it, but she did.

There was hardly any alcohol left. It was the aftertaste of whiskey that touched her tongue, carried by a sip of cool water. Whiskey and something like... him.

Shade's gaze lingered on her for a moment, the look in his eyes completely inscrutable, before he stuffed his hands in his pockets and stepped around her. Had she passed the test or failed?

She had no idea, but something told her he'd *won*.

The shadows followed him, drawn like the ends of a cloak toward his body and away from her in a slow, steady drag. Something deep and neglected in her stirred at the sensation even as her arm, bereft of his support, fell limp by her side. The cool glass dangled from numb fingers.

"You're leaving?" she croaked.

"Sure am." He passed her. On his way, he pulled one hand out of his pocket to flick her hair off her shoulder.

Petra whirled around. "But you didn't say what you wanted?"

He gave her a pitying look, like he thought she was a little slow on the uptake. "Didn't I?"

"No, you didn't."

"Hm." He kept walking. Shadows pulled away from the walls, the table, the floor. Like miles of black gossamer, they folded and draped and slithered back to him.

Petra watched with wide eyes. She'd met demons before, but never one who could manipulate shadows like *that*.

"Wait," she gasped, lunging for his arm. "Are you going to help me or not?"

Shade patted her hand once before he pried her fingers off of him, one by one. "I'll help you, but right now I'm leavin'."

"How can I get a hold of you?"

"You don't."

She was very, very close to stomping her snakeskin boot. Or crying. Either one. Maybe both. "How is this supposed to *work?*"

Shade cast her a boyish smile over his shoulder. "You don't get a hold of me and you don't do the work. That's my job. Don't worry, little goddess, I'll find you."

Petra could only watch, helpless and confused, as those long legs took him out of the bar. Behind her, the lamp flickered back to life.

CHAPTER THREE

SILAS CHOSE HIS SEAT IN THE PEWS OF ST. EMAINE'S cathedral carefully. Sitting in the front row would afford him the delicious benefit of seeing his High Priestess try to ignore him up close, but sitting in the back was better for observing her when she felt at ease, in control. That was when he liked her best.

Well, maybe second best. There'd been something altogether new and intoxicating in seeing her off-kilter in the bar, too.

In the end, he split the difference by choosing neither the front nor the back. He picked a seat in the middle, on the left side of the cavernous cathedral, mostly because he enjoyed the way everyone in the pews around him squirmed.

They had no choice but to sit near him, though. There weren't exactly a bevy of options.

Silas lounged against the hard, polished wood of the pew, his arms stretched out along the back and his legs spread. He didn't need the space, but he thought it was funny how no one dared to give him a pointed look or a discreet cough in protest to his unabashed use of the cramped seating arrangements.

Dawn service hadn't even begun, but the cathedral was packed.

The scent of incense and metallic candle smoke hung in the

air, mixing with the natural musk and perfumes of countless bodies. Despite the fact that every seat was full, people still shuffled in through the towering double doors at the far end of the cathedral. They stood in the back or squeezed in around the behemoth columns that supported the arched ceiling, jockeying to get a good view of the altar.

Still, the spaces on either side of him were empty.

Silas drummed his claws on the wood, his lips quirked in a smile. All were welcome in Glory's Temple, but some were clearly more welcome than others.

It wasn't a great surprise. Although the world advanced in leaps and bounds, some superstitions were hard to shake — and some people, like him, quite enjoyed indulging in them.

Silas eyed the dark stained-glass window, easily two stories tall, that loomed over the altar. A statue of the goddess Glory, a little greater than life-sized, stood between the altar and the window, her arms outstretched and her eye sockets empty.

Candles burned all around her, casting the altar space in a flickering glow. Silas tilted his head to one side and watched as the shadows moved in response. They were a little more lively than they ought to be.

There you are.

It was funny, he thought, as the choir began to lift their collective voices in a dawn hymn, that Glory's worshippers reviled the very darkness she created — and that which would eternally be drawn to her light.

Silas's attention was drawn away from the shadows to the red and topaz-robed acolytes who filed out, one by one, from a discreet door nearly hidden by a carved and gilded wooden screen. Their lips moved with the hymn, and each one carried a hammered bronze dish in both hands. One after the other, they set the dishes on the altar and then took their places on either side of the statue, hands folded and gazes cast out into the crowd.

The sky behind the stained glass window was just beginning to lighten when he caught the first glimpse of blonde hair.

He wasn't sure why he tensed, the muscles of his abdomen contracting as if preparing for a blow, nor why he felt compelled to sit up straight, his arms rising to grip the back of the pew in front of him.

There you are, he thought again.

This wasn't the first time he'd attended her services. Even so, he was always surprised by how little fanfare came with her entrance. He expected a little more pageantry, but his prey breezed out from behind the screen with a half-smile fixed in place. A ripple went through the crowd, a sudden upwelling of noise, then a thunderclap of silence descended over the cathedral as she took her place behind the altar.

She didn't even need to raise her soft hands. All Petra needed to do to command the room was lift her eyes.

Silas's grip on the pew tightened. He couldn't exactly claim to be shocked when his cock stirred. Seeing her in control of so many people was delicious.

Petra, dressed in a blood-red velvet robe and white dress with a neckline so deep, it nearly touched her navel, raised her hands in a welcoming gesture. Silas swore he could *hear* the people around him holding their breath.

"It is a blessed dawn," she announced, "as all new days are, when we live to greet them."

A hushed murmur filled the air, mumbles of agreement and recognition. Silas narrowed his eyes. He generally considered the gods only good enough to go fuck themselves, so he wasn't exactly a regular worshipper, but he got the impression that her greeting wasn't the standard opening sentiment. It never was. Every service he'd attended was a little different, a little more... weighty. Something in how she spoke seemed constantly layered, as if she were having several different conversations with the crowd at once and all of them were of the gravest importance.

Maybe that was a symptom of all the masks she wore over that striking face, an ability to say something different with every one.

It was a remarkable talent that made every worshipper believe she was speaking directly to *them*.

Petra Zaskodna was a liar, but she was a deeply compelling one.

Silas watched her move through the motions of accepting the offerings on the table, all of them donated by worshippers seeking favors from the gods. All the while, she spoke in that calm, carrying voice about not taking Glory's gift of life-giving light for granted, and how that light existed in every life, every relationship, every choice made throughout the day.

As usual, he only half-listened, since he found the sentiment rather trite, but he enjoyed the sound of her voice and her graceful, practiced movements as she blessed the offerings.

The sunrise crept into the panes of the stained glass window behind her and those that loomed over the pews, inch by inch. Each welded shard of glass, once dark, blazed with color — candy yellow, violet, navy, orange, and electric teal. Colors splashed down around her, crowning her golden head in a wreath of rainbow light, even as *she* began to glow.

It was almost unnoticeable at first, but he saw it. It was his favorite part of her services and the image that glowed on the backs of his eyelids when he tried to sleep.

Silas inched forward on the uncomfortable bench, his gaze fixed on her striking features, refusing to miss even a second of her glorious transformation. It still annoyed him that she'd hidden her face under an impressively complex glamour the night before.

It was cute, the way she thought he wouldn't know exactly who he was dealing with, and the face she'd crafted wasn't bad. But *this* face. *This* woman...

Silas bit the tip of his tongue as he watched her tanned skin begin to radiate its own light — gentle at first, then a blaze. The air over the crowd's heads heated until a wave of summer heat crested over them, stirring hair and loosely clutched shawls. He wasn't the only one at the edge of his seat when the white-hot shape of her bones radiated from beneath her skin.

She was magnificent.

She was *terrifying*.

His blood rushed so fast in his veins that he couldn't hear the rest of her service. He watched her set the kindling at the base of Glory's statue aflame with a single touch and wondered how much she'd restrained herself when she simply scorched his lapel.

His little goddess was pure, destructive magic.

Exactly what I need.

The dawn service was quick, designed to be enjoyed before the start of a busy day, and all too soon it was over. A long line of worshippers shuffled into the red carpet that delineated the center aisle, waiting for their turn to approach Petra as she stood in front of the altar, offering bowl in hand.

While she was occupied, Silas slipped out from his row and cut a swath through the crowd, which couldn't decide between staying for a longer look at the High Priestess or leaving as quickly as possible.

It would have been a pain to get through if people didn't hurry to get out of his way, usually at the cost of those around them.

He strode confidently toward the front of the cathedral, his gaze trained on the wooden screen and its hidden door. Realistically, he knew all he had to do was wait for Petra to notice him and he'd have her undivided attention. He didn't *have* to sneak into the bowels of the cathedral, let alone at the busiest time of the day.

But where was the fun in that?

Worshippers swarmed the marble floor in front of the altar, either waiting for their turn or stopping to light one of the hundreds of candles in the bronze racks on either side of it.

Acolytes milled around, speaking quietly to people who sought them out and, perhaps unknowingly, guarded the way to the door.

Silas stopped by one of the racks. He glanced to his right and was a tiny bit put out that Petra hadn't noticed him yet. She was engrossed in a hushed conversation with an old woman, their heads bent as they spoke about whatever it was people who believed in bullshit cared about.

He lingered there by the candles for a while, until a middle-aged dragon wandered up, wings folded against his back, to light a candle with his own breath and whisper a prayer into the blue flame.

Silas stepped around the dragon and, with a tiny nudge of a shadow, sent the entire rack tumbling into him. Tea candles in small violet glasses tumbled down the dragon's front and onto the floor with a fiery clatter. Shouts of alarm went up at the same time the dragon's clothes did.

Speaking in a mild voice, he said, "Someone should really weigh those racks down."

One of the acolytes went running for a fire extinguisher while another tried to help the vexed dragon pat out the flames. While they worked, the red runner that led to the altar caught fire as well. The shouts got a little louder.

Silas slipped behind the screen.

CHAPTER FOUR

HE WATCHED QUIETLY FROM HIS SHADOWED CORNER AS Petra closed the door to her wood-paneled office. It was fascinating, seeing her set aside a mask.

Even after handling the fiasco he'd created, Petra Zaskodna, High Priestess of Glory's Temple, stood tall and regal... right up until the door clicked into place. Then she became something else. Something a little smaller, a little dimmer, as her shoulders rounded and her forehead dropped against the polished wood.

She reminded him a bit of a dove sitting peacefully on a ledge, unaware that a cat lurked just behind her.

Silas wanted to see her wings flap a little.

"D'you know that your office is bugged?"

He couldn't help but smile at the way she jumped. *Flap-flap.* Even the big blue eyes she turned in his direction reminded him of a pretty bird.

To her credit, she didn't do what most normal people did when they found him lurking in a place he ought not to be. Rather than immediately demand to know what he was doing there — a question no good criminal ever answered, surely — Petra drew herself up and watched him silently for several seconds.

"You must be mistaken," she answered in a tone that made it obvious she did not, in fact, think he was mistaken.

Silas's cheek cramped. It did that the previous night, too. It was a result of smiling so much, but it was hard not to grin when one held something so very entertaining in the palm of their hand.

She'd drawn up another mask, slightly different from the one she wore behind the altar. This one wasn't quite as warm. It was still regal, though, like she was a pretty queen staring down her long, sloping nose at a peasant who'd wandered where he shouldn't.

That was the kind of look that made him want to see her beg.

"There's no need to worry," he lied, "I've disabled them."

That, at least, wasn't a lie. He had disabled the six audio and visual surveillance devices he'd found hidden in her office.

Obviously, she still needed to worry, though, because now she was alone with him.

"You *what?*" Petra's face went very blank and disconcertingly pale. "Why would you do that?"

Silas stepped away from the corner to examine her cluttered desk. It was the kind that folded up, allowing its owner to lock everything away when they weren't using it. Petra hadn't, though, perhaps because she felt safe with her surveillance, or because she had nothing to hide.

Or, he amended, peering at her stricken expression from beneath his lashes, *she knows she's being watched by someone else and a lock won't keep her safe.*

The desk's fold-out writing surface was littered with small bits of paper, a sketch pad covered in sigil variations, and an old tablet. He plucked the sketchpad up and examined her work. "D'you want me to leave them on?"

"Yes," she answered immediately.

Silas turned the sketchpad. He couldn't make horns or tails out of what she was trying to accomplish with them. Distracted, he asked, "Why?"

"*Because* disabling them means that the person who put them there will know *I* know they exist." The heavy velvet of her robe rustled. The sound of her engaging a lock came next, a moment before her white, soft-soled slippers whispered across the floor. "You shouldn't even be here."

He turned the sketchbook the other way. "I go where I want. I disable surveillance equipment when I want. If you have a problem with that, then you should have said something."

"If I'd known you would show up here, I would have!" Petra snatched the sketchbook out of his hand. Her cheeks had gone a dark pink and her eyes, cornflower blue rather than the golden brown they'd been the night before, glowed with a ring of fire.

He wondered if she knew that the glamour hadn't been able to suppress that. If she didn't, then he certainly wasn't going to tell her.

"What're those for?" he asked, unbothered by her anger. People got angry at him all the time. "Those sigils aren't good for any type of spell or ward work I've ever seen."

And he would know. He was one of the best sigilworkers in the world. Maybe *the* best, if one didn't count Ruby Goode and a few crotchety old witches in Hong Kong. The only leg up he had on them, of course, was his lack of ethical boundaries. Otherwise they'd kick his ass six ways from Sunday.

"They're *marriage* sigils," she answered, hissing through her teeth like a fierce animal. He liked it when she did that.

Silas shamelessly poked around her desk some more, picking up papers and testing pens before discarding them as haphazardly as he found them. "Useless, you mean."

Demons didn't do frivolous displays like ceremonies and useless, nonsense sigils carved into their foreheads to declare ownership over a mate. They just *took* one. They wrapped their shadows around them, owned them, worshipped them.

If anyone had anything to say about that, then they also probably had a death wish, because nothing, even in his extensive experience, was more dangerous than a demon protecting their mate.

"They aren't useless. They're reminders— You know what, I'm not going to debate this with you. What are you doing here?"

"To make our deal, obviously." He glanced over his shoulder. "D'you want me to turn the mics back on?"

"It's too late now," she answered, a grave note of exhaustion in her voice.

He wasn't stupid enough to actually take them *out,* but he wanted to see what she'd do if she thought he had. Silas initially suspected that they belonged to her — paranoia was always smart and Petra Zaskodna was, if nothing else, *smart* — but her distress felt genuine. There were no lies this time.

Petra hadn't bugged her own office, but she knew *someone* had.

Silky red curtains partially obscured a small, diamond-paneled window. Silas fingered the material as he watched her set the sketchpad back on the desk. It was so fine as to be almost imperceptible, but a tremor shook her hand.

The smell of fear, faint but sour, pierced the cloud of sunshine and rich incense that filled the air around her. Silas frowned. *I don't like that.*

His brother was always telling him he needed to be more conscious of other people's feelings, but Silas argued that he was plenty conscious. He just didn't care. That's why it was an awfully foreign feeling, that pang of dissatisfaction he experienced when that sour scent singed his nose.

"Who bugged your office?"

Petra sighed. "Tell me what you want, Shade."

Silas flicked the curtain away. Normally he found it funny when clients tried to negotiate with him or withhold information he wanted, but something about *her* doing it was... annoying.

No matter how much self-reflection his brother or his clan urged him to do, Silas never cared to examine where his impulses came from. His urges were unerringly straight lines. They didn't weave or tangle or circle around in uncertainty. He had an urge and he acted. Easy. It hadn't steered him wrong yet. Why fix a system that wasn't broken?

Those impulses, alongside a childhood promise, had brought him to San Francisco when he'd gotten wind of a suspicious bounty weeks prior to the announcement of the m-generator. They'd brought him to Petra, who unknowingly held the key to fulfilling that promise. Now they urged him to close his fist around the little goddess and hold fast, no matter how hard she squirmed to be free.

Silas canted his head to one side, fascinated by the way light from the window played across her sunshine hair and golden skin. Maybe that was why he wanted to possess her so viscerally. Demons were creatures of the dark, which meant the thing they craved most was a taste of the light.

Or the thought of having a perfect priestess, all sunshine and bite, stooping to ask for his help just made his cock hard.

Bit of both.

When he'd let the silence hang long enough to make the spark of anger reappear in her eyes, he answered, "It really would be better if you just got me into the Tower, you know."

Solbourne Tower, where the top-secret research and development of the m-generator prototype was planned to take place, was perhaps the only building in the world he couldn't break into. He'd tried, of course. Too bad the crazy bastard who built it, Thaddeus II, had been as paranoid as he was cruel. The damn skyscraper had wards pressed into every steel girder and panel of triple-reinforced glass.

He *could* get through eventually, but Silas wasn't exactly known for his patience. Using a cunning, desperate witch with good connections was much faster. *And pleasurable.*

Petra's expression tensed. "I said no."

Silas clicked his tongue against the roof of his mouth. "So loyal to your sovereign's mate. Seems a bit silly to me."

Most loyalties did. He'd never been able to get a good grasp on why people felt the need to *cling* to one another, especially when it went against their best interest.

"Margot is a friend," Petra replied, voice tight. "Now drop it."

Turning her wooden desk chair to face her, Silas plopped into it and spread his legs. He balanced the heel of his boot on the floor and twisted his ankle one way, then the other, his attention drawn to her tiny reflection in the polished leather stretched over the steel toe box. "It's cute that you think you can order me around. Does that normally work for you?"

"I'm High Priestess. Of course it does."

"Ah, but you're a scared High Priestess, aren't you? Scared enough to beg a monster for help." He dropped his foot and leaned forward to brace his elbows on his knees. "You're at *my* mercy, little goddess. Might be good to remember that."

The memory of how she'd fought him about the whiskey and how much that enhanced the urge to make her bend rose unbidden, sending a lick of flame down his spine. The way she'd looked up at him when she finally did as she was told... Yes, that was something he planned to repeat.

Silas liked having her at his mercy. A lot.

He was impressed by the way she approached him then, dressed in her service finery but holding herself like a sheathed switchblade, ready to spring at any moment. Petra stalked across the room to stand just between his knees. She looked down the slope of her proud nose with an expression of stark finality when she said, "Listen to me, demon: I don't have time to play games with you. I'm not negotiating terms. If you don't want my money, then you can *get the fuck out* of my office."

Silas couldn't help but marvel at her. *Tal is going to love her.*

His brother had been against Silas's back-up plan — which, he argued, wasn't really a *back-up* when it would lead to the generator eventually. Tal was all for murder and mayhem, but apparently this was a line even he wouldn't cross. The poor thing simply didn't have the stomach for it.

In fact, he didn't have a stomach at all.

But instinct, the straight line of his urges, told Silas he was on the right path. Petra's abysmal attitude and general lack of good sense only confirmed it. She was perfect.

"Don't you want to hear my proposal?" he asked, not even trying to keep the laughter out of his voice.

Petra's lip curled. "No."

"Too bad." Silas reached out to run the tip of one claw over the golden embroidery that decorated her white dress. She went stiff as a board, but she didn't slap his hand away like he expected her to.

Mulling over whether that pleased him or not, Silas told her, "If you can't get me the generator, then I want you."

There was a pause and then, with impressive venom, "Absolutely not."

Silas plucked at a single thread, tugging it ever-so-slightly out of place. "Calm down, little goddess. I only mean your witchbond."

Another lie.

"...You're joking."

"I find most things very funny," he replied, "but I rarely joke."

It was a thing of beauty, seeing the stunned look on her face — a face he'd seen splashed across newsreels and in press releases and in the cardstock pamphlet he'd tucked in his pocket just before the first service he'd attended. Weeks later, it was so creased from being opened too many times that he'd had to cut her picture out to preserve it. Now it lived in the breast pocket of his suit jacket.

Silas wanted to lick the shock from her parted lips and savor the taste. It was a shame when the look melted away. Petra's expression transformed into one of incredulity. He knew that expression well. It was the first one he remembered seeing on his parents' faces; the *'Silas, baby, what have you done?'* look that preceded horror.

His parents and the rest of the Cuttcombe clan were good folks, which was why they tended to look at him like a bomb put together upside down. They couldn't make sense of him, and they *definitely* couldn't disarm him.

"Why would you want that?" Petra's fingers flexed at her sides. "Do you even realize what that would *mean?*"

It was a little insulting, the way she kept thinking he didn't know things. Silas gave her a reproachful look from under the shade of his brows. "'Course I do."

"But... but a witchbond isn't something that can be undone. We'd be tied together for *life*. Why would you ask that of someone you've only just met?"

"Strictly speaking, ma'am, I've known you for a bit longer than you seem to think."

Of course he'd done his recon on high and mighty Petra Zaskodna, even before fate had dropped her in his lap so prettily. He wasn't ashamed to admit his fascination began long before he managed to find a reason for it. All it took was the sound of her throaty voice playing in a thirty-second news clip and he'd been hooked.

The fact that he'd found a justification for his fascination was not really necessary, but it was convenient.

She seemed like the easiest entry point to getting into the Tower, seeing as elves, who controlled the territory and more specifically the skyscraper, were a pain in the ass to manipulate. Not to mention the fact that people in power *always* had weaknesses to exploit. Petra was no different. In fact, he'd been watching her work with children in a community garden, attacking a clump of weeds with an incongruously grave expression, when he got the meeting request from Rasmus.

He'd felt a pang of annoyance at being pulled away from his prey, but only until he uncovered who he was actually dealing with.

Before she could recover from the revelation that he'd been watching her, Silas continued, "And a witchbond is only as permanent as life is. Who knows? You could put a bolt in my brain tomorrow. Easy fix."

"If you think I might kill you to be rid of you, why would you want this?"

Petra paused. He liked watching her mind work behind those cornflower eyes. There was an almost visible spark in them when she finally made the connection. "You wanted the generator... and now you want my witchbond because you want power."

Silas nodded. "Good girl."

"There are other ways. Other people."

His smile fell. The way she said *other people* struck a discordant note in his mind, a strike against the perfect line of his impulse. He didn't like it. He really didn't.

"I need a source of magic," he told her, voice dropping with displeasure. "M-siphons are a hassle, the generator is off-limits and untested, and I have you in the palm of my hand. Why would I use anyone else?"

Not only was Petra a gloriana, the most powerful designation a witch could be born and the equivalent of a walking magical power plant, but she was also too damn tempting to leave for another.

Even if she never let him slake his lust, Silas knew he'd be viciously content with the knowledge that she belonged to him and him alone.

"You're asking me to put my magic, my *life*, in your hands." Petra looked positively queasy at the prospect. Silas could hardly blame her. He doubted he was any witch's dream bondmate.

"Aren't you already doing that?" He had his doubts about how serious her problem really was, but *she* certainly believed the stakes were life and death. He wasn't above using that belief to his advantage.

Petra looked away. For several long seconds, her attention drifted around the polished wood paneling of the office, as if she might find her answer there rather than sprawled in front of her, waiting, watching. She breathed deeply, once, before the tension in her features eased.

"You're right," she answered. "I guess it doesn't really matter."

Silas narrowed his eyes. "What doesn't?"

"What I do with my life." Petra shook her head slowly, a rhythmic movement that rippled her golden hair. It reminded him of sunlight glancing off the water of the creek that ran behind his parents' house. So pretty. So unattainable.

"Fine. You can have it."

His frown deepened. *Where's the fight?*

"You're gonna tie your soul to mine," he said, skeptical, "and you're gonna let *me* filter your magic for you, something essential to keeping you alive for the next two or more centuries. Really."

It was an unsettling thing, seeing a new mask slip over her face like that. In between one blink and another, Petra was colder, more serene, as she stepped away from him. When she replied, she was all business, as if she hadn't just been too shocked to speak a moment ago. "Well, it's not like I have very many options. It is getting to be that time for me, anyway."

Smoothing her mass of hair over one shoulder, she offered him a cool, practiced smile. "However, I would request one thing: since this *is* such a big commitment, I can't agree to it prior to getting what I want. I'm sure you understand."

Something primal in him, rarely heard from, snapped its jaws at the thought of waiting. *She could run,* the animal snarled. *She could try to get out of it.*

Ridiculous, he reasoned. *She'll never escape me.*

People had tried before — granted, no one he'd been so keen on keeping alive — but his reach was long, his resources endless, and his ruthlessness... well, that's what made him so very good at his job.

"You can't play with me, little goddess," he warned. Silas stood up from the chair to tower over her, not necessarily because his height was often intimidating, but because he liked crowding her. Being near her. Feeling the heat that rolled off her body like the waves off blacktop in the summer. "You won't win. I promise you won't."

Petra's half-smile didn't wane, but it didn't reach her eyes.

Those were blank. Two circles of perfect, empty blue. "That's where you're wrong about me, demon."

"How is that?"

"I'm not playing to win."

The primal thing went very still. Around the room, deep in the corners where soft sunlight couldn't reach, shadows unfurled like the seeking arms of the damned. "Who are you afraid of, little goddess?"

"Is it a deal, then?"

Dissatisfaction again. That's what he felt when she wouldn't bend, wouldn't just *answer*. He hated the feeling and strove never to endure it, which was why he always did exactly what he wanted, when he wanted to.

But unraveling Petra's secrets, bleeding into the cracks of her defenses, was a campaign of finesse, not hammer blows. That was why it would be so damn satisfying when he eventually got what he wanted.

I always do.

Maybe not right away. Maybe at great cost. Maybe people would die along the way. But Silas always, always got what he wanted.

His shadows, an extension of him and yet independent of him, wove around her delicate ankles, shackling her as he closed the space between them. Petra held perfectly still as he chucked her under the chin. "We have a deal. Your bond for my help. Now..." He pressed the tip of one claw into the cushion of her lower lip, rumbling, "Give me a name."

Her lips moved, brushing the pad of his thumb. "The Protector of the Gloriae, Antonin Vanderpoel."

Chapter Five

Petra had not been the first choice to take the position as High Priestess of St. Emaine's cathedral. She hadn't been in the top five, or ten, or even one hundred. In fact, she hadn't made the list at all.

But her boss had.

A ponderous old man with a weakness for card games, High Priest Gurney and his assistant had been summoned from St. Raoul's cathedral in Seattle to negotiate a crisis in the Elvish Protectorate. Theodore Solbourne, barely a year into his sovereignty at the time, had created a political firestorm by demanding changes to how Healing Houses — under the purview of and partially funded by the Temple — were run.

Gurney, a well-liked man known for his ability to negotiate with prickly leaders, had been dispatched to reason with the young sovereign. Too bad his assistant had come down with a terrible case of food poisoning the night before their departure. It was a bad omen, surely.

Luckily Petra, a priestess who had previously never shown much interest in politics but fell just below his assistant in the hierarchy, was there to fill the gap.

It was even luckier that she happened to be there, ready to step into the old man's shoes, when he came down with the same bout of illness and couldn't meet the sovereign when he'd come by unexpectedly, demanding a wedding to Margot Goode.

She'd been all too happy to accommodate him — on the condition that he recommend to the High Gloriae, the secretive ruling body of the Temple, that she replace Maximilian Dooraker as San Francisco's highest ranking acolyte.

It was a shock, to be sure, when the name of a completely unknown priestess was announced. Gurney had been the popular choice, but the position was a powerful one, so the debate over who would take the seat had been raging for months. The news that she would take it hadn't been well-received.

At first.

For reasons she couldn't quite understand, the people of San Francisco warmed up to her almost immediately, and that political pull quieted most of her detractors. Some of it was certainly due to her appearance, but she hoped they also saw a bit of Max in her. A pale shadow of the warmth he'd brought to his services, the genuine compassion he'd felt for the suffering, perhaps, but *something* of him.

She couldn't say the same for the Temple, let alone the Gloriae. They, like most in Glory's service, were a tangled mass of vipers.

They weren't all bad. Few groups of people were, in her experience, but she'd been in institutions almost all her life and that meant she'd seen exactly what power structures did to even the best of people. There'd been a moment of hope, when Max had finally tracked her down and pulled her from the children's home, that life among Glory's acolytes would be different, but that hope was extinguished within a week.

The truth of the matter was that, for all the violence, deprivation, and abuse she'd suffered on the streets and then in the children's home, Glory's Temple was far more dangerous.

The prospect of real power made snakes out of even the sweetest souls eventually. And if it didn't, then they hadn't lasted long enough for the transformation to take place.

That was why she had trouble understanding how Robert had survived as long as he had.

Her assistant found her, as he usually did at this hour, standing at the balcony railing of the columbarium to eat her lunch. She could hear him huffing and puffing his way up the spiral staircase long before she caught a glimpse of his balding head or flapping robes.

Petra let out a quiet sigh. The columbarium, a two-story, octagonal tower where ashes were interred, was not often visited by staff or worshippers. Situated at the front of the main building, the balcony overlooked the full stretch of the cathedral below. It was also the only part of the entire cathedral complex where she could find a little peace.

Fitting, she thought, swallowing a bite of her turkey sandwich without tasting it, *that the only comfort I can find these days is amongst the dead.*

"Your grace," Robert huffed behind her, as was his habit.

"Call me Petra, Rob," she replied, as was hers.

"The contractors are done with the guest suite's bathroom and the chef has finished with the menu. It just needs your approval." He lumbered up to the balcony, where he turned to face her, sweaty hands tucking away into the depths of his red sleeves. His long gold necklace, similar to her own, hung so far from his neck, Glory's symbol bounced against his belly whenever he moved.

Petra stared out across the yawning expanse of the cathedral, eyeing the exposed ribs of the arched ceiling and the play of light through the massive stained glass windows. Curls of sweet smoke rose from the statue of Glory's eye sockets, drifting over the head of a praying worshipper in the first pew.

Even from so far away, she swore she could feel those empty eyes fixed on her.

"None of us walk alone," Max once told her. *"Even when it might feel like we're in the dark, Glory's eyes are watching. Remember that, Pet. She expects great things from you."*

Petra bit back a snort. *Great things?* So far *great things* appeared to be paranoia, poking at predators, making deals with demons, and seeing that the nicest suite in the complex was even *nicer* for their esteemed guest and his entourage.

Antonin had complained, in his benevolent way, about the guest suite during his last stay. It didn't matter that he hadn't given the staff any notice before he showed up at their door, nor that he hadn't stayed a full twenty-four hours. She'd gotten the message.

He would be coming back for her, and he expected her to be ready.

"Your grace?"

Petra turned her attention back to her flushed assistant. A tightness settled in around her ribs. She *liked* Robert, but that was a dangerous thing in their world. Even if she could afford to bestow favor on people, she couldn't protect everyone. Petra didn't have the reach, the resources, or the ruthlessness required of a real High Priestess.

She was an angry little girl playing dress-up and trying to catch a murderer.

"I'll look over the menu tonight," she assured him. "And thank you for handling the suite. Did the new furniture come in?"

"It did." Robert pursed his lips, as he liked to do whenever he had something to say but wasn't sure he should.

Petra gave him a look. "Out with it, Rob."

A held breath exploded past his lips. He went downright ruddy when he whispered, at speed, "It just doesn't seem fair that he gets everything he wants when this isn't even *his* cathedral. Your suite hasn't been updated since the sixties! You should be the one getting new furniture, not the Protector."

Petra took another bite of her sandwich and prayed for

patience. They'd had this fight before. Twice, actually. "First, it's not just for him. The guest suite is for any visiting member of the Gloriae. Second, I don't *want* new furniture or my suite to be taken over by construction. It's fine."

If she wasn't certain that there were listening ears even in the columbarium, she might have told him that making sure the Protector had nicer sheets than her was the *least* of her problems. Antonin was the source of most of them, but Shade was rapidly hurtling to the top of the list.

But even if everything was perfect, she wouldn't have wanted to renovate her suite anyway. It didn't matter that the bathroom was outdated, the water pressure abysmal, and the furniture not to her taste.

The suite had been Max's. Sometimes, when she stared at the ceiling, struggling to sleep, she thought she could feel him in the air. A foolish, sentimental part of her worried that if she modernized the suite, his essence would disappear.

And then she'd really be alone.

Of course, besides her sentimentality, there was always the secret passage to worry about. It was just about the only reason she could sleep at night at all, knowing that she could escape if she truly wanted to. An illusion, perhaps, but one she needed to stay even a little bit sane.

But she couldn't tell Robert that even if there *weren't* listening devices in every nook and cranny of the cathedral, so Petra gave her assistant a quelling look.

Robert pursed his lips again. Grumbling, he conceded, "Fine." He looked out over the balcony. "We found a new runner, by the way, to replace the burnt one. And I've ordered a couple sandbags to place on the bases of the votive holders."

Petra hid her grimace in her sandwich. *Fucking Shade.*

He hadn't admitted to being the reason not one but *two* worshippers needed to be hit with a fire extinguisher, nor why the very expensive, antique altar runner needed to be replaced, but she'd seen it in his smug grin.

It was the same smile he'd given her just before he climbed out her office window, saying, "By the way, I only jammed the surveillance devices. They'll come back online as soon as I'm gone. Just thought I'd warn you, in case you wanted to say something really filthy while you have the chance."

She recalled how she'd returned from the bar after their first meeting and shuddered. It turned out he hadn't actually removed her glamour. He'd somehow managed to modify it so only her hair was revealed.

Fear crawled from the atavistic part of her brain at the display of raw magical skill. It was one thing to break a glamour, but never, in all her life and magical instruction, had she heard of someone so powerful they could *change* a spell with a simple swipe of a finger.

What have I gotten myself into?

After Antonin's first visit, it hadn't seemed like she could get into deeper shit than she already stood in, but Petra could practically feel it oozing up her legs.

Her only solace was in the fact that she could count on one man, at least, to do what he said he would.

"Good work, Rob." Finishing off the last of her sandwich, she dusted the crumbs off her fingers over the railing and turned to head back down the stairs. Since she didn't have a future to speak of, she let herself ask about Robert's. "How's the search for a surrogate going?"

"We've got it down to two interviews," he answered, sounding both scared out of his mind and breathtakingly happy. He followed her as she headed for the stairs. "We think we've settled on the right one already, but you have to have back-ups in case— Well, you just have to."

Petra paused to look over her shoulder at him. Her heart was a clenched fist in her chest, drawing tighter every time she recalled that she would probably never get to meet the baby her assistant and his husband were trying so hard to bring into the world.

Her voice came out a little throatier than normal, a little more raw, when she said, "If I can do anything to help you, name it. Time off, recommendations, a good healer. Whatever you need."

Robert's throat bobbed with a hard swallow. "Thank you, your grace. You'll be the first to know, I promise. Hopefully we'll know something before you go on sabbatical."

There was a strange, uncanny weight to the word *sabbatical*. She hadn't discussed why she planned to take time off after Antonin's visit, but it didn't matter. Everyone had come to their own conclusion.

She could tell he wanted to say something about it, maybe offer a warning, but she cut him off. "Even if I'm away from the cathedral, I want to know everything. Promise you'll send me a message."

It was unlikely that she'd ever see it, but she needed to know he would. That someone would think about her in a moment of joy even when she was... wherever she'd end up.

The skin around Robert's eyes tightened. Quietly, he replied, "I promise, your grace."

Petra liked babies. She liked them a lot. It hurt like a motherfucker to know she wouldn't get the chance to know Robert's.

Forcing herself to smile, to keep walking, to keep moving lest she stall, crack, and shatter there in the columbarium, she playfully admonished, "It's Petra, Rob."

"Sorry, your grace. I'll remember next time."

She shook her head and kept walking. All around her, names and dates engraved on tiny bronze plaques glinted in the lights of a hundred tiny candles, each one set into its own special tray to mark the souls connected to those names.

There'd been questions about why Max wasn't interred there. Rumor was that he'd left a request to have his remains sent to his only living relative, but no one could say for certain where they'd gone.

No one knew that his ashes were in her suite, carefully stored in a warded box in the cabinet next to her bed. She'd already drafted her will, instructing Robert to place her and her adopted father together in the columbarium, but a cold feeling in the pit of her stomach told her that she wouldn't get even that simple courtesy.

Death was a scary thing to imagine, but it was far better than the alternative: a life tied to the Protector himself.

CHAPTER SIX

ANTONIN VANDERPOEL WAS A GHOST.

Silas encountered so few of them that he was taken by surprise when, despite his best efforts, he couldn't dig up anything on the man.

He sat in the office of his newly purchased house — a mansion, really — and glared at his various computer screens. The office wasn't quite as sophisticated as his lab back home in the Neutral Zone, but it had everything he needed. Everything *they* needed.

What's wrong? Tal's voice was gentle, a low rasp in the back of his mind. In the far corner of the office, where the shadows were deepest, the vague shape of a person only visible to Silas wavered. *You look upset.*

"I don't get upset," Silas lied.

Shadows couldn't roll eyes they didn't have, and yet... *You throw tantrums every other day.*

He quibbled over the use of the word *tantrum*, but Silas could admit that he wasn't exactly pleasant to be around when he didn't get his way. Tal, his brother in every way that mattered, knew that better than most.

What's bothering you? The shadows stirred, as they often did, whenever Tal's interest spiked. *Is it the witch again?*

Silas glared at the screen. He'd been certain that he would be able to get all the information he needed to satisfy his curiosity with a few keystrokes, but just like everything else involving his little goddess, he found himself thwarted.

One line next to a generated placeholder image rather than a headshot. That was all he'd come up with after hours of sifting through available and less-than-public databases.

Antonin Vanderpoel, a lifetime member of Glory's Temple and accomplished High Priest, was appointed as Protector of the Gloriae March 12th, 2038.

"Is the name Antonin Vanderpoel familiar to you?" He leaned over, his ergonomic office chair squeaking under the strain, to peer at the shadows.

Tal was a person as surely as he was, just without a body. He identified as male, had a keen mind for crime, and nearly a thousand years of accumulated knowledge from which he pulled regularly. He was also Silas's first and only friend — a being he'd called his brother for as long as he'd known the meaning of the word.

They'd been nearly inseparable since Silas first began speaking to the shadows at three years old, so sometimes he forgot that Tal was an ancient being who'd seen and done more than he could comprehend. He was a wealth of untapped information, just as all wraiths with the ability to speak were.

Despite what people wanted to believe, demons weren't the only intelligent life that could thrive in the dark. The trick was knowing where to look.

No, Tal answered. *Should I?*

"I don't know." Silas drummed his claws on the desk, the puzzle that was Petra turning over and over in his mind. "My witch thinks he's important enough to trade her magic for."

Tal's shadows crept along the wall, edging out of the way of what little sunlight Silas let in through a crack in the blackout blinds. Normally he chose hole-in-the-wall apartments for their hideouts. Since Tal couldn't function well in the light — a fact that wounded him, though Silas couldn't understand why — they preferred places where sunproofing wasn't a hassle.

But Silas hadn't been able to pass up the purchase of this particular house, perfectly placed as it was, and Tal had only given him a knowing sigh when he chose it, saying he'd make it work.

"You can have your own house soon," Silas had promised him. He didn't do that lightly. There were vanishingly few beings in the world Silas would even open a door for, let alone break all the laws of man and gods.

And Tal had waited long enough for Silas to fulfill his biggest promise, one he'd made when he was a little boy. The least he could do was tack on a house for the trouble.

But he really didn't appreciate the skepticism in Tal's voice when he asked, *She really agreed to it?*

Silas shrugged. "She's desperate."

Now, *why* she was so desperate was something he was keen to discover. His dominant theory was an over-dramatic threat in the convoluted and incestuous power structure of the Temple, but it could have been anything.

Is that an ex-lover of hers, do you think?

A muscle in Silas's jaw twitched. "Could be."

It wouldn't be the first time he'd been dragged into a lover's quarrel. People with extraordinary amounts of money had a tendency to get into extraordinary amounts of trouble when it came to sex — either seeking it, through the dissolution of a relationship, or in trying to maintain one. Some poor sap up in the Sierras had even paid him millions just to ward a woman's tiny, rundown house. Not because there was any real threat up there in the mountains, but because he *worried* about her.

Silas didn't think he'd ever understand what drove people to madness over someone else. Lust was one thing, a quantifiable physical urge that could be aroused and satisfied, but to completely lose your head over someone? *Stupid.*

He wanted to believe that Petra was smarter than that.

"She said that he's coming for an official visit next week," he explained, ignoring the odd, bitter taste in his mouth. "He's the one she wants me to steal from."

What could he have that she wants badly enough to trade herself in exchange? Tal almost sounded sad for her.

They'd argued for hours over Silas's plan, but even after conceding defeat, Tal clearly couldn't accept the fact that it really wasn't that big of a deal. People, witches in particular, made calculated exchanges of power every day.

Petra would not be the first to hand over her witchbond in exchange for something other than domestic bliss, and Silas was not the first bastard ruthless enough to accept it.

As far as he was concerned, if she consented to it, then there really was nothing to moan about.

"She wants whatever information he's got with him when he visits," Silas answered. "That's all she'd tell me."

I once overheard someone say that the most powerful currency in the Temple is blackmail, Tal mused. *But that was... a very long time ago. When the Temple thought it could control the world. Maybe things have changed.*

Silas pushed away from his desk with his heel. "Besides losing all their power? I doubt it."

Glory's Temple had once been a fierce thing — unified, coordinated, and wealthy. They'd crowned kings and played empires against each other, controlling cities and whole countries from their lofty cathedrals, protected by a radiant shield of religious impartiality.

And then the Burning Years began, when the tide turned against them. Witches, considered Glory's most vulnerable children, had borne the brunt of the fury as governments and acolytes of other gods sought to tear them down. No one knew how many innocent witches who had nothing to do with the Temple were burned, drowned, hanged, or beaten to death by mobs.

A century of bloodshed had driven witches across continents to found the Coven Collective, the small but mighty territory in the Pacific Northwest, but the Temple itself had never quite recovered from the blow.

Now they named their new cathedrals after those who'd been martyred and played at politics with a delicate but no less ambitious touch.

Silas had no patience for hypocrites, and the Temple was positively bursting with them.

He wasn't a good man, but at least he never pretended to be one. People either accepted that or they didn't. What did he care? His clan was safe. His promise to Tal was on the brink of fulfillment at last. He had more money than Glory herself.

And he'd made all of that happen by being as bad as he wanted.

The only thing he *didn't* have was power. Not enough, anyway. Not like Petra.

Normally he made up for his deficit with borderline blasphemous sigilwork. He could mold magic to suit his every whim, but razor-sharp skill could only take him so far. He needed the raw, burning core of magic at the heart of his witch.

Silas wandered over to his lab table, where sleek metal, encased in his own proprietary black enamel, lay scattered across the brushed steel surface. At first glance, it might have appeared disorganized, but he knew exactly where every scrap, every wire, every tube, and every plate ought to go.

He'd spent a century working on prototypes with Tal, getting everything exactly right in between Silas's jobs. Sometimes those jobs were chosen deliberately, allowing Silas to steal research or parts for their work, but mostly he'd picked his clients for the fun of it — and the money, of course.

He did love money.

Silas. The warning note was back in Tal's disembodied voice, which was never a good sign.

As much as Silas liked having Tal around, he got tired of his sanctimonious lectures. The only reason he could tolerate it at all was because, unlike a certain golden priestess, Tal actually *believed* in what he preached.

I really don't think this is a good idea, he cautioned. *Witch-bonds aren't like hats. You can't just put one on and take it off again when you get tired of it. You're asking this woman to be your mate. That's sacred, Si.*

Silas shot the shadows a frown. "I am not. Witchbonds aren't just for mates."

His father, a witch himself, had explained it to him extensively when Silas hit puberty. Being half-witch, no one had been quite sure what Silas's needs would be, and his dad wanted to be sure his son didn't accidentally bind himself to an unsuspecting person in a hormone-driven passion. Really, it was more for the public's protection than Silas's.

You're obsessed with her, Tal challenged. *You want her. Do you really think you're going to be able to keep your hands off of her when she's tied to you, body and soul? That's like catnip to you.*

Unspoken between them lay another truth: that Silas's obsessions burned hot but fleeting. While he'd never been so invested in another person before, he'd had passions in the past. None of them lasted.

After a moment of silence, Tal added, *Rut's coming. You know how stupid demons get this time of year.*

"I've never been stupid," he argued. "And rut has never been an issue for me." A blessing of being only half demon. While he went through a seasonal rut, it had never completely robbed him of his personhood as it so often did with others, turning them into mindless animals desperate to fuck.

Normally he just hired someone to deal with his cock for a week or two. He never bothered learning names or trying to find someone to stick around, and he certainly never enjoyed the same partner twice.

Rut, like any biological function, was simply a fact of life that, once handled, he didn't need to think too hard about. For a few weeks out of the year, he got a little temperamental and extremely horny. Then it was over. Never, not once in his life, had he felt the urge to actually *mate* that drove so many of his cousins out of their minds. And he'd never gotten so lost in the rut that he abandoned his logic.

Yes, Tal said, clearly at the end of his patience, *but you've never been this stuck on a woman, either. Si, you've done nothing but stalk her for weeks. For the gods' sakes, you bought this* house *two days after seeing her for the first time.*

"So? It's a good house." Sure, it was a little bigger than he needed, and definitely in an exposed position that made the wild, demon heart of him antsy, but...

It was close to her. A perfect position to track his target's every move. There wasn't more to it than that.

Tal couldn't sigh without lungs, but the sentiment was clear when he said, *Sometimes I really can't tell if you're lying or just willfully blind. Either way, I'm warning you that this is different.*

Silas could see the reason in Tal's concerns, but something more than his natural combativeness bucked at the well-meaning redirection.

That didn't mean he thought she was his mate. Silas wasn't sure even Petra, hypocrite that she was, would deserve that cosmic punishment. But he'd decided to play with her, and he so loathed giving up his toys.

Silas rested his knuckles on the cool lab table and fixed Tal with a dangerous look. "I'm doin' this."

Why?

"Because I want to," he answered simply, "and because you'll understand when you meet her."

Shadows slid along the floor and across the walls like a liquid spider web. Silas sensed them, sensed Tal's familiar energy in them, as he reformed by the table. *I have a bad feeling about this plan.*

"This is borin' me." Luckily a tiny vibration drew his attention to his wrist. Silas glanced at his watch — a sleek cuff he'd designed himself — and his heartbeat picked up speed. It'd alerted him that sundown was nearly over, which meant Petra would be wrapping up her second service of the day. Within an hour, she would be headed to the dining hall for dinner with the cathedral's small fleet of staff and young initiates.

You're going back there, aren't you? Tal had gone from concern to outright reproach.

Silas rolled his eyes. "'Course I am. D'you want to come along?"

No, I don't, Tal replied, sharp. *I'm not going to help you make a mess of this. This— this is* sacred. *Matehood shouldn't be bought and sold. You deserve better than that. She does, too. It's too painful, knowing you don't care.*

Silas blinked. "I care."

Tal's shape shivered like hot air. *You don't. You only care about what you want in the moment, but someday you* are *going to care about something other than yourself, Silas, and I pray you realize what that means before you break it beyond repair.*

He opened his mouth to point out that there was nothing he couldn't fix, but in an instant, Tal was gone, his form melted back into the natural darkness of the room. *Off into the ether,* he'd once said. Back to wherever it was that wraiths dwelled when the tangible world became too much.

He'd been doing that more often lately — descending into moods, arguing over Silas's methods, and disappearing for long stretches into the ether. He assumed Tal's snippiness came from impatience, which was why he'd decided to push their plan along in the first place. Finding a way into the Tower had led to Petra, and now Petra herself would lead to getting Tal what he craved most.

So why was he so damn *testy?*

Silas scowled, unsettled by the impassioned declaration, and turned to eye the metal on the table. Since his brother wasn't there, he settled for flicking Tal's helmet with the tip of his claw.

"Asshole," he muttered.

CHAPTER SEVEN

Breaking into Petra's private suite wasn't nearly as fun as breaking into her office, mostly because it didn't involve setting anyone on fire.

In fact, it didn't take any effort at all.

A bubble of anger burst in his chest as he seamlessly slid through the basic wards guarding her door. In another building, his witch and the rest of the cathedral staff were busy enjoying whatever it was they ate for dinner, leaving a perfect opportunity for him — *anyone* — to trespass.

Silas stood by the door for several seconds, his eyes narrowed as he peered into the darkness. Like her office, the walls were paneled with wood, the windows were narrow but tall, and the furniture in the sitting room was elegant but clearly aged. The rich scent of her was strong, too, all warmth and spice that made the primal thing in him flex its claws.

And like her office, the room was bugged.

His wrist cuff vibrated twice in a specific pulsing pattern, alerting him to the number of surveillance devices it'd picked up.

Normally, he found the existence of surveillance amusing. Cameras had trouble picking up the presence of a shadow-cloaked demon even when they were the most advanced kind, and he liked the challenge of dismantling audio equipment while some unknown lackey listened on, oblivious.

But that thing in him stirred at the thought of Petra's space being invaded. Not by him. *He* had every right to be there, but by unknown others. Who knew what they'd seen? What they'd heard? He understood why someone might have eyes on her office, where she took meetings and kept information, but in her private space...

Dissatisfaction rankled him anew.

With a flick of his claw across the screen on his wrist, a low, nearly inaudible whine broke the silence. There was a low pop, the sound of a mic's natural feedback, and then quiet.

Silas stalked across the room, noting that, despite spending three years in the suite, Petra had no personal effects scattered around. No pictures on the walls, no throw blankets over the back of the couch. He couldn't say it was pristine, necessarily, not when the suite had the distinct feeling of being *lived in,* but it didn't feel like *hers.*

Maybe she knows she's watched in here, too, he thought, ire growing as he threaded a path around the low coffee table and toward the walnut-paneled door across the room.

His body moved differently when he took on his shadow form. While he could never manage the pure liquid grace of Tal and other wraiths, he didn't walk like a human, either. Silas glided across the old wood floor without hitting a single creaky board. His hand, fingers unnaturally long and swathed in shifting darkness, curled around the brass doorknob of Petra's bedroom.

An explosion of scent stopped him there in the doorway.

A deep, involuntary rumble worked its way up his throat as he savored the smell of incense, sunlight, and lush woman. He'd never been particularly scent-motivated, unlike his fully demon cousins, but this...

He now understood what'd driven them so crazy when they encountered something sweet around this time of the year.

The concentrated scent of Petra was enough to make blood rush to his cock so fast, he actually swayed.

Silas bit back a groan as he adjusted himself, trying to ease the pressure. He was there on a fact-finding mission, not to roll around in her bed and maybe paint her sheets with his come. Not yet, anyway.

Maybe later, when he had his little goddess on a pretty golden leash, he'd let her watch as he stroked his cock to the scent of her. If she was *extra* good, he'd even let her sleep on the sheets he soiled.

Oh, but the primal thing inside him liked the idea of her sleeping cocooned in his scent. It liked it almost as much as the thought of her walking around in her sacred robes, her thighs and pink cunt wet with his release. Any predator would know the sharp, musky scent of come and understand the pious priestess was well-fucked.

It wasn't in the cards for that night, but he couldn't stop himself from drifting toward the dark shape of Petra's simple canopied bed. The itch to stroke the pillow where she laid her golden head was too—

A vibrating pulse stopped him in the center of the room.

Motherfucker.

At once, territorial rage crackled through his shadows, whipping them out across the floor in search of a target. The shadows that were him and yet not craved destruction, but it was as if they sensed what was Petra's and what wasn't. The seeking tentacles didn't want to destroy her den. They wanted to find the intruder who'd made the colossal mistake of touching something Silas claimed.

It was one thing to know her outer suite had been bugged. It was quite another to discover her bedroom was, too.

Silas activated the sensor on his watch and waited for it to ping a signal around the room. His jaw clenched hard as he held himself still. It took less than a minute for the information to flicker across the shielded screen.

Barely warded, bugged, and watched.

Audio and visual surveillance had been detected in her bedroom. Just one device, but one was more than enough.

Silas turned slowly, until he stood facing the wall opposite Petra's simple bed. Glory's symbol, a blazing sun cast in polished bronze and glass, was mounted to the wall. When he lifted his wrist toward it, a quick pulse followed.

He tilted his head to one side. *I'm gonna kill you,* he silently promised the person behind the camera and, should they be separate entities, the one who'd ordered it placed there. *I'm gonna let her watch, just like you've watched her.*

It wasn't fun being angry. He preferred to laugh, to do things that interested him and made him feel alive. Very little stirred him to true anger because very little made him feel much of anything at all. But sometimes, when the mood struck, he didn't mind a bit of rage. It added a little something special to an act as mundane as murder.

This was different. This was a sort of anger he'd never experienced before, and it was about as pleasurable as having a tooth pulled.

Silas reached into his pocket and withdrew a notebook, small enough to fit into the palm of his shadowed hand. He flipped the cover over with his thumb claw, opening the notebook to the tiny, wax-lined pages he sewed in himself. Each one held a variety of tiny, clear-backed stickers, and every one of those stickers held a sigil, crafted of hair-thin wire, a battery too small to be seen, and a similarly-sized microchip.

Like most everything he used in his line of work, he'd crafted them himself, and each one had a specific function.

Using the tip of his claw, Silas carefully peeled a sticker off of the paper before tucking the notebook back into his pocket. That done, he raised his arm and, gently enough to not accidentally move the ornament, placed the sticker just out of sight.

A flare of magic, hot and bright and metallic, filled the air.

Silas rocked back on his heels, gut still roiling with anger but at least momentarily satisfied that no one would watch her now.

Except him, of course, but that was okay. She was his.

He would have liked to rip the ornament off the wall and smash it under his boot heel, but that wasn't smart. It was better to have Petra's watchers simply view the loop of the last week, as he'd programmed into the sticker. It usually took days, sometimes even weeks, for people to notice they were watching the same footage, especially if there was a rotating crew assigned to the surveillance.

That bought him plenty of time to get information out of Petra, track down who was behind it, kill them, and then delete any footage they'd saved.

Silas turned his head back and forth, judging the line of sight from the hidden camera. Fury snapped again, a lightning bolt through his very being.

It was situated directly across from Petra's bed.

There was no telling what they'd seen, but even if it wasn't those manicured fingers pulling sad little orgasms from her pretty pink cunt, it was too much. He didn't *like* the thought of someone else watching her sleep. He didn't *like* knowing that they'd seen her dress. He didn't *like* sharing Petra and all the mundane, private things she did when she thought she was alone.

He didn't like it at all.

Silas wasn't entirely sure what he expected to find in Petra's bare little bedroom, but rigidly folded clothing, a box of cremated human remains, and three separate caches of non-perishable food wasn't it.

There were no frills, baubles, ornaments, or hidden luxuries. Her makeup kit fit in one tiny bag, neatly stored on her small bathroom counter. The entirety of her wardrobe was contained in the top two drawers of her dresser. The most lavish things he discovered were her formal robes and the Crown of Glory, the elaborate headdress and veil she wore during the equinox services.

Well, that and a disproportionate amount of lingerie. It appeared his witch had a weakness for satin and lace, but only a small one. The only reason it was notable — besides his obvious interest — was because she had so little clothing to begin with. All of it was high quality, elegant, and well-cared for, but there was so *little* of it that he actually went looking for more.

But no, in the closet he found only a thick peacoat, her lavish and jewel-encrusted ceremonial gown, and a small, dented suitcase.

The only things he discovered in abundance were food and the ashes of a man named Maximilian Dooraker.

Silas sat on Petra's bed, his boots off and her softest night-gown draped over his shoulders. Around him were her caches — each one squirreled away in a discreet but accessible spot. He'd discovered one in her office as well and hadn't thought much of it, but *three* stashes of food seemed excessive. Granola bars, crackers, bottles of water, fruit snacks, trail mix... It looked like an assortment of things one might filch from a snack table at a convention.

Or, he thought, brows bunching, *from the dining hall of a cathedral.*

Something about that bothered him, and it wasn't just because the more he dug into Petra's life, the more questions he had. He stared at a flashing neon sign and yet somehow couldn't make sense of what it was telling him.

More troubling, of course, were the ashes.

Silas turned the box over in his hand, examining the plain, waxed wood and the simple plaque on top. He knew the name, of course. Maximilian Dooraker had been the previous High Priest of St. Emaine's cathedral and died unexpectedly some years prior, leaving a small power vacuum Petra, a no-name witch, had filled.

It made sense that his remains would be interred in the cathedral and, perhaps in the interim, be placed into the care of the new High Priestess, but something about it seemed off to him.

Silas scowled at the box. *Why does she keep you next to her bed?*

He gave the box a good, hearty shake, but he wasn't sure if it was to startle an answer out of a dead man or to listen to the tell-tale rattle of bone fragments and dust.

Tal's innocent question rose unbidden: *Is that an ex-lover of hers, do you think?*

Dooraker would have been centuries her senior, but odder pairings had happened, particularly in corrupt power structures like Glory's Temple. So long as she was a fully-grown woman who knew her own mind, something as inconsequential as an age gap certainly wouldn't have stopped *him* from fucking Petra. He didn't relish the thought of dying long before her, though.

Centuries was an awfully long time for her to have to stay single.

"Tough shit, old man. She won't be doing that for you," he told the box. Silas gave it one more resentful rattle before he leaned over to tuck it back into its hiding place beside her bed. He didn't particularly care if she knew he'd gone through her stuff — that would be obvious — but he tried to be measured about these things.

Petra would be upset knowing he did it, but *seeing* him casually inspecting the remains of her dusty lover would take that to a level he didn't have the patience to deal with.

She didn't *seem* like a shrieker, but the more he peered past her masks, the more she surprised him, so he really couldn't be sure.

I'm about to find out, he thought, lounging back against her too-soft pillows. He listened to the sound of her opening the outer door as he ripped open a pack of chocolate candies with his teeth. His other hand mindlessly bunched her nightgown, rubbing the petal-soft fabric against the callused skin of his palm.

Her skin was softer, making the nightgown a pale substitute, but he liked knowing she wore it to bed. The fact that it smelled like her, all warm and sexy, made it irresistible. The fact that it now smelled like him, too, was a delicious bonus.

Silas chewed on his candy quietly, holding the rest of his body very still and cloaked in deep shadow, as the sounds of her footsteps approached the bedroom door. Petra walked briskly, on the balls of her feet, with long, purposeful strides.

The knob turned. The muscles of Silas's abdomen flexed with anticipation. Chocolate melted on his tongue just as the door swung open.

His breath caught.

She glows in the dark.

Not a lot. Maybe not enough for the average person to notice. But for a demon whose soul was welded with shadow, the faint luminescence of skin was striking. It was the afterglow of a warm day, the memory of sunshine, and something about it made him want to sink his claws into her and never let that warmth go.

CHAPTER EIGHT

PETRA FLICKED THE OLD FASHIONED LIGHT SWITCH, bathing the room in an artificial glow. Silas scowled. Her shine disappeared in the harsh light. *Annoying.*

She spotted him immediately, of course, but she didn't scream. Instead, she froze there in the doorway, her hand hovering above the switch and her wide-eyed gaze locked on him.

He wondered what she made of the sight: a transformed demon, body larger and more monstrous than any other bipedal being, lounging on her bed and eating her food.

Lifting the bag of candy to his lips, he complained, "I liked the lights off." His voice was deeper, more growl than human speech, but Petra seemed to understand him well enough.

In a measured tone, she replied, "And I'd like you to stop invading my spaces."

He cracked a candy between his molars. "Nah."

Petra's attention dropped to the bag of candy in his hand. A strange ripple crossed her strained expression, a flash of intense emotion that passed too quickly for him to identify. "I see you've made yourself at home."

"In this sad little room? Hardly." He swept his disapproving gaze around the room, taking in her aged furniture, the lack of *any* luxuries, and the ornament on the wall.

It was a far cry from the luxurious home he'd purchased, and seemed like an odd fit for someone as radiant and powerful as Petra. Shouldn't a woman who wore a crown at least have nice pillows?

He knew some religious orders, particularly Loft and Burden's followers, preached various levels of asceticism and deprivation, but Glory's Temple had never shied away from worldly goods.

"You can't be here." Petra snapped the door closed. Though her expression was stony, her willow frame nearly vibrated with tension. "There's no reason for you *to* be here. If someone caught you—"

Silas offered her a slow grin. "What? Afraid you'll be judged for having a demon in your room?"

She would be. Oh, she would be. He could already see the headlines that would spawn. The scandal might even be enough to cost Petra her precious position as High Priestess.

Demons weren't reviled, but they weren't exactly celebrated, either, when thousands of years of superstition lingered like a cloud around their heads. Even non-religious people were likely to look askance at demons. For those who *were* religious, they were the children of Blight, god of disease and decay.

Over the years, he'd used that reputation to his advantage again and again — as well as all the other handy attributes that came with being more demon than witch. So what if the world was afraid of them? At least in his case, they *should* be.

A fully grown demon, mature and in control of his shadows, was nearly indestructible. They lived long, could survive even grievous injuries, and had strong, interconnected clans. In the UTA, they minded their own business, but on the European continent, whole swaths of territory were held by fierce, shadowed hands.

Silas didn't have any grand ambitions on that score, and he wasn't particularly sentimental, but he did have pride.

And that pride was delighted to think that many people would shudder with horror at the idea of Glory's High Priestess, a witch blessed with power over her light, considered the living flesh of the goddess, being *debased* by his unworthy hands.

He expected Petra to scoff at the idea of sleeping with him, or perhaps confirm what he already knew about how sex between them would be viewed, but she didn't.

Instead, she asked, "Did you disable the camera?"

The half-full bag of candy crunched in his suddenly tense fist. "'Course. Now, I'd love to know why you've been *knowingly* living with—"

He didn't get the chance to finish, because as soon as he'd answered her question, she marched up to the bed, snatched one of the water bottles, and threw it at his head. He dodged it easily, but even if he hadn't, it would have bounced harmlessly off his shadows.

Petra had an impressive throwing arm, though.

"That's not very nice of you, High Priestess," he admonished her.

"Gods, if I'd known how much trouble you'd be, I never would have sought you out!" Her movements were quick, jerky, as she began to grab as much of the food as she could. "I just need you to spy on Antonin for me. I don't need you *here*. I don't want you here! Can't you just do your job and leave me the fuck alone?"

His hackles rose as he watched her gather what food he hadn't pilfered, her beautiful mask cracked to reveal not just anger, but real panic.

"Petra."

"I have less than a week before he gets here. I don't have time for your games. I don't have time for anything. You think this is *fun,* but I'm the one living on the edge of a fucking knife. It's not fun for me!" There was no screeching, but he might have preferred that over her breathless fury.

"I just need you to do your job, not break into my room and eat my food." She spoke so fast the words began to blur together. A bag of pretzels tumbled from her overflowing arms. A low, wounded animal sound escaped her throat as she made a desperate grab for it.

It was with a great amount of alarm that Silas realized her eyes were glossy.

Suddenly, *he* was the panicked one. The animal part of him balked at the sight of her unshed tears and the way she frantically gathered her things, as if she feared he'd snatch them from her at any moment. It disturbed the logical part of him, too, because something about seeing the perfect, regal witch unravel over a packet of candy was... wrong.

Without thinking, Silas's shadows spread, blanketing the bed and reaching for her. Petra made another animal sound, this one of pure frustration, as she tried to twist out of their reach. More snacks slipped from her grasp.

"Stop it!" she hissed.

Silas discarded his candy in favor of restraining her the good old fashioned way. Instinct compelled him to shed his shadows as he banded his human hands around her upper arms. Touching her skin to skin was like reaching into a beam of scorching sunlight: it burned, but it also felt *good*.

His voice was as sharp as a whip's crack when he commanded, "Calm down."

Petra's shoulders rose and fell with the force of her breaths. She wouldn't look at him but rather curled in on herself defensively. Wrappers crinkled where she pinched the packages against her chest.

Speaking in a strangled voice, she said, "You think this is all a game, but it's not. This is my life, Shade."

Grasping for some way to get the fun Petra back, he promised her, "I won't eat any more of your candy."

Petra let out a watery laugh and twisted, not to get away, but rather to sit on the edge of the mattress. He forced himself to let go of her. Gradually, her arms fell by her sides, allowing the snacks to tumble to the floor.

She braced her palms on her knees and dipped her head. Her eyes closed. "It's not about the food."

Silas eyed the packages on the floor warily. "Sure seems like it."

"That's—" She cut herself off in favor of taking a deep breath. "I don't like people touching my stuff, that's all. I get defensive."

He could understand that. He usually killed people who touched his things. But there was more to it than that. It was written in the purple smudges under her eyes, the way she braced herself, as if she needed to lock her joints to keep from slumping to the ground.

This was not the woman who stood proudly before worshippers, giving succor and false promises of hope in the light of sunrise. This woman was... brittle.

He didn't like it at all.

Disquieted, Silas threw his legs over the side of the bed and, careful to avoid the food on the ground, began to stalk around the room. Movement helped clear his head. Demons weren't supposed to be kept pets, nor city-dwellers. They had too much energy, too much wildness. Even if they didn't experience the volatility of the rut every year, they would have chafed under the restrictions of city life.

Mostly he did okay. Moving to a new place every few weeks helped. Controlled explosions of violence and lust did, too. His family attributed his tolerance to being half-witch, but he believed it was his unrestricted lifestyle that did it. After all, if he was never controlled by anything more than his own whims, what could a city do to rein him in?

But something about Petra's little meltdown disturbed the animal in him. It pushed out, clawing for freedom, and made the bedroom seem even smaller and grimmer than it was.

Temper snapping, Silas demanded, "You don't like me

touching your things, but you're fine with someone watching you sleep?"

Petra rubbed her eyes. She looked tired, her shine worn down by some tarnish he couldn't see. "That's different."

"How?"

"It's not your problem," she replied, firmer. Petra opened her eyes to give him a pleading look. "Please, just do your job. I already promised I'd give you what you want."

A niggling suspicion paused his stalking of the room's perimeter. Eyes narrowing, Silas asked, "Is the entire cathedral under surveillance?"

"I believe so. That's why I need your help."

But it wasn't the full story. That was clear enough. "Who's watching?"

Petra's expression went carefully blank. "I can't say for sure."

"But you have suspicions."

"Yes."

"And it's not *you*, the woman who ostensibly *runs* this place."

Petra's eyes didn't change, but the skin around her mouth went tight. "Was that a question?"

"You're awfully blasé about having your most private spaces violated," he observed, surprising even himself with the level of venom in his voice. Everything about this situation bothered him, and the more she spoke, the more certain he became that she was hiding something vital from him.

Nothing about her situation made a damn lick of sense, and that was completely intolerable.

A sweeping gesture drew his attention back to the mess of her caches spread across the floor by the bed. "Apparently *not*," she dryly challenged. "But when you've lived with it for years, demon, you learn to adapt."

"Were you gonna tell me about the surveillance before or after I attempted to rob Vanderpoel?"

Petra stood up from her bed. Without looking at him, she padded over to her plain dresser, its surface completely devoid of knick-knacks or keepsakes or accessories, and wrenched open the top drawer.

"You're the best at what you do, aren't you?" she mocked, shoulders shrugging beneath her blood-red robe. It slid down her arms, left bare by the simple pale blue blouse she'd changed into after the dawn service, until she could fold it and tuck it into the drawer. "I assumed you'd figure it out."

It was impossible to resist the draw of her, he realized, and he didn't want to even if he could.

Silas stalked across the room to press himself against her back. She stiffened, but didn't turn when he grasped the edge of the dresser on either side of her, caging the witch in.

Speaking against her ear, he hissed, "Do you know why I'm the best, little goddess?"

Petra's breathing slowed, as if she knew instinctively that any quick movement, any sign at all that she might bolt, would make the predator at her back pounce. "Because you don't care who you hurt?"

"Because I always know when a client is lyin' to me," he answered. "And before you ask, yes, withholding the truth is the same as lyin' when both will get a plasma bolt stuck between my eyes."

"And what do you think I'm hiding, Shade?"

The urge to bite her was a living thing in him, a roar from the animal who wanted nothing more than to conquer the inscrutable creature it had captured. "Whoever bugged your office, whoever bugged your *bedroom* — they're the one you're afraid of."

Petra remained stubbornly silent, so he continued. "Whoever it is needs to have more power than *you*, the highest ranking member of Glory's Temple in the Protectorate. They need to have enough power to make you do nothin' even after having your privacy invaded, day after day. Enough to make you afraid for your life. Enough to make you come to *me.*"

His mind raced with possibilities, filling the silence she

refused to break with a thousand scenarios. Each one pissed him off more than the last.

Silas gradually drew his arms in closer to her sides, pulling the edges of her cage in. His right hand left the dresser to press flat against her stomach, drawing her back into his chest as he stooped over her, lips pressing against the shell of her ear.

"Is it the Protector, little goddess?"

Theoretically, there were at least a dozen, probably more, members of the Temple who had the power to keep the High Priestess of San Francisco on a short leash, but it was Antonin Vanderpoel, the ghost he couldn't track, who sprang to mind.

He expected to feel her tremble, but he was quickly learning that he never really knew what Petra would do next. Instead of squirming to be free or shaking with adrenaline and fear, she relaxed her shoulders and the curve of her spine. For just a moment, she leaned her weight into him — trusting him, however unconsciously, not to let her fall.

"You're wrong," she answered, soft and flat.

Silas's claws snagged in the fabric of her blouse. His voice went harsh, the syllables clipped, when he replied, "Then give me a fuckin' name."

Petra shook her head. "Not about that. About me being afraid of dying."

"What are you talking about?"

She turned, ever-so-slowly, in his arms. When she tilted her face up, her eyes were no longer dull, but shone with razor-thin circles of pure white light around the pupils. "I'm not afraid of dying, Shade. There are much worse things that can happen in the world, and I've seen most of them."

Petra said it with such frankness, such calm finality, that it made the unfamiliar weight of dread sink into his belly. "Something is *wrong,*" she continued, "not just here in St. Emaine's, but in the whole Temple — and that man is at the heart of it. I'm not afraid to die. I'm afraid to *fail.* I've spent three years trying to get to him on my own, living under constant surveillance, so I'd really fucking appreciate it if you didn't get me killed before I saw this finished, okay?"

She pressed a palm against his chest. He was so taken off-guard by her that he let her direct him back a step, allowing her to slip around him. Silas watched her pause at the scattered packages of food on the floor, before she reached out to snatch her discarded nightgown from the bed.

"If you want my witchbond, then you're going to have to start taking this seriously," she warned him, "because if Antonin gets his way, you won't get it."

"What does he want?" Silas demanded. "Power? Sex?"

Those were the usual suspects in cases like this, when a woman became desperate enough to hire him to deal with a man. Whatever the motivation, it wouldn't save Vanderpoel from his wrath, but Silas was a man who liked to go into situations armed with every bit of knowledge he could.

Petra knelt to gather the food with one hand. Placing each package on the cabinet by her bedside, the one that hid Dooraker's ashes, she arranged them with an unsettling gentleness. It was as if she were afraid that one wrong move would make the little packets of cookies and pretzels and trail mix disappear.

Secrets, he thought, dissatisfied again. *Secrets on secrets on secrets.*

"I wish I knew what the reason for all of this was," she finally answered, head down and eyes fixed on her task, "but I don't."

"You're in the center of the shit storm. How could you not know?"

"The center?" Petra paused. The golden curtain of her hair shimmered when she lifted her head to look over her shoulder. There was a dreadful sort of amusement in her expression when she told him, "Shade, whoever you think I am, I'm not. I'm no one. If I'm at the center of anything, it's because I've made room for myself there, not because I'm the one pulling strings."

The longer the conversation went, the more confused and annoyed he became. Silas ran a palm over one of his curling horns

— a restless, anxious gesture he hadn't done since he was a child — and then hissed with annoyance when he realized he'd done it.

"Why would you involve yourself in this, then?"

Petra remained in a kneeling position on the floor, her nightgown in one hand and an unopened packet of chocolate candies in the other. At any other time, he would have enjoyed the pose, the way she looked up at him from so far below, as if she wished to offer him a prayer from her pretty, sacred mouth.

But in that moment, her blue eyes cut right through him. They saw clean through muscle and bone to the wild, confused thing in him, the part that wanted nothing more than to get on its knees with her.

"Have you ever cared about someone so much that you'd risk everything for them?" It was a soft question, but the words landed like bolt shots.

Silas's mouth went oddly dry. "No."

Tal didn't count. Not really. He could handle himself, and were Silas to die, he would continue on for millennia more. They had an unshakable bond, but it was different from the thing they both knew she spoke of.

His clan didn't count, either. Against all good sense, they loved him. His aunts and uncles, his cousins, the dozens and dozens of little baby demons they seemed to pop out every year, about ten months after every rut. He felt enough for them to know it was in their best interest that he keep his distance, but would he risk *everything* for them?

No. The answer was obvious to him, but clearly not to her, so he asked, "Why would I?"

A small puff of air escaped Petra's nose — the tiniest, softest, most heartbreakingly disappointed sigh he'd ever heard. "That's answer enough. I guess there's no point in trying to explain it to you. You'll never understand it."

Dissatisfaction came again, hard and mean, but Silas couldn't rightly tell if it was directed at her or himself.

CHAPTER NINE

PETRA DIDN'T SLEEP WELL AND NEVER HAD, BUT SHE could admit to herself that knowing Shade had disabled the camera in her bedroom made rest come a tiny bit easier.

Unfortunately, rest was a relative thing when her worries still kept her up half the night.

She spent most of it agonizing over her uncharacteristic lack of self-control in front of *Shade*, of all people. *You can't afford to break,* she'd admonished herself. *Not now. Not after all this time. You just have to hold on a little longer.*

Normally, she held onto her emotions with an iron fist — a necessary thing when every one of her movements and words were tracked. If it wasn't the cameras and the microphones she discovered during her first few months in the cathedral, then it was the acolytes, none of whom could be entirely trusted not to report back to Antonin to curry favor.

If it wasn't *them,* then it was a worshipper. A photographer for *The San Francisco Light.* A child who'd wandered away from the nursery.

Not once since she'd taken Max's position had she been *alone.*

Really, she had no reason to trust that she was at that moment, either. Shade very well could have installed his own camera, or simply lied about disabling the one she already knew existed.

But for reasons she couldn't quite explain, she believed him.

Maybe it was the rage that had glowed in his molten metal eyes or the quick, raw look of panic he wore when she'd begun to unravel. Or perhaps it was the almost childlike confusion he'd expressed just before he left.

Shade was undoubtedly a monster. Only the gods knew how many people he'd killed, the secrets he knew, and the money he'd raked in with bloodied claws. But the more they interacted, the more she thought she understood the way his mind worked.

Shade was a monster, but he was an honest sort of monster. Unlike her.

Petra tossed and turned, trying to find a comfortable spot in a bed that had never really felt like hers. Now it felt even less so. No matter where she settled her head, she could smell him there.

Thyme, citrus, and amber.

Every time she breathed, she could almost taste him on her tongue. Memories of walking into her bedroom to find him there, transformed into his monstrous shape, lounging amongst her pillows, haunted her as surely as her mortification did.

Why was the sight so *compelling?*

Why had something hot and heavy curled in the pit of her stomach when he pressed himself against her back and hissed into her ear? It had to be the stress. Finally, after so many years of constant vigilance and grief, she'd begun to lose it.

No wonder, she thought, drawing her pillow a little closer to her nose for a deep breath of thyme.

The stress was bound to catch up with her eventually. It wasn't just her situation, either, but running the cathedral and all its programs, carrying the weight of so many lost souls seeking comfort... add Antonin's ultimatum, and her meltdown didn't look so unreasonable.

That didn't clear the bitter taste from her mouth, though.

Being exposed was never comfortable for her. Being exposed

to *Shade,* a man who seemed to take great pleasure in taunting and humiliating her, was a different level of pain.

It was impossible not to lose it with him, though. He apparently boasted a preternatural sense for exactly where her buttons were hidden. He picked and picked and picked. *Why* he took such great delight in hounding her, she really couldn't say.

That man wants me to bind myself to him. Her stomach turned at the thought.

Petra couldn't say she was sentimental. That had been beaten out of her early on, when her parents sold her toys to pay for food and when her friends at the children's home snitched on her to save their own skin. Life in the Temple wasn't kind to the soft, either.

Despite what the High Gloriae preached to the public, witchbonds weren't always the result of a fated love connection. In the Temple, they were used to carve out alliances that could never be broken. It was hard to stab someone in the back when your souls were tied together. The Gloriae encouraged the practice of exchanging witchbonds amongst acolytes, since it tied all involved parties to the fabric of the Temple that much tighter and, if they were lucky, could result in a new crop of magically gifted children.

Petra had entertained a handful of offers herself before her machinations brought her to San Francisco and some small measure of power. But she hadn't been a rising star then, and the people who'd proposed matches were as low level in the hierarchy as she was.

Out of all the ways her plan to discover the truth Max's murder could have gone awry, never, not *once,* did she suspect it would have to do with her suddenly being a desirable match.

A cold sweat broke out across her skin. Shade's demand rang clear as the cathedral's bells in her mind.

Ideas of what it would be like to give her magic over to the demon, what he might *do* with that power, made her gorge rise. She could admit that some stupid, tiny part of her was attracted to him — surely a byproduct of her dysfunctional upbringing amongst criminals — but she could never imagine *willfully* tying herself to him.

And that was why she lied.

The likelihood that she would live past Antonin's visit was slim, and that was the best possible outcome. Because surviving meant one of two things: either she tied her life to a half-mad, sociopathic demon...

Or she tied herself to Antonin.

≈

Two days crawled by after Shade broke into her bedroom, and Petra knew for certain she was going crazy.

The cathedral was in an uproar. There'd been no time to panic before the Protector's last visit, when he'd shown up with his entourage and his easy smile just after sundown service.

"I was in town to meet a friend," he'd said, oozing charm even as her staff quivered with fear behind her in the dining hall. *"But I couldn't pass up a chance to visit our rising star. I hope you don't mind."*

No one knew much about Antonin Vanderpoel besides two essential facts: firstly, that he was the head of investigation and security for the entire Temple and secondly, that the people around him tended to simply disappear.

Not his closest entourage, of course. *They* were a terrifyingly dull-eyed, silent unit rumored to be packed with intensely magically gifted witches he'd hand-selected as children.

But everyone else, from esteemed Priestesses to lowly acolytes to domestic staff, seemed to vanish with a snap of his fingers.

Max had warned her to steer clear of the Protector's all-seeing eye long before he'd shocked her by accepting the position as San Francisco's High Priest. But when she pressed, he refused to elaborate on the danger. She still wasn't entirely certain what he'd tried to warn her about, only that Antonin Vanderpoel was a very dangerous man.

She would know, since she was certain he'd had Max killed.

Whether the staff knew that or not, they were, to a one, terrified of his upcoming visit. In the three years she'd been in charge of them, she'd never seen the marble floor of the cathedral shine so brightly, nor the brass fittings on the doors and archways gleam like gold.

One by one, the paintings of Glory were freed of dust and the greasy leavings of reverent fingertips. Curtains were pulled down and beaten outside. Young acolytes redoubled their studies of ancient epics, tales of the gods and their trials and triumphs, in the library. She swore even the staff's children, who normally frolicked in the nursery attached to the cathedral's living areas, were more subdued than normal.

And against this tense backdrop, Petra swore she was being followed.

Not in the way she might have expected, and not by the usual crawling eyes she knew so well, but by *shadows.*

At first she thought it was Shade, hiding in the corner of her office again, or haunting her as she walked up winding staircases. It made sense. He'd already demonstrated how little he cared about breaking and entering.

But whenever she caught sight of a shifting shadow, an unnatural movement in the dark, there was nothing there. It would have been unnerving on the best of days, but with Antonin's visit rapidly approaching and the way Shade seemed to have disappeared after her breakdown...

Petra sat at the head table in the dining hall and pushed food around her plate. A hum of anticipation filled the air in lieu of conversation. Normally she could eat no matter how she felt and she always, *always* cleaned her plate, but even her knotted stomach had its limits.

It seemed absurd to miss the damn demon, but *not* seeing him actually caused her more worry than when he was right in front of her.

They needed to talk. She'd gotten her hands on the floor plan for what would be Antonin's suite and it was essential she tell Shade exactly what she needed him to find, then what to do with it.

Not to mention that there will likely be five to ten terrifyingly loyal witches standing guard at all times.

Petra's lips thinned as she speared a roasted potato the size of a marble. *No, I'll handle that.*

Based on their last meeting, the bulk of Antonin's entourage went where he did. Theoretically, when she joined him for the private meal he'd requested, he'd bring them with him. She doubted he'd leave his things unguarded, but dealing with one or two lackeys on guard duty was infinitely better than the half a dozen bodyguards he boasted.

They would be her problem.

Petra popped the buttered potato into her mouth and tried to savor the rosemary and salt it had been seasoned with, but even the absurd spread of food the chef arrayed on her table couldn't distract her from a thousand ways her plan could go wrong.

If Shade didn't show back up, she'd be screwed. If Antonin caught onto her, she'd be screwed. If Shade's tampering with the surveillance in her room was discovered, she'd be screwed. If Antonin caught him breaking into his suite...

Screwed, screwed, screwed.

A faint buzzing in the pocket of her slacks nearly startled the fork right out of her hand.

Petra froze. For just a moment, a wild, mad hope bloomed in her chest.

That particular phone never left her side. Not even when she slept. It was paid for by a buried account held under a false name, one not even connected to the money Max had hidden away for her.

The phone was one of a pair. It only had one number saved in its contacts, and its twin had been destroyed at some point between the last conversation she'd shared with Max, when he quietly but urgently begged her to leave the Temple, and his murder.

She knew it had been destroyed because she found the pieces hidden beneath a loose tile in her bathroom. Petra remembered the terror that had pierced her when she realized what he'd done, how scared he must have been when he did it.

Max hadn't just crushed it, plucked out the SIM card, or factory reset it.

No, he'd first removed the SIM card, then melted it. Next, he'd drilled a hole in the battery, effectively incinerating the phone from the inside, before he crushed it to pieces and buried what remained beneath the tile.

That was why, when she discreetly pulled it from her pocket beneath the table, her heart lurched at the sight of the screen lit with a text notification.

For a single second, the span of a blink, Max was alive again.

And then he wasn't, because the number on the screen was marked as *private*.

Petra's stomach sank so fast, she worried she might actually be sick. Her hand shook as she unlocked the screen and, after checking to make sure no one was watching her, glanced at the message.

It was an address.

She blinked and read it again. As she did so, another message came in.

Don't make me wait, little goddess.

The blood drained away from her face in a woozy rush. Petra shoved the phone back into her pocket and stared, sightless, at her half-finished plate. *How?* How had he gotten the number to her phone? The implications of that were... sweeping. Horrifying.

She had to hold her breath to stop herself from hyperventilating there at the high table as she considered everything that would mean. Either she and Max hadn't covered their tracks as well as they thought they did, or Shade was much, much better at his job than she could ever have imagined.

"Your grace?"

Petra swallowed a scream, shoved it down deep enough to echo in the cavern of her belly, and turned her head to meet the questioning look of a young acolyte carrying a tray.

"Do you want me to ask the chef for something else?" The acolyte, no older than eighteen and newly initiated, was a sweet-faced dragon named Yelizaveta — a rarity amongst the sea of witches and arrants who dominated the Temple's hierarchy. Pale gold eyes flicked back and forth between Petra's half-finished plate and her superior's face. "I'm sorry you didn't like dinner. Please let me—"

"I'm fine, Yelizaveta," Petra sighed. "Really. I'm just tired."

Life was hard for young acolytes. They were the workhorses of the Temple, given the menial and often humbling tasks, and tended to be abused to varying degrees by those who forgot what it was like to be in their position. Like Max before her, Petra had made it *very* clear that new initiates were supposed to report any hazing or misuse of power directly to her — and those who mistreated them would be met with the harshest possible punishments.

That, of course, had the unintended consequence of making her a bit of a mother hen to the gaggle of wide-eyed devotees who came from San Francisco or were transferred to St. Emaine's from elsewhere. On the whole, they were good kids.

However, they loved to *hover.*

Yelizaveta lingered by her elbow, unaware of the jolt of alarm that ran through Petra at the feeling of yet another incoming message.

"But your grace, I noticed you haven't been eating as much," she whispered, wings folding and unfolding anxiously against her back. Like all initiates, she wore a pale yellow robe over her clothing. The color stood out starkly against her night-time coloring: a navy so deep, it looked like a starless sky.

Petra could only offer her a wan smile. "The stress of the visit is getting to me, I think. Here—" She stood up from her seat and gently extracted the empty tray from the initiate's clawed hands. "I know you haven't had dinner yet, so how about you finish what I can't?"

The dragon's eyes went as wide as saucers as they took in the spread of plates on the table — more than enough to feed several people. Petra hated waste, so all Temple leftovers were served to worshippers in need the following day. Not even a hungry dragon could eat enough to make a dent in what they gave out.

"I can't do that," the initiate protested. "I'm not allowed."

Technically, no, she wasn't. Initiates were expected to eat together in the kitchen after dinner was served to the rest of the staff, and usually far simpler fare than what everyone else got.

Normally Petra would have been more cautious about breaking a stupid taboo like that, as well as the implication of favor it might give, but she was anxious, exhausted, and had to sneak out to meet a mad demon.

I might die in a few days, she thought, firming her spine. *So who gives a fuck?*

"Sit, initiate," she commanded.

The room went curiously silent as all eyes turned to watch the girl sit nervously in Petra's silly, gilded chair while the High Priestess herself stood at her elbow, a sticky food tray tucked under her arm.

Her pocket buzzed again. Petra drew her shoulders back and faced the room. Projecting her voice, she announced, "All of you have been working exceptionally hard the past few weeks to make our cathedral ready for the Protector's visit. I can't express my appreciation enough." Pausing to lay a hand on Yelizaveta's shoulder, she continued, "But as you all know, nothing would be possible without the hard work of our initiates. In light of that, I'm ending dinner service early tonight. Initiates, please drop off your trays, grab some chairs, and join Initiate Yelizaveta at the high table to enjoy a well-earned break."

It was a credit to her staff, or perhaps how well her staff knew her, that there was only some minor grumbling when she added in a steely tone, "Everyone will be bringing their own dishes, as well as all communal plates, bowls, and cutlery, to the kitchen tonight. If I find out that *anyone* left their work for another, I'll speak to you personally tomorrow."

Buzz, buzz.

"Thank you," Yelizaveta whispered, head down, as her fellow initiates scrambled to leave their trays in the kitchen and race back to the dining hall.

Petra gave her shoulder a squeeze. "Enjoy your dinner."

Her pocket buzzed again, but she ignored it as she strolled out of the dining hall, the tray tucked under her arm, and toward the kitchen. A chorus of appreciation and breathless smiles greeted her as the gaggle of initiates ran by her.

I'm not beholden to you, she thought, imagining Shade's dangerous smile as she informed the kitchen staff about the change to dinner's usual structure.

She wasn't certain how he'd found out about her secret phone. She didn't know if he was watching her from the shadows. She had no idea what he wanted with her power or what he'd do to her when he found out she had no intention to go through with their bargain.

But she wasn't powerless.

They were playing a game of cat and mouse. It was well past time she showed him that he wasn't dealing with some soft, pampered priestess who shook in her vestments whenever he said something crude.

She was a motherfucking witch, and she'd bite any hand that dared hold her leash.

Chapter Ten

It was a dim sum restaurant.

Petra wasn't entirely sure what she'd expected when she snuck out of the secret passageway in her suite, but a cheerfully lit, hole-in -the-wall restaurant with a cartoon dumpling dancing across vid screens in its windows wasn't it. That should have been her first tip-off that something was wrong.

The second, she realized too late, was the low purr of a well-tuned engine.

It happened too fast for her to scream, and even if it hadn't, she couldn't have risked it. One moment she stood on the curb, trying to peer past the glare of over-bright screens showing tempting dishes she would have liked to try on any other night, the cartoon dumpling bouncing between each one like a cheerful little rubber ball, and the next an arm banded around her middle and darkness shrouded her eyes.

Within a handful of seconds she was thrown in a car, her wrists and ankles locked together by something insubstantial and yet unbreakable.

"If you were hungry, you should have met me earlier." The deep, southern drawl of Shade's voice was too loud in the dark cocoon he'd wrapped around her. Petra thrashed, magic bubbling beneath her skin, as he pulled away from the curb.

Willfully misinterpreting her struggles, he added, "I did text you asking you what you wanted, but you didn't reply, so I just got you some tea. I'll let you have it if you promise not to throw it in my face. I don't want to have to get this car detailed again."

A heavy hand, hot and familiar, settled on her thigh. "Will you be good, little goddess?"

I'm going to kill you, she silently promised, nodding. *I'm going to burn your cock off like a hot dog left on a fucking grill.*

"Good girl," he praised. It didn't sound like he really believed her, but rather that he found the situation funny. Giving her thigh a little squeeze, he cajoled, "Remember, girls who keep their promises get rewards."

She couldn't even *begin* to imagine what kind of reward it would require for her to ever, in a million years, willingly follow the sociopath's directions, but Petra didn't say that. She couldn't, not with his shadows sealed over her eyes and mouth like ethereal duct tape.

The shadows lifted. Petra reacted on pure instinct and fury.

Without thinking, she twisted to throw a punch directly at the side of his smug head.

Shade caught it, of course. He held her fist in his much bigger hand and shot her a disapproving look. "Really? When I'm driving? If we get in a car crash, it's not me who'll die. You're the fragile one, baby."

Baby? Petra showed him her teeth. "You *kidnapped* me!"

"Only a little." He pried her rigid fist apart with his thumb —*just his thumb* — and brought her palm to his mouth for a searing kiss.

That simple, shocking contact of lips and scraping teeth, was more terrifying than being shoved, blind and gagged, into a car. Petra gasped and jerked her arm. Her magic, already hot and roiling, surged toward that small point of connection until it seared her palm, desperate to be free.

Shade let out a hiss as his face was suddenly bathed in a yellow-orange glow. "Like trying to kiss the fuckin' sun," he muttered, going in for another like it was some mad challenge.

"Do that again and I'll burn your lips off," she snapped.

Those amber-on-black eyes cast her a heavy-lidded look even as he lowered her hand to rest on *his* thigh, dangerously close to bits she was certain he didn't want scorched. "I like that you've got claws, little goddess."

It would have been wonderful to react, to have some quick retort to wipe the smug, lustful look off of his handsome face, but she didn't. For a moment, she could only sit there and gape at him.

She didn't even have the presence of mind to take her hand off of his tense thigh when she noted, "Something is seriously wrong with you, Shade."

And there was clearly something, perhaps many somethings, seriously wrong with her, too, because, *gods help her,* she was almost certain her panties were wet.

The way his grin widened in that slow, unspooling way as his nostrils flared all but confirmed it long before he drawled, "I think you like that about me about as much as I like it about *you,* little goddess."

She knew that her childhood, the way her parents had raised her and the people they associated with — Max excluded — had probably predisposed her to finding certain less-than-societally-acceptable traits attractive, but it was a humbling thing, actually experiencing it.

"Any attraction I might have to you is strictly involuntary and immediately canceled out by how much I'm learning to hate you."

"Nah, it's not. Your body knows I'll be a good fuck. She's just gotta wait your head out." Shade lifted the hand that had been loosely covering her own on his thigh to reach behind him. His eyes never left the road as he pulled a small paper bag out from the back seat and dropped it unceremoniously into her lap. "Drink your tea and buckle up."

Petra finally had the presence of mind to pull her hand away from his thigh, but the fact that she experienced a moment of hesitation at all was galling.

"What is going on?" she demanded, ignoring both of his instructions on principle. "Seriously, Shade, what the fuck is happening?"

"I'm taking you for a drive," he answered. His tone was infuriatingly glib. Nothing in the relaxed way he steered the car — a small, sporty thing that zipped along the streets at speed that *definitely* wasn't built into the m-grid — indicated that their situation was in any way unusual.

Petra wanted to claw his spooky demon eyes out. "Where?"

"Good girls get answers," he sing-songed, "and good girls buckle their fuckin' seatbelts."

It cost her greatly, but Petra did, in fact, put her seatbelt on. Not because her stomach did unwelcome little flips when he praised her, but because she worried she really would attack him again if she didn't occupy her hands.

She opened her mouth to demand answers again, but he beat her to it. "Tea, little goddess. And maybe a bite of the snack I brought you."

Petra's fingers clenched in the paper bag. Her throat went oddly tight when she asked, "You *did* buy me food?"

Shade didn't look at her. He simply shrugged, his wide shoulders moving under his tight black t-shirt, as he guided the car onto the Golden Gate Bridge. "You haven't been eating much."

And just like that, any uncomfortable feelings she might have felt tickling at the back of her mind vanished.

"You're watching me."

"Of course I am." Shade rested his right arm on the console between them. His long fingers dangled over the edge, just enough to tickle her knee with the very tips of his claws. "You think I'd let you run around unsupervised when I still don't have my half of the deal?"

"It's not like I have mine either," she argued. "All I've gotten is a demon invading every aspect of my life! And now *kidnapping.*"

"Don't forget a drink you'll love and egg rolls for naughty priestesses who don't finish their dinners."

It was absolutely shameless, the way he talked about watching her, the way he mocked her. He didn't try to hide it or even make it overtly threatening. It just *was*. The fact that he knew she hadn't eaten much at dinner was as much a simple fact as it was a power play.

"Did you tap into the cameras? Do you have an informant? Tell me, Shade," she demanded.

"None of the above."

"Then *how*—"

"Easy, Petra," he drawled, giving her knee a little tap with his fingertips. "I'm just protecting what's mine. Now that I'm back from my little trip, no more surveillance." He paused, jaw working from side to side, before he added in a darker tone, "No one and nothing has been in your room. That's a promise."

"Why on Burden's Earth would I *ever* believe you?"

"Because," he replied, finally losing patience and reaching over to open the bag himself, "starting tonight, you aren't leaving my sight."

Petra recoiled so fast, the back of her head hit the window. "Excuse me?"

Shade rooted around in the bag for a moment before he extracted a bottled drink. Pale green liquid sloshed against the sides and what looked like cubes of dark pink jelly tumbled around the bottom. Still somehow watching the road, he stuffed it into her limp hand. "You heard me. We're going to go for a little drive, have a nice chat—" he cut her a disconcertingly hard look "—without glamours, and then we'll go back to the cathedral. I have my bag packed and everything."

Petra's fingers closed weakly around the chilled bottle. "You can't do that."

"I can do whatever I want."

So much for showing him who's boss. Petra felt a bit like she was drowning. Her breath fought to come faster, but she ruthlessly clamped down on her panic, trying to will it out of existence. "No, you *can't*. I'm the one who hired you, remember?"

Shade released a long, slow breath and tipped his head toward her. "Petra," he drawled, "if you think you're the one in control here, then you aren't nearly as smart as I thought you were."

It was ludicrous to argue when she had been kidnapped not fifteen minutes prior, but still, Petra had to try.

"This is my deal, Shade," she rasped, "and if you aren't going to listen to me, then I don't have to honor it."

The truth was that she had no intention of making him her bondmate, but he didn't know that. Shade had proven to be far more volatile than she could have ever guessed. It was well within her rights to call off their deal now, since neither of them had fulfilled their end of the bargain yet.

I should have called this off days ago.

She should have done it the moment she discovered him in her room, his shoulders draped in her nightgown. Maybe even as soon as she met him.

She couldn't control this man. No one could. And now that he'd been unleashed on her life, she worried that he was becoming an even bigger problem than the one she'd sought to solve.

Shade was quiet for a moment as they joined the flow of traffic toward the Marin side of the bay. She held her breath, waiting for an explosion, or a threat, or even violence as he processed her ultimatum.

But he surprised her.

His drawl was calm, *almost* patient, when he ordered, "Drink, little goddess. You're gonna need the caffeine."

CHAPTER ELEVEN

Even disguised by the glamour she wore, Petra looked a little shellshocked as she nibbled on a crispy eggroll and drank her tea. The expression in her eyes, illuminated in pale blue-green from the controls on his modified dashboard, was lost.

Good.

It was always best to keep wily opponents wrong-footed, and Petra Zaskodna was, if nothing else, wily.

"Where are you taking me?"

Silas brushed the backs of his claws against her kneecap again. He hadn't quite been able to stop himself from finding reasons to touch her and didn't care to besides. He didn't like her glamour, impressive though it was. He wanted to see *her*, but since he was driving, he couldn't find where she'd placed the sigil to anchor it in place.

Smelling her but not *seeing* her made the animal in him restless, aggressive. It urged him to pull over the car and pin her in place as he searched for that damn sigil. Then he'd wipe it away, revealing golden hair and pale blue eyes and a lush mouth and the too-striking cheekbones that made her features almost brutal.

The animal craved a look at that face. It wanted to spend the upcoming frenzy of the rut with her, yes, but it also just wanted to *bask* in her. But Silas had a destination in mind, so he soothed the animal by stroking her tense knee and breathing her in.

He wasn't typically one for explanations, but he made an exception for her. "We're going somewhere I know there won't be any listening ears."

"We couldn't have stayed in San Francisco?"

"San Francisco is one of the single most surveilled cities on the *planet.*" That's why he preferred to work pretty much anywhere else on the continent, though the Draakonriik was also a royal pain in his ass.

Elves were worse, though. Enriched by the technological boom and a collectively ruthless business savvy, they kept a tight fist on their territory — who came in, who left, and what a person did nearly every moment they were there. The EVP was known for being one of the most highly controlled areas of the continent, but what few average people understood was that it also boasted a correspondingly intelligent and ruthless underground network of spies, criminals, and black markets.

What even fewer knew, even among his ilk, was that those underground activities were closely monitored and sanctioned by the EVP itself. Nothing, not even crime, happened in an elf's territory without their consent.

Which was exactly why he stayed the fuck out. Usually. Silas didn't play within the EVP's rules for criminals nor did he care to report to Kazimier Le Roy, the orcish attack dog secretly in charge of the intelligence unit that patrolled the underground. They would be stupid to trust Silas even if he said he would.

He'd been playing a little game with the orc for years. Whenever he snuck across the border, he made sure to let Kaz know — after he'd slipped back out. A sort of mutual respect existed between them, something developed over years of near-misses and exchanges of information. Silas let Kaz know where the holes in his security were, which he thought was awfully generous of him. In exchange, Kaz continued to let him come and go with only cursory attempts at capture.

Silas had nothing against Kaz other than the fact that he would probably put a bolt between his eyes the second the orc saw him in San Francisco. There were no hard feelings about it one way or the other. It was a matter of principle and winning the game.

It would become much, much more than that if the orc knew Silas was only *in* the city to steal the plans for the m-generator his new mate co-created.

Silas rubbed the backs of his claws against the denim covering Petra's knee once more. That restlessness in him only grew when he thought of what might happen should Kaz — very distracted as of late, apparently — discover that Silas was a threat to his mate.

Normally, he would have rolled his eyes at the dramatics he imagined, loads of snarling and threats and piping hot plasma bolts ready to melt a hole through his brain, but now...

He understood it. Just a little.

He didn't like people touching his things, either.

"You understand that women generally don't like being kidnapped and then driven in the dead of night to some undisclosed location, right?"

Silas rolled his eyes. "Why would I kill you if I need your bond?"

Petra went quiet again. After some time, she said, "There are worse things than being murdered, Shade."

"You seem to know an awful lot about the worst things in the world," he replied, careful to keep his voice level. "I wonder why that is."

She said nothing, but he didn't expect her to. As he'd learned over the last few days, his little goddess wasn't entirely what he thought she'd be. She remained a hypocrite, certainly, but everything else he thought he knew was smoke and mirrors.

Petra was a far better liar — a far more *experienced* liar — than he ever would have given her credit for.

His words hung in the air as they drove for an hour in silence.

Silas noticed that she'd finished every drop of tea and even licked the tiny crumbs of the eggroll off the tip of her finger, but he couldn't tell if it was a task to keep herself occupied or some other compulsion.

Tal told me she hasn't been eating much, but I didn't think she was starving.

He'd tasked his reluctant brother with watching over her while he did his recon, but the update he'd received upon returning to the city had been more confusing than helpful, particularly in light of what he'd learned.

Every day, she woke up before dawn to perform her service. She ate breakfast afterward, usually in her office, where she took meetings with worshippers, planned weddings, and did administrative tasks. Lunch was eaten amongst the dead, hidden in a tower above the main cathedral, and the rest of the day was spent either running community programs or instructing the initiates under her care. Then dinner, bed, and it began again.

She's good to her people, Tal had told him, sounding even more troubled than when Silas left. *Doesn't take shit, but is always patient. She works hard, plays with kids in the nursery, never gets angry when someone accidentally messes up. I don't think she knows it, but most of the staff adore her. I didn't see one suspicious thing, Silas. Not one. I don't think she does anything other than live and breathe her work. I don't even know if she actually sleeps.*

Someone else might have wondered if they'd misjudged her, but not Silas. Because no one, no good, *normal* person, sought him out. Ever. So he had to wonder who the real Petra was, hidden beneath so many masks. Who was the real woman? The one who performed so well under constant surveillance, or the one who felt comfortable seeking the help of a known killer?

He thought he might get some answers from his trip up north, but he'd only gotten more questions.

Because, as it turned out, Antonin Vanderpoel wasn't the only ghost.

It was nearly midnight by the time he pulled into the gravel driveway of the tiny coastal shack he kept for emergencies. It was too dark to make out much of the squat wooden home or its red walls, tucked in amongst towering, spindly trees sloped by the wind, but he knew every inch of the land on which it sat.

Like all his properties, it was warded so tightly, no one but him and whoever he allowed could step foot on it. Even if they wanted to, it was almost impossible to see. He'd crafted funhouse mirrors of magic and power, distorting the image of the land, the road, the home, until what an outsider saw bore no resemblance to what was actually there.

Silas cut a glance at Petra, wondering what she'd make of it. He wasn't disappointed.

She sat ram-rod straight in her seat, the empty bottle of tea in her white-knuckled grip, and stared out the windshield at the cottage with eyes that were wide enough to show white around the edges.

His home in the city was equally well warded. A bomb blast wouldn't have made a dent in his defenses there, though that house was, by necessity, far more exposed to the public than the shack and therefore required more finesse in his work. Despite what he told her, she would have been safe and their conversation private if he'd simply taken her to his home in San Francisco.

But she wouldn't have been as unsettled there, and that part was essential. Shaking her secrets loose wouldn't happen if he didn't rattle her a little.

"What are you hiding in there?" she asked, voice pitched so low he almost missed it.

Silas unclipped his seatbelt and then, because she seemed to have turned to stone, reached over her to do hers, too. "Nothing but some furniture, a fireplace, and canned soup."

He was bent over her, contorted to twist over the console, when she turned her head sharply to face him. Nose to nose, their breath mingling between them, he thought he could *just* see between the shimmering layers of her glamour.

Petra nearly breathed the words against his mouth when she hissed, "Is this where you take people to kill them?"

Fuck. The urge to snake his tongue along her plush bottom lip, undisguised by her illusion, was a visceral thing. He'd never been one for kissing, really, but with Petra... Yes, he could understand why others enjoyed it so much. He wanted to suck the breath from her lungs until she came to *him* for air.

"No," he answered, unlatching her seatbelt's mechanism. His voice sounded like crushed gravel. Shadows stirred around the car, awakened by the deep, dark thing in him that reached for her. "Mostly I kill people in their own homes. You think I'd go through all this effort just to clean a bunch of brainmatter off my own walls?"

He *tsked.* "Baby, I'm not gonna kill you. I'm gonna *interrogate* you. If you're a good girl and answer all my questions, I might even fuck you after." Silas fought the desire to kiss her, knowing he should save that for another time, and instead brushed his lips, so very gently, against the silky curve of her cheek. "Even little goddesses like to come, don't they?"

He said it mostly to get a rise out of her — gods knew she needed to do so very little to get one out of him — but he was pleased as punch when it did something else.

The thread of scent in the air was unmistakable. He was pretty sure it was branded into his brain the first time he smelled it, but *now,* up close and stronger than before, it was a siren's song.

Petra's desire was like ambrosia on his tongue.

Her expression was shuttered, her glamoured eyes almost hateful, but her scent couldn't be controlled — and demons had damn good noses.

Silas couldn't help it. He laughed.

My pretty hypocrite, he thought, pressing a quick kiss to the tip of her nose, *you're more fucked up than I thought.*

CHAPTER TWELVE

STILL CHUCKLING, SILAS CLIMBED OUT OF HIS CAR AND circle around to open her door. Petra didn't move. She didn't look at him. She didn't do anything at all except say, in a flat voice, "Nothing in this world could compel me to go into that house with you."

"Baby." He crouched down next to her and gently extracted the paper bag and empty bottle from her hands. Setting it down in the footwell, he grabbed her calves and guided her legs out until the tips of her little black boots touched his thighs. "How much do you want that information from Vanderpoel?"

She still wouldn't look at him, but she couldn't hide the way her throat bobbed with a hard swallow. "Not enough to do that."

It took him a second to follow her train of thought. Silas blinked. "That's not part of the deal."

Petra's lips went thin and bloodless. It took her a second to find the words, but when she did, they were brimming with venom. "Isn't it? When you say things like that, what am I supposed to think? Apparently you have all the control here and now you're saying you want to fuck me. That makes it part of the deal."

Silas really had to think about that. Normally he never

mixed sex with business, so it hadn't occurred to him that he was doing exactly that. To him, fucking his little goddess and making a deal with Petra were two different things. Two straight lines running in the same direction, perhaps, but they never touched.

Something oily and uncomfortable squirmed in his gut the longer he looked at her rigid body language. *She feels powerless.*

He wanted that. He liked knowing he'd bent Glory's favorite to his will, that she'd take food from his hand, that she might come begging on her knees for a taste of demon cock.

But, he realized with an unsettling jolt, he didn't want it to be *forced*.

None of it would satisfy him unless she wanted to give him the power, because what attracted him to Petra *was* her power. He wanted her to hand it over to him because he valued it, *her*, so very much.

It didn't appear she noticed that even at that moment, he was knelt before her. She didn't know that he was asking, not taking, nor that by doing so, he was freely admitting how much power she had over *him*.

He thought she understood the game, but like with everything else involving her, Silas had apparently miscalculated.

Masks and secrets and more. Every time he thought he knew her, Petra revealed something new facet that threw him off balance.

"Look at me."

When she stubbornly refused, he grabbed one of her ankles and gave it a good wiggle. "Petra, give me your eyes."

Bless her, she did try to kick him then, which was exactly what he wanted. With her extended leg caught in his grip, she couldn't help but glare at him, her brows turned down and her soft mouth pinched.

"You need to understand something," he told her in a voice as close to gentle as he could get. "You are one of the very few people in this world who can say no to me."

He understood why she looked at him like he'd grown a different set of horns, but he really didn't appreciate it.

"I've *been* saying no!"

"I mean about everything *other* than our deal," he amended. "That's set in stone. Your bond is mine, Petra, and the methods I use to fulfill our bargain aren't up for debate."

"Then how—"

He gave her ankle a squeeze. "Let me finish before you give me a dressing down, woman."

The look she gave him could have peeled paint. He loved it.

It was hard work suppressing his grin when he continued, "Our deal is our deal, but it also means two things: first, that I need you alive, and second, that if I'm going to be stuck with you for the rest of my life, then you can't hate me *too* much."

He wasn't sure what he wanted from her besides her bond and the deeply satisfying knowledge that she belonged to him alone, but hate wasn't it.

"I get a thrill out of fuckin' with you, but the only reason it's fun is because you're a powerful woman. You are a *High Priestess.* Every room you're in, you shine so bright you blind everyone else. You're a gloriana with the ability to wield fuckin' *light.* You think I want you beaten down or backed into a corner, giving me whatever I want because you're scared?"

Silas leaned into the passenger's side of the car. Bracing his hands on either side of her thighs, he pressed his lips against the shell of her ear and breathed in the scent of her ridiculous glamoured hair. "Baby, the fun comes from knowing you *want* me to have the power. I'd like nothing more than to know for a fuckin' fact that you are desperate for my cock. I want to know I own a goddess — body and soul."

She began to breathe faster. He was desperate to see the look in her eyes, but he held himself there through will alone. Silas intended to settle something between them tonight, and though he hadn't thought of this before, he realized it was vitally important they get this straight, too.

"If you don't want it, I'll never force you," he promised.

The thought had never even crossed his mind. Everyone was capable of violence, but demons were particularly sensitive to sexual coercion. Ruts made things messy and often dangerous, so clans had to be extremely strict about sexual boundaries. Not to mention the fact that they damn near worshipped the very concept of matehood.

He couldn't say he fit into much of clan life, but those things had made an impression on him. Silas doubted he'd ever be a mate, but he would never stoop to coercing a woman into something she didn't want.

The thought of *Petra* — strong, stunning, powerful Petra — worrying that he might do that to her made that sick, oily feeling return with a vengeance.

He wasn't sure he really meant it, but he tried to when he added, "You can call this thing between us off, Petra, if you really can't believe I wouldn't ask that of you. But if you go into that house with me, then there's no backing out. This is the line. Once you cross it, you're never getting rid of me."

Truthfully, he wasn't sure there was ever much of a chance of that, but if there was, then she needed to get as far from him as possible *now.*

He couldn't promise that he wouldn't chase her down, but he'd let her get a headstart first.

Silas pulled back enough to see her face and was annoyed anew at the sight of a stranger peering back at him. But he knew Petra. He knew his little goddess's soul, even if he didn't know her past. He could make out *her* in the oddly dark eyes, the expression that tightened those foreign features.

"How do I know I can trust you?"

"You can't," he answered simply. "I wouldn't even trust me."

He expected her to get angry at that, but she didn't. Petra seemed to anticipate that answer and, perhaps sensing the honesty in it, only nodded. "No sex unless I say so explicitly, and I need something from you to make this feel equal." After a thoughtful beat, she demanded, "Give me your name. Your *real* name."

Gods, she's magnificent.

People a thousand times more dangerous and powerful than her had killed for the knowledge she demanded so easily. No one had ever come close to figuring it out and he intended to keep it that way. Silas's clan had nothing to do with what he'd made of his life. They were good people with kids and feelings and shit. He was a monster, but he protected and provided for his clan because they were *his.*

Giving Petra his name was like giving her the key to them.

She could use it against him. She could sell it to a hundred different people who wouldn't hesitate to slaughter everyone in the little town they occupied. She would hold one of the very few precious things he guarded in the palm of her hand.

And, for reasons he didn't truly understand, he wanted to give it to her.

Silas lifted her right hand to his lips. Pressing a kiss to the back of her hand, he murmured, "My name's Silas Augustus Cuttcombe. It's a pleasure to meet you, ma'am."

Petra let out a short breath. If she was surprised by his concession, she hid it behind an immediate and amusing burst of suspicion. "What do you expect in return for that?"

He didn't pretend to hesitate. His witch was canny enough to know he'd never give something like that up for free because *she* wouldn't.

"No more glamours."

"I can't walk around the city without being recognized," she protested.

"You won't be recognized." He dug into his back pocket. It was awfully dark for her eyes, but she must have been able to see well enough because the moment he extracted the necklace from his pocket, she made an odd, squeaky sound and slapped her hand against her chest. She groped around, feeling for the chain that hung there.

"Is that my necklace?"

"A replica," he assured her, without explaining that it was a much nicer necklace than the one she wore every day. Hers was gold *plated*. His was solid twenty-four karat.

Setting it and its long, delicate chain into her palm, he guided her to run her fingers over the flat side of Glory's sun symbol. It was the side that would rest against her skin, and it was engraved with a hundred tiny sigils he'd carved with a jewelers drill.

"Wear this instead. I've personalized it to you. Every time you activate the glamour, it'll create a different set of features so you're even less likely to be recognized."

Petra's hand trembled under his. "Why would you do this? I thought you didn't want me to wear glamours."

"I don't want you to wear glamours *I* can't see through," he corrected her. "And even though you have impressive skills for an amateur, yours can be wiped away by a careless napkin." *Or a demon's seeking fingers.* "This is much harder to remove."

There was more to it than that, of course. A simple glamour charm would have done the trick, but he was never one for simplicity. She didn't need to know what else he'd packed into the small pendant, though.

Petra tried to force the necklace back into his hand. "I can't afford this."

That was true. Unless she had several million dollars squared away, she couldn't have afforded even half the work he'd put into the necklace. Imbuing objects with magic, even with sigilwork, took finely-honed skill and patience. It was just lucky for her that, after decades of secret research, he was an expert in that sort of thing.

"You aren't paying for it," he replied, annoyed that she'd turn down a gift. The animal in him didn't like that at all. "Consider it an insurance policy to keep my investment safe."

"I..." Her words died on her tongue. Rather than the angry silences she'd fallen into before, this one seemed genuinely baffled.

Silas clicked his tongue and, knelt there in the gravel driveway, helped her remove the original necklace. She was docile as he looped the long chain over her neck and only watched, wide-eyed, as he transferred it to himself.

Once it was in place against his chest, deliciously warmed by her body heat, he plucked the replica from her limp hand and did the same process for her.

"There," he announced, exceedingly pleased now that everything was sorted. "C'mon."

She was quiet as he helped her climb out of the car. With one hand tucked behind her back, he guided her toward the shack. The necklace bumped his breastbone with every step. He imagined it was an echo of her heartbeat, thumbing away in time with his own.

Beside him, looking lost in the dark, Petra whispered, "Thank you, Silas."

CHAPTER THIRTEEN

WALKING INTO THE TINY, DARKENED COTTAGE WAS maybe the single stupidest thing Petra had ever done.

Once upon a time, she'd taken pride in her self-preservation instincts. She'd survived circumstances that would have landed most people face down in a gutter solely because she kept her eyes open at all times and trusted no one. She didn't take risks. She didn't believe kind words unless they were backed up by cold, hard facts.

But that was before Max's murder.

The Petra that had survived, the one content with a safe life obscured in the hierarchy of the Temple, died the day she received his ashes in the secret post office box they'd set up so many years prior.

Every day since, a little bit more of her caution had been rubbed away by the grit of grief and anger. By the time she stood in the doorway of Shade's — *Silas's* — cottage, she'd been worn down into a new shape, a different sort of woman.

That woman took risks because she had nothing left to lose.

Petra watched Silas stride into the dark entryway of the cottage, his movements almost feline in their grace, and felt the weight of the necklace he'd given her. It rested beneath her shirt, heavier than the one she'd received upon accession from initiate to priestess, and imbued with enough raw, wild power to hum against her flesh.

Silas. His name is Silas. The thought carried more weight than the necklace. More power. More everything.

It was an odd thing, to realize one stood on the precipice of the end of their life. No matter what she chose in that moment, her life as she knew it would end, and she felt the weight of it in the necklace, pulling her down until her spine strained under the force.

The old Petra would have balked at following Silas. She would have rejected the burning coal of attraction smoldering in her stomach. She would have walked away.

But that woman had the luxury of a long, independent life. The new Petra did not.

Her time to make choices had narrowed into days, not months or years or the centuries she should have had. To some degree it hadn't truly felt *real* until that moment.

If she didn't die by the Protector's hand, then she would become his creature, bound to him by magic and blood. Either way, her world would end.

She'd accepted that weeks ago, but now, here, she realized she'd been given a gift — not a reprieve, not a savior, but a chance to make a choice before all else was stolen from her.

Fuck it, she thought, forcing her feet across the threshold.

She didn't trust Silas, but it didn't really matter because something had shifted between them, a great leveling that she felt more than she could truly articulate. Silas hadn't just given her his name — real or fake, she couldn't say — but the knowledge that she held power over him.

In a moment when she knew her agency would be snatched from her, it was a heady thing.

So she followed him, risks be damned, and watched him with new eyes as he flicked a light switch on, revealing a quaint little sitting room and corner kitchen. A short hallway led to what she could only presume was a bedroom and bathroom.

"Sit," he ordered, gesturing to a small couch situated across from an old fashioned iron stove.

It was a habit to argue, as she'd never been one to take direction well, but she was so overwhelmed by the turns things had taken that she shrugged it off. Petra sank onto the couch's cushions and watched in a daze as the demon knelt to open the stove's grate. He expertly piled kindling from a basket in the belly of the stove and reached for a box of matches.

"I can do that."

Petra wasn't entirely sure why she offered. The season rested on the cusp of summer and though the night had a coastal coolness to it, she wasn't cold. Even if she was, he had matches to light the thing. It was pure habit, she realized, to help him light a fire.

Silas turned his head to give her one of those knife-sharp smiles. "Does the little goddess wish to bless the flame for me?"

She could do nothing about the flush that infused her cheeks. "Figured you might not want to waste a match is all."

"By all means." Silas shifted away from the stove and gestured grandly toward the kindling. "Go ahead, your grace."

His taunting drew her spine up, but she got up from the couch anyway. Kneeling as close to him as she dared, Petra reached into the stove to press her fingertips against the kindling.

Magic bubbled up from somewhere deep in her body — a molten core of power that was both a gift and a curse from Glory herself. For those like Petra, witches powerful enough to be called gloriana, that same power would eventually eat their soft, human bodies alive without the assistance of a witchbond.

The very same power that manipulated the light around her, refracting it and honing it to suit her will, was the thing both Silas and the Protector craved. She never had ambitions for her abilities, preferring to keep the elemental force of her magic tucked close to her heart. Petra used the gift Glory had given her to bless others, lighting sacred fires, burning marriage sigils into flesh, and offering comfort to worshippers.

This was no sacred fire, but she worked her magic on it all the same. In an instant, her will narrowed the focus of the light around her and within her, refracting it like the lens of a magnifying glass, to set the kindling ablaze.

Petra withdrew her hand slowly. She savored the warmth of the fire like the touch of a loved one. In every lick of flame, she felt the life of the goddess and those who'd basked in her light. Sometimes, she even imagined she could feel Max there, speaking in the crackle of wood and sparks.

"What do you see in there?"

She sat back on her haunches, her attention drawn to the demon who'd sprawled on the floor beside her, one knee drawn up to his chest and his unnerving eyes fixed on her.

Wiping her fingers on her pant leg, she answered, "Glory isn't just the goddess of sunlight, you know. She's also the wielder of flame. She exists in all fires."

Silas quirked a brow. His expression wasn't just mocking. It was *disbelieving*. "You don't honestly believe in all that, do you? You're too smart for that."

"Believe in what? The gods?"

"Yes."

Petra scrutinized him for a long moment. Slowly, she asked, "Do you think I get up in front of hundreds of people every day and lie about what I believe in?"

He didn't even have the grace to look abashed, but then again, she never really expected him to. "You lie about other things. Why wouldn't you lie about that?"

Silas had unknowingly touched on a nerve, but Petra did her best to keep her temper in check when she answered him. "I don't necessarily agree with all the pageantry and ceremony and hierarchy of the Temple, but I believe in what I say."

"If you don't like the pageantry and the ego of the Temple, then how come you're the High Priestess of San Francisco?" That smile played around the corners of his mouth. "I find it hard to believe that someone who doesn't play by the Temple's rules would skyrocket to power like you did."

The hair on the back of Petra's neck stood on end. "And what would you know about that?"

Silas braced his weight on his hands. The firelight bathed the angles of his face and curve of his horns in gold and orange when he answered, "Good question. That's what I wanted to talk to you about, actually. See, I took a little trip up the coast to see if I could answer some of the questions I had about you, but the more I dug, the more questions I had."

She wasn't sure why she was shocked, but she was. There was nothing for him to find in her past. Max had made sure her records were clean, that there would be no trail back to her parents or organized crime or the children's home. After that, she'd lived in perfect obscurity, content with a safe life in Max's shadow in Seattle.

"What do you want to know?" she asked, trying to keep her tone as neutral as possible.

Silas was quiet for a moment. He studied her from under half-lowered lids, before he leaned close enough to brush a lock of hair behind her ear. "Remove the glamour."

"Can't you?"

She held her breath as he skated his fingertips over the curve of her ear and side of her jaw. "I would, but you were smart enough to put the sigil in a different place this time."

It was deeply worrying, the way something warm sparked in her chest at the hint of pride in his voice. Instead of dwelling on that, she ran her fingers through the hair at her temples, pressing the pads against her scalp until she felt the slightly oily texture of the eyeliner she'd used to draw the sigils.

Two were needed to anchor the "mask" in place. Usually she used concealer just below her ears or under her jaw, but with how easily he'd spotted them the first time, she'd taken the extra precaution of drawing tiny ones just inside her hairline. If anyone caught a glimpse of them, they might simply pass them off as freckles, which was helpful, but being in her hairline meant she could easily fidget and wipe them away.

Not that it matters now, she thought, nose tingling with the metallic scent of magic that burst in the air with the release of the spell.

Silas's smile fell. A new expression tightened his features — a thing of such intense scrutiny, she almost recoiled from it. His thumb skimmed the curve of her jaw again, only stopping when he could pinch her chin and turn her face one way, then the other.

Her heartbeat throbbed in her ears when he murmured, "Ah, there she is."

And just like that, he was back to lounging, the smile firmly fixed in place as if it had never disappeared. "Now, I want you to tell me *everything.*"

Chapter Fourteen

In a bid to buy herself a little bit of time to compose herself, Petra arranged herself into a more comfortable position. Settled with her spine against the coffee table, she managed to reply, "That's a tall order, Mr. Cuttcombe."

The addition of, "*and one I'm unlikely to fulfill*" went unsaid but not unheard between them.

She thought she detected real amusement in his amber-on-black eyes when he suggested, "Start with how it is a witch of no real rank or power went from a glorified Temple teacher to the head of one of the most powerful cathedrals in the UTA overnight."

Petra fought the urge to swallow the lump in her throat. "How do you know I had no real standing? The Temple hierarchy is obscure even to those of us in it."

"I know that someone in charge of initiates is basically the equivalent of a high school teacher," he answered, "and I know that no one of real power is given a room the size of a broom closet."

There it is. She knew what he implied when he said he'd taken a trip up the coast, but to hear him confirm that he'd been up to Seattle, that he knew where she used to *sleep,* was a chilling thing.

It was a power play, just like everything else he'd done, but it was also its own form of honesty. He wasn't trying to entrap her in a lie. Silas was letting her know what he knew — or thought he knew.

Petra watched him closely, cautiously, when she chose her words. *What's it matter? There isn't much time for him to use it against me, anyway.*

And deep down below the fatalistic veneer, Petra just... wanted to tell someone. She'd been playing a character for so long that she was exhausted by the effort. The urge to connect, even shallowly, with another person was a deep, guttural scream in the cavern of her gut.

"I wanted the position," she answered, "so I found a way to take it."

Silas leaned forward until he rested his forearm on his bent knee. He tilted his head in that predatory, assessing way she was becoming used to when he asked, "What naughty thing did you do?"

"Nothing horrible." She hated how defensive she sounded, how quick those words tumbled out of her. Petra had spent years unlearning so many bad lessons from her childhood that she felt a reflexive, cutting guilt whenever she recalled what she'd done to get her place in St. Emaine's. Even knowing it was the right thing to do, the shame bit at her, ridiculing her for falling back on lessons she'd long ago left behind.

Silas pursed his lips, clearly holding in a laugh. "D'you think I'm gonna judge you? Little goddess, you could tell me you'd castrated someone and it'd only make me want you more."

"That's really troubling. You know that, right?"

"You don't seem too troubled to me." He bit the tip of his tongue between his teeth and offered her a cheeky smile. "I think you actually *like* me."

Petra gave him the look that assumption deserved. "That's pushing it."

The demon had been nothing but trouble since she made the

mistake of seeking him out. He was crude, cruel, and entirely uncontrollable.

But she could allow that she did feel more comfortable around him than she'd felt with anyone else since Max's death. This wasn't because she was particularly fond of him, nor because she was attracted to him. It was because for *once* she didn't have to hide every little bit of her true self behind layers of masks.

She could never be vulnerable with him, but she could shake a little bit of the weight off. After all, he already knew she wasn't what she pretended to be. What was the point in keeping up the ruse when she could just *breathe* for a second?

Averting her eyes from his ever-widening grin and that annoying beauty mark above his lip, Petra continued, "When the sovereign poked his nose into the High Gloriae's business, my boss was asked to step in and help him see reason. Unfortunately, my boss's assistant wasn't able to make the trip, so I volunteered."

Petra couldn't look at him as she told the story, not because she worried she'd see disapproval there, but because she believed he'd like it *too* much. Instead, she buffed her thumbnail, covered in a semi-transparent pearlescent coat of polish, against her thigh and watched the fire.

"It was pure luck that my boss ate something that disagreed with him as soon as we got to the cathedral and that I just happened to be in the right place at the right time to intercept the sovereign and his consort when they came by looking for a wedding."

She'd never forget how her hands shook as she addressed the sovereign like she was anybody worth talking to. She rode on a wave of pure adrenaline as she negotiated with him, even daring to withhold her services as their officiant if he didn't help get her the seat.

Her, an orphaned street rat. A covenless witch with no connections, no family. All she had was a steely will and the ability to lie through her teeth.

Warm, callused fingers gripped the sides of her jaw. The tips of

Silas's claws pressed into her skin as he turned her face back to him. Petra's breath caught.

He was close, crouched before her like an animal about to pounce. Those molten eyes held her own, unblinking, when he growled, "Did you poison and *lie* your way into your position?"

Petra licked her lips. "Yes," she answered, soft but without the shame that wanted to force its way into every word. "I lied right to the sovereign's face and then told him I wouldn't marry them unless I got the seat. And, for the record, it was only barely a poisoning. They lived."

"You went from no one to one of the most influential witches in the entire UTA overnight based on a bluff."

She could feel her cheeks heating, but she refused to back down or break eye contact. No, she wasn't proud of what it'd taken to get where she was, but sometimes doing the right thing in the wrong way was the only option.

"Yes."

In hindsight, she probably should have seen the kiss coming, but even if she had, there was nothing Petra could have done to prepare herself for it.

Silas sealed their mouths together with all the heat and power of a welding torch. They fused instantly. Petra opened her mouth on a gasp, shocked by the roar of magic in her veins and the heady taste of him as he kissed her — *consumed* her. Silas's tongue traced her bottom lip, hot as a brand, before it snaked into her mouth to seek hers.

He held her head in place, tilting her how he liked, as she scrambled to find something to hold onto. Her fingers curled into the fabric of his t-shirt, stretched tight over his shoulders. Her mind went blank in a white-hot rush of sensation.

The scent of him. The heat of his body. The slick glide of their mouths as the kiss got messier, more carnal with every second. The taste of him on her tongue as he tipped her head back and devoured her.

She forgot that they'd made a deal. She forgot that she was

supposed to keep her head on straight and hold him at arm's length. She forgot and she *loved* it.

It had been so long since she'd had any kiss at all. Even before she set out to uncover the truth behind Max's death, she'd been leery about who she shared intimacies with. Relationships in the Temple tended to be fraught with expectation and political intrigue, making casual sex both commonplace and dangerous.

Her last partner had been a fellow initiate instructor. She'd liked him, but when he began asking leading questions about bonding, she was forced to end things.

Sex was certainly something she'd never risk in St. Emaine's, so she'd simply cut herself off from thinking about it — no great hardship when every day was a trial by fire.

Petra didn't even realize she missed the feeling of another person's body until Silas stroked his tongue along hers in a deep, ruthless kiss. Heat seared a path down her spine and then out, sparking every nerve until the warmth matured, turning syrupy and insistent.

A swirl of molten desire settled low in her middle, building pressure in her core as he somehow arranged her so she was straddling his lap. He rocked her down, against the hard ridge of his erection, and made an animal noise of want so guttural, she felt it between her thighs.

Silas fisted one hand in her hair, knotting it at the base of her skull, and reared back suddenly. His lips were swollen and red, but the look in his eyes was indecipherable. It was like he couldn't decide if he was turned on, delighted, or absolutely furious.

"Every fuckin' time," he rumbled, twisting his fingers in her hair until she was forced to tilt her head back, arching her neck. "Every *fuckin'* time I think I have you figured out, you trip me up. How?"

Petra's brows pulled together. Breathing hard, she bit out, "Maybe you should stop making so many assumptions about me."

He loomed over her, lips curled in a snarl. "I'll stop making assumptions when I figure out exactly who you are."

She couldn't help it — she *laughed*. It was either that or she start crying the big, ugly tears she'd been holding in for so very long. Gasping for breath, she asked, "Don't you get it yet? Gods, for someone who's supposed to be so smart, you can't see what's right in front of your fucking face."

The gleam in his eyes got even more unsettling when he brushed his lips against hers. It was a deceptively gentle gesture, contrasted sharply against the way her scalp stung. "Tell me, little goddess."

Petra's eyes closed automatically, against her will, as he whispered the words into her mouth in that silky drawl.

"I'm no one," she murmured. "Honestly, truly no one. There's no great truth to uncover in my past. I don't have ambitions. I don't want to be a member of the High Gloriae or play politics. I'm no one. Nothing."

Silas pulled back slowly. In the glow of the fire she could make out a flush in his pale skin and a dark, dangerous look in his eyes. "I don't believe you."

"Why?"

"Because someone who's *nothing* doesn't lie her way into power. *No one* doesn't have secret phones, secret accounts, and a past that begins halfway through their adolescence. *No one* doesn't bargain with a fuckin' king like it's her right. *No one* doesn't make me want to take you apart so I can finally fuckin' know what makes you tick. You're more than nothing, and you have a damn good reason to do what you did. So *tell* me."

"Tell you what?"

The drawl deepened into a raspy growl. "Tell me what you *want.*"

At that second, all Petra really wanted was to feel his lips on hers again. She didn't want to talk about the mess of her life or think about the rapidly approaching future. All she craved was the sensation of clawed hands on her skin and a cruel mouth forcing her to yield, to let *go*.

But something in the rigid set of his mouth told her he wouldn't accept that answer, no matter how desperately his hard cock strained against her through the barriers of their clothing.

Petra curled her fingers into his shoulders, hoping he felt the bite of her nails into his tough demon skin.

Her eyes stung. She hadn't realized how desperately she needed a tiny taste of oblivion until it was taken from her. Of all the things he'd done and said to her, this was by far the cruelest.

"I need to know who killed Maximilian Dooraker," she admitted, each word like broken glass in her throat. "I *have* to know."

Something cold skittered in Silas's eyes. In a voice gone disturbingly light, he said, "The dusty friend I found in your room? Ah, yes, I wondered about that."

It was a confusing experience, wanting to kiss and hit someone at the same time. Since it didn't look like the kissing would be happening any time soon — and she was rapidly losing the desire to do so — Petra leaned into her anger.

She squirmed in his lap, trying to free herself from his unyielding grip. "Damn it, Silas, if you touched—"

"Let me get this straight," he drawled, speaking over her, "you did all of this for a dead man? You lied to Theodore Solbourne's face, stole a powerful position, tracked me down, and traded yourself for a *man*."

Petra stilled. It was a natural, instinctive reaction to the quiet menace that permeated every syllable, every soft word that left his lips. She wasn't sure why she felt like she was suddenly sitting on a time bomb, but she knew it was true.

Hair still caught in his grip, it was all she could do to watch him as he digested that information, plucking out what he thought he knew and what he could only assume.

Her throat was almost too tight to get words out, but she did it. "I can't tell if you're jealous or disappointed."

"Both." It was a single, flat word, but it was somehow more terrifying than anything else he'd ever said to her.

Petra didn't owe him any answers. If he wanted to believe that she'd risked everything for the memory of a lover, then that was his issue, not hers. But something in that blank stare, that flat inflection, the way he went almost preternaturally still beneath her... It wasn't just scary. It *bothered* her.

A mean little part of her, embittered by the cruelty of the world, urged her to let him think whatever he wanted, but the part that had worked so hard to learn compassion felt almost *bad* for him.

It was ridiculous. He didn't have real feelings. He didn't care about her. He wanted to use her just as Antonin did. What did it matter if she saw something almost hurt in that immediate withdrawal from her? Even if she had all the time left on the Earth to try and fix whatever it was that was broken in Silas, she doubted she could.

But she didn't like lying to him about this, either.

It pissed her off, but still, she said, "Well, don't bother. Max and I weren't like that."

Silas didn't thaw, but his fingers flexed in her hair. "What were you?"

"Family."

If she expected him to soften, she would have been sorely disappointed. Silas appeared utterly unmoved. "What kind?"

"Does it matter?"

"Yes," he answered, eyes narrowed until the amber centers were barely visible, "because you're a liar."

It stung because it was true. It didn't matter that he said it without any particular judgment — which would have been rich, coming from him. She still felt the sting of shame.

Max had worked so hard to break her of the habit. *"You're safe now,"* he'd gently coached her, again and again. *"You never need to lie to me, Pet, when there's no chance I'll abandon you. No matter what you do or say."*

But he had. He'd abandoned her *twice*. And that wound had festered, pulling out old poisons until they oozed out of her in a constant, sour drip.

What would he think of me now?

"I'm not lying," she snapped. "If you don't believe me, that's your problem. It doesn't make a difference to me."

Perhaps anticipating the direction of her thoughts, Silas stopped whatever it was she was about to say by pressing the pad of his thumb against her lips. He smoothed it back and forth when he growled, "If you think none of this matters, then you're lying to *yourself*. There is a fuckin' world of difference between you sending me to get information on a professional rival and you doing *all of this* because a family member was murdered."

She saw it — the moment he put the pieces together. That dark, cold thing slithered back into his eyes. "Antonin Vanderpoel. You think he murdered Maximilian Dooraker."

Petra had never spoken the words aloud. She didn't dare. Even at that moment, when she believed no one would know except Silas, she hesitated.

"Petra." Her name came out like the crack of a whip — not a shout, but with such quiet intensity she felt it land with all the snap of broken-in leather.

"Yes," she finally forced herself to answer. "But it's more likely that he ordered one of his followers to do it."

"His followers?"

"The Protector of the Gloriae is in charge of investigations within the Temple, but he also commands the Ardeo." She broke out in a fresh wave of cold sweat just saying the name aloud. Petra tugged on Silas's shirt, trying to force him to really *listen*. "The Ardeo is what keeps every cathedral and every high ranking member of the Temple in check. They handle all Temple security and assets and secrets. They're *powerful*, Silas."

"The Ardeo was disbanded. Glory's Temple hasn't had a military since the seventeen hundreds," he argued, infuriatingly dismissive.

"Publicly. *Publicly* they haven't had a military since the Collapse, but they do. It's not something most acolytes know, but we all feel it. Max told me— He *knew* it was real. They have eyes and ears everywhere. That's why the entire cathedral is bugged. That's why any one of my staff might report my suspicious behavior at any moment. Even if they can't put a name to it, we all *know.*"

When he didn't appear convinced, perhaps thinking her *dramatic* again, Petra's desperation clawed up and out at last. Her voice was raw when she continued, "Max knew something about them. He said that there was something happening within the High Gloriae, that there'd been some shift after Antonin was appointed Protector. He said he was worried something really awful was brewing and then... And then a month later I got his ashes in the mail."

She had to suck in a breath to stop her voice from breaking. *Remember who you're talking to.*

"I don't expect you to care about any of that," she croaked, "but if you want the context, the truth, that's it. Antonin doesn't have a fixed headquarters. He travels from temple to temple, and that means he has to bring his shit with him wherever he goes — including whatever files he keeps. *Your* job is to find the proof that he ordered Max's murder and deliver it to Elise Sasini at *The San Francisco Light.*"

Silas was dreadfully quiet for several beats. His expression was inscrutable. She had no idea if he believed her, let alone took her claims with even an ounce of the seriousness they deserved.

Just when she couldn't take the silence any longer, Silas eased his fingers out of her hair to slowly drag his palm down the column of her throat. Speaking in a soft voice, he asked, "Why did he put a camera in your room, baby?"

Petra shook her head. "I... I miscalculated. I knew I needed to take Max's place if I ever wanted a chance to figure out the truth, but I didn't anticipate I'd draw Antonin's attention as much as I did. He's had his eyes on me from the moment the sovereign put my name in as his preference for the seat."

That was the truth. Or at least most of it.

A certain amount of surveillance had already been in place when she arrived, but things escalated significantly after the Protector's visit. Max's warnings to keep away from Antonin meant little when the man himself sought her out.

And she could do nothing but keep the horror and disgust under a thin veneer of calm when the look in the Protector's eyes had gone from coolly assessing to avaricious.

Petra held her breath again, praying that Silas would take what she'd given him at face value. She didn't want to have to explain the proposition she'd received, nor that the reason for the Protector's visit was to get an answer from her — one way or another.

Something told her he'd take the news that another man sought her witchbond poorly. If he pressed, she would be forced to lie.

At length, Silas let out a long, put-upon sigh. "Looks like my little goddess has made a mess. I can't tell if I'm annoyed or impressed by the sheer scale of your fuck-up. You really do need my help."

A bitter taste filled her mouth, wiping out whatever remained of her lust. "If you're referring to the fuck-up where I thought asking *you* for help would actually get me somewhere, then I agree with you. I'm also impressed by the scale of bullshit it's brought me."

Rubbing his thumb over her throbbing pulse, Silas gave her a long, mocking look. "Asking me for help was probably the smartest thing you could have done."

"Why is that?"

He stooped to press a featherlight kiss to her pursed lips. It was as silky and dangerous as the flat side of a knife sliding across her mouth. "Because I would have killed anyone else you asked."

Chapter Fifteen

I<small>F SHE WASN'T STRUNG OUT ON ADRENALINE AND</small> anger, Silas suspected Petra would have been dead on her feet by the time she reluctantly escorted him through the short, utilitarian secret passage connected to her closet.

It annoyed him that he'd missed the secret door when he went through her room, but not so much that he regretted it being there. That door would make coming and going much easier for him. Silas made a mental note to inform Tal of its existence in the morning.

Not that his brother needed doors. Tal could move from shadow to shadow in a way only a wraith could. If he wanted to, he could have hidden himself away in any tiny corner and no one but Silas would have known.

Not that he *would,* though. His brother wasn't allowed into Petra's den unless it was an emergency. Silas had made that very, very clear.

No one was allowed into her den but him. *Ever.*

He'd timed their little date to coincide with a morning when she wouldn't be expected to give dawn service, but his witch was used to early mornings and therefore struggled with the late hour. Considering how badly she'd begun to flag, he was impressed by how strongly she fought him on the sleeping arrangements.

"I'll sleep on the floor," she insisted again. She'd only just given up on trying to convince him to leave the cathedral grounds entirely and seemed to have swung hard to putting all her weight behind a ridiculous notion that they wouldn't be sleeping together.

Silas dropped his backpack on the floor next to his side of the bed — the one closest to the hidden door, because one never knew — and rummaged around for his sleep pants.

His preference was to sleep nude, of course, but quick escapes were a pain with a cock out.

"Sleep on the floor and I'll just join you there," he said, extracting his clothing.

"*Why?*"

"Besides the fact that I want to wake up with your ass cradling my cock in the morning? Well, tonight I learned that you do a lot of stupid, reckless shit when no one is watching, so it's now in my best interest to make sure I have my eye on you at all times."

If Petra went any redder, she'd match her formal robes perfectly. When she spoke, it was through her teeth. "You can keep an eye on me just fine without *sleeping next to me.*"

"Nah, that's an essential part of the process." Silas toed off his boots and reached for the collar of his shirt. Pulling it over his head, he told her, "Besides, I wanna try it. Never slept a night with a woman. I might hate it. Who knows?"

Going by the way Petra made a gurgling noise and spun around, averting her eyes from his naked chest like she hadn't sucked on his tongue earlier, he was *pretty sure* he'd like it. He was growing to like just about everything about Petra.

My little puzzle, he thought, grinning at the back of her head as he popped the brass button of his jeans. *I'm going to take you apart to see how you work.*

Once he'd crushed Vanderpoel's head under his boot and presented his witch with whatever part of the man she preferred, he'd take great pleasure in unraveling Petra strand by strand, discovering how all the little contradictions of her interconnected.

Power-hungry but self-sacrificing. Loyal but alone. Powerful but powerless. An open book with so many pages missing.

"Put your nightie on, baby. The one that smells like me," he ordered, just to get a rise out of her.

As he hoped, Petra's head swiveled around to glare at him just in time to see him sliding his jeans and briefs down his thighs. His cock, pretty much constantly half-hard since he saw her for the first time, gave an enthusiastic twitch when her eyes dropped.

"Good *gods,*" she hissed, marching over to her dresser to angrily yank out a different nightgown. "You keep that thing to yourself, Silas, or so help me Glory, I'll burn it off."

"Careful, little goddess, that's not as much of a deterrent as you might think. I *like* it when you get all hot on me."

Pulling the loose waistband of his airy sleep pants over his cock was a little bit like torture. He was sure it'd only get worse as he burrowed in her sheets, imprinting his scent not only on her bedding, but her skin as well.

Silas padded over to her and bent to murmur in her ear. "I bet when your cunt is wrapped around me, it'll feel like you're burning me alive."

He dodged the wadded up socks she threw at his head by inches. She stormed around him, nightgown in hand, and very nearly slammed the door to the bathroom before apparently thinking better of it.

The way she flicked the lock into place was awfully cute, though.

Silas's grin cramped his cheeks as he turned off the glaring overhead light and moved back to the bed to wait for her. It was hardly big enough for him, but he'd slept in worse positions than curled on his side so his feet didn't hang off the edge. Certainly his accommodations during his little trip hadn't been half as comfortable as Petra's bed.

He'd been in a bad mood during his time away from her. It

was soured further by the discovery of so very little. The demon part of him, animalistic and hungry, took every unanswered question as a challenge to his claim. The man part of him, on the other hand, was both delighted by her mystery and increasingly vexed by it.

Silas thought he knew Petra. She was a fixed quantity in his mind: a beautiful hypocrite caught in a web of Temple intrigue and an easy mark to exploit. The fact that he wanted to fuck her was just a happy bonus to a mildly entertaining diversion from his usual pursuits.

He'd expected their bargain to be a simple and a relatively tidy affair once he'd gotten what he wanted. With Petra tied to him and the first half of his promise to Tal fulfilled, he could then use her dependence on him to get access to the m-generator.

And then their business would be done. She could have her lofty seat in St. Emaine's and he wouldn't think twice about abandoning her, bond or no bond, because there were no real ties between them save magic and lust.

That was before. Silas slid his hand beneath the pillow on his side, checking to make sure his gun was safely tucked out of her reach.

Now he understood that he'd vastly underestimated Petra, and he wouldn't put it past her to try and shoot him in the night if he pissed her off too much. Silas kind of hoped she'd try it.

Listening to the rustle of fabric and the running faucet in the bathroom, he made himself comfortable under the sheets and immediately stifled a groan of pleasure at the waft of rich scent that enveloped him.

That scent was his new favorite thing. *Well,* he allowed, imagining he could still taste her on his lips, *maybe not the only new favorite.*

A deep, sensual craving tightened the muscles of his abdomen. That craving was a solid wall in the face of his previous plans to leave her to her own devices as soon as their business was done.

Silas frowned at the canopy of the bed. Even if he got everything he wanted — a foregone conclusion — he balked at the idea of letting the puzzle of Petra lay half-finished, forgotten.

He needed to know what filled those blank fifteen years before she became an initiate. He needed to know why she'd had a secret phone under a pseudonym and a PO box under another. He needed to know who Maximilian fucking Dooraker really was and why she'd put herself at such risk simply to uncover the truth of something she couldn't change.

Silas blinked into the darkness.

I need to understand her.

It wasn't a want. It wasn't a passing fancy. It wasn't even a fixation, like the many, many times he'd lost himself in sigilwork or hunched over a sea of wires, soldering gun in hand.

It was a *need.*

Shadows rippled up and down his body, restless as they sought something beneath the sheets. Encountering nothing, they spread out across the floor, seeping into the natural darkness of the bedroom like a living net.

There was faint magic in that darkness — a whisper, soft as a breath, of intelligence. But it was unformed, too young to be more than a spark, and vanished under the dominance of Silas's own overbearing shadows.

When Petra walked out of the bathroom a few minutes later, it was to discover him with his nose pressed into the pillow that smelled strongest of her. Her voice was strained, pitched high, when she demanded, "What are you doing?"

"Savoring it," he answered, unashamed, "and adding to it."

"Adding *what?*"

He rubbed his cheek against the pillowcase, his eyelids lowering as the lushness of her scent sent his instincts into a tailspin. Beneath the sheets, his cock had gone hard as steel. He was pretty sure there was a wet spot on his thigh, too.

"Adding me," he answered. Silas flipped her side of the sheets over, beckoning her to climb in. Around her, perhaps invisible to her untrained eye, his shadows writhed at the edges of the shaft of light she stood in. "C'mere."

She looked very small and un-priestesslike as she stood there in the glow of the tiny bathroom. Her nightgown was not the one he'd covered in his scent, but he knew she wouldn't listen to him. It fell to a modest mid-thigh and looked like a soft, unadorned cotton edged with eyelet lace. It was an incongruously modest garment for someone who routinely wore dresses with V's so deep they almost touched her navel.

It was positively virginal compared to all the scraps of lace and mesh he knew she possessed.

He wanted to push it up around her breasts and feast on her cunt until she screamed. When he was done, he'd take great pleasure in arranging it around her thighs again — like a doll, all virginal and sweet for him and him alone.

Of course, he liked all the strappy lingerie she had in her drawers, too. He wasn't picky. If she wanted to be his vixen for a night, he'd take that just as happily as this sweet little bite who lingered uncertainly in the bathroom doorway.

I'm a man of multitudes.

She must have seen something of his fantasies in his eyes because the look on her face grew increasingly alarmed. "That sounds like a *very* bad idea."

"It is, and that's why it sounds like something you'd do, doesn't it?"

He counted it as a win when her face screwed up like that. It meant several layers of her masks had fallen off, revealing more of the mysterious woman who'd managed to fool even him into believing she was the same as all her ilk.

"It's awfully bold of you to assume I won't try to kill you in the middle of the night."

"I haven't assumed anything," he replied, loving the bite in her voice. "That's why I'm sleeping with a weapon, baby."

Petra's eyebrows hiked up her forehead. "Is that a threat, demon?"

The only real threat was that his cock might go off the second she brushed her skin against his. Anything else wouldn't stand a chance against him. Petra needed him too much to follow through on any bluster, and her enemies...

Every fine muscle of his body, from his fingers to the strong ropes of flesh bracketing his spine, tensed. "No one is getting into this den," he promised her. "No one will ever touch you but me, Petra, and it's not your pain I'm after."

Her toes curled at the smudged edge of the light cast on the floor. Maybe she sensed the reach of a predator in the darkness. His shadows weren't weakened by light, not like a wraith's were, but it was instinct to wait, hiding just out of sight, for the right time to pounce.

They were an extension of him. If demon tradition was to be believed, they were a manifestation of a demon's soul, tied to all those of their line, and each demon's shadow was unique. His would never be confused for another's. They existed within and without a demon, a symbiotic parasite they were all born with and one that acted on base impulses as well as will — a being that would, as old demon stories claimed, survive far beyond that of its bodily host.

Silas had always had finer control over his shadows than other demons, but around Petra they were in constant flux, desperate to be near her and yet rippling with unease in her light.

That disquiet seemed to have melted away at some point while he was away from her, however, because now they surrounded his witch, crawling up the walls and just outside of her little fortress of light. A deep growl, more motion than sound, shook his chest as he waited for her to step into the dark with him.

The glow of light silhouetted her body within the thin material of her nightgown. It formed a halo around her golden head, making her appear both untouchable and irresistible when she murmured, "Are you saying I'm safe with you, Silas?"

"With me? Yes." His claws bit into the empty side of the mattress, curling around a body that instinct demanded already be there. Silas's voice was gritty with want when he promised, "From me? Never."

She stood there a moment longer, her expression unreadable, before she slowly reached back to flip the old fashioned switch on the wall inside the bathroom.

He wouldn't have blamed her for squeaking or even screaming with alarm when the trap sprung around her bare legs, but his witch was always full of surprises. Petra merely stumbled to a stop, barely a step outside of the bathroom, with a quick, forceful exhale.

Her tone was carefully measured when she said, "Silas?"

He shuddered. Awareness of her filtered in through his shadows: the silky warmth of her skin, the smooth glide of shadow over the slopes of her legs, even an impression of the salty-sweet taste of her as they curled around her limbs to squeeze possessively.

He was rarely taken by surprise, but it seemed to happen every few minutes in Petra's presence.

Silas had been through many ruts before. He knew the power of instinct, the senseless urge to breed. He understood the demonic urge to seek out a mate and hoard them close, to fuck them well and often enough that they wouldn't seek out another.

And yet the sight of Petra, glowing faintly with her own precious light, nearly swallowed by his seeking shadows, inspired such a blistering wave of desire in him, he was forced to take his cock in hand and squeeze hard enough to hurt. It was the only way to beat back the release that screamed down his spine.

He liked the idea of coating her bed in his come, but not when he had her within arm's reach.

Still holding himself with punishing force, Silas rumbled, "Come here. Now."

"I can't move!" She waved her hands over her body, her eyes wide in her striking face. "It's *touching me.*"

"They're learning you," he explained, though he was only

moderately certain of that himself, "but if you don't start walking toward this bed, they'll bring you to me. I'd start moving. Now."

She didn't move as fast as he would have liked, but Petra did make her way over to the bed. The shadows clung to her like long sheets of cobwebs, a cloak of hungry darkness that couldn't decide if it wished to protect her or consume her.

Bit of both, I imagine.

Chapter Sixteen

Petra didn't quite scurry under the covers, but she wasn't exactly relaxed, either, as she slipped between the sheets and laid down as far from him as she was able.

Not that it mattered. His shadows were a second mind, a second body. They draped over her, molded to her lush shape, as she lay rigidly beneath the blankets. Through them he could feel her racing pulse, the tremble of her thighs as they squeezed together, the pucker of her nipples against her nightgown, and the intoxicating buzz of her magic just beneath her flesh.

A new hunger roared in him as he sensed that deep well of power just beyond his reach — not for the power itself, but for what it represented. That magic was *her* soul, just as the shadows were his, and it chafed to realize it was hidden away from him.

They both lay there in the dark for several long minutes, their breathing harsh in the quiet. Outside, beyond the thick walls of the cathedral's living quarters, cars rushed by.

He thought he would feel more content with her in the bed, but the opposite was true. Silas was more tightly strung than before. His erection throbbed angrily in his rigid grip and his instincts spun in a dizzying circle, unable to settle on what they wanted him to do.

Eventually, one need won out over all the others.

"Relax," he snapped.

Petra's voice took on its own sharpness when she replied, "A bit hard when I'm being smothered to death by shadows."

He traced the tense profile of her face with his gaze. She lay stock still beneath the sheets, arms at her sides and legs straight, near enough to the edge that any small nudge might send her off the side.

Not that his shadows would allow that. No, she was anchored to him now, though he doubted she knew it, and until he worked up the desire to release her, she wouldn't be going anywhere.

But her clear discomfort made the oily, squirming feelings reappear, tempering the sharpest edge of his lust.

"What do you know about a demon's shadows?"

Petra's eyes swung in his direction. He wondered what she could see in the blue-black darkness. Did he look like a monster or a man? Silas couldn't decide which he wanted more.

"I know they're an extension of a demon's will," she answered, a bit tart.

Finally feeling like he wasn't going to spill at any moment, Silas slowly eased his grip on himself. "They are. Mostly. They have their own magic, though, and are connected to our instincts more than our higher minds. That means sometimes they act independently of what we want."

"Are you trying to say you aren't controlling this?"

He shrugged, though he wasn't certain she'd see it. "Right now, it's a little of column A and B."

It was a good thing *he* had no trouble seeing in the dark, otherwise he would have missed the absolutely withering glare she sent his way. She wriggled a bit under the sheets. "Was that supposed to make me feel better about this?"

"No," he answered, shuddering anew at the sensations the shadows fed back to him, "but you might be interested in the fact that a demon's shadows are almost indestructible. Right now, you're basically wearing full-body armor. Not even a bolt gun shot could hurt you."

Silas cast the bronze symbol of Glory hanging on the wall across the room a venomous look. Not that anyone would get the chance to get a shot off before he slit their throats, but it settled something fundamental in him to know she was safe even in enemy territory.

I'll feel even better when she's in my den.

He hadn't considered sharing a space with her before, but now that the thought was there, it seemed like the most sensible and enjoyable choice. Locking Petra away in his warded, booby trapped, and guarded home where she could sleep in his bed, draped in his shadows?

Fuck. His hand snuck down again, squeezing his abused cock hard enough to bruise.

"But that also means I'm at your mercy."

Petra wriggled again. The shadows weren't pinning her down, but he knew she felt something when they touched her. Perhaps she felt confined and that was why she wouldn't stop fidgeting. As if a little wiggle would ever stand the chance of freeing her.

Silas scowled. "You're at my mercy regardless. Might as well get used to it."

Her eyes, mostly sightless in the dark, still managed to flash with temper — and no small amount of magic. "I thought you said I had power. That doesn't sound like it."

The urge to cover her with his much heavier body, replacing the shadows with his flesh to pin her to the bed, was almost as strong as the one he felt to nip her proud nose in reprimand.

His voice took on a dry, strained quality when he replied, "You do. If you didn't, I would be inside of you already."

By some miracle, he wasn't even *touching* her, despite being only about a foot away from all that lovely golden flesh. Despite every rousing, furious instinct, he remained on his side. And if his hand happened to be on his cock, it was only so he didn't make a mess of the sheets involuntarily rather than to covertly take his pleasure beside her.

The idea might have had appeal if the animal part of him could stand the thought of being so near to her and not... well, doing anything. At the very least, his basal instincts demanded he throw off the sheets and let her watch. *Preen* for her.

A novel impulse, that. He'd never felt the need to impress anyone in his life. *How galling.*

While he wrestled with that revelation, Petra went very still again. "Is this you respecting my boundaries?"

He really didn't appreciate the note of incredulity in her voice. "I said I would, didn't I?"

"So you're not going to try anything?"

His eyebrows lifted so high, his clan's matriarch would have said they were touching his horns. "Is that disappointment I hear?"

"No," she answered, too quick. "I was just making sure you planned to keep your word."

"No sex unless you say so *explicitly.*" He propped his head up with his palm, narrowed eyes locked on her glowing face. His eyes and nose worked in tandem with the shadows, telling him everything she refused to say.

Her heartbeat was elevated, her breaths short. Her cheeks were flushed. Her nipples were hard. The rich, spicy scent of her desire was a curl in the air — as real and tantalizing as the incense smoke she used in her services.

If he wanted to test himself, to drive them both insane, he needed only to use a slight amount of will to nudge his shadows between her thighs, where he was absolutely certain he'd find her wet and needy.

Lust was its own beast in his mind, but it had a new shape. Silas wasn't just desperate to relieve the painful pressure in his balls, but to satisfy *her.*

She needs me, the suddenly pitifully desperate demon side of him wailed. *She needs me!*

Silas was at once split in two. One half roared with vicious pleasure at the thought of righteous High Priestess Zaskodna squirming with need for him, while the other was certain it'd die if it didn't fix the issue immediately.

His clan had gone on and on about a demon's famed devotion to a mate, how they prided themselves on their care and comfort, their impeccable instincts, but since he had no mate, the impulse to please was very confusing. He'd never sought to please anyone in his life.

Suddenly needing to claw back a bit of the power over himself, Silas used his coldest, silkiest purr when he said, "Baby, if you want me to fuck you, you're gonna have to beg."

There was a slight pause as she absorbed the sudden shift in his demeanor. "That isn't going to happen. I don't need to *beg* for anything."

"Oh? Even when your cunt is wet enough to drip down those pretty thighs just by being *next* to me?" He had no intention of informing her that he was in a similar state, if not considerably worse off.

"No," she answered, back to using her cool priestess voice. "If I wanted sex that bad, I wouldn't need to beg you for it. I could find someone else to—"

He didn't make the choice to move, nor command his shadows to act, but it happened anyway. Silas wasn't even sure if she finished her sentence. He couldn't hear a damn thing over the sudden roar of blood in his ears as he dragged her back to his front. One hand still held his head up and the other pressed hard into the mattress in front of her navel, caging her in while his shadows did the rest of the work of keeping her there.

"Watch it," he hissed against the shell of her ear. "Demons don't share, little goddess."

And a demon on the brink of rut would kill anyone who tried to touch what was his. Aggression ran furious and wild the closer they got to the hottest months of the year, though the exact timing of one's rut varied based on a variety of factors like genetics, environment, and exposure to certain delicious, musky pheromones.

Those same pheromones clouded the air around Petra. They were heavy on the back of his tongue — complex and rich like the finest wild honey he loved to eat by the spoonful as a child.

Silas canted his hips against the soft curve of her backside, fitting them together like two pieces of a puzzle, but he still kept his hands to himself when he warned, "If you want me to kill someone, keep taunting me. If you want me to make you come harder than you ever have in your life, then *beg.*"

He had to hand it to her. Petra had a spine of steel. That was the only explanation for how she could turn her head to look at him over her shoulder and snarl, *"No."*

Silas was not a man to lose control. That implied he was a slave to emotions he just didn't have, no matter how hard he tried. He'd never flown into a jealous rage, never felt the impulse to possess another, and never wanted to howl with rage at the thought of his partner challenging him.

Not until then.

Because Petra's *no* wasn't a denial. It was a challenge. She was exerting her power over him because she knew what *he* wanted. This was both a dare and a punishment. If he didn't keep his word, the fragile trust between them would be shattered, even if sex was truly what she was angling for. If he *did* keep his word, she would do this again and again — a worrying prospect when his rut seemed to be hurtling toward them faster with every second.

What she wanted, he realized, staring into those eyes blazing with a hair-thin ring of pure light, was for *him* to beg.

Before he could come up with some way to punish her for that, Silas was knocked off-guard by the one-two punch of Petra squirming against him and the sudden, shocking pleasure of feeling the bare flesh of her ass against his cock.

She'd hiked up her nightgown, dislodged his loose waistband, and, with the help of his over-eager shadows, parted her legs just enough to let his cock slip between her thighs, which she promptly snapped shut.

Silas hissed, claws digging deep holes into the mattress in front of her, and bucked his hips involuntarily.

"See?" Petra's voice was breathy but absolutely *dripping* with superiority when she used quick, efficient touches to press him between the slick, swollen folds of her cunt. "I don't need to beg you for anything, demon. I can get off without your help, or anyone else's."

The witch had the audacity to rock her hips, allowing him to glide between her wet thighs and over the hot little pearl of her clitoris.

Fuck. Silas's instincts, already wild, were whipped into a frenzy as he comprehended her challenge, the fact that his cock was sliding through her slick with every taunting roll of her hips, and that losing this game was absolutely, entirely unacceptable.

He guessed that she'd be hot as fire, but *feeling* it...

Gritting his teeth against the searing friction — too much, not nearly enough — he fought for control enough to speak into her ear. "You want to get off, baby? Go ahead. But I'm not touching you, no matter what you do or the sounds you make. My hands are staying right here." He couldn't help but fist one hand in the soft strands of her hair, forcing her to arch her neck as she ground into him, but the other stayed put, claws buried in the mattress.

Just to make things fair, he made sure his shadows bound her hands to her sides, making it impossible for her to reach an orgasm in any other way than by the use of his cock.

After a moment of half-hearted struggle, Petra's breath hitched and her eyes slid closed. "Fine."

It was adorable that she thought he'd settle for *fine*.

When she eased into a rhythm, Silas pressed his lips against the smooth skin behind her ear and breathed her in, tasting her desire on his tongue as she used him. "Pretty little goddess," he whispered, determined to see her unravel before he did, "do you like the feeling of demon cock sliding between your thighs?"

She ignored him. Petra's brows drew together in an expression of pleasure-pain. A soft, nearly inaudible noise escaped her throat as she angled her hips, her thighs tightening around his shaft, and picked up her pace.

Silas fought the compulsion to assist her — and himself — by rocking his hips into hers. Letting her take the lead was torture. *But she asked for this,* he reminded himself. *She wanted to play this game, so she's going to find out what happens when she challenges me.*

"Ah, there you are. I think you do like it. I think you're imagining what it would be like if I were inside you right now." *Gods know I am.* "But my little goddess isn't ready to beg yet, is she? So you're going to get a sad little orgasm, like all the ones you've had before. You know what *I'll* get?"

"What?" She gritted the word out, but the way her hips moved faster, the stuttering beat of her breath... *She likes my voice,* he realized, grinning.

He licked a short trail from the curve of her jaw to the lobe of her ear, tasting the thin sheen of sweat that had accumulated there. Speaking directly against her skin, he answered, "My demon come all over Glory's precious High Priestess."

Her rhythm stuttered. A low sound escaped her throat as she desperately tried to find it again, but her movements were too frantic. Petra chased her orgasm like it was hovering just out of reach, taunting her. She moved like she needed help. Like she needed *him.*

She needed him to take control of it, of them, *her.*

Silas's chest sawed with every deep breath. It took every ounce of self-control to hold perfectly still. He didn't lift up her thigh and slide into that ready, hungry cunt. He didn't grab her hip and jerk her forward and back as roughly as they both needed. He didn't turn her head and shove his tongue so far down her throat, she'd never be rid of the taste of him.

He lay there, his own orgasm building in painful lurches, as their bodies made slick, sloppy noises against one another. Silas rumbled words in her ear — mostly taunts, but those gradually gave way to demands. He couldn't use his hands or his cock to wring the brutal orgasms out of her like he wanted, but the demon in him wouldn't be denied.

It knew what she needed and it'd be damned if he didn't see her satisfied, even partially, by the end of this.

"Faster," he bit out. He refused to thrust, but he gave into the impulse to cant his hips at a slightly different angle, making it easier for her to grind the head of his cock against the most sensitive part of her soft pink cunt. "Petra, move your *fuckin'* hips. Yes. *Yes.* There you go. No, I didn't tell you to stop. *Move!*"

He doubted either of them could pinpoint exactly when her power play became his, nor when she started eagerly obeying his commands, but it didn't matter.

In that moment, there was nothing more important that the desperate little sounds she made, so hushed and secretive, like she was afraid she'd be caught, and the way they fit together so perfectly even as they tried their damnedest to torture one another.

Petra began to tense. Her heartbeat thundered in her chest. He could feel it through her back, through his shadows. They were connected skin to skin, but they were also linked by a potent, drugging force neither of them could really control.

"Give it to me," he ordered, fingers tightening in her hair until the back of her head touched his shoulder. Silas crushed his lips against her jaw, a snarl contorting the touch into something too brutal to be called a kiss. "Petra, I want that orgasm *now.* Give it to me!"

A noise not unlike a muffled sob bubbled from her as she bore down on him, her thighs pressed tight and drawn up a bit, as if she were trying to get him as close as possible without her hands.

And then she snapped. Her spine bowed, releasing her from

her curled position, and her hips rolled erratically as she gushed over his tortured cock.

He almost missed it over the sound of blood rushing in his ears, but no, breathed out on a long, low moan, was his name.

Telling her my name was the best fuckin' decision I've ever made.

Baring his fangs against her skin, triumphant and miserable all at once, Silas at last closed his claws over the soft swell of her hip and jerked her backward. Petra was pliant and perfect as he used her, rutting between her thighs and rumbling like an animal until he came, lashing her perfect flesh with pearly release and his unique musk.

For a time they lay there like that, tangled and sticky and panting. He'd won, he thought, savagely pleased as he dragged his hand through the mess he'd made. Silas spread it as far as it would go across her thighs and stomach. When she complained, voice scratchy, he shushed her with a quick nip of her ear.

"I get to have this," he told her. "Next time, if you don't want a mess, you can beg me to come inside you instead. If you're good, I might even say yes."

He suspected she was too tired to fight and that was why she simply let out a heavy sigh and relaxed in his arms. Still, she asked in a voice thick with sleep, "Why are you so obsessed with me begging?"

Silas fixed her nightgown over her thighs before he banded his arm around her waist, drawing her even more tightly against his front. He took his time answering her. When he finally decided on what to say, she was already dozing off.

Whispering into the crown of her head, he answered, "Because if you don't, I'm pretty sure I will."

Chapter Seventeen

Petra was fairly certain she was self-destructing. That was the only reason she could come up with for why she would do what she'd done with Silas.

She didn't exactly feel shame about it, but she wasn't proud, either. Particularly when she woke up with him watching her like a cat who'd gotten the cream.

Sure, she knew there was a not-insignificant chance she was going to die in twenty-four hours — or at least wish she'd died — and that meant she had some leeway in regards to sexual expression and bad choices, but that one seemed extreme even for her.

Because now that she'd opened that door, there was no closing it.

Silas made himself comfortable in the center of her bed, one arm thrown behind his head as he watched her scramble around for her robe. He let out a low chuckle when she grimaced at the odd, tacky pull of her skin around her thighs and belly.

"Why the face?"

Petra shot him a glare as she cinched her bathrobe around her waist. "Shut up."

It was deeply unsettling how Silas so effortlessly embodied both boyish charm and menace. His chocolate curls were tousled around his horns, his eyelids were lowered to a drowsy half-mast, and everything in his posture screamed of perfect ease. Even the damn stupid, *wonderful* beauty mark above his lip added to his air of early morning effortlessness.

But one couldn't miss the glow of his eyes, molten bronze on black, nor the twitch of his smile — an expression that on anyone else might have been soft, but on him was as beautiful and deadly as a sharpened knife.

"You have the day off today," he drawled. "Come back to bed. Now." He smoothed his free hand over the side of the bed that should have been hers. In reality, he'd hogged the whole mattress all night and used her as his personal body pillow, manhandling her this way and that depending on his preferences every few hours.

She had a crick in her neck, she hadn't gotten the amount of blankets she preferred, he *breathed* in her ear all night—

And it was the best sleep she'd had in three years.

I'm losing my mind.

"My breakfast will be delivered any minute," she explained, "and just because I *technically* have the day off doesn't mean I don't have things to do." Petra paused, adjusted her robe with another grimace, and muttered, "I also need a shower."

"You shower my scent off and I'm just going to put more on you."

He said it so calmly, almost *cheerfully,* that it took her a moment to hear the threat there. Her hand rested on the doorknob of her bedroom when she craned her neck to glare at him over her shoulder. "And what would that entail, demon?"

She had no idea why she asked. She knew what he meant. The man had been alarmingly gleeful as he rubbed his release into her skin the previous night. She had absolutely no doubt that he'd try it again, whether she washed it off or not.

Silas's smile melted into a sensual curl of his lips over sharp fangs — the same fangs that had left little streaks of fire along her jaw and down her throat. It was *that* smile that reminded her exactly why she'd lost her mind the previous night.

Because *that* Silas, *that* look... It wasn't just the end of her life hurtling towards her that made desire a constant pressure in her stomach. It was the way he looked at her like his sole focus was to watch her come.

As if he knew that his look alone said it all, Silas purred, "Go get your breakfast, baby, and hurry back to me."

"Why do you keep giving me orders?"

"Because you like it."

Petra didn't dignify that with a response. Internally, however, she grumbled, *I hope they only brought enough for me.*

And then, of course, she felt a pang of guilt at the thought of him being hungry, which sent her spiraling into yet another whirlwind of silent complaints about how he'd wedged himself into her life.

She didn't have grand plans for her final days, but Petra also never thought that she'd spend them sparring with a demon apparently just as determined to get into her underwear as he was to use her magic.

Doing her best to act normal for the cameras in her sitting room, Petra quietly closed the door behind her and padded toward the entrance of her suite. Like every Saturday, a simple cart waited outside the door, laden with a spread of breakfast foods, fruit, and coffee.

The cathedral was closed to the public on Saturdays, allowing for a day of rest for the staff. An initiate was responsible for bringing Petra her breakfast, but the rest of the day all the acolytes were free to do as they pleased. She suspected the cathedral would be even more abandoned than usual. With how hard everyone had been working and the pall that hung over them, she wouldn't have been surprised if every last acolyte got as far as possible from the premises on their day off.

Petra's stomach turned as she pulled the cart into the suite and shut the door. *Antonin will arrive tomorrow.*

Suddenly, whatever appetite she'd woken up with vanished. Normally her anxiety over wasting food or missing a meal was far greater than any worry she might have entertained, but when the Protector's face flashed to the forefront of her mind, her stomach went as heavy and solid as a boulder.

She swallowed the bitter taste of bile as she stared down at the tray. Would it be the second-to-last breakfast she ever had? Or would she only *wish* it was?

Petra felt removed from the thought. It was as if she stood a great distance away from her own mortality — near enough to see it, certainly, but little more than that. She was simply an observer of her own fate.

No, I'm not an observer, she admonished herself as she pushed the cart toward the bedroom. *I might not have a choice in the end, but I haven't let the universe push me around.*

It was a good reminder that there was still work to be done.

The finish line drew near, but she wasn't quite there yet. One more push. One more great, terrifying hurdle, and it would be over — one way or another.

Steeling her spine, Petra opened the bedroom door just enough to slip the cart and herself inside. "Silas, we need to talk about—"

Firm hands closed around her waist, drawing her back into a naked chest. Body heat radiated along her spine as Silas pressed himself against her. "That shower? I agree. I changed my mind and decided it would be a great idea to give you a scrub."

Petra curled her fingers into his forearms, but she couldn't tell if the bite of her nails was to urge him to let her go or to keep him close.

Her heart raced as he rubbed the top of his chin against the crown of her head, nuzzling her in an odd, animalistic way. A deep thrumming noise, more vibration than sound, rumbled against her back.

A sharp ache took up residence between her thighs. Not because the purr meant anything to her, really, but because her body seemed to have associated the memory of that sound with the crushing orgasm she'd worked out as she slid her body over his cock.

Silas's deep breath was noisy and large enough that his entire torso seemed to flex against her back. "Mm," he hummed, palms skating up her stomach to cup the undersides of her breasts. "That's my *favorite* smell."

Petra tried very hard not to wheeze. "Coffee?"

He *tsked*. "No. My little goddess's wet cunt." Silas tilted his head to run the tip of his tongue over the shell of her ear and down her cheek. Petra shuddered, toes curling against the cool wood floor, when he added, "Should I have that for breakfast, baby?"

Her body very much wanted her to say yes, but the existence of the cart before her, the fact that Silas was in her room at *all*, demanded she focus. As much as she would have liked to spend her final days having wild, borderline hateful sex with a demon who liked to torment her, she couldn't.

Petra put her hands on the backs of his and was a little surprised when he let her pull them away from her breasts. *It's only fun if I give him the power willingly,* she reminded herself as she turned to face him.

It was easy to forget when he was... well, *him,* but Silas showed her again and again that he respected her boundaries. Mostly. It helped when she knew what they were, which wasn't always a given when she couldn't decide if she wanted to live in debauchery for her final days or do the things she *needed* to do.

Silas watched her from under lowered brows, his hands hovering over her hips. He still had that sleepy look about him, which was awfully distracting. Especially when he was half naked, all of his pale skin, pink nipples, and smattering of dark moles on display.

"As much as I would like to say yes, Silas, I just don't have time for any of that right now." She hadn't meant to put so much real regret into her voice, but there it was. Petra *did* wish she could let him have his wicked way with her. Carnal delights hadn't been an option for her for so long, it felt criminal to pass them up now, with so little time left.

But that was precisely why she couldn't.

"In the shower, then," he drawled. "Let me clean you up so I can make you dirty again."

Petra eyed his sturdy frame dubiously. "There is no way on Burden's green Earth you and I will both fit in that shower. I don't even know if you'll fit in there on your own."

"It's worth a try."

She shook her head. Needing to get some breathing room, Petra stepped away under the guise of pushing the cart toward the bed. Her gaze stayed away from him as she hopped onto the mattress and began filling her cup with coffee. "Listen," she began in her most professional voice, "last night was— interesting. But the situation I'm in isn't one where I can just fool around and do whatever I want. Until the Protector is handled, I can't afford to play games with you. We *have* to make a plan."

For a man of his size, Silas moved with shockingly little noise. Her only indication that he was near was the sudden dip of the mattress behind her. Petra's breath caught as he slid into place at her back, caging her legs in with his own and reaching around her to pluck a wedge of apple from the bowl of fruit.

After a wet crunch and some contemplative chewing, Silas informed her, "I have a plan."

Petra clutched her cup of coffee close to her chest as she twisted her torso, trying to get a good look at the suddenly clingy demon behind her. "You do? What is it?"

Silas curled one arm around her waist and hunched a little to offer her the other half of his apple slice. "Eat, baby."

"What's your *plan*—" He cut her off by tucking the juicy chunk of apple past her lips.

Watching her chew belligerently, he informed her, "If I could trust you not to do something reckless, I'd tell you. Since you're a cute liar with a penchant for trouble, I won't be telling you shit-all."

Petra swallowed the bite of apple as quickly and furiously as she could. "You have no damn idea what you're walking into!"

He shrugged and reached for a wrinkled slice of bacon. "Then tell me."

"Oh, so you want to know *my* plan. How convenient."

"You're the one who needs this done," he reminded her. "So you can tell me and hope I'll take what you say into consideration, or you can watch me do whatever the fuck I want. Your choice."

Petra took an angry sip of her coffee, immediately blamed him for the fact that she'd forgotten to douse it with sugar and cream, and lowered it again to scowl at the clawed hand rummaging around the cart.

For a moment, she strongly considered telling him off. But that was pride talking. She had no room for pride in her life now.

Letting out a cleansing breath, she forced out, "The Protector arrives at six PM tomorrow. He's supposed to stay in the visitor's suite, which was recently renovated. That means I've got blue-prints for you."

She ignored the rumbling purr at her back and its accompanying silky murmur of *good girl*.

It took another sip of bitter coffee to brace herself before she could continue. Tension made her desperate for some distraction, so she leaned forward to flavor her coffee as she explained. "I have a dinner meeting with the Protector at seven. That's the only time I know for certain he'll be completely occupied, so that's when you need to sneak into his room and get whatever you can from his computer — or whatever else you find. Anything will help."

Silas went very still behind her. "You're having dinner with him?"

"Unfortunately." She strove to sound calm, collected, but tension bled into her voice anyway. There was no hope of hiding it, only obfuscating its origin. "It's not the first time I've had to. He stopped for a surprise visit several weeks ago — never told me why — and took the opportunity to inspect the staff, the buildings, and...”

“You?”

“Yes.” She found herself making her usual plastic, High Priestess smile reflexively, though he couldn’t see it. “He was very curious about me, probably for the same reasons you are.”

“Was he now?” The tangled mass of her hair shifted over to one shoulder. An incongruously soft mouth whispered over the side of her throat. It was a delicate touch, but shocking, even after the previous night, for someone who hadn’t been touched intimately in years.

Petra froze, the muscles of her abdomen tightening as opposing impulses roared to life. Three distinct wants clamored for attention: the desire to get as far from a predator like Silas as possible for the sake of self-preservation, the pressing need to see her task to the end without distraction, and the desperate sort of lust that begged her to take what he offered while she still could.

Seeing as they were all equally strong positions, she could do little more than sit completely still and make no choice whatsoever.

Chapter Eighteen

"HE WANTED TO KNOW WHERE I CAME FROM, HOW I got the seat so many other people wanted, et cetera," she said, though she barely breathed.

"Hm." Something squeezed around her legs and slithered upwards — the strange there-and-not sensation of Silas's shadow's curling around her like the vines of a great, carnivorous plant. "Is that why a man puts a camera in a woman's bedroom? Because he wants to know how *ambitious* she is?"

"The Protector has eyes everywhere," she replied, though she knew exactly what he was implying.

"I wonder how many of them are fixed on you and you alone."

Many, she silently answered. *Too many.*

It hadn't started like that. She knew the cathedral was bugged because it was an open secret amongst the higher ranks that *all* of Glory's Temple buildings fed information back to the High Gloriae — every secret, every tryst, every muttered complaint. Even if it wasn't true, the rumor had a devastatingly effective chokehold on dissent.

The other reason she knew was because Max had told her so.

He mentioned it only once, during that last concerning phone call when he told her he was confronting the Protector about something he'd found. The city sounds had been loud in the phone's speakers and she'd asked him why he was outside at such a late hour.

"There are eyes and ears everywhere in the cathedral," he'd explained, sounding exhausted to the point of tears. *"There are cameras everywhere but my room. I did a sweep there, but now— I can't risk anything. Not until I see him."*

When she took over his old suite, she'd used her own black market sensor to confirm what Max had confessed. For three years her bedroom had been safe.

And then Antonin showed up at her door, asking so many deceptively pleasant questions, and by the time he left...

Trying to divert the conversation back into a more productive avenue, Petra said, "Well, he'll be focused on me tomorrow, which is good for the plan. Last time he traveled with six guards. Two were with him at all times, two stayed in his suite, and the other two joined the staff security team. If everything goes right, you should only have to avoid the two guarding his suite while I have dinner with him."

Silas was curiously quiet for a man who seemed to love the sound of his own voice so much. He merely sat there, arm and shadows tight around her, listening as she rambled at increasing speed. "Once you get something incriminating — *anything* — you have to take it straight to Elise. She knows to expect something. If it's incriminating enough, she should take it to Patrol."

"And what happens when the Protector discovers his secrets are out?"

Petra swallowed. "Well, theoretically, he'll have no reason to tie it back to either of us, since I'll be having dinner with him and he won't know you're here. Nothing more than suspicion, anyway, if you do your job well. And if the news gets out about who he is and what he's done, then... then he'll go to jail."

She didn't need to feel Silas's deep, deep sigh to realize how naive she sounded. Petra was painfully aware.

She was also lying.

The daughter of two criminals, orphaned by a turf war, victim of a system that didn't know what to do with magically gifted children no one wanted, and pawn in a vicious power structure — of course she knew better than to trust the system to achieve justice.

But in this instance, she had to believe *something* would happen to Antonin. She could only speculate about the extent of his crimes, but there was no way they stopped at the mysterious death of her predecessor.

Some terrible dread itched at the back of her mind — a shadow not cast by her own looming demise, but the feeling that something much bigger, much more terrible loomed just out of sight.

Max knew what it was and it got him killed. It would likely do the same to her despite the fact that she barely had the smallest inkling of what it might be. The only difference between them was that Petra suffered no delusions about her own ability to change the course or scare the Protector enough to confess.

Antonin would not give up power. Even faced with credible accusations, the High Gloriae, who benefited immensely from his spy network and surveillance, would never remove him even if they wanted to.

But the public? The major players of the UTA? Oh, *they* could do something.

In fact, Petra had a letter drafted and ready to be delivered to Margot Goode in the event of her death, explaining everything in great detail. Even if Petra's plan completely failed, that letter would still reach her.

A steady hand tipped the bottom of her coffee cup toward her lips. Petra took a drink reflexively as he shrewdly noted, "You would have been smarter to bargain with me to kill him."

Before she could think better of it and censor herself, she answered, "I didn't have the money for a hit that risky."

She didn't expect him to let out a low groan of pleasure, nor for him to drop his head to rest on the curve of her shoulder. "You're perfect."

"You're deranged for thinking so."

No one *sane* would take her blithe confession that she'd considered having a man murdered as a mark of perfection. It made sense that he would, but it was important to her that he understood the crucial fact that it didn't make it *normal.*

"You have no idea how much it turns me on to know I never have any idea what you're going to say next." Going by the press of his heavy erection against her ass, she thought she had a pretty good idea, but decided the safest option available to her was silence.

"How much money do you really have?" he asked, still sounding horrifyingly pleased with her. "I was able to find a few of your accounts, but none of them had more than ten thousand in them."

"Was that how you found the cellphone?"

"Yes. Next time, don't honor a long-term contract. Use it, burn it, cancel it. If you keep using the same phone, it's relatively easy to eventually pick up on the repeated location pings in the satellite network. Find enough of them and it's child's play to work backwards and get the source."

Petra swallowed a mushy lump of oatmeal with great difficulty. "Thanks for the tip. I'll remember it for next time." She forced down another bite. "But I didn't set up the phones. Max did. He also handled all the accounts."

The humiliating truth was that she only had a grasp on half of what he'd explained to her in painful detail. It was partly because she hadn't wanted to listen, believing him understandably paranoid, and partly because no bit of her had ever, *ever* considered that he would not be around to make sure everything was okay.

How stupid that was, considering he'd left me before. She hated how bitter she still was about that, but childhood wounds never truly healed, no matter how much time passed.

Picking her words carefully, she explained, "The biggest account has a few million dollars in it. That was his major back-up in case we ever needed to run. The others were insurance and emergency funds."

"The accounts, the secret phones, the back-up plan to run — that sounds like a criminal's safety net, not a High Priest's retirement plan." Silas grasped her chin and urged her to turn her head. When she caught his eye, she found his expression as keen and sharp as a blade. "Who was Maximilian Dooraker?"

"A good man," she answered, grief squeezing her so tight, she wondered if it would at last snap her in two.

Silas grazed her jaw with the tip of his claw and drawled, "Baby, good men are boring. *That* man wasn't boring."

Petra closed her eyes to keep him from seeing how they watered. She'd already cried in front of Silas once. There was absolutely no way she'd make that mistake again.

There was a part of her that balked at revealing the memory of Max to someone like Silas, but another part, something beaten and starving, was desperate for someone, *anyone* to know how and why she grieved.

"Max wasn't always *Max,*" she whispered, as if such a secret could still hurt the man who existed as a pile of ash in her cabinet. "He grew up in a crime family from Baltimore, then moved with his siblings to Los Angeles after the war ended. He mostly ran guns — which is where he made his money."

There'd been so much opportunity in the chaos that followed the war. So many ways to make money. Max might have made even more if the elves hadn't gotten their act together and began cracking down on crime — specifically the du Soleil family, which controlled the vast majority of southern California with icy benevolence.

"Shit happens," she continued, referring to the horror of that life in the way of her people, "and eventually he got sick of people dying. Around then he got shot and nearly died. Max decided it was as good a time as any to get out of the game, so he faked his death and rebuilt an identity in the Coven Collective as an acolyte."

He meant it, too. The years of violence and grief had scarred him. Glory's light, the peace of religious instruction and service... it healed him in ways it had never quite done for her.

Her peace had been found in a little life, helping young, wayward teens find their footing — in or out of the Temple — and spending time with the only family she had left.

All of that was gone.

"That's all there is," she finished, shrugging like her nose didn't sting with tears. *A whole life summed up in a couple paragraphs. How depressing.*

Silas's voice took on a curious note when he asked, "Where do you come in?"

She risked opening her eyes to gauge his expression. It was stiff with some intense emotion she couldn't name, but also avid, like he couldn't stop himself from asking for more information.

Her first instinct was to deny him an answer, but she checked it before the words could make it past her lips. *Why shouldn't I?*

There was nothing he could do with the information besides turn on her to curry favor with Antonin, but he had more than enough on her already. Knowing her connection to Max wouldn't dig her grave any deeper.

And she imagined it would feel... good to say it. To have the words out, heard. No one else in all the world knew about their bond and that bothered her. When Max lived, it was a sweet secret she could cherish always. After his death, it was a too-small cage for her grief, forever dooming her to screaming in the silence of her mind.

But I don't have to do that now.

Looking at him, she knew that he would not offer her comforting words or a big hug to ease the pain. He was perhaps the least receptive ear for her grief that she could imagine.

But he was there and he was listening, and if she died the following day, at least one person would know about the relationship that saved her.

Speaking softly, she answered, "Max was my uncle, and the only family I had left. Everyone else is dead."

CHAPTER NINETEEN

UNFORTUNATELY, PETRA STILL HAD A PART TO PLAY. She couldn't sit in her room all day with Silas even if she wanted to — something she was very much undecided on — because there were more cameras than the one in her suite to perform for.

If she never emerged from her bedroom, it would arouse far more suspicion than if her routine was slightly irregular, because Petra never hid away. There was simply too much to do. Besides, discovering the truth about Max's murder wouldn't happen in her bedroom.

So Petra did her best to ignore the demon who watched her every movement, his powerful body stretched out across her rumpled bed sheets. He looked perfectly at home as he sipped from her half-finished coffee and absently petted her pillow.

Not for the first time, she felt as though she were drifting through some bizarre dream. That was the only logical explanation for why she was the one caught in a web of intrigue and murder, and it only *barely* explained how a demon known across the continent as both ruthless and mad watched her with glittering eyes as she emerged from the bathroom.

She expected him to say something. Perhaps a remark about her thin, everyday robe of office, or the way she'd put her hair up, or how she'd gotten dressed in the bathroom rather than endure his scrutiny as she pulled her linen skirt over her thighs.

But he remained silent, his lips a wicked curve over the lip of her coffee cup.

Unsettled and more than a little flustered, she shoved her feet into her low, serviceable pumps and reflexively checked to make sure her necklace was in place. She was startled to feel the new one there, smoother and heavier than her old, simple pendant. The gold hummed with a dark, wild power beneath her fingers.

Why does he need me?

The thought came unbidden as she smoothed her fingers over the symbol of the sun. *He has so much power, so much skill. What could he possibly need my bond for?*

It was unusual for a demon to have such fine control over magic. That was the purview of witches — the *one* advantage they had over the rest of the beings in the world. Humans were weak in all ways except for the lucky few who were born with open m-paths, the channels that mirrored the nervous system and allowed the use of magic.

But with that came the unfortunate side-effect of burn out, when the m-paths began to deteriorate and magic leaked out into the nervous system, essentially frying a witch from the inside out. Any witch was susceptible, but for the most powerful, like herself, it was an inevitability.

Petra had only just begun to consider her options on that front when her life fell apart. Now she had no need to.

She would never bond with Silas, but she still wondered why a man as powerful as him would need an energy boost the likes of which her bond would provide. If he could pack as much power as he had into the necklace, if he'd done even a small sliver of the things she'd heard whispers of...

The possibilities made her shudder.

Silas set the plain ceramic mug down on the tray and stood up from the bed with an enormous stretch. Her old necklace gleamed against his creamy skin. It should have looked innocent enough, but somehow it seemed blasphemous. *And thrilling,* some dark part of her whispered. *Because it feels like I've left my mark on him, too.*

"S'pose it's time for me to get ready," he announced, padding toward the bathroom.

Passing her, he raked his claws through the fall of her ponytail, making her scalp tingle with the memory of how he'd pulled her hair and demanded she come. Going by the dark gleam in his eyes, she rather suspected he was recalling the same thing.

Petra took a hasty step back and smoothed her suddenly clammy palms down the front of her crisp blouse. "What are you getting ready for? You might as well stay in your pajamas all day, since you'll be stuck in here."

Silas crossed the threshold into the bathroom. "Sounds like you forgot what I told you yesterday."

Frowning, she trailed after him to peer into the bathroom, where he was reaching into the shower to turn on the water. She had only a moment to admire how comically small it looked compared to him before the meaning of his words sunk in.

Her hiss cut through the sound of water spraying against old, pastel green tiles when she objected, "You are *not* following me around the cathedral all day, Silas!"

Not only was it too risky, but she was looking forward to getting away from him. Being around Silas for more than a few moments at a time was like locking herself in a cage with a tiger. Every moment that ticked by made her feel a little less secure, a little more certain that she'd get her head bitten off.

"I am," he replied, casual as you please, as he hooked his thumbs under the waistband of his sleep pants. She didn't even get a chance to avert her eyes before he dropped them.

Standing in all his nude, *definitely not flaccid* glory, Silas continued, "I told you I'm not letting you out of my sight. What part of that wasn't clear?"

It took her brain an embarrassingly long time to move past the ripple of his muscles beneath smooth, alabaster skin as he pushed the shower curtain aside and stepped beneath the spray. The showerhead was laughably short compared to him, so it mostly drenched his chest, magnificently solid abdomen, and the heavy, erect cock hanging between his legs.

Silas had a powerful body, but it wasn't the finely sculpted, glamorous form of a man who spent his days in a gym. It was rangy, strong, but layered with enough flesh for him to feel real, *solid*. The crisp line of chestnut hair that drew her eye down his stomach to his cock was a tantalizing addition to an already perfect form — as were the shadowed hollows on either side of his ass.

Petra had to mentally recite a hymn and shift her eyes to the ceiling before she could remember what in the world they'd been talking about.

"You'll be caught."

"No, I won't, because no one's around except you today. We both know that, baby."

Baby. She couldn't rightly tell if she liked that better or worse than *little goddess*. Both were certainly mocking, meant to make her feel every inch the hypocrite she was, so why did she like them at *all*?

"The cameras," she gritted out, unable to keep herself from glancing toward the shower. Silas had put one hand on the wall, hunching his shoulders to dip his head and horns beneath the spray, while the other—

All the moisture evaporated from her mouth when he curled his fingers around the base of his cock for a slow, firm stroke.

"I've got my signal jammer." He spoke so calmly, so casually, like he wasn't masturbating right in front of her. Like he wasn't *watching* her through narrowed eyes, water catching the light in his long lashes.

For some reason she couldn't even begin to decipher, Petra stood there, rooted to the spot, and continued the argument. She could barely hear herself speak over the sound of her own pulse and the splash of water against the tile. "T-That is a terrible idea.

If you... if you follow me around, then it'll block me, too, which will raise—"

At last, a little bit of breathlessness entered Silas's steady voice when he cut her off. "Petra, I know what I'm doing."

Hard to argue with that, she thought, a little dazed, as he began to stroke himself in earnest. Not once had his gaze strayed from her. It raked over her from head to toe, leaving a blazing path of heat in its wake.

Silas pinched the tip of his tongue between his teeth, his brows furrowing with a look almost like rage, and she had the insane urge to step into the shower, grab him by the horns, and suck the pink flesh of his tongue into her mouth.

"It's not worth the risk," she forced herself to say. "I'm going to do what I always do. Stay here or don't, but you *aren't* following me."

A deep, hair-raising growl echoed off the tile. Silas's restless hand stilled, squeezing the ruddy tip of his cock with what looked like an alarming amount of force. "Little goddess, get over here."

Why she continued to bait him, she couldn't say. But she did it anyway. "I already took my shower, thanks."

"So why are you looking at me like you wish you were already on your knees, sucking my cock?" He tilted his head in that predatory way of his. It was almost like he could *see* the way her core pulsed, the ache so sharp it was almost painful. "If you're good, I'll let you do it however you want. If you're bad, you do it how *I* want."

Power. He loved the idea of making her bend. Silas got off on the fact that she was a priestess and what it meant for her to give him free rein to use her. Not only was it taboo for her, a high-ranking member of the Temple, to have sex with a notorious criminal she'd *hired,* but it held an echo of a grudge carried on through millennia.

After all, it was Glory who enticed the god Blight to her bed, and it was Glory who spurned him in the end.

Petra wouldn't lie to herself and try to pretend she *didn't* want to take him up on his offer, but that didn't mean she'd do it.

Because this was about power, and if Silas wanted to exert his over hers... Well, he'd have to fucking work for it.

Her heart raced at the thought. She knew that if she played this game, *really* played it, then there was no backing out. The previous night had been an impulsive choice. A taste of what grew bigger, darker between them with every passing moment and one she'd been unable — unwilling — to resist. But this... If she challenged him here, now, then it would be open season for however long she had left.

It was *that* fact that solidified her resolve.

Petra drew her shoulders back and boldly, coolly dragged her gaze over his body. She took in every dark constellation of moles, the faint scars barely visible against his pale skin, and the livid flesh of his wet cock when she answered, "Enjoy your shower, Silas."

When she met his eyes again, her breath stuck in her throat. A hungry, disturbingly primal thing lurked in his molten gaze when he softly warned her, "If you make me chase you, there's no going back."

I know. But what does it matter when this will be over tomorrow anyway?

Petra didn't say that. She didn't say anything at all. Instead, she held his gaze as she took a step back, over the threshold of the bathroom.

All at once, Silas's expression went taut, the skin around his eyes and mouth pulling sharply until he looked ready to snap. "*Petra.*"

Even in the brightly lit bathroom, she became aware of all the shadowed nooks and crannies as those tiny pockets of darkness began to roil, stretching boldly across the floor to reach for her.

She slammed the door shut just in time to feel it shake under the force of his roar.

Chapter Twenty

Petra regretted her decision almost immediately.

Stress, mortal dread, and chronic lack of sleep had addled her mind to the point of breaking, apparently. That was the only explanation for why she would *knowingly* bait the sociopath who wanted into her panties and then *run*.

I'm not running, she tried to convince herself. *Just walking fast.*

There were still cameras everywhere. She couldn't sprint through the halls like she wanted to, hollering that she didn't mean it, that she took it back. All she could do was walk *quickly*.

The living quarters were deserted, and only pigeons greeted her as she hustled across the courtyard to the side entrance of the main building. The sound of a cable car trundling along, bell dinging with discordant cheerfulness, made her jump as she fumbled with the biometric lock on the door.

It took everything in her not to glance nervously over her shoulder.

The haze of lust that had robbed her of what little good sense she had left had evaporated as soon as she left her suite. Now all she felt was the anticipation of prey about to be eaten.

Not that she believed Silas wanted to hurt her, necessarily, but she probably should have found some other way to savor her last taste of life. Petra's mind was a chaotic swirl of regret and panic as she stepped through the door and slammed it shut behind her.

I should have taken myself out for a really nice dinner. Maybe gone to the beach. I haven't gotten a chance to go to the Fairmont and see that new exhibit yet. I could have done that instead of basically taunting an amoral demon into—

What, exactly? Petra's core tightened at the kaleidoscope of possibilities. She had no doubt that Silas could get awfully creative in the bedroom.

She normally enjoyed the solemn silence of the empty cathedral on Saturdays. Glory's presence felt nearer when she was alone, surrounded by towering columns and shafts of light painted bright colors by the two-story stained-glass windows. The rhythm of her heel strikes on the marble floor were normally even, a metronome for her strained mind to drift to as she did the small tasks around the altar and Glory's statue that needed doing.

But at that moment, her heels clicking on the floor sounded as loud as bolt gun shots. Her breathing was raspy. Her mind was a whirlwind unable to settle on one worry for more than a moment before it screamed to the next. It took everything she had to keep an even, steady pace down the center of the cathedral.

At the last minute, she swerved away from the high altar and the statue. She was torn between hiding away in the columbarium, which she normally tended after cleaning the altar, and hiding away in the sanctuary.

Both were out of the way, but the columbarium was part of her regular routine, which meant that Silas would probably look there first. *Sanctuary it is.*

She didn't have any hope that he *wouldn't* find her, but she wanted to buy herself a little bit of time before the reckoning came down on her like Tempest's wrath.

The decision was reinforced by the fact that the sanctuary boasted a wrought iron gate and lock.

Petra took a hard left at the altar and slipped through the shadowed gap between a towering column and the decorative ones that framed the high altar's niche. A few brisk strides brought her to the massive iron gate that guarded the sanctuary. Though the beautifully designed scroll work filled the entrance from floor to ceiling, most worshippers didn't even know the sanctuary was there. They rarely ventured so far past the high altar, preferring to bask in the light of the windows or kneel before Glory's statue.

Not that they would have been able to get in even if they knew it was there. The sanctuary was open by appointment only, due to the value of the relics held within it. Day to day it was used by Temple staff for personal worship and religious instruction, but its most important role was in prestige.

Goosebumps erupted across her body as she stood before the gate, her palm pressed to the scanner designed to hide amongst the wrought iron filigree. She stood in the dimmest part of the main cathedral floor, where not even the light from the windows reached. Only soft ambient light got that far past the high altar, though there were normally many racks of candles lit — each one a blessing or a prayer left by a worshipper.

On Saturdays, there were no candles lit. The small cups were dark, their pretty glass turned dark violet without the glow of a candle to illuminate them from within.

As she waited for the scanner to recognize her, Petra realized she'd made a miscalculation. While the sanctuary was the most secure place she could hide without drawing Antonin's attention, it was also a perfect playground for a man who thrived in shadow.

Her stomach sank as she quickly glanced from side to side, eyeing the shadows that never quite looked right since she met Silas. Even when he wasn't around, they appeared more alive than they had before.

She regretted not taking the time to learn more about how demons interacted with shadows. Everyone knew they controlled their own, but what could a man like Silas do with natural darkness?

The scanner vibrated beneath her palm. Half a second later the lock clicked, allowing her to hastily push the well-oiled gate open and step inside. She wasn't foolish enough to breathe a sigh of relief as she closed it behind her, but she did feel a bit better when the lock clicked again.

Petra walked past the four rows of mahogany benches, much more elaborately carved than the pews in the main part of the cathedral and approximately three hundred years older, to the alcove at the far end of the room. All around her were relics of Glory's worship from across the world — bargained for, traded, donated, and stolen a thousand times by too many people to count.

Each one cost a fortune, but the centerpiece was the fifteenth-century solid wood and gold altar on the dais. Worship had evolved since its creation, making its design outdated, but the beauty of the piece couldn't be understated. Unlike the altar she used every day, which was essentially a very fancy fire retardant table, the antique was more like a massive, semi-enclosed cabinet at which one was meant to kneel.

Services could be performed in front of it, but it also acted as a private worship space for whatever extremely wealthy person commissioned it. Wooden screens could be extended out across the open end, allowing a worshipper to kneel in the small, enclosed space before the elaborate altar and its gold-plated statue of the goddess.

Petra didn't dare touch the screens, worried about the great age of the piece, but she did tuck herself close to the altar. This deep into the sanctuary, no one peering through the gate would be able to see her anyway.

Ridiculous. She shook her head. How long could she hide there before she either tipped off Antonin's men that she was acting strange or Silas found a way to get her out?

The fact that she was hiding from him at all made her cringe.

Not only would it not work, but it would only make her seem weak. The right thing to do would have been to either follow through with her destructive impulse or eat crow and explain that she'd temporarily lost her mind.

But she'd done neither of those things and instead knelt on an embroidered cushion within a priceless fifteenth-century altar cabinet, staring up into the sightless eyes of her goddess.

"Don't give me that look," she muttered, reaching out to light the incense at the goddess's feet. "Like you've never gotten in too deep with a demon? I need support here, not judgment."

"Your goddess didn't fuck a demon. She fucked our father."

Petra swallowed a scream. Whirling around on her knees, she found Silas — or what *mostly* looked like Silas — grasping the two sides of the folded wooden screens and fearlessly dragging them across the floor. She could only watch, horrified, as he latched them together, completely enclosing them in the shadowy altar cabinet.

And then he turned to face her.

Good gods.

Silas looked wild. It wasn't that his hair was damp, nor that he wasn't even wearing shoes. It was the way his body had changed, blending with darkness to make a being half-transformed. Shadows rippled across the harsh, hungry lines of his face and over his body. They flexed like muscles when he prowled across the marble floor, but never seemed to settle into one definitive shape.

It was like he couldn't decide if he wished to be a monster or man. Maybe it didn't matter when both sides only wanted to consume her.

"You know, I think it's fitting," Silas rumbled as he came to a stop just behind her cushion.

Petra reached out to brace herself against the edge of the altar. His presence, the *look* in his eyes, the shock of him finding her so quickly, and the heady curl of rich incense made her head spin. "How did you get in here?" she croaked. "It's supposed to be—"

Silas spoke like she hadn't said anything at all. "Do you know why Blight is known as the One Who Weeps, High Priestess Zaskodna?"

"Silas..."

He *tutted* and grasped the base of her ponytail. She held her breath as he slid his hand down its length before he began to coil it around his palm, looping it end over end until the meat of his palm touched the crown of her head once more. Her scalp prickled, making her wince. Not a moment later he used his grip to guide her around, forcing her to kneel on the cushion before him, her back to the altar.

"Tell me the story."

Petra's throat was painfully dry. She stared up at Silas with wide eyes, her breathing too fast. There was no reasoning with him. It was in that violent, taunting grin and those eyes that were so full of want they were almost *cruel*. His unstable form was backlit by the soft light that filtered in through the sun-shaped cutouts in the wooden screen behind him.

She reached out reflexively, steadying herself by bracing her palms on his knees as he stepped closer, herding her back against the altar. Her shoulders touched the gilded wood.

It was a form of madness, the thing that took over her body when he bore down on her like that. Petra had never been particularly adventurous in bed, probably because she'd never been able to let her guard down, but with Silas that wasn't an option.

There was no guard. He took a sledgehammer to her doubts and insecurities. They couldn't exist under the sheer, brutal weight of his lust.

For all the agonizing she'd done as she ran away, Petra found herself going liquid under that all-consuming stare. Blood rushed to her skin in a head-to-toe flush. Her mind went wonderfully blank. The ache between her legs returned, tripled. Her core felt swollen, feverish, and slick when she tightened the muscles of her thighs.

Seeing no better option than to give him what he wanted, Petra whispered, "Blight fell in love with Glory the instant he was made. When she chose Burden as her mate instead, it broke his heart."

Silas cocked his head to one side. For as wild as he seemed, he didn't appear to be in any hurry to address the intimidating bulk of his erection hovering in front of her face. "Is that the version you teach kids?"

"I don't know what you're talking about."

She wasn't playing obtuse. That was the tale she'd been taught: that the love story between Blight and Glory was doomed due to the god's covetousness, how he'd sought to smother her light, and that she'd left him for the god Burden, who wished only to bask in her warmth for all time.

"Hm, it figures demons would tell it differently." Silas raised his free hand to cup her jaw. Staring down his nose at her, he rasped, "Glory and Blight were mates. He came to life only because her light made shadow. He created forests so life could worship her. He loved her, *wanted* her so fiercely, that when she came to him, he entered the first rut."

He pressed his thumb against her lower lip, forcing her mouth open just enough to slip the digit past her teeth. His voice took on a knife's edge when he ordered, "Take my cock out, little goddess."

A protest jumped to her lips, but those were occupied. All she could do was stare incredulously up at him. *Here? Now?*

There were cameras. They were in a place of worship. They were surrounded by a priceless antique altar cabinet. Glory's statue was right behind her, *watching*.

But the lines of Silas's face were utterly implacable. Speaking in a quiet voice far scarier than his growl, he warned, "Don't make me tell you twice."

A zing of adrenaline raced through her, as potent and bright as a lightning strike. Before she'd even thought it through, her hands were already sliding up his legs to shakily unbutton his jeans and pull down his zipper.

"Good girl," he purred, watching from under lowered lids as

she hefted the weight of his cock in her palm. It was rigid, silky soft and blazing hot against her skin. Petra swore she could feel the beat of his heart when she curled her fingers around his girth.

The amber of his eyes gleamed when he demanded, "Tell me you want it."

For the span of a handful of heartbeats, Petra considered refusing. For all that Silas was demanding, crude, and dominant, she understood that if she *truly* couldn't do this, he wouldn't force it. This was all a part of the game. If she didn't willingly do this for him in such an inappropriate place, playing into whatever fantasy he had about debauching Glory's priestess, then there was no game. No pleasure.

In his place, she thought she could understand the appeal of someone like her *choosing* to get on her knees and give him a blowjob under the reproachful gaze of Glory's statue. She also understood that Silas's pleasure did not primarily come from the act itself, but rather her submission.

It was far, far more satisfying to have her hand over control than it was for him to take it by force.

So while she hesitated, Petra didn't truly *want* to say no.

Anything could happen tomorrow. There was every possibility that this was her last chance to do something reckless and sensual. No, it wasn't going to be the lovemaking someone else might want for their last day on Earth, but at least it was interesting.

Her voice was barely a whisper when she said, "I want it."

Silas's lips curved. "Now suck my cock while I tell you the rest of the story. If you do a good job, I might forgive you for running away. Or I might not."

If Antonin's cameras were going to catch him, she reasoned as she pressed the flat of her tongue to the underside of his cockhead, *it's already done. Might as well enjoy it before the consequences come.*

If they come at all, a small, soft voice whispered in the back of her mind. That silly thought came from the helpless, drowning girl she'd believed long buried — the one that, against all damn reason, actually *trusted* Silas to keep her safe.

That part of her really needed to get a grip, because the man who pressed his fingertips into her cheeks, forcing her mouth open wider, was no savior. Even if she did like it when he did that.

Silas let out a low rumbling sound from deep in his chest as she learned the contours of his flesh, the taste of him on her tongue. "Show me how sweet that sacred mouth can be."

There was no way on Burden's Earth she was going to be able to fit even half of him in her mouth, not when she was so long out of practice, but Petra gave it a shot. *It's a game. That means I have to play, too.*

Neither of them wanted her to be completely crushed under his dominance, no matter how readily she might submit to him. There had to be push and pull. Petra had to enjoy herself, too, or that would disappear.

So while she hollowed her cheeks, her fist pumping what her mouth just couldn't take yet, Petra kept her eyes boldly raised to watch every flicker of emotion pass over his shadowed face.

Silas's brows were furrowed, his lips curled back from his white teeth. "Do you know what a rut is, little goddess?" He clearly didn't expect an actual answer, because he timed his question with a shallow pump of his hips, encouraging her to take him a little deeper. She couldn't tell him that she only knew the very basics afforded by state-sponsored sex ed because she was far too busy trying to get her throat muscles to relax.

"It's demon breeding season," he explained, grip tightening in her hair until her eyes watered, "when we go mindless with the need to fuck. Some demons like to call it *Glory's gift.*" His tone and the derogatory lift of his upper lip heavily implied that it was not complimentary. "It's what your goddess left Blight with when she ran off to be with Burden instead — the frenzy of need and aggression that takes all of us every year. Unable to find another mate to ease him, Blight was left to wander the forests in agony for all eternity."

Out of the corner of her eye, shadows writhed across the floor, moving toward her in slow-motion waves until they lapped at her legs. They were a slight weight, but when she tried to shift away, they held her there like bands of steel.

"Focus." Silas's order snapped down her spine. Petra straightened, her attention flying back to him in an instant.

"Eyes on me at all times," he commanded. "You're going to want to pay attention to what I'm telling you, baby, because you are about to experience Glory's gift for yourself."

Her jaw was beginning to ache, but the muscles controlling her gag reflex were weakening, allowing her to pull him deeper even as she gave him a look of wide-eyed incomprehension.

Silas's grin was slow to spread and dark with promise. "Yes, baby. You think I'm gonna fuck someone else for weeks when I have this pretty mouth and that perfect pussy at my disposal? Not a chance." A curl of incense smoke traced the contour of one horn when he promised, "I'm going to lock you up in my den. I'm going show you what it's like to be bred by a demon. And when you're so covered in my come that the scent is in your fuckin' pores, you're gonna give me your bond. You're *mine,* Petra."

Petra experienced several new feelings at once: terror at the idea of enduring this man's attentions during a rut, a pang of sadness that it would never happen, and a furious burst of jealousy over the very idea of him spending it with anyone but her.

She didn't know what to do with any of that except try to exert her own power over him while she could.

Silas's breath began to saw in and out of him as she snaked her tongue around the head of his cock, tasting sticky pre-come and the salt of his skin. Her free hand snuck down to cradle the soft flesh of his sac as she slowly pressed forward, determined to take him as deep as she could go.

He grunted, back bowing, when she was at last able to overcome her body's instinctive reaction and take him down her throat. It wasn't all of him, but it was damn close.

"Fuck," he breathed. "Good. *Good* girl. Such a pretty mouth — perfect for prayers and cock."

She had only a moment to bask in the glow of that profane praise before a startled squeak erupted out of her. Silas's shadows had curled around her legs and pulled them wide. Her skirt bunched around her upper thighs and waist as they drifted up her legs like ghostly hands.

She was so shocked by the sensation that she nearly pulled back from Silas altogether, but the hand in her hair stopped her retreat. He smiled down at her when he ordered, "Hold still."

There was little else for her to do when his shadows kept her pinned to the floor and his hand stalled any retreat she might have instinctively tried to make.

Silas began to shallowly shuttle his hips back and forth, using her mouth, as his shadows slithered under the gusset of her panties. Petra's back spasmed, the muscles along her spine tightening with the shock of pleasure that came with a phantom stroke through her slippery flesh.

It wasn't quite like fingers rubbing her, nor was it like the smooth glide of a vibrator. It was a bit like the touch of an extremely dexterous tongue. A pitiful whimper made its way around the cock thrusting in and out of her mouth when the shadows rolled over her again and again, parting her and licking her and providing a delicious amount of pressure.

She began to rock her hips, seeking more to ease the ache of her core contracting around nothing, and didn't even mind when Silas's chuckle washed over her head.

"Do you need something, baby?"

Petra rocked her hips again, more forcefully this time, and leaned forward until he took most of her weight. The benefits of this position were twofold: it allowed him to go deeper down her throat and it gave her leverage to grind down, though there was nothing truly there to grind *against*.

"*Greedy girl,*" he panted. "You need to be filled up."

Petra's eyes nearly slid closed at the very idea, but they

snapped open wide when he gave her hair a warning tug. Silas raised his eyebrows, looking down at her regretfully — like his cheeks weren't flushed or his shadows weren't in a riot around him as he clearly neared his own climax.

"I'm sorry, baby, but you're not getting cock today." He punctuated his declaration with a stiff roll of his hips, one hard enough to make her shoulders hunch as she fought a gag.

Before she could even think of a way to protest his decision, Silas's attention drifted over the top of her head. His lips twitched with a cold smile. "But I'm gonna fill you up anyway, right here where your goddess can see."

In a dizzying series of quick movements, Silas pulled out of her mouth and stooped to lift her off the ground. Shadows swept behind her, sending the incense burner clattering to the floor. Her ass landed on the hard, smooth surface of the altar and her back hit the gold statue as he hiked up her skirt and tore her panties down her legs, leaving them to dangle off one of her black heels.

Speaking with a cool calm that was completely at odds with his actions, Silas warned her, "From now on, you follow my rules. You do as I fuckin' say when I say it. You ever run from me like that again and I'll choke you on my cock."

"You already—"

"You think that was bad?" Silas gave her a cruel smile. "Baby, that was gentle."

"Silas, I— *Oh!*"

Petra's knees drew up and her fingers locked around the edge of the altar as something wide and firm slid inside of her. For a wild second she thought he'd done exactly what he said he wouldn't do, but no, that was impossible because Silas was on his knees before her.

He'd thrown her calves over his shoulders and appeared to be watching as his shadows pumped inside her, their movement like nothing she'd ever experienced in the past.

Petra's spine bowed as she bit back a cry. For all that they were a magical construct, they felt *real* as they thrust inside her. Her thighs began to shake. She held onto the altar for dear life as he made the shadows a bit bigger, their movements a bit more forceful, until she felt like she was being split in two.

And then Silas's mouth closed over her clitoris, sealing with perfect, borderline painful suction, and the world went spotty.

She came with a muffled sob, her lips tucked between her teeth. The shadows gradually stilled, but Silas remained between her legs for several long minutes afterward, prolonging the aftershocks with slow, ravenous kisses.

Just when she believed she couldn't take anymore, he rose up, elbows hooked beneath her knees, and settled the heavy weight of his cock onto her core for several quick, jagged thrusts.

"Gorgeous, gorgeous, gorgeous," he chanted, almost to himself, as thick ropes of come splashed across her mons and upper thighs.

Exhausted, Petra dropped her head back against the priceless statue and stared up at the goddess through dazed eyes. *Glory help me,* she thought, working her sore jaw back and forth. *I've unleashed a monster.*

Chapter Twenty-One

It took an enormous amount of willpower for Silas to peel himself out of Petra's bed. Instinct fought every minute shift and flex of his muscles as he forced his arms to release her. Petra twitched, suddenly restless as he carefully arranged her limbs beneath the blankets. She'd dropped into a deep slumber almost as soon as her head hit the pillow, but now her expression crinkled and her fingers grasped at the pillow beneath her cheek.

A muscle in Silas's jaw twitched. *Stay,* instinct implored. *Guard her.*

But logic and a certain amount of pride reminded him that he protected her just as well outside her bed as in it. A small kernel of resentment made itself known as he dropped his bare feet onto the cool wood floor of her bedroom.

He didn't resent *her.* He resented the sudden wild internal fluctuation he experienced every moment he was around her.

At first it was fun. Entertaining. A little extra spice sprinkled on top of what would otherwise be a pretty mundane job.

Now, though...

Silas stood up from the bed to swipe his pants off the floor. A deep internal pressure began to build as he paced away from

Petra's bed. On the cabinet beside it lay a copy of the blueprints she'd promised him. He grabbed them and quickly folded the paper until they fit nicely in his back pocket.

After their intensely pleasurable diversion in the sanctuary — a place he'd gleefully informed her was not *nearly* as secure as she believed — he'd spent the day shadowing her around the cathedral. A game had developed between them as she pretended to do her normal day off tasks while he lurked in the shadows, waiting for an opportune time to haul her into a dark corner for a quick, filthy orgasm.

The only place she objected to it was in the columbarium, claiming it wasn't right to let him slip his fingers into the blazing heat of her cunt with the dead all around. He agreed wholeheartedly. That was why he'd gotten on his knees and used his tongue instead.

For all her initial reticence, Petra turned out to be game for just about anything he wanted — a fact that should have delighted him if only it didn't make some latent instinct bristle with suspicion.

That feeling had dogged him ever since her little breakdown over her snacks. He thought it'd been vanquished after he had most of his questions about her answered, but that was only a temporary lull. Everything she'd said since made him wary, as if an opponent lurked just out of sight, threatening to steal her from him if he dropped his guard.

Alongside that feeling came the unnerving unpredictability of his own internal landscape. Silas had been certain that satisfying some of his craving for Petra would settle him, but the opposite was proving true.

He couldn't seem to relax, nor even work up the normal titillation he experienced the night before a job.

He couldn't control his impulses, which were going haywire at the lack of security in her den and the knowledge that she made even less sense to him now than she did a few days prior. Everything became even more unstable after discovering another man wanted her.

Petra had been awfully cagey about why the Protector was visiting, but he didn't need her to say it aloud. No man who installed video cameras in a woman's bedroom did it simply for information. It was for blackmail or pleasure. Always.

Her admission to being the daughter of a crime family — something he'd be looking into when he had a damn *second* — made the blackmail option slightly more likely, but only just.

Silas had exactly zero doubts that Vanderpoel had taken one look at the mysterious, shining facade of Petra's masks and wanted what he did: *more.*

If he hadn't already planned to kill the man, that would have clinched it.

Silas couldn't stop himself from glancing over his shoulder as he knelt on the floor by the bed. He was still looking at her, unable to tear his eyes away from her slumbering form, even as he rooted around in his backpack for his invisible ink marker.

It was large, with a thick chisel nib, and dried quickly enough to be useful for swift sigilwork. Exactly what he needed if he wanted even the smallest chance of his instincts allowing him to leave her side for a moment.

Teeth grinding, Silas forced his attention to the task at hand.

A few minutes passed as he worked. The astringent, chemical scent of the marker sliced through the rich haze of Petra's fragrance, wrinkling his nose as he drew a protective ring of unique sigils around her bed.

He'd only be gone for a few minutes, but anything could happen in that time. Silas aimed to make sure that anything was *nothing.*

His hair still stood on end after he finished, but it settled something in him to know that nothing could cross that invisible boundary without their insides liquefying.

Silas's lips quirked at the thought. He wondered if, like the story of Blight and Glory, the nastier sigilwork was another thing Petra hadn't been taught in school.

Where did she go to school?

His smile fell. Another question, another gap in his knowledge. Normally he didn't care to learn anything about a woman besides what her cunt tasted like, but the blank slate of Petra's formative years gnawed at him.

In fact, the sweet, musky taste of her cunt only made him want to know more.

Damn.

Shaking his head, Silas shoved his feet into his boots and strained to keep his eyes forward as he crept towards the closet and its hidden door.

His skin felt a little tighter with every step. His jaw tensed. His shadows were a furious, roiling mass just beneath his skin, desperate to get back to the treasure they'd left vulnerable in the bed.

But he kept moving. He turned the knob on the closet door. He slipped inside.

The short, dank hallway — barely big enough to fit the width of his shoulders — seemed much longer than it had before. Every step took more effort and the walls, unsealed, rough concrete, seemed to loom around him like a tunnel of brambles.

His heart, normally steady even under the most dire circumstances, throbbed in his chest. By the time he squeezed out of the concealed door into the gap between two buildings, he was covered head to toe in a layer of cold sweat.

Silas braced a palm on the filthy wall and tried in vain to catch his breath. *What the fuck is wrong with me?*

Are you wearing Glory's symbol? He didn't think he'd ever heard Tal sound so incredulous, which was saying something.

Silas smoothed his palm over the cheap gold necklace. It was warmed with his body heat, but he thought he could still feel a bit of Petra in it. "Yes."

Why are you—

"Worried I'm becoming religious?"

Fuck no, Tal replied. *It just seems a little blasphemous, even for you.*

Silas scoffed. Of all the things to be pulled out of bed for... "What do you care? The gods aren't real."

People don't think wraiths are real, either, but here I am.

Rolling his eyes, Silas demanded, "What did you find?"

You won't like it, Tal answered from somewhere deep in the murky shadows of the alleyway.

Silas unconsciously ran his palm over a horn as he paced a tight circle, his boots dodging the usual alley detritus not even the squeaky clean EVP street sweeper bots could fully eradicate.

"I don't like any of this," he grunted.

You could back out. Tal's shadows undulated and his voice, soft and low, carried a distinct note of unease. *But I don't think you should.*

Silas stopped pacing long enough to send his brother an incredulous look. "Weren't you the one who told me I shouldn't do this?"

Not that he was considering backing out. Silas couldn't imagine walking away now, not after he'd just begun to peel back Petra's layers with his clawtips. But it was unlike Tal to approve of a plan like this. He didn't really have a problem with murder and mayhem for profit, but Tal was staunchly against using innocent people — an amorphous, blurry line to draw in the moral sand.

I still don't think you should bond with a witch you don't care about, he explained, *but that doesn't mean I think you should just leave Petra high and dry. Something is seriously wrong here, Silas.*

"I know. She's given me enough bits and pieces of the truth to put that together on my own."

No, you don't understand. Tal's voice was a whisper in his mind, a low hiss of urgency. *I followed a couple of the acolytes tonight after they came back from dinner. They weren't using explicit language, but I could tell they were discussing Petra's meeting with the Protector.*

A deep rumble built in Silas's chest. He didn't like the idea of people discussing Petra behind her back, and he *loathed* her plan to meet with the man she believed was a murderer.

It wouldn't happen, of course, but the fact that she even considered it made him want to bite her someplace tender.

When she told him the plan, it was only the knowledge that she'd do everything in her power to thwart him that kept him from telling her she wouldn't be going into a room alone with that man under any circumstances. He didn't care that she might be wrong about his involvement in Dooraker's murder. He didn't care that there was no proof the man wanted her as anything more than a political ally.

She was *not* having dinner with him. Period.

"What did they say?" Silas resumed pacing.

They were speculating about her meeting, Tal answered, *and worrying.*

"Worrying? About what?"

About Petra. They wouldn't say it aloud, but it was clear they were talking about whatever it was Vanderpoel wants from her. They kept whispering about how they hoped 'she has a choice'.

Silas stopped abruptly, his head swinging around to stare out through the opening of the alley to where the cathedral complex glowed with an impressive array of decorative lights. He and Tal had chosen to meet across the street, despite the fact that Tal had long since established himself in the shadows of the cathedral. Although Silas was confident in his abilities to jam any surveillance equipment, the most prudent option when exchanging information was to simply do so when one wasn't surveilled at all.

He narrowed his eyes. *My little liar, what aren't you telling me?*

Speaking to Tal, he said, "Petra believes he killed her uncle.

Apparently Maximilian Dooraker was at one time a criminal from Los Angeles by way of Baltimore."

He could almost *feel* Tal's dismay as his form, indistinct but more solid than any other wraith Silas had encountered, shimmered like hot air over a blacktop. *So she's doing this to get revenge?*

Silas snorted. "No, worse. She wants to bring the man to *justice.*"

She hadn't said it in so many words, but it was there. Despite her apparent consideration of simply ridding the world of the man, he doubted she would have gone through with it even if she'd had the money required for a hit. For all her lies and scheming, Silas had begun to suspect that something soft and naive lurked within his little goddess.

Normally that would have been enough to put him off anyone, explosive sexual chemistry be damned, but just like everything else related to Petra, the knowledge seemed to have the opposite effect.

It made his gut churn to think about, but Silas actually *wanted* to see that softness, if only so he could hold it in his fist. *No one else can have it,* he reasoned. *That's why I want it so much. I won't let anyone else touch her — any part of her.*

Tal drifted along the filthy walls, avoiding the dull shaft of light cast by the street lamp just beyond the opening of the alley. *I told you she's a good person, Silas. I told you.*

"I never said she wasn't a good person," he argued, temper flaring. "I said she was a liar and that she would get us what we need. What *you* need."

He wasn't the only one beginning to lose his temper. Tal's shadows stretched out along the wall in a sticky wave of black threads, like he was adhering himself there to keep himself from doing something rash. *What I need? Don't you put this on me, Silas. You aren't doing this for me. There are a thousand different ways we could have gotten the power we need for the body! Petra was a barely viable option, but you took one look at her and—*

"What?" Silas rounded on his brother with a snarl. He wasn't even entirely certain why they were fighting, but something about Tal's criticisms, his staunch belief that he'd known Petra's character better than Silas himself, made him want to rake his claws through the shadows. "What happened, Tal? Because all I remember was making a deal that'd get you a fuckin' body back, just like you wanted."

Tal's voice took on the tone that drove Silas up a wall — an infuriating combination of patience and condescension. *I'm not saying I didn't want it. I'm just trying to explain that maybe this is more complicated than you're ready to deal with. I want you to help Petra, Silas, but I don't think you're ready for her bond, or what being tied to her would do to you. Look at you! You look like you're barely keeping it together.*

"You think I should let her go."

The words were a tiny, insignificant pebble dropped down a dark well inside him. At first there was nothing, no reaction, as it sailed into the depths of him. Then, all at once there was a splash — a great, echoing cataclysm that rippled through the very core of his being.

Petra wasn't just a mystery. She was *his* mystery. Her magic was *his* magic. Her body was *his* body. All her little secrets, all her lies, all her curious soft spots — they all belonged to him. They had since the moment she dared to walk into that bar and lie to his face.

Silas's fingers curled into a fist, one by one, when he announced, "No."

No?

"I'm not letting her go. I'm *never* letting her go."

Silas, listen to yourself. Tal lost the patience and exchanged it for outright concern. *You're obsessed with her now, but what if this is just the rut? I don't want you to tangle yourself up in this poor woman's life, only to break her heart when you don't want anything to do with her come fall. Say it's not the rut— What are you going to do if you actually want to keep her? I'm just asking you to think this through.*

Dissatisfaction wasn't a heavy feeling then, but a sharp sting inside him. "You think I'm going to hurt her."

It wasn't the first time Tal had warned him away from hurting someone he felt didn't deserve it, but something about *this* warning made the muscles of Silas's throat tighten.

I think you're stepping into something far more complicated and dangerous than you accounted for. And I'm not just talking about whatever is going on with the Temple and Vanderpoel.

That, at least, Silas could agree with. He didn't care about whatever was rotting the Temple from the inside out, but he was beginning to understand that whatever it was that existed between himself and Petra had taken on a life of its own.

It was its own kind of predator, and he sensed that it was simply biding its time before it swallowed them both whole.

But he couldn't articulate that feeling even if he wanted to, which he didn't. Silas was intensely possessive of his relationship with Petra, and things he'd normally feel nothing about sharing with his only friend in the world were suddenly precious little jewels to be hoarded.

He didn't want anyone else to see them when he took them out and held them to the light, inspecting every facet and color. He wanted to keep them close, locked where no one could touch them, and know they belonged to him and him alone.

Not even Tal would get the privilege of admiring the treasure he'd found.

Trying to end the conversation before he really did rake his claws through Tal's barely-there form, he said, "I'm not leaving Petra to fend for herself. I'm going to handle this for her and then figure out the rest."

That's all I ask, Tal replied, sounding relieved. *Just use your head, Silas. That's all. I know you hate being told what to do, but I'm worried about you. I'm worried about her, too.*

"Well, stop worrying about her. She isn't fuckin' yours."

Silas's teeth clicked together as his jaw snapped shut. A beat of silence passed. In the distance, a flurry of honking horns and a lone disgruntled voice interrupted the relatively quiet city night.

Then, in his whispery voice, Tal asked, *Do you hear yourself? Tell me what you sound like, Silas.*

He turned on his heel to pace again. Anger was a burning coal in his stomach, its heat fueled by the urgent need to get back to Petra's den, where she lay vulnerable and soft beneath her sheets.

"I sound like a demon on the edge of rut," he grunted. "It's not that fuckin' deep, Tal."

You seem to forget that I've known you for decades, Silas. Long before you entered your first rut. And before that, I went through them myself. I know the fucking difference.

It was on the tip of Silas's tongue to ask what Tal's own experience had anything to do with this, since he could barely remember something that happened a lifetime and a millennia ago, but that was too cruel even for him.

"What do I sound like, then?" he snapped instead.

You sound like a mate.

Silas rolled his eyes in such a way that his matriarch would have warned him that they'd get lost in the back of his head. "I'm not anyone's mate."

Are you sure? Because you seem awfully tetchy for a man who just wants to get his cock wet in a pretty priestess.

Silas turned his head so fast something in his spine cracked. "Watch your fuckin' mouth!"

See?

"She's not my mate," he ground out, disturbed by the very idea. Not because he disliked the thought of Petra being bound to him for the rest of her life — that was a lovely benefit of her bond, after all — but because *his* instincts were out of his control. Demons didn't get to decide who their partners were, unlike witches, and he'd always gotten the feeling that he would be one of those pitied few who never discovered his other half.

Silas wasn't ignorant to the fact that his clan whispered that though it was regrettable for any demon to never meet their mate, in his case it was probably for the best. After all, who could be that unlucky?

He didn't take offense. His family meant well, as they always did, and he was certain they would be delighted if he *did* find his mate, but he had historically agreed that it was for the best that he didn't. Silas had never felt the craving to find a mate like his cousins and couldn't stomach the maintenance of one besides.

Until now. What had long been considered a blessing now felt... wrong.

Despite Silas's combative tone and posture warning him to back off, Tal kept pushing. *How do you know?*

"Because my shadows haven't— It hasn't *happened.*"

When demons met their mates, a piece of their shadows lived within their partner and acted as a brand of ownership. No other demon would mistake them for being unmated when a piece of living shadow possessively curled around their arm, ankle, waist, or throat. Demons and their clans shared a unique fingerprint, a tenor to their shadows that could be perceived by any of their kind, giving even more depth to the claim. If Petra wore his shadow, it would be the equivalent of having his name and that of his clan tattooed across her forehead.

...Which, in hindsight, helped him understand the appeal of a marriage sigil a little bit more.

It doesn't always happen right away, Si, Tal argued, *and you're a hybrid. Who knows what that means for mating?*

The thought of Petra wearing a brand of his shadow, telling all the world who she belonged to, reminded him of how her lush cunt stretched around the very essence of Silas's soul. A fresh wave of cold sweat broke out across the back of his neck. Want curled in his gut, syrupy and sweet like molasses.

But if she *was* his mate, surely his shadows would have known *then,* when they were literally inside her. *Right?*

Unfortunately, that wasn't a question he could ask without telling his brother things he should never, *ever* know about his witch.

Silas drove a knuckle into his eye, trying to thwart the beginnings of a headache. "Fuck this," he muttered, striding toward the entrance of the alley. "I'm not having this conversation with you, Tal, so drop it. I'm going back to bed."

Tal wasn't happy, but he begrudgingly allowed, *Fine. What about tomorrow? What's the plan?*

He paused, shrugging. "Tomorrow? We kill the motherfucker who put cameras in my witch's bedroom."

CHAPTER TWENTY-TWO

It was sweet relief to slide back under Petra's sheets, but rest eluded him.

He didn't usually sleep through the night. He preferred to work, either doing whatever job struck his fancy or tinkering with his machines in his lab while Tal drifted in and out. Silas tended to sleep about four hours a night, supplemented with sporadic naps during the day.

But it wasn't his sleep schedule that kept him awake as he draped his limbs over Petra, pressing her into the mattress and shielding her from... nothing.

Silas bit the inside of his cheek. *Damn.*

He'd never been protective of another being in his life. Possessive? Certainly. His clan belonged to him, and therefore anything that threatened a member of his family fell under his protection, even if they technically outranked him in the loose hierarchy of the Cuttcombe clan.

Tal fell under that umbrella, too, but he didn't need protecting. There was vanishingly little, as far as they knew, that could harm a wraith. Even if there was a threat, Tal was almost as ruthless as Silas. He could defend himself.

But a compulsive anxiety about the safety of another being?

No, he'd never felt that before. Not with his family, not with Tal, not with his rut partners.

Just Petra.

A deep growl of discontent worked its way up his throat. Silas pulled her closer, annoyed that they were still in her den, annoyed at his instincts, annoyed at Tal, annoyed that she was so soft, annoyed that she trusted him enough to sleep so deeply in his arms, and annoyed that she wasn't awake so he could talk to her.

As if sensing his growing restlessness, Petra stirred beneath him, her long blonde hair dragging across the pillow as she turned her head toward his. Eyes still closed, she murmured, "Demon?"

A soft hand touched his back. It settled in the dip of his spine, fingers pressing into firm muscle and ridged bone, before going lax.

A band tightened around Silas's chest. For an unsettling moment, he found it hard to breathe — something that only got worse when she blindly turned her nose into his throat and let out a drowsy sigh.

Silas tightened his arms around her. Sounding unreasonable to his own ears, he demanded, "How can you sleep so well with me here? Do you have any idea what I could do while you're knocked out?"

It hadn't bothered him a bit the previous night, but Tal's questions had pricked something in him, a volatile vein of... *feeling*. Now the contentment he'd felt in her presence was gone, replaced by a foreign tension he struggled to grapple with.

Somehow those feelings transmuted into being angry at her when she blinked owlishly up at him, those painfully blue eyes soft with slumber.

"Are you going to hurt me?"

"Of course not," he snapped. "Why does everyone think that? I'm not gonna fuckin' hurt you, Petra. You're mine."

Petra's brows drew together slowly. "Who's everybody?"

Disgruntled anew, Silas commanded, "Go back to sleep."

His skin felt too tight, his body too small to contain the thing that craved her. The familiar sensation of shadows bleeding through him, out of him, to drape over her body only relieved a small amount of that pressure.

A small, weak voice he didn't recognize whispered in the back of his mind, *Take. Please take to her. Make her mine.*

His lip curled in disgust as he shook the thought loose. *Since when do I beg?* He was a motherfucking demon. He'd decided Petra was his and she would be — shadows be damned.

Her huff drifted over the skin of his throat, but she was apparently too tired to fight him. Instead, she wiggled beneath him, trying to get more comfortable. His first instinct was to scowl and press down, holding her in place until she settled, but he quickly realized what she was up to and forced himself to relax.

Petra turned on her side, one arm slung over his waist, her knees drawn up and her forehead cradled by the divot between his collar bones.

His pulse thundered there at the base of his throat as the scent of her hair tantalized him. *She came to me,* he realized, lips parting in confusion. It was the first time she'd initiated any sort of contact between them, though she'd certainly enjoyed his touch before then.

But this was... different.

Silas lay frozen for several seconds, half expecting her to immediately change her mind and seek out the other side of the bed, maybe lunge for his weapon, but when she didn't, he threw his arm over her. Curling his fingers around the nape of her neck, he compulsively rubbed the underside of his jaw over the crown of her head.

"Tell me something about you," he demanded, his voice a harsh rasp in the quiet.

"Silas, do you want me to sleep or not?"

"I don't know. Both."

He was amused to feel a small pinch. "You're a lot needier than I ever could have imagined."

"My clan could have warned you about that," he replied,

surprising himself almost as much as her. Petra went stiff in his arms, but the words were out.

Silas never discussed his clan with anyone but Tal, and he'd certainly never intended to allow Petra near them, but he couldn't summon any regret now.

Savoring the warm silk of the skin of her nape, he doubled down. "They'd tell you I've always been a terror — especially when I don't get my way."

They'd love you.

Not because she was famous or beautiful, but because she was probably the only person in the world who didn't fear him. Not really. Not in her heart. Not as much as she should.

She didn't quite relax again, but she did press her lips against his throat when she murmured, "Well now, that I could have predicted."

"Tell me about you."

"It's late, Silas."

"I don't care. I want to know something about you." That was a partial truth. He wanted to know *everything*, but he could grant that it was too big of an ask for two AM.

Another drowsy sigh tickled his skin, making his toes curl. "Ask me a real question and I'll answer."

He fished for a second, trying to decide between the dozens and dozens of questions that only ever seemed to spawn more. Gaze darting around the dark bedroom, he finally settled on one that had nagged at him for days.

"Why do you keep caches of food?"

A long stretch of silence followed his question. Silas waited with all the patience he was capable of before he gave her nape a quick squeeze. "Did you fall asleep?"

"Unfortunately, no." Petra's chest expanded with a deep inhale. She held it for a moment, her breasts a soft pressure against him, before she released it slowly. "That's a complicated question."

Silas rolled his eyes toward the ceiling. "I'm *shocked.*"

"What's that supposed to mean?"

"It means that for every damn question I get answered, ten more take its place."

Her fingers curled into a small fist against his back. "I'm really not that interesting, Silas. Everything you think I am — it's all smoke and mirrors."

"You let me decide what's interesting about you," he deadpanned, "because so far you've had shit judgment on the subject."

"For the love of—"

"Quit stalling and answer the question, baby."

Petra took her sweet time, but eventually she said, "It's something I do to help with anxiety."

Anxiety? Silas's eyes narrowed. "Explain."

"It's a long story that I'm way too tired to get into right now, but suffice it to say I spent most of my formative years without regular access to food. It wasn't so bad when I was really young, but after— well, when I was a teenager I'd go days without food. So I learned to ration and snatch whatever I could for the days when things were thin." Her shoulders shrugged under his arm. "I haven't gone hungry in decades, but I get... anxious when I don't have *something* around, just in case. Having my caches helps me not think about food all day."

Dissatisfaction again, worse than ever before. Silas was stunned by the force of it. The squirming in his gut was more like the lash of a whip inside him.

I ate some of her food. A wave of pinpricks rushed over his skin. It was an ugly feeling, the thing that whipped him again and again. Bad. Very bad.

The animal in him choked. It could hardly comprehend the reality that she'd revealed to him. Not only was she threatened in the present, but she'd been vulnerable all her life. *Hungry,* deprived of the most basic of needs. If that hadn't been met by the people who should have protected her, then what other horrors was she keeping locked away in her murky past?

Silas floundered. He had no idea how to make the ugly feeling

go away. All he knew was that he needed to fix this in some way —
by any means necessary.

Voice rough, he promised her, "I'll get you more."

She'd never have to think about food again. He'd make sure
her cabinets were never less than bursting, her fridge overflowing
with fresh fruit and takeout and fancy cheese and anything else
her heart desired. He'd pack caches himself and place them in
every room of the house.

He had to, because the thought of Petra worrying about
something as fundamental as whether she'd go hungry tomorrow
caused him a near-physical discomfort.

His little goddess, radiant and powerful and cunning, anxious
about her next meal? Petra motherfucking Zaskodna, the witch
who outshone everyone she met? *His* witch, who'd connived her
way into power despite having no coven, no name, no family?
The woman who held the adoration of an entire city and one
fucked up demon who couldn't get enough of her?

Over my dead fuckin' body.

Petra seemed to hear some thread of that intense feeling in his
simple promise. Her breath hitched as her blunt nails dug into the
meat of his muscle. "Silas..."

"I won't take your food anymore." The memory of how he'd
gleefully eaten those chocolate candies on her bed and how she'd
cried as she carefully scooped the packages off the floor was like
acid churning in his stomach.

"I didn't mean—"

"And," he bit out, "I'll make sure you never have to think
about it again. Not once. Clear?"

Petra was quiet for the span of several heartbeats before she
whispered, "You're forgiven, Silas. Really."

That drew him up short.

He stared at the opposite wall, unblinking, and rolled the
words over in his mind. *You're forgiven, Silas.*

Was he asking for forgiveness? He'd never done it before, so it hadn't occurred to him that maybe the ugly thing in him wasn't just dissatisfaction, but guilt.

Huh.

As if sensing his unease, Petra stroked his spine and asked, in a lighter tone, "Can I go back to sleep now?"

It was hard to speak around the lump in his throat, but he managed to rasp, "Yes."

If every nerve in his body wasn't straining to pay attention to her slightest shift, Silas might have thought it was his imagination that conjured the soft, seeking touch of her lips to his throat. "Goodnight, demon. Sleep tight."

"Goodnight, little goddess."

After a few minutes, Petra's body went soft again, her breathing even and deep. Silas didn't follow her into slumber, though. He stared into the darkness and thought, *Maybe Tal's right.*

And then, like there might be some benevolent god listening, the pathetic, newborn thing in him prayed, *Please be right.*

Chapter Twenty-Three

The last day of her life as she'd known it began with a demon breathing in her ear. All things considered, it wasn't a bad start.

As Petra lay there, nearly suffocated by the weight of a full-grown demon, she tried to summon some great swell of feeling about what was to come or what she'd allowed to happen the previous day.

But there was nothing. After so much work, so many sleepless nights, and too many quiet tears, she found an unnatural stillness within herself now that the day of reckoning had arrived.

As for regret...

Petra turned her head as much as she was able. It wasn't easy, since Silas had apparently decided to become a sentient blanket in the night. She only just managed enough movement to see a sliver of his face, nearly obscured by a fall of chocolate brown curls. She expected him to look relaxed in sleep, but he appeared quite the opposite.

His brows were drawn tight together, his lips pressed into a flat line. This close, she could even see that the skin around the base of his dark, slightly ridged horns was tense.

But the arm around her middle wasn't too tight. His

breathing was even. His smell, thyme and *him,* created a hazy comfort in the warmth of her bed. Which was ridiculous, because nothing about the man could be clinically defined as comforting.

Liar.

Petra let out a slow sigh. She had to acknowledge, if only to herself, that though Silas was clearly off his rocker and deeply amoral — at *best* — she hadn't exactly suffered in his company. At the very least, he'd done marvelous work in taking her mind off of what was to come, and gave her several shattering orgasms on top of it. If nothing else, he deserved a bit of credit for giving her a lusciously sensual penultimate day.

And sometimes, if she really squinted and turned her head *just so,* she thought she could see something almost boyish about him.

Dim memories of the previous night's conversation bubbled up as she admired the fan of his lashes, thick and sooty, where they lay against the tops of his cheekbones.

She remembered waking up to his low drawl and complaining about it, though she hoped she didn't say anything about how she'd been enjoying what might be the last good night's sleep of her life. There were clearer memories of bickering, their bodies shifting, and the odd, comforting pressure of his shadows wrapping around her body.

And then he asked her about food.

Obviously, it wasn't something she'd talked about with anyone besides Max, but even he hadn't known the true extent of her anxious habit. He knew enough about what had happened to her between the time when he faked his death and when he tracked her down years later to riddle him with guilt. She never wanted to add onto that load with something she could manage on her own, and she'd certainly never told him how she'd pawed through trash for food scraps or stolen things like shoes and blankets when the cold became unbearable.

But with Silas, the words had simply tumbled out. Not because she thought she'd find some deep well of compassion in him, but rather the opposite. There would be no pity from Silas. He was too frank, too removed from ordinary feeling, to weep for a hungry child.

Petra didn't want pity or tears. Her life was what it was. The past couldn't be changed, and she wasn't special. Many children, particularly those who didn't quite fit into the fabric of respectable society for one reason or another, ended up with worse fates than hers. She'd been rescued. Others hadn't.

If she came out of it with scars, then she didn't want someone to look at them and flinch. She wanted someone to see them plainly, with neither pity nor scorn, but with admiration for how she'd survived.

In the moment, Silas seemed like the perfect person to tell because he wouldn't offer her platitudes or false praise for coming through adversity mostly okay in the end.

What she *didn't* expect was the almost panicked note in his voice when he told her he'd *get her more.*

He didn't ask more questions. He didn't get angry on her behalf. His first reaction was to immediately connect her explanation to what he'd done and how she'd reacted to it.

Her half-asleep mind could barely comprehend it, but she thought she'd heard an almost childlike, anxious guilt in that simple promise and those that came after it.

Maybe she was reading too much into it. It did seem a little outlandish to assign guilt to a man who, rumor had it, had once been hired by three separate clients who all put hits out on one another and somehow managed to collect his payment for every single one of them.

But Petra didn't want to think too hard about it. She didn't want to regret wringing the last drops of pleasure out of her life in the most inappropriate ways possible. She wanted to live in the fantasy world where Silas was actually kind of sweet in his own awful little way for a moment longer.

Unfortunately, wanting something had never stopped the gods from doing as they chose with her life, and it certainly never hit the snooze button on her alarm — which picked that moment to ring.

Petra's chest clenched. *Here we go.*

"Dawn service is too fuckin' early." Silas's growl rumbled through the bed a moment before he scraped his teeth over the corner of her jaw, eliciting a sharp gasp. "But if I have to get up at the ass-crack of dawn, at least I get to watch you up there by the altar and imagine what it'll be like fuckin' you on it."

I've changed my mind, she decided, pushing him away with a disgruntled huff. *I actually hate this man.*

"That's not happening."

"You didn't have a problem with the idea yesterday," he murmured, a hand sliding down her side to slip beneath her nightgown. Her body responded instantly to that proprietary touch and the gravelly purr that rattled his chest.

"I temporarily lost my mind yesterday. It won't be happening again." Not because she didn't want to, but because there was no future in which she and Silas could pursue the electric chemistry between them. Whether she lived or died, their relationship would end the moment the Protector stepped foot on cathedral grounds.

A sharp blade of grief sliced her. *Gods, I can't believe I'm actually going to miss this man.*

Silas's shadows nudged her legs apart. She could have fought that slight pressure, but she didn't want to. The thought that this was truly her last chance to experience pleasure made her soul shrivel and her body ache.

What's one more orgasm before the end?

"Is that so?" Silas slowly slipped his fingers through the seam of her cunt, already slick and hot with arousal, and let out a dark chuckle. "Is that why you're so wet already, baby? Or is it lying that gets you off?"

Neither. She hated lying and she didn't love the idea of having sex in public places, let alone her cathedral. Not that Glory would care, of course. The only god who seemed to have a problem with sexuality in all its expressions was Loft, and that was only because their followers believed true worship could only be achieved in a lack of worldly attachments.

Petra canted her hips into his hand, slowly swiveling to match the rhythm of his slow, swirling touches. His shadows drifted across the sensitive skin of her inner thighs and up beneath her nightgown until her breasts were cradled by ethereal hands.

"Has it ever occurred to you," she breathed, "that what gets me off might just be your touch, demon?"

Silas dragged the flat of his tongue over her jaw as he increased the pressure of his touches. A raw note in his voice sent a frisson of heat down her spine when he rasped, "Oh, I know you like it when I touch you. This cunt was made for me." He turned her head, allowing him to lick and nip at her lips. "This perfect mouth was made for me, too. Your body is my pretty toy, isn't it? Always ready for whatever I choose to give it. Because it's mine."

It really wasn't fair that he tasted as good as he smelled, even in the morning. Petra rocked her hips and met his tongue in a slick tangle. Speaking in the gaps between luscious, filthy kisses, she challenged, "Demon, if you can make me come before my second alarm goes off, you can use me all you like."

"Ah, my little goddess..." He startled a yelp out of her with a small, sharp slap to her core. "There's no universe in which you aren't mine to use, and there's no alarm in this world that'd stop me from making sure you know it."

Chapter Twenty-Four

Petra had worried that the day would drag, each second prolonged by the torture of grim anticipation, but that wasn't how it went. Instead, the hours seemed to flash by. They whirled past her in gusts of activity, last-minute preparations, nervous questions from her staff, and the uneasy feeling that losing sight of Silas gave her.

He'd watched her from the front row during her service, his lips curled in that arrogant, mocking smile as worshippers gave him a wide berth. Though he didn't seem to care that no one wanted to sit close, the sight of empty spaces on either side of him sent a lightning bolt of irritation through her.

Who were they to think a demon didn't belong in her cathedral? The sight made her wonder just how many other demons might have wanted to attend her services but felt unwelcome. San Francisco's demon population was small, certainly, but it wasn't zero. And yet she couldn't recall ever seeing a demon in the pews before.

That pissed her off.

She didn't have any time left to make a proper statement about who was welcome in her cathedral, but that didn't mean she did nothing. Without thinking it through, she altered her prepared service and blessings about Glory's gifts — a term she absolutely could never use again — to speak, with a touch more vehemence than normal, about how all were welcome in her divine light.

She'd staunchly refused to look at him then, but she could *feel* his amusement from his seat in the pews.

Petra couldn't decide if it was a boon or a bad omen when he simply disappeared after the service. On one hand, she appreciated the lack of fires. On the other, she got nervous when he wasn't in her direct eyeline.

Not because she'd grown used to his steady, if vexing, presence, but because today was not the day for him to get up to shenanigans.

Unfortunately, there simply wasn't the time for her to try and track him down. There was too much to do. On top of her regular duties, the staff was in a frenzy as they hurried to make the cathedral and themselves as presentable as possible.

They also wouldn't leave her alone.

If she wasn't answering questions or giving orders, she was constantly fielding anxious, even pitying looks. A few of the higher ranking priests and priestesses had been so bold as to assure her in the vaguest of ways that everything would be well and they hoped the visit would go smoothly for her.

Not them. Not the cathedral. Her.

Even if no one but Robert dared ask her directly what the Protector wanted from her, they all seemed to have a good idea. Even the initiates, mostly kept out of the loop of Temple politics until they were sworn in as acolytes, fluttered nervously around her. Eventually she'd been forced to give them extra craft study — the worship of Glory through artistic pursuit — in order to get them out of her hair once and for all.

Through all of this, Silas lingered in the back of her mind, his presence there its own type of specter. That wasn't helped by the constant reminder of their time together: the soreness between her thighs.

Despite the fact that there'd been no penetrative sex, technically speaking, every step sent a little twinge up her spine, an echo of every tiny, stinging slap he'd given her until he forced not one, but two orgasms just before her back-up alarm rang.

On any other day in her previous life, she might have found that satisfying, but in this one, it only reminded her of what she would no longer have.

By the time the Protector's entourage was due to arrive, Petra had a tension headache, she never wanted to hear the words *'do you think we need a...'* again, and she really, really wanted to know where Silas was.

Every hour that passed without a snide comment, a proprietary touch, or the weight of his shadows doing something they shouldn't made her nerves ratchet up another notch.

No, his presence wasn't what she would call traditionally reassuring, but he was the only one who knew what was really going on, and he was the only who knew *her,* and—

Damn, I just want to see his smug face.

Something about him not being by her side as she faced the predator from her nightmares made her feel deeply unmoored. Not because she worried about what he was up to unsupervised, but because she'd come to actually like the man. He made her feel safe.

Good gods.

It was very much against her will, but it was there: a thread of something warm and a little prickly tying them together.

There was no time left to examine that, nor the curdled feeling that settled in her gut at the thought that the thread would never have a chance to grow into something stronger, warmer, fiercer.

It's for the best, she thought as she took her place by the grand bronze doors of the cathedral's entrance. *We would have been a disaster, anyway.*

Her staff fanned out around her as three sleek black town cars pulled into the courtyard. Normally no one was allowed to park

there, but nothing was off-limits to the Protector. Certainly not
the landscaping.

Robert nearly vibrated with tension from his place beside her
as he watched one of the cars swing a little too close to the large,
extremely expensive marble fountain in the center of the
courtyard.

Petra didn't bother sending him a reassuring look. They all
knew that the Protector would do exactly as he wanted. If that
meant taking out a million dollar water fixture donated by a long-
deceased worshipper, then he would do so and there was absolutely nothing any of them could say about it.

This was her cathedral, but they all understood that as of this
moment, she didn't have the power to protect them from
anything, let alone the entourage's carelessness.

That's not entirely true.

In one secret way, she had power. She had Silas.

Petra had to believe that things would work out — even if she
didn't live long enough to see it.

Drawing her shoulders back, she watched the middle vehicle
come to a slow stop in front of the stone steps. A cool breeze, a
summer in San Francisco specialty, threatened to tear her hair
from its carefully crafted chignon and sent her robes of office fluttering around her legs.

Silas's necklace hung heavy and warm between her breasts,
tucked safely beneath her silk blouse. Not too far away, a cable car
rumbled along its track and dinged its bell as it passed between the
cathedral and the stately mansion grounds on the other side of the
street.

Breathe. You've got this.

A man she didn't recognize left the front passenger's seat to
open the back door of the car. He wore a sleek, wine-red uniform
and was clearly a member of Antonin's entourage, but she didn't
recall seeing him during the last visit.

Not that it meant much. She'd been flying by the seat of her
pants and surviving off of pure adrenaline last time, so there was

every chance that she simply didn't recall every member of the Protector's personal security unit as well as she thought.

There was no forgetting the man himself, though.

When Antonin Vanderpoel climbed out of the car, one shiny designer shoe at a time, it was as if the world around her held its breath.

He was slight of build, handsome in a finely aged, old money way, and wore an expression that could only be described as benign. His three-piece suit was perfectly pressed, the fabric a dark charcoal with barely visible pinstripes. A deep crimson tie and simple gold chain were the only pops of color on his person.

Antonin's hair, once dark, was streaked with more salt than pepper and swept back into a classic style. Not a single strand was out of place. His beard was similarly well kept and colored, giving him a mature attractiveness that might have been devastating on any other man.

The smile that creased his cheeks when he locked eyes with her was blinding. Bile crawled up her esophagus.

Petra had no proof that Antonin killed Maximilian with his own hands, but her intuition screamed when he climbed the steps, his movements lithe and graceful for a man approaching his elder years, and extended his arms to her.

You took the only family I had left, a wounded thing in her moaned, too hurt to carry the fire of fury. *You took everything from me.*

But she was more than that wounded creature. She was more than a starving child. She was more than a witch with no name.

She was a woman with steel in her spine and a demon on her side. Petra would see this to the end, no matter what that was.

So she summoned her practiced smile, just as false and shining as Antonin's, and slowly descended two steps to meet him. A hug was too much to bear, but she was able to smoothly move into clasping his hands. They burned with sickly heat against her own — the unnatural meeting of two luminists with Glory's light in their souls.

"Welcome back, your eminence," she murmured, leaning in to feather a kiss to both bearded cheeks.

Antonin's fingers curled around hers, holding tight, as he reciprocated the gesture. The only difference was that *his* lips actually touched her skin. "It's a pleasure to see you again so soon," he replied, voice as smooth and warm as a sunbaked river stone. "I regretted how short my trip was last time, so I'm looking forward to savoring your company, my dear."

Petra swallowed the bitter tang of bile as they pulled back, hands still clasped. "You're a busy man. I'm honored to get even a moment of your time, let alone this much."

"Ah, but who could resist the siren's call of High Priestess Zaskodna?" He cast his gaze over her shoulder, as if he wished to commiserate with her staff over how irresistible she was. "And in such a beautiful city, no less. I'm afraid it was too much for even my schedule to compete with."

Desperate to get his hands off her, Petra stepped back and to the side, as if to show off her pale-faced staff to the predator at their doorstep. "You didn't get the chance to meet them properly last time, so I'd love to introduce St. Emaine's staff to you, your eminence."

Forced to release her, Antonin instead held his hands out, palms forward, to her staff as she rattled off names and titles he almost certainly already knew. When she was finished, he greeted them with a fatherly smile. "I look forward to speaking with you all during my stay. May Glory's light shine on you for welcoming me and my entourage so warmly."

Going by the way several staff members flinched, Petra wasn't the only one who heard the threat woven into the polite response.

Before an awkward silence could settle in, Antonin clapped his hands together and turned his smile back on Petra. "Now, my dear, how about a tour?"

"Would you not like to get settled first? I'm sure you and your entourage could use a moment to decompress from so much traveling." She glanced over his shoulder under the pretense of concern for his entourage, but really she was counting the number of guards that had climbed out of the vehicles. It was hard work keeping her expression smooth when she realized he'd brought more than she anticipated.

All of them were blank-faced, their mouths set in neutral lines and their eyes a little... off. Just looking at them made the hair on the back of her neck stand on end.

One's missing. Petra did another quick count, but the somber face of Antonin's assistant didn't appear in the rows of red-clad guards.

"Ah, that's very kind of you," Antonin replied. "I'm used to all the travel, but my entourage will get settled while you guide me on a tour. I'm sure they'd appreciate a hearty meal, too."

"Of course. That shouldn't be a problem." She glanced at Robert, who was already turning to scurry across the courtyard and, she had no doubt, the kitchens.

Gods bless that man. Petra looked back at Antonin. "Is your assistant coming?"

Stepping closer, he hovered a hand over the small of her back. Unnatural warmth radiated between the skin of his palm and her spine. "Nicolas is on sabbatical," he answered as he guided her up the steps and into the womb-like darkness of the cathedral.

Keenly aware that *sabbatical* could be code for anything, including rotting somewhere in an abandoned building or chained in a top secret Temple dungeon, Petra chose the mildest possible response. "I see. I hope he's well?"

Antonin tossed her another charming smile. "I'm sure he is. Speaking of sabbaticals— I heard you're planning one for yourself quite soon."

Their steps were soft on the marble floor of the cathedral, but to her the beat sounded like a funeral march. "I am," she answered evenly, her mind racing with all the different ways he could interpret her decision. His expression gave nothing away. Antonin's mask was as good as hers.

Choosing her words with the utmost care, she explained, "I've been enormously privileged to be given this seat by the High Gloriae and try to earn it every day, but I can't give Glory's worshippers the guidance they deserve if my well is empty."

"You haven't missed a service in three years," he pointed out. "Most High Priests do one or two a week. I'm quite sure you've more than earned a month or two off, my dear. I doubt it will put a dent in your shining reputation amongst the EVP's populace."

Violently uncomfortable with his smooth praise, Petra demurred, "I am lucky to serve so many good people, your eminence."

"Aren't we all?" Rather than let her guide him as he claimed to want, the Protector steered her toward the high altar. She had to work very hard to not glance in the direction of the sanctuary.

His hand settled more firmly on the base of her spine, just above the divots of her tailbone. "Though I heard you had a mishap recently. Something about a fire after a service?"

Petra's mouth went painfully dry. *He doesn't know about Silas. He doesn't.* "An accident. An over-eager worshipper bumped into one of the votive stands and our runner unfortunately paid the price. We've temporarily fixed the issue with a few discreet sandbags, so hopefully there won't be incidents like it in the future."

She could just see Silas's smug face when she said that. His imagined voice, low and taunting, drifted through her mind. *"It's cute that you think that'll stop me."*

"Ah, that explains it," the Protector murmured, his voice dropping to an intimate drawl. "Someone was just trying to get a closer look at your radiance. That's an urge I understand completely."

A cold trickle of dread ran down her spine. "You're too kind to me, your eminence."

"Hardly. But I do believe I asked you to call me Antonin last time we spoke."

Was Max on a first name basis with you too, asshole?

"My apologies," she murmured. "With your position and responsibilities, I'd hate to imply favoritism."

Antonin stepped lightly onto the dais, his hand sliding away to grasp her elbow and guide her up as well. The sun shone through the great stained glass masterpiece of Glory's window, casting them and the dais in a thousand different colors of light. Glory's statue, towering but lifeless without a sacred fire lit within it, stared out sightlessly over their heads as Antonin inspected the offerings on the altar.

For half a second, she thought she spied a flickering shadow out of the corner of her eye, but she didn't dare turn her head to see what lurked in the gaps between shafts of colored light.

For once, the thought that something might be in the darkness watching her didn't unsettle her. She *wanted* it to be Silas. He couldn't save her from Antonin, but having him there made her feel less alone.

Without thinking about it, she lifted a hand to run her fingertips over the delicate gold chain of her necklace. Wild magic thrummed against the sensitive nerves in her finger pads. She could almost hear his southern drawl in her ear.

Thinkin' about me, baby?

She wished for one awful moment that she could rewind time and go back to the previous day, when he unknowingly chased away her fear with brutal touches and slithering shadows and barked commands.

It was a taste of bliss, letting him take control and wipe away her worries.

But she couldn't go back. All she could do was hope that he'd do exactly as he said he would, that Elise would get the information, and that something — anything — would come of this.

Petra stood beside Antonin, her heart thundering, and held very still when he leaned in close to whisper, "My dear, there's no harm in implying favoritism when it's the truth."

Chapter Twenty-Five

Even knowing it was coming, it was still a shock to be by Antonin's side for hours. She'd planned. She'd agonized. She'd practiced what she'd say and how she'd act.

None of it prepared her for the way being friendly with the man tore her in two.

Petra existed outside of her body as she gave the Protector his tour through the facilities. They chatted amiably, even flirtatiously, as if some foreign being inhabited her body while the real Petra huddled in the back of her mind, screaming into her palms.

The only thing the being in control of her couldn't handle was his touch. Antonin seemed to take every excuse to lay his hands on her, though it was carefully calculated to never cross any polite boundaries — just push them. She thanked the gods for her staff, who despite their anxiety seemed grimly intent on having at least one person with them at all times. Petra wasn't sure what he'd do without an audience, or even if said audience was a true deterrent for a man like him, but she was fiercely grateful for her staff all the same.

Unfortunately, it was imperative that he not suspect anything, so Petra was forced to endure most of it, though she did manage to slip away once or twice under the guise of coy flirtation.

The minutes dragged as she danced on the edge of a knife. Adrenaline was a constant hum in her blood. Fight or flight instincts battled with her need for calm, with the masks she'd worn for so long. As dinner approached, Petra would have done just about anything to be able to run screaming from his side, but there was no reprieve, no escape, and certainly no chance for her to look into his eyes and demand answers he'd never give her.

When it became too much, Petra imagined Silas. She pictured him skulking around the cathedral, those molten eyes gleaming in the dark. She imagined his cold, dangerous smile as he slipped into Antonin's suite and rifled through his things as he'd so gleefully done to her.

She pictured him there, standing just behind her, keeping her safe even as she stood in the path of disaster.

Their tour ended at the door to Antonin's suite. Two guards flanked it. They were joined by the two who'd trailed the Protector throughout the tour. All of them wore the same blank expression and not once did they speak a word.

Standing between his guards, Antonin lifted her right hand to his lips for a lingering kiss to her knuckles. Her skin crawled.

He didn't lower her hand right away, but rather rubbed his thumb over the tops of her fingers. "Not even one ring? You wear a shocking lack of jewelry, my dear."

His tone made it impossible for her to decipher whether that was a rebuke or not, so Petra settled on a neutral answer. "I prefer to keep attention on Glory, not my body."

Antonin *tsked*. "There's no way to outshine the goddess of the sun. Gilding yourself in jewelry that reflects her light is an act of worship and a sign of your station." He gave her fingers a quick, slightly too-tight squeeze and met her eyes over the ridge line of her knuckles. "I'll have pieces shipped here for you. You should always sparkle, my dear, particularly when you stand beside me."

She knew he assumed what her answer to his proposition would be. No one would be stupid enough to turn a bond with *him* down, after all. But it was deeply jarring to hear his confidence aloud.

Worried her hand would begin to shake, Petra gently extracted it from his own. She covered the tactical retreat with a featherlight touch to his arm. Disgust scalded her when he gave her a heavy-lidded look of approval.

She was rapidly losing her ability to pretend, so Petra pitched her voice low and hoped it came out as a private whisper rather than a croak when she said, "Thank you, Antonin. You're too generous with me."

"For Glory's rising star? My dear, you deserve far more than gold." His smile was sharp under the perfect curl of his gray-streaked mustache. "But we'll discuss that over dinner."

"Of course. We'll be taking our meal in the belltower, since it has the best view of the city." It was also the most remote part of the cathedral, which would hopefully give Silas plenty of time and space to do what he'd promised.

Antonin arched a brow. The look was teasing, but too practiced to come off as anything other than predatory. "Not your suite?"

Gods, no. The thought of inviting that man into her private space, even knowing it had been invaded by him already, made her gorge rise.

Summoning a slight, private smile, she replied, "My suite is in the heart of the staff living quarters. I believed you'd prefer more privacy than that."

Antonin shot her a cheeky wink. "Clever girl."

Truly unable to stomach more, Petra accepted his praise with a nod and turned to go. She hadn't made it more than a handful of steps before his voice stopped her.

"Petra?"

She turned her head, but couldn't make her body face him. "Yes?"

His eyes were dark when he commanded her, "Wear something beautiful. It's an important night. I want to make it special."

Bile really did threaten to make its appearance then. Petra swallowed a mouthful of excess saliva before answering. "Of course. It will be... very special. I can't wait."

∾

It was with a shocking splash of bitter disappointment that Petra discovered her room was empty.

Silas, where are you?

Surely it was a good sign that he'd made himself scarce, but she'd gotten used to having him in her space. It was unsettling to get ready without the weight of his attention on her at all times. She'd somehow even gotten used to the feeling of his shadows writhing around her legs like seeking hands.

It was disorienting to find herself suddenly unscrutinized as she pulled her white cocktail dress out of her closet and slipped it on. A part of her desperately wanted to take a second to breathe, maybe even sit on the edge of her bed and stare into the middle distance for a while, but she worried that if she gave in to the impulse, she wouldn't be able to force herself back out the door.

The secret passageway hidden in the back of her closet taunted her.

You could run, it said. *Max wouldn't blame you. He'd tell you to save yourself, that this isn't worth it. He'd want you to live.*

But the fact that Max wasn't there to tell her that himself was the whole reason she'd gotten into this mess. And every time she thought of simply slipping into the night and disappearing with all the money he'd set aside just for this situation, she remembered the shaky way he sounded when he confided his suspicions that something horrible was about to happen.

The scared little girl in her, beaten, starved, and feral, hissed from the safety of her hiding place in Petra's mind, *I'm going to finish what you started, dyadya Matvei.*

So she didn't take whatever chance remained to escape her fate. Instead, she did as so many women in her place had done before: she got ready for her date.

She curled her hair. She washed her face. She carefully applied her makeup — neither too much nor too little. She slipped her feet into red heels, the toes sharp points tipped with gold, and said a short prayer for her feet on the one hundred and fifty steps they would climb up to the belltower.

When there was no part of her left to primp, prune, or decorate, Petra stared at her reflection for several seconds. An unknown woman stared back at her.

"For Matvei," she mouthed. Even then, when he was nothing but dust and crushed bone, she couldn't bring herself to betray him by speaking his real name aloud. Petra had always been fiercely loyal. That intensity had nowhere to go now, but...

She swallowed hard as she curled her fingers around the gold charm Silas had crafted for her. The back of her nose stung with unshed tears. A deep pang of grief struck her — not for her uncle, but for the fact that she hadn't gotten to see Silas's violent smile, those molten eyes, or that stupid little beauty mark above his lip one last time.

There's no loyalty between us, but there's trust. Just enough.

Petra turned away from the mirror. Her heels clicked on the old wooden floor as she made her way back to her closet for a light coat. Summer nights were always unpredictable in San Francisco, and she didn't want to die shivering in the wind.

Swinging the closet door open, she stepped inside to grab her favorite white coat off its hanger. Her fingers had just closed around the soft wool collar when the light vanished.

Shock held her there for the span of heartbeat, but she didn't get the chance to recover, let alone fight. Without warning, the darkness yanked her forward, squashing her into the clothing with a rattle of hangers. Petra squawked, her body instinctively thrashing to throw off an assailant that didn't truly exist.

"Sil—" His name was cut off by a clinging film of shadows

covering her mouth. Behind her, the closet door swung shut. Petra screamed into the dark, but the sound was trapped in her throat.

No! She tried to struggle, to fight like a fox caught in a snare, but it was no use. The shadows were everywhere. They were gentle, gentler than she remembered Silas's ever being before, but they didn't give her an inch.

The musty smell of the closet, the texture of her coat pressed against her cheek, the way the darkness seemed to be *petting her hair*— Petra wanted to throw back her head and howl in outrage.

She *knew* it'd been too easy. She *knew* he'd been too accommodating.

Something had seemed off about his easy acceptance of her plan to have dinner with Antonin, but she'd ignored it because there was no other choice. Now she saw how stupid that was.

She'd underestimated Silas. *Again.*

Gods knew what he planned now that she was stowed away like old camping equipment. A garbled sound of pure outrage escaped her throat. *I'm going to fucking kill him!*

But that could only happen if she found a way to escape. Most likely he'd come back for her, but she didn't have time to hope for that. She needed to get out of the closet, climb one hundred and fifty stairs, distract Antonin, and *then* murder Silas with her bare hands.

Fury was a roaring fire in her chest. Her breaths quickened, her lungs like twin bellows fanning the flames.

"I have my own plan," he'd said.

Petra bared her teeth against the shadows covering her mouth. Her skin burned hot, her magic bubbling up to the surface like an upswell of magma. The shadows around her stilled, then began to move in earnest, pressing down on her as if they could stop the white-hot glow of magic from bursting from her pores.

They couldn't.

Shadows can't hold me, motherfucker. Not unless I let them.

Chapter Twenty-Six

Petra made it to the belltower with less than a minute to spare.

Her feet screamed in her heels and her lungs burned from exertion, but she plastered on a smile for the two guards standing at the utilitarian door that blocked the final short flight of steps.

They gave her nothing in return — just that ever-present blank stare that made her stomach turn. Something was wrong with the members of the Ardeo. Not that they'd ever been a particularly saintly group, but the way these men looked...

Petra shook herself. *There's no time to speculate.*

That would be Elise's job, or whoever it was who took on the monumental task of unraveling what exactly was going on within the heart of Glory's Temple.

The guards let her pass with twin, crisp nods. One of the men opened the door for her. It swung inward with a groan, its hinges creaking and a little rusted by the cool, wet air that drifted down the staircase every day.

Petra sucked in a deep breath of night air and willed her magic to settle. It still boiled under her skin, unsatisfied with the way the shadows had recoiled from it, fleeing to wherever it was shadows went. She wasn't one for wanton destruction, but when roused, her magic craved an outlet.

Her temper did, too.

Settle, she urged herself again as she curled her fingers around the cold metal railing. Each step she took made the balls of her feet howl in pain, but she forced herself to walk steadily, to appear poised as she climbed the stairs and emerged onto the enclosed roof of the tower.

She wasn't lying when she said that the belltower had the best view. Standing two hundred and fifty feet above the ground and atop a hill, it allowed her to look out at the sprawl of San Francisco glittering in the night. To the northeast, Solbourne Tower was a distant, glowing shape on Treasure Island, lit to show its majesty and protected by sigils carved into the very face of the building itself.

During the summer solstice and after the grand public celebrations, Petra and her staff liked to gather there to watch the sunset. They feasted on sweets, drank too much, and danced to music. It was the one day a year she'd been able to truly feel at ease with them, but she'd miss it this time around.

Because the person waiting for her by the sumptuously dressed table was not a member of her staff. The solstice was weeks away. The air was chilly and there were no cakes, no too-sweet alcoholic beverages.

"Petra." Antonin stepped away from the table to help her ascend the final step. His hands were hot on her arm and the dip of her waist. Again, she cursed Silas. In her desperation to get free and not be late, she'd left her coat behind. That meant Antonin touched her bare skin when he took her elbow in hand.

"Thank you," she murmured, casting him a close-lipped smile.

The belltower wasn't huge, so thankfully he didn't have to touch her for too long as he guided her to their table. Antonin gamely pulled her chair out for her. As much as she didn't want to have the man at her back, Petra forced herself into the seat.

He didn't step back right away. Instead, he covered her shoulders, bare save for the thin straps of her dress, with his hot palms and leaned down to whisper in her ear, "You look divine, my dear."

His breath brushed her skin. His scent, all expensive cologne and something *off* she couldn't place, wrapped around her. Petra swallowed hard. It took an enormous amount of self control to not shy away or gag reflexively.

Instead, she replied, "I'm glad you approve."

Antonin squeezed her shoulders, his touch lingering, before he finally released her. Circling the table, he slid into his seat with a small, pleased smile.

The gold chain around his neck winked in the light cast by the candles arrayed around them. The glow flickered in his eyes, too, giving them a sinister, glassy look as he reached over to fill her empty glass with red wine.

"Your cooking staff outdid themselves," he complimented her.

Petra gave the spread a good look, but she saw none of it. Not really. Her mind was split between focusing on every minute movement the Protector made and agonizing over what Silas was doing.

"We're lucky to have such skilled staff," she replied, reaching for her wine.

Antonin poured himself some wine as well, just a splash of bloody liquid at the bottom of his glass. "Very much so. I'm looking forward to my stays here."

Stays. The wine soured on her tongue. She had to force her sip down with great effort.

Knowing he expected her to say *something* now that they were alone, Petra asked, "Do you plan on staying long?"

After a small sip, Antonin set his glass back down on the table. He peered at her from under gray-streaked brows, his lips set in a small, benign smile. "That depends."

"On?"

"How long it takes to get you pregnant."

A deep internal tremor tried to work its way out of her, to rumble down her bones all the way to her fingertips and toes, but she somehow managed to shove it down, to stay calm. She knew he wanted an heir. That had been part of his proposal all those weeks ago, but *hearing* it...

For some reason she couldn't possibly explain to herself, Silas's face flashed to the forefront of her mind. Not because of the filthy promises he'd made about *breeding* her, but because—

Doesn't matter.

Even if everything was different, there was no future with him. She didn't even know why she thought of it. Besides, the idea of having Silas's children made her shudder for different reasons. The man was a menace and lived an objectively dangerous life. There was no possibility of a family with him even if she wanted one.

Those thoughts bombarded her, one after another, in the space between heartbeats. It was a certain kind of madness to think of it on a normal day, let alone when the Protector was sitting a foot away from her, gauging her reaction.

Petra draped her cloth napkin in her lap and smoothed her fingers over it. "Forgive me for questioning you, Antonin, but I'm still... It's still shocking for me. Are you certain that I'm your best match?"

The crow's feet around Antonin's eyes crinkled with his widening smile. It was unfortunate that something in him was rotten. If he'd been a good man, or even just not *cruel,* she might have found him attractive.

"If I wasn't certain, I wouldn't have asked," he replied, picking up his fork with deft, ring-clad fingers. "I've had my eye on you for years, Petra. A woman of your ambition— It's like catnip to a man like me. I've waited a *very* long time to find a partner worthy of me, you know."

Petra nodded. Unlike her, he had the luxury of time. As a

witch much farther down the magical power scale than her, the threat of burnout didn't put a ticking clock on his choices.

Taking his fork and knife to the perfectly seared tuna filet on his plate, he continued, "And of course, if I *hadn't* been certain after meeting you, then I would have been after discovering how you got your position."

Anxiety ratcheting up another notch, she asked, "What do you mean?"

Antonin flashed her a white smile. "Ah, my dear, I'm talking about how you poisoned Gurney and his assistant."

For just a moment, she considered denying it. But what use would that be? He clearly knew the truth, and she didn't hold out any hope of deceiving him.

Her limbs felt wooden, her stomach a painfully tight ball of nerves, but she forced herself to mimic his casual air as she reached for her own utensils. "Poisoning is a bit of a stretch, I think. They were fine after a couple days."

"Deliciously ruthless of you all the same." He popped a bite of fish into his mouth and chewed thoughtfully for a moment. "You can't imagine how interesting it was to hear of some nobody witch from the mouth of the sovereign himself. The Gloriae were absolutely scandalized."

That didn't shock her, though she'd never been deemed important enough to meet the secretive group who ruled the Temple. She hadn't even been invited when Theodore Solbourne met with them in a high-stakes meeting to negotiate his authority over Healing Houses in his territory.

"I'm sure it was quite a shock," she murmured, spearing a halved cherry tomato drizzled with vinaigrette on the tines of her fork.

"They tried to refuse, you know," he told her, as if he was imparting some great secret, "but the elf stood firm. I've been dying to know why that is."

It seemed he appreciated her scheming, so Petra dared to

answer honestly. "I told the sovereign that I'd only consent to marrying him and his consort if he vouched for me. To be honest, even I was surprised when he kept his word."

Petra was startled when Antonin sat back in his seat, his head tipping back with a roar of laughter. "Clever girl! I don't know any beings — besides maybe dragons and weres, barbaric creatures that they are — who take mating as seriously as elves do. It was a stroke of genius to use that to your advantage."

She didn't tell him that she *hadn't* known how seriously the sovereign took his union to the witch. It was all a bluff. But if Antonin wanted to believe she was some diabolical genius for playing on the elvish mating urge — something she doubted very many people knew about — then that was fine with her.

"It seemed like the most expedient way of getting what I wanted," she demurred.

Antonin nodded. Smoothing a hand over his beard, he agreed, "Efficiency is an overlooked but vital element to a successful rise through the ranks. *Your* rise has been truly spectacular to witness, my dear. A covenless witch working as an initiate instructor to High Priestess of St. Emaine's in a single stroke. Absolutely breathtaking."

He leaned forward to rest his forearms against the edge of the table. His expression was eager and the tops of his cheeks a rosy red. In any other situation, he would have looked like a date thoroughly enjoying himself. "I admire that, Petra. I can't say how much. You and I have such similar backgrounds. We both came from nothing and were chosen by Glory, not given magic through the happenstance of family. It took me over a century of service to get into the Ardeo and another to become Protector, but *you*... If there was anyone worthy to become my bondmate and have my children, it's you."

"Well, that's very kind of you—"

Antonin interrupted her with a soft sound, his brows scrunching to give him a look of almost painful adoration. "Even now that I know all about your connection to Dooraker... You're perfect, my dear. Truly perfect."

Ice crystallized in her veins. "Excuse me?"

"Your uncle," he continued, breezily, as he turned back to his meal. "It took me too long to discover the link, but when I did, everything became quite clear. The man was very clever — a trait that runs in your family, apparently."

Petra slowly lowered her utensils back onto the table cloth, afraid that if she didn't do so voluntarily, her numb fingers would simply lose their grip. Her mind didn't race so much as it went curiously blank.

He knows.

He *knew.* For how long she couldn't say, but he knew the truth. Petra stopped feeling the cool air, nor the warmth of the wine in her stomach. She didn't exist at all. She was outside of herself, protected from the horror of the situation by some great internal distance.

Apparently unaware of her distress, Antonin continued, "It was smart of him to keep you a secret. I do have such a soft spot for luminists, you know, seeing as we're Glory's favorites. And with your mind, I certainly would have plucked you from the flock early on. It's for the best, I suppose. This way I got to see you rise to your true potential without any interference from me."

He chuckled. The tines of his fork slid neatly through a roasted and glazed carrot when he added, "Well, a little interference. We both know St. Emaine's seat wouldn't have been vacant if it wasn't for me, don't we?"

Her voice came from somewhere far away. "I had my suspicions, yes."

Speaking like he was inquiring about how she liked the color of his suit, he asked, "And what are your feelings on those suspicions, my dear?"

Hatred. Disgust. Fear. Grief.

There was so much, too much, and yet she couldn't feel any of it. Not at that moment. Not when she was standing over her own shoulder, watching the conversation happen to the mirror version of herself.

Buy time, she urged the other Petra, the one who endured it all with a neutral expression and even voice. *Buy Silas time. Say whatever you have to.*

Her stomach rolled again as a new, terrible suspicion wrapped its fingers around her throat.

Did Silas tell him?

No, it had to be a coincidence that the Protector admitted he knew about Max so close to when she told Silas the truth. It had to be.

Because if it wasn't, if she allowed herself to believe the cynical part of herself that had come out of that children's home, then something fragile would shatter. Something she hadn't even allowed herself to look at but knew was there in the comfort she took in his arms, the tightness in her chest when he looked at her like he was a lost little boy.

If Silas had betrayed her, that last little bit of hope and trust that had somehow managed to survive everything she'd suffered would be snuffed out forever. And it would be her own fault for letting her loneliness talk her into actually trusting the demon.

For just a moment it'd felt like she had someone to trust again, as mad as that sounded to her own ears, but now she was back to where she started — with the only person she could count on sitting in a plain wooden box in her nightstand, nothing but ashes and bone.

"I'd have preferred he retire," she heard herself say, "but these things happen."

Antonin nodded sympathetically and let out a long sigh. "They happen too often, but that's the reality of the Ardeo, I'm afraid. We must do what's best for the Temple, even when it's not what we would personally prefer." He reached across the table to lay one too-warm hand over hers. "I am truly sorry, Petra, but I'm glad we'll both benefit from your uncle's unfortunate choice to go against the Temple. I'm sure he's happy by Grim's riverbank, hearing the news that he brought us together in the end."

She never imagined she'd actually have the chance to find out the truth, but now... Petra found herself back in her body, staring across the table at the man who murdered the only family she had left, and asked, "Would it be possible to know what happened?"

Antonin gave her another sympathetic look and squeezed her hand. "I'm afraid I can't share all the details before we're bonded and married, but I will say that he approached me personally with several outlandish accusations and threatened to go public with them. I was forced to take care of the situation. You understand."

So it was exactly what she'd thought. Her once street-hardened uncle thought he could handle Antonin on his own and paid the price for it. Petra really couldn't say whether it was better or worse to know that.

"But let's not dwell on something so negative!" Antonin lifted his glass and tipped it toward her. "Tonight is for celebration, my dear! After all, we'll be bonded by tomorrow morning. If we're truly blessed by our goddess, you might even be pregnant."

An electric current ran down her spine, jolting her out of her haze. "Tomorrow morning?"

Swallowing a sip that stained the inner part of his lips burgundy, he answered, "Of course. Tonight you'll bond with me and we'll try for that heir. Tomorrow we'll announce our engagement and begin planning our wedding. I've got business to attend to in the city, so there's no rush there. You should have at least a few weeks to get everything in order."

"I... didn't realize you wanted my bond tonight."

"Why wait?" He gave her a slow, sultry smile. "In fact, I'll have your bond as soon as we finish dessert. You'll do it here, now, and then we'll head back to my suite."

She wasn't sure why she was fishing for excuses, knowing that there was no good outcome for herself either way and that she was only there to buy Silas time. Still she asked, "I've heard the bond can take a toll on the body. Are you sure we should do it here? What if you—"

Antonin waved a hand dismissively. "Only the weak and magicless suffer when the bond is forged. I'll be fine." He gestured for her to pick up her glass. She did so under automation. Clinking their glasses together, he toasted, "To Glory's own rising star — my bride. Let's conquer this world, my dear."

Chapter Twenty-Seven

He couldn't say he felt bad for calling Petra dramatic, but he *could* admit that he underestimated how fucked up the heart of Glory's Temple was.

Silas knew it was corrupt because all institutions were. He knew the higher-ups were liars because everyone was. He knew they had a history of blackmail, indoctrination of gifted children, and much more because... well, that shit was all in the history books.

After all he'd seen and done in his long criminal career, Silas thought he was unshockable. Turns out he was wrong.

A dead, red-clad guard stared up at him with glassy eyes. He was sprawled on the floor, disabled by one of Silas's nastier wards when he made the mistake of checking on a mysterious noise in the sparkling, freshly renovated bathroom. The ward hadn't been his cause of death — not technically, anyway. Neither was it Silas's boot, which had come down hard on his windpipe as soon as he stumbled to the ground.

No, his demise came from a beautifully woven mesh of magic draped over his mind. One that, once disabled by Silas's own ward, had set off a cascade effect that terminated in what he could only speculate was an aneurysm.

Whether that was an intentional design or simply bad luck, Silas couldn't say.

"Damn," he muttered, peeling his boot off the guard's throat. He didn't like dealing with brainwashed folks. It grossed him out about as much as m-siphons did. Yes, it was a quick way to get things done, but where was the art in it? The *skill*?

Besides the fact that it was just lazy, it was also prone to failure. The guard was a perfect example. The mind could only take so much pressure, so much fiddling, before it became as fragile as an eggshell — a bad trait to have in a henchman.

Sighing, Silas stooped to drag the body across the bathroom floor and into the brand new bathtub. Normally he didn't care about leaving a mess, but this was Petra's territory and he didn't want to complicate her life *too* much.

Thinking of her made him even more restless and agitated. Now that he knew he was dealing with a man who carted around carloads of armed and brainwashed guards, he enjoyed the thought of her out there entertaining Antonin for most of the day even less than he had before.

The only thing that stopped him from abandoning his plan for Vanderpoel's suite was the knowledge that she was safely locked away in her closet, guarded by Tal. For all his warnings and complaints, Tal would look after Petra with all the ferocity of Silas himself.

Mostly. Tal wouldn't set fire to this city for her. I would.

It was a struggle to put her out of his mind for most of the day as he set up his wards in the Protector's suite well ahead of his arrival. It was a new and humbling form of torture to force himself to sit in the alley that the Protector's bathroom window opened up into, waiting, knowing that Petra was out front facing the man himself.

He considered spiriting her away before Antonin arrived, but that was an instinctive urge, not a logical one. Petra was right in that she was a perfect distraction, and killing the man would be much easier if he wasn't already on his guard due to a missing High Priestess.

So as much as it went against something deeply fundamental, Silas let her greet the Protector and, according to the flat updates passed between the guards he heard moving in and out of the suite, give him a tour.

He drew the line at dinner, though. Not just because it was objectively too risky, *especially* now that he knew the man brain-washed his guards, but because the jealous, possessive monster in him simply couldn't abide the thought of her sharing a private meal with a man who wanted her.

Silas had been sure of that before, but after a quick scan of the belongings his entourage had unpacked and set about the suite, he was absolutely certain of it.

Luxury women's bathing products had been placed alongside the Protector's shaving kit, the bottles new and unopened. Two robes, one small enough to fit his witch and one slightly larger were carefully hung on hooks on the other side of the bathroom door. When he stalked into the bedroom, he found the bed sheets turned down.

Both nightstands held covered glasses of water, and at the foot of the bed was a sheer negligee in deep crimson, just the right size for *his* witch.

Silas's stomach turned. When it settled back into position, it began to fill with the liquid fire of pure fury.

Clearly the man expected dinner to go well. It was just too bad for him that Petra wouldn't be sleeping in anyone's bed besides Silas's — and also that she wouldn't be making their date. She was safely locked away in a closet and guarded by one very determined wraith.

Reminding himself that he'd kill the man as soon as he returned to the suite, hopefully feeling jilted, Silas turned his mind to getting his job done as quickly as possible.

The bedroom had little of interest save for a few strategically hidden guns and portable wards, which had been effectively muted by the ones he laid around the suite before the Protector's arrival.

The sitting room held far more of interest.

I'll be damned, he thought, eyeing the impressive portable command center the guards had set up in a corner. *Petra was right. He did bring everything with him.*

Not only was there a bank of screens showing the entire cathedral, but also several neat red trunks lined up against the wall. When he skated his palm over them, magic screamed out from the very pores of the leather, warning him away.

Silas debated for a moment over which to investigate first. He eyed the empty seat in front of the screens. Fury roared out from where it simmered in his gut.

The guard who lay dead in the bathtub had almost certainly been stationed there, scanning the screens for anything amiss — including the one that showed the manipulated view of Petra's bedroom.

You're lucky you're already dead, he thought, stalking over to the station.

Yanking the chair back from the desk, he fought the urge to swipe his arm across the whole thing, sending every bit of machinery onto the floor where he could stomp it into nothing but trash.

You promised her.

He'd get her revenge, but he had to do this, too. If he didn't, he wouldn't get her bond.

Silas gripped the edge of the desk so hard his knuckles bleached white. At some point his objective shifted from needing her power and connections to needing *her*. It was a subtle thing, a movement of inches when he wasn't looking, but there it was, clear as day.

If his shadows refused to take to her like they should, then her bond was all he had to tie her to him. *Not* having her tied to him was so fundamentally unacceptable, he simply refused to contemplate it.

So he pried his claws out from where they'd gouged holes in the desk and got to work.

She wouldn't have any excuses after this. No reason to deny him. He'd give her Vanderpoel's head, the proof she believed she needed, even hand deliver it all to her journalist friend — whatever it took to chain her to his side so he could satisfy the craven, desperate thing in him that howled for her every second they were apart.

While Silas downloaded the contents of the surveillance station and the various tablets and phones he'd found locked away in a safe onto a few hard drives, he got to work on the red trunks.

Their hardware was burnished gold and the red leather was stamped with the Glory's symbol on the lid, but otherwise they were nondescript. The only thing that truly set them apart were the wards.

A few had been voided when they were brought into the suite, but whoever had worked on them knew what they were doing. Failsafes and multiple layers meant that they were still a bitch to unravel.

Normally he would have savored the challenge, but his nerves were strung too tight to enjoy it.

The wards required all his focus — if he didn't want to lose a finger, or be immolated, or perhaps have his gray matter turned to jelly from a controlled sonic impact — but a small part of his mind couldn't be diverted from his anxiety over what Petra was doing, whether Tal was keeping her safe.

Of course he was. They had, after all, gone around in circles over the point just the night before. Even if Tal didn't suspect how deep Silas had sunk into his obsession with the witch, he trusted his brother implicitly.

Like him, Tal had a heavily skewed moral compass but he was unerringly loyal to those few who earned it. If he said he'd keep Petra safe, he'd do everything in his power to keep his word.

And yet *Silas* wasn't the one watching her. She wasn't in *his* den. She'd been fully prepared to meet another dangerous, unpredictable man for dinner. She probably even had Antonin's scent on her — the cloying, artificial amber of the expensive cologne that lingered in the bathroom.

It was enough to drive a man to distraction, even when he handled borderline explosive magic-infused objects.

He did get them open, though, one by one.

Within each trunk were hundreds and hundreds of painstakingly organized files, hard drives, ancient disks, and much more modern organic computing chips that could store a mind-blowing amount of data. At a glance, the information in the trunks seemed to span at least two hundred and fifty years, but probably much more than that.

Some of the paper files were labeled with names, some with codes. Some held compromising photos, bank records, politically damaging testimony. Some were almost an inch thick and some held a single piece of paper. In one he picked at random, he found a thin file on a sweet-faced initiate dated to the eighteen hundreds. Twin girls, their hair braided, stared out from beneath a later portrait of just one of them.

Something tickled his brain about the shape of their faces, the canny, almost vulpine look to their features, before he quickly flipped through the rest of the file. A blur of information went over his head — initiate intake paperwork, a two-hundred year old marriage license registered in the Coven Collective, yellowed letters with increasingly erratic handwriting, a plea for help scrawled on the back of a hymn ripped out of a book, and a death certificate.

Huh, he thought, eyebrows hiking up his forehead as he read the name on the certificate. *Ellouise Goode.* He flipped back to the pictures. The resemblance clicked. *I didn't know Sophie Goode had a sister.*

Silas let out a put-upon sigh. He slid the file back into place and closed the trunk before he moved onto the final one. *Petra will want all of this.*

It was a good thing he'd parked his car in the alley and cloaked it. Otherwise getting all the damn trunks out would have been an even bigger pain in his ass.

After a glance at the download progress of his hard drives, Silas opened the last trunk. Unlike the others, it was only half full, and what it did have was mostly personal effects.

An ancient-looking leather-bound journal that smelled of stale smoke, a small, well-buffed briefcase, several velvet boxes containing gold and platinum, more files...

Silas popped open the briefcase and tensed. Within it was a slim red file with Petra's name on it. He couldn't say he was surprised, but it was still jarring to open the cover and see a picture of her there, glossy and candid.

He skated his fingertips over the curve of her cheek and made a silent promise to burn it for her as soon as he was able.

Unable to stop himself, he turned it over to see what lay directly beneath the large photograph.

What the fuck?

Silas stared, uncomprehending, at the half-finished marriage license. It was registered to San Francisco and the names, birth dates, and ID numbers had already been filled out.

All it was missing was a couple signatures.

He'd never blacked out in his life, but in that moment, Silas's mind went completely blank, his senses mute. The declaration on the innocuous piece of paper, the *intention* behind it, was so outrageous and so offensive that he could not assimilate its existence into his reality.

It was one thing to know that Vanderpoel wanted Petra. Of course he did. Silas could understand that better than anyone, though that understanding wouldn't save the man from his wrath.

What had never occurred to him, however, was that he would want to *keep* her. The implications of that desire were far, far more dire than that of a man who simply wanted to have sex with a beautiful, powerful woman like Petra.

Does she know?

A bitter taste coated the back of his tongue. His ears rang. He didn't even realize what he'd done before the remnants of the shredded document floated back down into the trunk.

Of course she knew. Hadn't she hedged when she explained why the Protector was so interested in her? He'd assumed she didn't want to admit that he wanted to fuck her, but now...

She knew that the Protector wanted to marry her. It stood to reason that he also wanted her bond.

Silas recalled the products in the bathroom with curious, deadly calm. The negligee. The turned down sheets.

Little liar, he thought, *you really have been playing with fire.*

A muscle in his jaw spasmed as he slowly placed the file back into the briefcase. The discovery of Maximilian Dooraker's file within the briefcase as well only made him that much angrier.

Obviously the Protector had discovered far more about Petra than she realized. Silas hated that. Not just because it put his witch at risk, but because those secrets didn't belong to Vander-poel. They, like everything else about her, belonged to *him*.

Petra had no clue how much danger she was in. She'd danced with two vipers, both trying to consume her, and thought she could survive.

We're going to have a very serious conversation tonight, naughty little goddess. A very, very serious conversation.

After he released her from her imprisonment, of course.

One by one, he shoved the trunks out into the alley and then into the back of his car. Downloads complete, he threw his hard drives into his backpack and then tossed that in the car as well.

Now all he had to do was clean up. Then he could rip Vanderpoel's throat out and retrieve his naughty witch.

Intending to save the body for last, Silas stooped over the surveillance station, inputting the program to wipe every bit of data from the servers and all connected to it, when the shadows in the corner of the room rippled.

A cold stone of dread dropped into the pit of his stomach.

Before Tal could even finish manifesting, Silas lunged for the door.

Chapter Twenty-Eight

She believed she'd thought through every way the moment would go, but as Petra spooned tiny bites of apricot mousse into her mouth, she was at a complete loss.

The possibility that Antonin would discover her connection to Max had always been a risk. His insistence that they bond had also been a real threat. But never, not in all her anxious imaginings, had she thought they would go hand in hand.

She assumed that he would simply kill her once he found out who she was, but perversely, it seemed Antonin actually found pleasure in the connection. He chatted amiably as they ate their meal and praised her several times for *taking the initiative* and *stepping up* when her uncle faltered.

He casually mentioned that he considered getting rid of her after his discovery, but she impressed him so much that he changed his mind. "Who am I to snuff out such a bright light?" he'd asked. "I figured it would be a waste, especially when I could just bind you to my side instead. A win all around, wouldn't you say?"

Petra endured it all because she had no choice.

There was no escape, not when the only viable exit was blocked by two armed guards. Her alternative was a quick trip over the railing of the tower — an option that's appeal grew with every word out of his mouth.

Her panic was a thick, blanketing thing. It didn't scramble her brain with a frenzy of possibilities and plans. It didn't tell her to run, no matter how futile that might be. It held her there in her seat. It quieted her mind. It was a perfect sort of helplessness that allowed her to continue spooning mousse into her mouth. It was an acceptance that she imagined one might feel on a sinking ship — yes, she was afraid and wished there was a chance to escape her fate, but if she couldn't do that, what was the point in screaming?

There was perfectly good food in front of her. She might as well enjoy it while the water rose.

Petra didn't want to die, but a part of her had always assumed she would never get this far. Disbelief mingled with heavy, sluggish panic as the tart, sugary sweetness of the dessert melted on her tongue.

She wasn't even aware that she'd finished it until her spoon clinked against the cut crystal bowl. Petra stared at the reflection of candle flames in the streaked crystal. Cool wind kissed her bare shoulders and exposed skin of her back. At any other time she would have bitterly wished for her jacket, but just then she didn't feel the discomfort of the temperature. She barely felt anything at all.

"Absolutely delightful," Antonin announced as he set his folded napkin onto the edge of the table. "Your kitchen staff is superb, my dear."

She must have made some sound of agreement or appreciation because he clapped his hands together and pushed his seat back from the table. "Well, I think it's about time we got on with the rest of our evening, don't you think?"

A jolt of disgust ran down her spine, rattling her out of the haze that had insulated her.

The delicate silver spoon slipped from between her fingers to clatter onto the table. Petra sat back in her chair and watched as Antonin stood up. He passed a hand over his mustache and beard, smoothing both to perfection, before he stepped around the table to ease her chair back.

Her fingernails bit into the armrests, as if a good grip would save her from the Protector's plans. As if anything, anyone could.

Silas's face flashed in her mind, his lambent eyes burning with intent. Something deep within her twanged, a plucked chord of pure, nauseating yearning. It was absurd to imagine him as any kind of savior, but that didn't stop her pounding heart from *wishing.*

A too-warm hand peeled her fingers away from the armrest. Petra forced the joints of her fingers to unlock as he helped her stand. He turned her to face him.

"So beautiful," he murmured, stepping close enough that their chests brushed. His cologne, spicy and cloying, filled her nose. He skimmed the pad of his thumb over her clammy cheek. "I didn't realize until tonight that you glow. The camera simply doesn't do you justice."

Her voice sounded thin even to her own ears when she asked, "You're a luminist, too. Don't you?"

His smile was wry. "I'm afraid I'm not nearly the same caliber as you, my dear. I'm but a humble brightling. A spark to your star."

In the modern world, one didn't need to boast the incredible magical power of a gloriana to be respected amongst witches, but still, it was shocking to hear that a man who so many feared sat at the very bottom of the power scale. Perhaps that was why he'd become so cunning.

Magic wasn't necessary to become a member of Glory's Temple, but the gifted were considered Glory's favorites and therefore tended to have the most pull. Luminists even moreso. While Antonin had that on his side, she doubted it was common knowledge that he probably couldn't even light a candle with his abilities, let alone burn so brightly from within it was as if he contained his own personal sun.

Ambitious but lacking in raw magical talent, Antonin had clearly turned to a different kind of power.

He cupped her cheek and leaned in close, until she could feel the tickle of his beard against her cheeks and chin. "I can't regret it, though," he whispered, "when it allows me to forge a bond with someone like you."

And it won't hurt having your own abilities boosted by my magic, I imagine.

Repulsion skittered down her back on light insect feet. It was like a thousand little bugs crawled out of his sleeves and over her, seeking a way in.

Her breath came faster. Her vision narrowed. *I can't do this.*

Antonin picked up her limp hand and guided it into place just above his heart. Picking up on her obvious change in mood, he crooned, "Easy now, my dear. There's no need to be nervous. We're going to make marvelous partners, you and I."

A scream was trapped behind her locked jaw — a primal, agonized sound of pure grief and the desire to escape a fate worse than death.

When his lips brushed hers, she tasted wine and apricots on his breath. Her stomach lurched. Everything in her rebelled against that familiar touch, the scent of him, the taste, the *feeling* of his body so close to hers. Even her magic, which had been so volatile around Silas, seemed to have curled in on itself, retreating into a protective ball in the core of her being.

It left her feeling cold, shaken. Helpless in a way that she hadn't since she was a little girl huddled under trash in a stinking alley in Los Angeles, crying herself to sleep because the hunger pains were too much, her parents were dead, no one cared if she lived or died—

"Do it, Petra," he ordered, the gentleness in his voice hardening into a hammer.

Her heart beat so fast, she had the fleeting hope that it might simply pop, freeing her from the nightmare she found herself in.

Maybe she'd pass out. Maybe she'd throw up all over him and he'd be so disgusted he'd leave her alone.

But those were childish, cowardly hopes. Petra knew there was no easy escape from the situation she'd put herself in.

She'd done this. She was the one who couldn't let sleeping dogs lie. She couldn't let Max's murder go unanswered. She had to scheme and plan and dig up the truth, knowing it was a fool's errand. Coming to Antonin's attention was an inevitability, something she'd known would have to happen when all other avenues failed to provide the proof she needed.

Petra tried to summon some violent will. It'd been there when she was trapped in the closet, but now that fiery surge of determination was nowhere to be found. Even when she'd considered having Antonin killed, Petra never imagined *herself* doing it. She'd always assumed she wouldn't have the opportunity, since he always had so many guards around, and even if she did, she didn't have the stomach for murder. Just like when her parents were killed, just like whenever something horrific happened in the children's home, she *froze*.

No matter how vehemently she attempted to talk herself into it, she couldn't do it. She couldn't move a muscle. She couldn't speak. She couldn't summon an upswell of fiery magic to end him.

Antonin pulled back just far enough to give her a stern look. "My dear, you're going to learn I'm not a very patient man, and I suspect I'll be a rather demanding husband. Let's not start this off on the wrong—"

A dull, metallic *thwump* echoed up the short staircase. Antonin dropped his hand from her cheek and half-turned to look at the dark shape of the opening in the floor.

Petra's heart leapt into her throat. That sound, the temporary reprieve from the Protector's penetrating gaze flipped a switch inside her. She sucked in a huge breath of cool air as a stinging rush of adrenaline scoured her veins.

One hand holding her upper arm, Antonin barked, "Sean, Val — What's happening down there?"

When a moment passed and still no response came, the line of Antonin's shoulders stiffened. His fingers gripped her arm a little harder, digging into her flesh, as he used his other hand to reach under his suit jacket.

His head swiveled to give her a narrow-eyed look. "What's going on?"

"I have no idea," she answered, eyes flicking down to where he still had his hand under his jacket. She'd once been the daughter of a prolific, if not particularly skilled, criminal. As a child, she'd been used to run cons and make deals more times than she could count.

Petra knew what it looked like when a man held a gun.

Antonin took a step closer. All the sultry warmth, the false gentleness, it vanished. The glow of the candles barely reached them this far away from the table, but tiny orange flickers danced in his dark eyes. When he spoke, it was in the patient cadence of an adult who already knew they'd have to discipline a child. "Petra, what have you done?"

An incredulous laugh tried its damnedest to bubble up her throat. "Nothing," she gasped, twisting her arm hard enough to break his grasp. A crackle of heat came to life in her belly. "I don't know what's going on, but *this*— I'm not doing this. I'm *never* doing this."

She backed up until she could almost feel the wide open archway of the one tower window behind her. A flash of white-hot heat rushed over her skin. Her fingertips tingled. Rage, an all-consuming fire, burned her fear to ash.

Now that she'd said it, Petra couldn't stop the words from falling out of her mouth, each one a rolling boulder picking up speed as it careened away from her. "I'm not going to bond with you. I'm not going to have your *children*. Are you insane? You killed my uncle. You— you took the only family I had left."

Antonin didn't approach her right away. Instead, he slowly drew his gun out from under his suit jacket. He didn't point it at her. He simply held it, the barrel aimed at the floor, and pressed the switch to turn off the safety. The low hum of the battery pack warming up was barely audible, but it was burned into her mind from so many secret trips to the firing range with Max that she would know it anywhere.

Speaking in a devastatingly calm voice, Antonin said, "I understand getting cold feet. This is a major life change for you. However, you seem to be laboring under a misapprehension — mainly that you can say no."

The wind tugged her hair back, out towards the glittering night sky and the San Francisco skyline. Petra braced her palms on the cold, gritty surface of the window's ledge and leaned forward. "I'd rather die."

If that meant that she joined her parents — and probably Max, too — in dying at the end of a gun, then so be it. Anything was better than being Antonin's perfect little bride.

He made a sucking sound with his teeth and tongue. "That is *very* disappointing, my dear." His expensive leather shoes whispered across the floor as he approached her, gun aimed at her chest. His smile was small, sharp, and icy cold. "I wanted this to be a partnership, but if you can't grasp that yet, then I have other ways of making you see reason. I don't have time for this right now, not when everything is finally coming together. Looks like we'll be making a trip to see a friend of mine in United Washington. I'd hoped to avoid it, but—"

The sound of hinges squealing made her jump. Antonin spun around and, in one agile movement, was next to her by the window, the too-hot barrel of his gun pressed against her temple.

"Stop! Name and rank before you come up the stairs," he barked.

There was no sound. No movement. For several terrible seconds, time seemed suspended, stretched into an eternity around her. Even the wind stopped blowing, leaving them in a suffocating stillness there at the top of the belltower.

And then the candles went out.

CHAPTER TWENTY-NINE

SILAS WAS ALWAYS AWARE OF WHAT HE WAS. HE'D known he was different from his parents, his cousins, his uncles, aunts, and neighbors. He didn't feel the same things, he didn't see people the same way as them, and he spoke to beings who didn't exist. In his adult life, he happily existed on the fringe and reveled in the freedom of criminal life.

But never, not in all the years he'd wrung money out of blood and joy out of other people's misfortune, did Silas feel more like a monster than when he saw a gun pointed at his witch's head.

Whatever civilized veneer he wore in order to function in a world that demanded niceties was shrugged off, abandoned. What was revealed was a beast. Higher function shut down. He melded with his shadows in a way he never had before. They were another set of limbs as they crawled across the rough concrete floor of the tower, telling him the speed and direction of the wind that tossed Petra's hair, the strength of the concrete, the taste of magic in the air.

The barrel of the gun pressed more firmly into Petra's temple as the weak little man demanded, "Who are you?"

The air had begun to warm unnaturally, but his shadows knew with the certainty of instinct that it wasn't Petra's magic that did it. This warmth was sweltering, sticky. The magic was clumsy. When the Protector's eyes began to glow with the hair-thin ring of white light around the pupils, even those twin circles looked pale and flickering in comparison to the raw radiance of his witch.

Silas didn't speak. He just stalked toward them, his mind quiet. There was no man left in him to reason with, and there was no mercy.

"Petra," the Protector hissed, backing them up until they both hit the window's ledge, "who is this? Tell him to stop *now.*"

 He didn't like Vanderpoel's tone. He liked it even less when the man clamped one hand on her arm, his other still pointing the humming gun at her head.

Petra appeared unable to speak. Her eyes were wide and her normally soft glow was a flickering, violent thing — the roar of a wildfire just beneath her skin. That roused the animal even more. His shadows moved with a hunter's deliberation around the pair, circling them both in a living net.

She glanced down, quick as lighting. "Silas?"

There was no room in his mind for speculating on the odd inflection in the syllables, let alone time. As soon as his name left her mouth, the gun swung away from her temple to aim squarely at him.

"Silas," the Protector said, voice smoothing into perfectly polished charm. "Call him off, Petra, or I'll shoot. Now."

Silas had seen many of Petra's masks, her secret faces and the soft thing she kept hidden beneath them all, but this was the first time he saw something truly vicious in her. Ignoring the gun between them, she rounded on Vanderpoel and hissed, "You shoot him and I'll kill you with my bare fucking hands, you son of a bitch."

The Protector was so outraged by that, apparently, he seemed to forget who the real predator was. He swung his gun back toward Petra and flinched reflexively at the white-hot glow of her.

Squinting, Vanderpoel tightened his grip on the gun. Silas had enough.

Things happened very quickly then.

The air went bright and hot, filled with a searing sort of light like the flash of a bomb blast. Petra's magic unleashed like a supernova just as the ward he'd painstakingly carved into her necklace released, throwing Antonin back with a wet crack of bone against one of the belltower's columns.

Sightless, Silas lunged, claws of compressed shadow aimed for where the Protector should have been. The whine of a bolt shot firing followed. Then another in quick succession. One he felt when the white-hot plasma struck the nearly indestructible armor of his shadow, but the other went wide. In response to the hit, the shadows around Silas exploded into action, arrowing toward the only thing that mattered: Petra.

In the time between heartbeats, the light guttered out and was replaced by the flickering glow of a man set ablaze.

A guttural scream erupted from Vanderpoel's throat as his suit and hair caught fire. He began to frantically wave his arms — one of which was already melting away, its flesh little more than sizzling fat and splintering bone. Petra collapsed against the ledge, the air around her thick with the scent of pure magic, at the same time that Silas's claws found the Protector's vulnerable throat.

He fell on the man like the animal he was, ripping and tearing with teeth and claws even as he burned alive. The flames didn't bother Silas, not when he was protected by his shadows, and not when his witch's magic was what fed them. They danced over Vanderpoel's flesh in unnatural waves, moving away from wherever Silas chose to attack next.

The stench of human fat, burning hair, and Petra's magic mingled in the air. Disgusted, Silas grabbed what was left of Vanderpoel's carefully crafted, half-burnt hair with one fist and raked his claws across the last remaining sinews holding his head to his neck. Before the body could fall to the floor beside Petra, he pushed it out through the window.

The flaming mass of flesh landed hard on the metal roof of the cathedral, where it rolled until it landed in a gutter. Silas lifted his arm and chucked the head in the same direction. It flew like a fiery bowling ball until it, too, hit the roof and rolled to rest face down in the gutter.

From the window, Silas watched the flames continue their work, burning with a heat so violent, so unnatural, that within a handful of moments, there was little left of the remains except smoldering bones and greasy streaks on the roof.

A stuttering breath snapped his focus back to Petra.

She was propped up against the wall, her hair catching in the rough surface to make it look like a mass of golden cobwebs behind her. Shadows writhed over her bare legs, over her middle, and around her throat to cradle her jaw. It was an infinitely gentle hold, but a jealous one.

And as they swirled over her, curling around her wrists, her ankles, her neck and waist and even through the locks of her hair, Silas knew.

She's mine.

Not just his toy. Not just a means to an end. Not just his little goddess.

She was *everything*.

He knelt down before her, slow and cautious. A profound sense of some great key slotting into place overtook him. Bolts slid, a tumbler was repositioned, and the thing inside him he hadn't even known existed until a few days ago was finally unlocked.

Silas crawled on his hands and knees until he was nearly on top of her. Petra was saying something, babbling, as her gaze roved over him in an unfocused way that spoke of shock.

"I killed him," she croaked. "Oh gods, I killed a man. I burned him alive. Silas, Silas—"

"Shush, baby. I've got you." He knew he must look terrifying, covered in gore and shadow as he was, but Petra didn't flinch when he leaned in close enough to nuzzle her pale cheek. Skin to skin, shadow to shadow, he was able to breathe at last.

"You ever scare me like that again and I'll invest in a riding crop," he warned. "You aren't allowed to leave me, do you understand? You're not allowed to get hurt. You aren't allowed to put yourself in danger like that. You did so good tonight, baby, but if I ever catch you alone with a man and a gun again, I'll—"

Her arms trembled as they wove around his neck and held fast. Petra buried her face in his hair. Her shoulders began to shake. This close, the salt of her tears managed to cut through the odor of burning flesh. "You came," she whimpered, so soft and pitiful it made him crazy. "I thought— I didn't think anyone would— Thank you. *Thank you.*"

Silas fisted his claws in her hair and sucked in a deep, deep breath of her. His voice was barely human when he reminded her, "You're *mine*, Petra. You think I was going to leave you to fend for yourself? Now stop crying. It feels bad and I don't like it."

"Shut up. I'm allowed to cry."

She sniffled, delicate fingers curling into his shirt. His shadows ghosted over her hands, soothing her in the only way it knew how, even as a different part of them settled around the base of her throat.

Silas turned his head a bit to see. *Well, I'll be damned. I guess wishes do come true.*

He'd known they'd settle somewhere on her, but it was an astonishing thing to actually see his shadows find their place around her throat — forever marking her as his in a place so visible it could never be missed.

My High Priestess, he thought, relishing the taste of victory, *a demon's mate.*

His clan would lose their ever-loving minds when he brought her home. The thought was a good one, but also unfortunately reminded him of all the things they still had to do. Pulling back enough to look into her face, Silas told her, "I'll take care of all this, baby, but you're gonna have some questions to answer when this is over."

Not just from her staff and likely the higher-ups of the Temple, but from him, too, because there was no way he'd let the discovery of that marriage license go.

Just when he'd gotten her to calm down some, Petra went all wide-eyed and shaky again. "I'm going to go to jail for killing Antonin, aren't I?"

Silas scowled. "Of-fuckin'-course not, Petra. Who do you think I am? Besides, I'm pretty sure I killed him, and I've killed plenty of people without any problems."

It was impossible to say what dealt the final blow, but it was hard to argue with a beheading. He did enjoy the thought of it being a team effort, though.

"Is that supposed to make me feel better?"

"Yes. Did it work?"

Petra was quiet for a beat. "I must be more fucked up than I thought, because it kind of did, yeah."

He could feel the shadows melting away from him, returning him to his more humanoid form. Feeling marginally calmer, Silas smiled at her. "Nah, you're just perfect for me. That's all."

Shaking her head, Petra made to stand. All at once, her face lost what little color it possessed. Her lush lips and the apples of her cheeks were left ashen. Alarm bells clanged in his mind.

He caught her a second before she swayed back into the wall, nearly smacking her head against the concrete.

"Petra? What's wrong?"

She stared up at him with big, liquid eyes. Petra looked surprised when she announced, "Demon, I think I've been shot."

Chapter Thirty

HE'D NEVER UNDERSTOOD WHY PEOPLE SAID FEAR FELT like ice in one's veins, mostly because he'd never really felt fear. The desire to live? Certainly. The fury that came with defending what belonged to him? Absolutely.

But *fear* wasn't something he really felt until he saw that gun pointed at Petra's head, and even that was a paltry thing to what he experienced when he skimmed his palm down her waist to find her ruined side.

He stared at the scorched flesh, barely comprehending a wound he'd seen a thousand times. Plasma bolts didn't just tear through the body like a bullet, but burnt it from the inside out, cauterizing a wound instantly even as it left a gaping hole.

Petra's wound was like someone had taken a small scoop of her side with white hot spoon. Intellectually, he knew that it wasn't the worst he'd seen by a long shot. It was a glancing blow, perhaps an accidental discharge of the weapon as Vanderpoel flailed his burning arms, but something about seeing *her* flesh torn, cauterized, the muscle around it seizing as the nerves began to register the damage—

The wards on her necklace hadn't protected her. His shadows hadn't, either.

For the first time in his life, Silas's hands shook. "You're fine," he muttered. "You'll be fine. You're fine."

Petra began to tremble in earnest. Her breathing grew ragged, each inhale coming faster than the last. Shock was setting in just in time for the pain to catch up to her. "Silas, it hurts. It *hurts.*"

For the second time that night, Silas went a little crazy. "I know, baby. I know. We're gonna— I'm going to take you to a healer. You need to just— Don't move. Let me fix it. I'll fix it."

She grabbed his arm. Her big blue eyes, navy in the darkness, shone with tears when she whispered, "I thought it was okay, but I don't want to die this way. I don't want to. I just wanted a nice little life, Silas, I really did." A sob stole her breath and chopped the words into pitiful little pieces. "I'm so sick of being scared all the time. I don't want to die like my parents. I want to be old someday. I want to have babies. I want to kiss you again. I don't want to die. *Please* don't let me."

Silas discovered another new emotion: *devastation.*

Sliding one arm under her back and the other under her knees, Silas climbed to his feet and snarled, "Shut up! You're not going to fuckin' die on me, Petra, so don't even try."

Her head lolled into the space between his neck and shoulder. Hot tears splashed his skin. "I really like you," she whimpered. "I don't want you to leave."

"You're not getting rid of me whether you like me or not," he snapped, aware that he was being unreasonable with her and yet fully unable to control the part of him that had gone senseless with fear.

Sí. Tal's voice rang in his mind. It was unusually strained. Silas turned to find his brother's shadows crawling out of the stairwell, a huge writhing mass of blackness that seemed somehow less corporeal than normal. *I'm blocking the door, but you won't be able to get out without being seen. Her assistant is desperate to get through. I think he might have heard the shots.*

"Fuck!" Silas clutched Petra tighter, like that would help anything at all. If he could have, he would have absorbed her into his chest and kept her there, locked away from the world that had tried so hard to steal her away. "Can't you do something? Kill him if you have to. I need to get Petra to a healer."

"Silas, who are you talking to?"

"No one, baby," he muttered, unwilling to explain Tal's existence *now* of all times. "I'm just trying to figure out the best way to get rid of your assistant. He's outside the door and I need to get you to a healer right fuckin' now."

Blunt nails curled into his chest. "Margot. Take me to Margot. Don't kill Robert, please. He's a good man." Her voice grew fainter, thinner, and the hands on his chest gradually lost their tension until they slid away.

"I'm not taking you into the damn elvish stronghold to be— Hey!" Wild-eyed, he gave her a tiny shake, not caring if he caused her a little extra pain if it kept her with him. Petra let out an animal sound against his neck. "Damn it, Petra, stay awake or I'll kill your assistant!"

Her shoulders hunched, turning her into his chest like she, too, wanted to find refuge there. "Don't. Please."

And then she went limp.

"Fuck!" Silas rounded on Tal. His mind fractured into a thousand sharp pieces. "I don't know what happened. The necklace should have— It failed. My wards failed."

She took a bolt shot from less than ten feet away, Si. Your wards worked. If they didn't, she'd be dead.

"Then my shadows failed!" he cried, stumbling back a step as his knees weakened. "She's my mate. My shadows should have protected her. How could they have failed, too?"

Si—

"Everyone was right. I never should have been a mate. I don't know how to do this. I fucked it up already."

Silas! Tal's shadows rippled with agitation. His normally soft voice was hard when he ordered, *Get your shit together. That's your mate. She needs you to focus. Do you want her to live or not?*

Desperation made his voice little more than a raw scraping sound when he asked, "What do I do?"

I think you should get Robert's help, Tal answered, once again calm in the face of Silas's complete lack of composure, *and then you need to get her stable so you can take her home to your dad. That wound isn't fatal, but only if we act fast.*

Tension rippled down his spine. "What if Robert's part of this?"

Now that he understood the true extent of what Petra was up against, every single member of Glory's Temple was on notice. No one would be free of his scrutiny, not until he personally uprooted any and all of her enemies with his bare hands.

I've watched him for days. I don't think he is, but I also think this is a risk you have to take. Either way, you have to deal with him.

And Petra had asked Silas not to kill the man, so really there wasn't much of a choice at all.

Swearing again, he told Tal to let Robert through. The priest burst out of the stairwell in a flurry of robes and strained breathing, his gaze swinging around to take in the table knocked on its side, the demon, and the wounded priestess.

Robert was a middle-aged man with a soft face, balding head, and an unfortunate predisposition to sweating. The look on his face when he saw Petra's ruined side was one of honest horror — a feeling Silas knew better than almost any.

"W-What happened?"

Silas stalked across the tower to loom over the red-robed man. "Antonin Vanderpoel shot her. I need a way out of this place *now.*"

"Who are you? Is she dead?" Robert looked like he was going to be sick, which Silas *really* didn't have time for. Words tumbled out of his mouth, one after another, a bit like vomit, as he gaped at the blood soaking Silas's clothing. "You killed the guards outside, didn't you? I saw the bodies. They... they were torn apart."

Speaking through his teeth, he asked, "Motherfucker, does it look like Petra's dead?"

"No, I—" Impossibly, the man went even paler. Spinning in a tight circle, he stammered, "Where's the Protector?"

"On the roof."

"Dead?"

Silas jerked his head impatiently.

"Oh, that's..." Robert spun back around, one hand clutching the gold necklace that bounced against his stomach every time he moved. "Gods, you need to get her out of here! His guards are everywhere—"

"What do you think I'm doing?" Silas started jogging the short distance to the stairs. Something in him cracked a little more every time the sway of his steps made Petra's unconscious form jerk in his arms. "I need a way out of here where I won't be spotted and immediately shot by the asshole's guards. Are you going to help with that, or am I going to have to kill you, too?"

"I'd really rather not die," he answered, throat bobbing. "My husband and I are expecting a baby. Or we will be soon. We just signed a—"

"I don't give a shit about you, your husband, *or* your baby. I only care that my witch doesn't fuckin' die!"

He expected some blubbering, maybe a frantic scramble to give him what he wanted, but what he got was a shaky nod. "Well, okay. I'm glad she finally has someone taking care of her. I really can't take losing another boss I like. Come on, we can take the service stairs they use to work on the roof."

Silas didn't want to trust anyone. He wasn't sure he *could*. But he had to trust Robert just enough to follow him down the first flight of stairs, into the dark heart of the tower, past the bodies he'd left strewn across the concrete floor.

He clutched his witch close to his heart, her body cloaked in such dense shadow that the eye could barely discern her shape. Following the priest's flapping robes through a small metal door in the wall partially hidden by storage boxes, he warned, "If you're lying to me, Robert, I'll kill you and your husband. Understood?"

Silas, Tal rumbled, *he's helping.*

He didn't give a fuck what Tal thought. Not when it came to this. To her.

Exiting out into the world's most narrow balcony, Silas took in the aerial view of the inside of the darkened cathedral for all of two seconds before he turned his gaze to Robert. Far below them, the dark shapes of the two-story tall windows looked tiny, and the flames from votive candles little more than specks.

Robert was breathing heavily, his face was ruddy, and his eyes were wild, but when he met Silas's stare, he didn't waver.

"Understood." Shuffling sideways, he squeezed his way across the balcony to where a small opening led to a catwalk. Being quite brave, he ventured, "I didn't know her grace had any friends besides the sovereign's consort. Who are you?"

"I'm not her friend."

"Then what—"

Silas bared his teeth at the back of Robert's shiny head. "I'm her mate."

The priest stumbled. Clumsy fingers grasped at the metal railing on either side of the narrow catwalk. "You're joking," he choked.

"If you don't start hustling your ass right now, I'll show you just how serious I am, motherfucker."

Robert must have heard the very real promise in Silas's tone, because he released the railing like it'd burned him. Nearly tripping over himself, he hurried across the planks of the catwalk. They flew over the great expanse of the cathedral, toward the opposite tower that was closest to Petra's office.

The shape of another low, no nonsense access door resolved itself in the darkness. Robert pried it open with a grunt. "Head through here and then go up one flight of stairs. On the right of the first landing, there'll be another door. It leads to the roof. Cross the front of the roof. There'll be another door. That will drop you down onto a staircase that'll lead you to the path between staff quarters and the main complex. You can get to the street from there."

Silas didn't bother replying. Shouldering his way past Robert, he made to duck inside the tower but was stopped by a hand on his arm.

Before he could snap the man's neck with his shadows, Robert rasped, "She can't be your mate and be High Priestess, too. Not after this. The High Gloriae would never allow it."

He didn't have time for this shit, but he couldn't stop himself from snarling, "Listen up, asshole: Petra can do whatever the fuck she wants. I don't care what you or the Gloriae think. I'll burn all you motherfuckers to the ground if you or anyone else tries to stand in her way."

"You'd take on the High Gloriae for her?"

Shoving the priest aside with his elbow, Silas snapped, "How about you ask Antonin what I'd do for my mate. Or the guards in the tower. Or the poor asshole in the bathtub."

Robert swallowed. "Who's in the bathtub?"

"A man who got in her way."

CHAPTER THIRTY-ONE

TIME DIDN'T MEAN MUCH WHEN PLASMA SCORCHED A hole in one's side.

Petra moved in and out of consciousness. She'd been injured enough times to know, in some slow, hazy way, that she was badly hurt, but the terror that had wrapped its fist around her throat in the belltower drifted away along with consciousness.

Sometimes, she could hear voices arguing. The familiar slam of a metal door. The roar of an engine. Silas's voice was the most common and comforting noise, though she couldn't always pick up what he was saying exactly. Mostly she just listened to the cadence of his drawl, not as smooth as normal, but familiar and soothing all the same.

Understanding was elusive. Why she was hurt, why he sounded stressed, where they were going — it all escaped her as shock insulated her from the worst of reality.

Her mind became a kaleidoscope of memory and sensation interspersed with periods of deep, restful darkness. She liked those moments best. They reminded her of how safe she'd felt in bed with Silas, when his shadows were a second skin and his weight settled on top of her.

She thought she recalled being scared of the dark once upon a time, back when her biggest fears were what might be hiding in her closet and hearing her parents argue while she tried to sleep, but now it was a place of refuge. The darkness was as soft as velvet, cradling her with the utmost gentleness, and she trusted it to hold her when consciousness trickled away.

Cigarette smoke and searing agony woke her briefly, but the memory had the uncanny glow of a dream, so she couldn't really be sure if any of it was real. It would be just like her to dream of the Broken Tooth, of Rasmus and Silas snarling at each other just out of sight as someone unseen sealed a huge, rubbery bandage over her side, of terrible pain.

Certainly it wasn't the first time she dreamed of wounds, real or imagined. Sometimes she woke up in the darkness before dawn still feeling bruises painting her ribcage, the agony of hunger cramps, and the grim imaginings of what it must have been like for her parents to die their ugly, ugly deaths.

But Silas was a new addition to the cruel landscape of her dreams. She could feel him there, his energy like the weight of a thunderstorm about to break, and somehow she was comforted by it.

Silas was a monster, *her* monster, and the only one terrible enough to make the darkness a refuge.

She didn't make a noise — or maybe she did, dreams being tricky things that they were — but Silas materialized by her side in an instant, his big hands cupping her cheeks.

"Shh. Easy, baby, you're okay. Breathe through it. You just gotta hold on for a few hours and—"

Rasmus, his hoarse voice as loud and furious as a bomb blast, bellowed, "If you won't let the best fucking healer in the territory see her, then let me call my—"

"No one's touching her but clan!" Even in her dream, Petra shied away from the rage that crackled in Silas's roar. "I don't trust anyone, *anyone* to touch her or know where she is. The only reason I'm here is because I didn't have bandages big enough to get her through the trip. If one more person so much as looks at her, I'm going to rip their *fuckin'* heads off."

"Shade, have you lost your mind?"

"Yes," he answered simply, raggedly. "Yes, I have. Can you blame me?"

He sounded so upset. Petra was compelled to reassure him, to tell him everything was all right and to stop yelling at Rasmus, but the dream was slipping away. The edges of her mind went fuzzy again, all soft and warm with darkness, and she was too tired to fight it.

She drifted back into the gentle hold of the shadows, each breath saturated with the scent of thyme, and let go.

Soft sunlight brushed her cheeks, and the fresh, green scent of growing things drifted around her on a warm breeze. The air was almost uncomfortably balmy even under the thin cotton sheet covering her.

Petra tried to turn on her side, her legs kicking to remove the sheet, but she was stalled by a heavy arm tightening around her middle. "Stop fussing," a sleepy voice drawled from somewhere near the top of her head.

"It's hot," she complained, shimmying again.

A deep sigh made her aware of the rest of the body squished against her side — a large, warm body made of sturdy muscle and bristly leg hair. There was some shifting before the sheet was pulled away from her sweaty skin. A heavy hand settled back in the curve of her waist.

"Better?"

"Yeah." She tried to crack her eyes open but closed them immediately. The room was way too bright for her poor, sensitive eyes first thing in the morning.

Is it morning?

The thought was a stone dropped into the placid water of her mind. Ripples followed.

Where am I? What happened? Who— No, I know that one.

Petra turned her head, which felt a little too heavy, a little too full, in her bed partner's direction. Smooth skin, satin over muscle and sinew, met the tip of her nose.

Thyme.

"Silas," she breathed, not entirely sure why her eyes stung with relief.

"Who else would be in your bed? Go back to sleep," he ordered, not quite gently, but as gentle as she'd ever heard him. "You need to rest."

But rest was an impossibility as her mind slowly came back online, a bit like an old-fashioned computer bank being booted up. Lights began to flash one by one, and screens flickered to life in the dark, hazy control center of her mind.

A full body shiver coursed through her, a symptom of an all-consuming, unmoored fear. Petra's muscles seized as if tensing in preparation for a blow. She didn't know *why*, nor what she was suddenly so afraid of. Her body acted on its own in response to something that was still too far away for her mind to make sense of.

Petra turned instinctively, curling into a tight little ball under the circle of Silas's arm, and pressed her face into the hollow at the base of his throat. It was warm and dark there, softly scented like skin and thyme and his particular musk. *Safe.*

A gentle pressure curled around her neck. It didn't squeeze, but held her carefully as she began to shake in earnest.

"Hey, hey," Silas grated, "you're fine, Petra. You're okay. Stop being upset."

He made it sound like she was doing it just to vex him. Of course she didn't want to be upset. In fact, she didn't even really understand why her body was going haywire in the first place.

"W-What happened?" Her teeth clattered, making it difficult to speak.

Silas shifted. His arm banded almost painfully tight around her middle. "You don't remember?" After a short pause, he sighed, "Dad was right. I think you're in shock."

Shock? The computer bank came on all at once.

Petra lost all feeling in her limbs when she breathed, "I killed Antonin Vanderpoel."

The events of the previous night — maybe, she had no idea how long she'd been out, which was its own terrifying thought — came back with all the noise and speed of an m-lev train.

Antonin knew about Max.

Antonin wanted her to bond with him *that night.*

Antonin had a gun.

Silas appeared from the stairwell.

Antonin's finger pressed down on the trigger, the gun aimed right at Silas's head.

She didn't remember making any choice or having a coherent thought at all. There'd only been the white-hot rage that overtook her when the Protector threatened to shoot her demon at point blank range.

Things got too bright, too hot, too volatile with magic after that. A blow knocked her down even as Vanderpoel's body ignited. A luminist of greater power wouldn't have been affected by the raw wave of magical fire she'd poured over him, but he didn't stand a chance. The fat in his body ignited immediately, immolating him from the inside out.

It was unfortunate that watching him burn was a crystal clear memory. She could see him in her mind's eye, his arms flailing as his fat cooked him from within, the marrow of his bones getting so hot so fast that the bone itself began to splinter and pop long before the flesh of his skin peeled away.

She knew logically that it had only taken a handful of seconds before Silas swooped in, gleefully tearing into flesh already beginning to char, but it felt like a lifetime. In the moments between ignition and beheading, she watched his eyes cook in their sockets and knew the instant his brain became little more than stewed gray matter in the chalky bowl of his skull.

A wave of nausea overcame her.

Petra squirmed so violently that Silas was forced to release her. She threw herself blindly out of the strange bed and stumbled across a wood floor to what she prayed was a bathroom. He called after her, barking orders she couldn't process, but she didn't have time to stop. She feared that if she opened her mouth to speak, she'd be sick all over the floor.

Blessedly, there was a bathroom behind the first door she wrenched open. Petra's knees met cool white tiles as she hunched over the bowl of an antique-looking toilet and expelled the contents of her last meal — the one she'd shared with Antonin.

Her stomach muscles tensed painfully with every convulsion. Tears streamed down her cheeks. Her fingers trembled so violently they struggled to grip the rim of the toilet as she desperately tried to hold herself steady against the storm.

While she retched, big hands pulled her hair back from her sweaty face. Silas knelt behind her, his body heat permeating the sudden internal chill that bit into every nerve.

His voice took on an unfamiliar edge of panic when he said, "Easy, easy. I've got you. Just try to breathe. You're okay. It's okay. I'll fix it. Everything's okay."

If she could stop throwing up for a second, she would have laughed. *It's okay?* Nothing was okay. She had no idea what was going to happen now, who she could trust, or what she was supposed to do.

For so long she'd been walking on a straight path. First it was following in Max's footsteps, content with a small life as long as it was a safe one by his side. Then it became a much more dangerous but still straight path toward the truth, toward justice. The end of that path wasn't one she wanted, but it, too, had a certain comforting finality to it.

What now?

Now her path had dissolved beneath her feet — or rather, it was burned away in a fire fed by greasy human fat and vengeance.

At some point her retching stopped, but her tears didn't. Huge, wrenching sobs shook her shoulders. She didn't even know what exactly she was crying for. Certainly it wasn't guilt over Antonin's death. But she couldn't seem to stop, no matter how hard she tried.

Her mind was fractured. She couldn't settle on one thought long enough to find a center point, a shelter to take refuge in, so her thoughts became a whirlwind of broken glass, cutting, cutting, cutting—

Silas was speaking to her, her voice strained enough to sound truly desperate. She didn't hear the words, but she tried to focus on the sound of his voice as he peeled her away from the toilet and hauled her against his chest.

Still, she cried. If anything, she cried harder as she recalled her suspicions that he'd told Antonin about her connection to Max. She so badly wanted to trust him. He'd come to her rescue. Hadn't he?

But nothing was certain anymore, and it terrified her to think that now he was her only real friend in the world.

If he betrayed her, she'd have no one.

That thought only made her sobs worse. She pressed on it like a bruise, exploring the pain it caused because at least it was straightforward, understandable. She didn't want to lose him. She didn't want to believe he'd betrayed her. She cared about him, *needed* him. Gods help her, but she thought she might shatter if he left her now.

A string of hissed curses broke through her downward spiral, but it was suddenly finding herself under the frigid spray of the shower that shocked her into stillness.

Petra opened her stinging eyes to find herself staring at an old but well-polished showerhead. After the initial shock of cold, the water that rained from it began to warm, soaking her nightgown until it clung to her like a second skin.

Silas was behind her in the tub, his legs framing her sides and his arms coiled around her middle, pinning her wrists to her front. His cheek pressed against hers. She could just feel the shape of one horn against the side of her head as he curved his bigger body over hers.

"You're okay," he crooned, voice breaking. "You're okay. You're okay."

The way he said it, she really wasn't sure if he was reassuring her or himself.

For several minutes, she watched the water rain down from the spigot, her mind blissfully empty. Her shaking gradually subsided. Silas rocked her gently back and forth, murmuring nonsense in her ear, as she went limp and numb in his arms.

The warmth of the water, the sound of his voice, the pressure of his arms around her — all of it brought her back to herself in inches.

Safe, the sad little thing in her whimpered. *I'm safe here.*

CHAPTER THIRTY-TWO

CLARITY SETTLED OVER HER AS SHE COUNTED THE water droplets beading in her eyelashes. Would a man who'd betrayed her come to her rescue? Maybe. But a man who betrayed her wouldn't care if she went into shock. A man who didn't care wouldn't hold her hair as she vomited wine and glazed carrots and bile. A man who didn't care wouldn't climb into a shower with her and rock her until her tears dried.

Whatever else Silas was, for some reason, in some way, he *cared*.

Even if that care was paper-thin and conditional, something ravenous in her lunged for it.

Her voice was as raw as her throat when she asked, "Did you tell Vanderpoel that Max was my uncle?"

Silas didn't waste time sputtering, being offended, or asking her why she suspected him. His answer came immediately, plainly. "No, baby."

Petra's neck lost its ability to hold her head up. Silas shifted, adjusting them so she could rest her head on the meat of his shoulder. "I didn't think so," she whispered.

Apparently sensing that she was no longer about to shatter into a million pieces, Silas's arms loosened enough for him to stroke her sides, her stomach, her upper thighs — anywhere he could reach, really.

"It's okay if you did," he rasped.

"You're not mad?"

He snorted. "Baby, if you *didn't* suspect me, you'd be stupid. And you're not stupid."

They were quiet for a moment. She licked the taste of fresh water off her lips and forced herself to take several deep breaths before she spoke again. "I don't know what to do now."

"The only thing you need to think about is rest. I know it's a new concept for you, but I trust you'll be able to manage it," he replied, a note of his usual sardonic drawl coming back into his hoarse voice.

Petra lifted a shaking hand to scrub at her face. "You're being weirdly nurturing. Stop it."

"Fuck you. I can be nurturing if I want." There was no heat in his voice but an unnerving intensity in the kiss he dropped on her shoulder. "You can't stop me."

Although it was disconcerting, Petra didn't actually want him to stop. Even if it was all an illusion that could be dispelled at any time, she clung to the reassurance this new side of Silas offered.

Pressing on her eyes to relieve some of the sting, she asked, "Where are we?"

"I brought you home."

Petra dropped her hand. Eyes popping open, she managed to lift her head just enough to give him an incredulous look. "You *what?*"

"I brought you home," he repeated, like that was a normal thing to say and that she'd have any idea what that actually meant. "You needed a healer, so I brought you to my clan."

His clan?

He'd mentioned something about his father, but she'd barely registered the strangeness of it in the moment. Now, though, Petra went into a different kind of shock. "Where are we, exactly?"

"Small town in the Smoky Mountains." He rubbed his lips

over her shoulder, back and forth through the warm water that poured over them both. His curls hung in dark tendrils around the blunt points of his ears and coiled against the pale skin at the nape of his neck, tempting her to trace their strange, alien shapes with the tips of her fingers.

"This is my house. Well, one of them. I own houses all over the world, but this is *home*. No one can touch you here."

Her heart thundered. For a moment, Petra really couldn't tell if she was going to be sick again. It wasn't fear that turned her stomach this time, but some other intense feeling too multi-layered for her to put her finger on. Her voice was barely a whisper under the patter of the water when she asked, "Why'd you bring me here, Silas?"

He lifted his head to give her a fierce scowl. "What'd you mean *why?* You were shot. You needed healing."

Her memories were disjointed and stretched into unrecognizable shapes by pain and shock, but Petra thought she recalled an argument between Silas and Rasmus about that very subject.

"You could have taken me to any healer," she protested, not entirely sure why she needed to get clarity on the subject other than the fact that it *felt* important. "I remember hearing Rasmus's voice. He knows healers. He could have called Healer M—"

"No." Silas's expression darkened into something thunderous. Those luminous, sinister eyes peered at her, but she wasn't entirely certain it was the man who looked out from within them. "I'll say this once and only once, little goddess: when it comes to your life, I don't trust anyone but clan."

Petra didn't have the courage to ask him why. She didn't want to argue, either, even knowing that the smarter and more convenient choice probably would have been to involve Margot or Healer Mason, her second-in-command and former mentor.

Except then they would know you're a murderer.

That gave her pause. It was a new and uncomfortable thing to realize she had a new title, let alone one of such profound emotional and societal weight. But the more she rolled it around in her head, the less she cared about the title itself and more the avalanche of consequence it came with.

There was no guilt for Antonin's death, only the floating feeling of grief for the new sort of life she would now have to live.

Silas was probably right to not let anyone in San Francisco or even the greater Elvish Protectorate heal her. Unless they were fully under the table and therefore untrustworthy, there was every chance they could report her injuries to Patrol. Even if by some miracle she wasn't recognized, she could still be reported simply for the anomaly of being shot in a territory that boasted its safety every chance it got.

In that light, going to Margot, who was not only a healer but the *co-ruler of said territory,* was an absolutely asinine thing to do.

There was no way she'd simply patch Petra up and send her on her merry way, no questions asked. And if Petra had to start answering those inevitable questions, then everything else would unravel.

A headache began to throb in the back of her skull. Exhausted by the sheer scale of her problems, she let out a shaky breath. "Thank you."

Silas held very still for a moment. She got the impression that she'd shocked him. She'd shocked herself, too. Not by being grateful, per se, but by how much she trusted him to have made the right choice when she couldn't.

"C'mon," Silas growled, slowly helping her stand.

Her legs felt like jelly and she slumped against him as he peeled her out of her nightgown. His hands were gentle but firm as he helped her wash. When he discovered that his black claws scraping her scalp as he worked shampoo into her hair made her melt, he drew the task out as she leaned her whole weight against him.

While he worked, she skimmed her fingers over the new, tender skin of her side. He'd been careful there, too, using a washcloth to cleanse the area so cautiously, it was like he actually feared the wound would split open if he pressed just a bit too hard.

She didn't care that she was nude and vulnerable with him in a way she hadn't been before. He'd seen her at her worst, her weakest. What did it matter?

It was hard to be self-conscious when the man stood in the shower with her, still wearing a pair of soaked briefs, and meticulously massaged conditioner into her hair. It was harder still to find any awkwardness when he turned off the shower, ran a towel over every inch of her, opened a fresh toothbrush for her, and then hauled her into his arms to put her back to bed.

She watched him from under the blankets, her eyelids heavy, as he prowled around the brightly lit room.

It was a nice bedroom. Simple. Lots of natural wood and whitewashed, textured walls. The furniture was obviously hand-made and well-crafted, the lines masculine but natural in a way that spoke of another century. If she'd expected some sort of deep, dank lair, she would have been sorely disappointed by the minimalist rustic luxury that was Silas's bedroom.

Her attention strayed from him occasionally, taking in the verdant greenery that shimmered in the breeze just outside the partially opened window or the simple linen curtains that whispered against each other in the breeze. Mostly she watched him, though.

Silas looked tired. The lines of his face were taut, strained. Even the skin around his horns appeared tighter than normal as he roughly towel-dried his curls and then stripped out of his wet underwear.

She admired the gorgeous, perfect curve of his ass as he dug around in his dresser for clothing, as well as the flex and contraction of his back muscles when he donned said clothing.

It should have been hard to reconcile the man before her with the shadow monster who'd appeared like a vengeful god in the belltower, but it wasn't. Something fundamental in her recognized that they were one and the same. He was a vengeful god forged of shadow and malice, but he was a man, too.

When he turned back to the bed, now dressed in a plain white t-shirt and low-slung, well-worn blue jeans, his feet bare and his hair still damp, she realized that it didn't bother her.

Silas, man and monster, was the only one looking out for her and... she liked him. A lot. Not in spite of what he was, but because of it.

"Here." Silas trotted back to her side and drew her attention to the nightstand nearest to her. There was a small collection of things there that she'd been too distracted by him to notice. "Drink that bottle of water and then take those pills. Dad said you're going to be depleted of a bunch of vitamins and minerals for a while, so you need to take supplements. You should also eat something. It's been almost a full day since you had anything."

He helped her sit up and then stuffed the bottle of water and a handful of colorful pills into her hands. Petra didn't argue but took them dutifully, one by one, under his hawkish gaze.

She'd never been so catastrophically injured before, but she knew that healing wasn't just a spontaneous thing where one went back to perfectly normal afterwards. Healers worked with what the body provided to close wounds, which meant that when something like blood was lost, they spurred bone marrow to make more at a hyper-fast speed. That meant that some of her fatigue likely came from her body's sudden depletion of essentials, not just the shock of what happened.

"Now eat," he instructed, handing her a protein bar as he sat on the edge of the bed by her hip.

She felt a little ridiculous for thinking it, but Petra couldn't help but feel like Silas was worried. Not the average kind of worry, but the *I-haven't-slept-in-three-days* kind of worry that changed the way one held their shoulders, the curve of their spine. Dark smudges were stark under his eyes. The corners of his mouth were crimped. When he circled the fingers of one hand around her calf over the sheets, his grip was stiff, manacle-like.

Using her thumbnail to open the stiff paper packaging on the bar, she tried to piece together what the events of the last twenty-four hours would have looked like for him.

Her stomach lurched, briefly threatening another meeting with the toilet, when she thought of what he'd been doing before her dinner with Antonin. It all seemed so far away now, and she shied away from asking him important questions about what he might have found.

She was certain that if he found anything at all, it was important that the public know what had been putrefying in the heart of Glory's Temple, but on a personal level, she was momentarily exhausted. She'd gotten what she wanted, right? Antonin admitted what he'd done and he'd died a horrific death. Was that justice?

It all seemed too big, too heavy for her to handle just then. It was much easier to imagine what it must have been like for Silas to sneak her out of the cathedral, take her to Rasmus, then smuggle her out of the EVP, across the continent, and back to his home town in... *Tennessee?* She wasn't entirely certain where the Smoky Mountains were, but that felt right.

Wherever they were, it made sense that he would look a bit haggard. Not even his mad spirit could come away from a marathon like that unaffected.

The soft, vulnerable part of her whose protective shell had been scoured away ached at the sight of his slightly rounded shoulders. Silas seemed just a bit more human now. Breakable.

And if her heart quickened at the thought of the source of that vulnerability being *her,* well... she didn't have to think about that just then, either.

After taking a tentative bite, she surprised herself by asking, "Do you want some?"

She wasn't entirely sure if Silas knew how monumental it was that her first impulse was to share her food with him, but she suspected he understood enough.

"No, baby," he said, his tone gruff, "that's for you. I put more in the drawer there, see? There's also energy gel packs and some fruit leather in there. It's not great, but that's what I had in the cabinet. I'll get you more from the market soon."

It hit her like a fist. Petra clutched the protein bar to her chest and curled over instinctively until her forehead pressed against his bicep.

"Who are you?" she gasped.

Silas cupped the back of her head. His claws threaded through the damp hair there, holding tight, when he answered, "I'm yours."

CHAPTER THIRTY-THREE

SHE HADN'T THOUGHT OF WHAT SILAS'S CLAN WOULD look like. Petra knew that many demons had close-knit family units, but for some reason, she never considered the fact that Silas might have one, too.

On top of every other uncertainty, Petra found herself listening to soft voices through the door of his bedroom and felt... odd. Out of place.

Through the open window, she swore she could hear the faint strains of a child's laughter. Silas had ordered her to sleep, but she couldn't stop herself from creeping out of bed after a short nap to peer out the window. A wild forest of trees insulated the home, but she thought she could just spy the shape of another house when the breeze moved the leaves just right.

Did that home belong to a member of his clan, too?

Petra's stomach tightened with acute discomfort. Letting the curtains fall back into place, she wandered back over to the bed. She sank onto the mattress, hands on her knees, and tried to sort through the chaotic jumble of feelings that were making such a mess of her head.

Why was it so strange to think of Silas in a clan? With a *dad?* He'd mentioned them before, of course, but...

Maybe it was because somewhere deep down, she'd assumed that someone as bad as him could only come from a world like hers — one where a healthy family life was a luxury.

Of all the things that could have made her uncomfortable in her situation, it said something truly grim about her that it was the fact that Silas might actually come from a loving, crowded home that unsettled her most.

Petra put a hand to her forehead. *Good gods. Maybe I'm the fucked up one in this relationship.*

She choked on nothing but air and spit. Were they even *in* a relationship?

On the heels of that thought, a new realization stole her breath. Petra's fingers moved to press hard against her lips.

That man is going to be my bondmate. Glory save me.

Her stomach did another uncomfortable convulsion. There were too many questions, too many unknowns. That was all her life was, apparently, now that her purpose had been more or less fulfilled.

Unable to dwell on that for any longer, Petra decided she needed to move around some more, Silas's growling about bedrest be damned.

She didn't exactly want to wander out into the middle of his clan — in fact, short of meeting Antonin again, she couldn't imagine something *more* undesirable — but that didn't mean she couldn't feel a little more human again.

The sun was setting, casting the room in a rosy glow as she went hunting for the clothing he'd apparently pilfered and brought with them in their escape. For once, she actually appreciated his lack of boundaries. It was a bone-deep relief to be able to don her own soft lounge pants and breezy shirt.

She picked through what he'd brought — little more than a backpack's worth of her belongings, but that was almost everything she owned, anyway. The back of her nose stung with a fresh wave of emotion when she discovered her little makeup kit at the bottom of the bag and, below it, safely wrapped in one of her blouses...

Matvei. Max.

Of all the things he could have grabbed, the fact that he remembered her uncle's ashes meant more to her than he could understand. Perhaps he hadn't done it for any sentimental reasons — *likely* — but that didn't make a difference to her. The thought of leaving her uncle's ashes and maybe never being able to retrieve them would have been too painful to bear.

But she had them, and the fact that she did made the new, fragile thing between her and the demon a little bit stronger, a little more real in her mind.

Petra tenderly covered the box up with her blouse and set the backpack aside. She was just considering stealing a pair of thick socks from Silas's bureau drawer when the door opened.

"I was gonna bring you dinner, but since you're ignoring orders anyway, you might as well come downstairs." Silas's annoyed drawl wrapped around her, familiar and comforting even when he sounded like he was considering turning her over his knee.

Petra turned away from his sock drawer and faced him without shame. If he got to go through her things, she wasn't going to feel self-conscious about stealing some of his comfy-looking, too-big socks.

"I'm not really hungry," she protested.

"Tough shit. Dad should have another look at you and you need food." He padded over, lambent eyes intent in a way that felt both predatory and something equally intense that she couldn't quite identify. Cupping the side of her head, he scowled at her. "You look pale. You should have slept more."

"I'm fine." There were approximately a thousand reasons she might look a little wan, not least of which was the prospect of meeting Silas's *father*.

"Little liar." He *tsked*. "You're coming downstairs, Petra. The only choice you have is whether you want to walk or be carried."

"Silas, I *really* don't think I'm in a good place to meet new people right now." Recently shot was bad enough, but when she might be a fugitive murderer *and* maybe, possibly about to bond with their son? That was too much.

Silas's eyes narrowed. "What is this?"

"What?"

"Are you *nervous?*"

Petra sputtered. "Nervous? Silas, I *killed a man* yesterday. You expect me to waltz downstairs, smile on my face, and make a good impression on your parents *now?*"

For a moment, Silas's expression was the very picture of incredulity, but that only lasted for as long as it took for the amusement to really settle in. "Petra, baby," he crooned, some of his old patronizing delight coming back. "You think this is the first time I've come home for supper after a murder? Please. You're fine. Mama wants to meet you and Dad needs to make sure you healed right, so we're going downstairs and enjoying a nice bowl of chili with cornbread together."

Petra could only stare. A tiny flare of hope sputtered to life in her chest when she asked, "Are... are your parents as insane as you?"

"Nah. They're normal, just used to my bullshit." He cupped the other side of her head and gently tilted it back, allowing him to press a skimming kiss to her lips. "Don't be nervous, baby. They already love you."

"Do they know—"

He shrugged. "Not everything, but the broad strokes."

So they're insane. Got it. Maybe her assumption that they were normal had been a bit premature.

Shoulders rounding, Petra admitted, "I don't want to meet them when I feel like roadkill, Silas."

She could barely comprehend the fact that she might actually, truly bond with this man, but if she was going to, then she didn't want to meet the people who would essentially be her in-laws when she looked like someone who'd had most of their right side blown off by plasma twenty-four hours prior. It was a little vain, but compared to all the other more serious reasons she didn't want to meet them, it was the one that she could articulate the best.

And really, it was easier than explaining the fact that she was insecure, uncertain about her ability to function in or around a family unit of any kind. She was suddenly painfully conscious of her background. Would she do or say something that would tip them off to the fact that she was a criminal's orphan, that she'd been institutionalized? It wouldn't be the first time.

Silas pulled back enough to give her a dark look from beneath his slashing brows. "Petra, are you fuckin' kidding me?"

"What?" she asked, her spine straightening with defensiveness.

Letting out a gusty sigh, Silas guided her toward what she assumed was a closet door. Pulling it open revealed a mirror on the inside. Placing himself behind her, he settled his hands on her shoulders and asked, "What do you see?"

Petra's sweeping gaze took in her mussed hair and comfortable, baggy clothing she never wore outside of her suite in the cathedral. Her face looked pale and strained, but not as sickly as she thought. What really drew her attention, however, was not any of that.

It was the slowly swirling band of shadow around her throat.

Reaching up to touch it, she felt nothing more than the suggestion of something there — easily missed if she wasn't paying attention. As she watched, the swirls curled around the tips of her fingers, almost as if the shadows sought to stick to her skin. The band itself was no thicker than her index finger and could have been mistaken for a choker if not for the unnatural movement.

Her throat bobbed. The shadow was his, and something about seeing it cling to her flesh made her feel... claimed.

He gave her a look of such profound satisfaction, it actually took her breath away. "You know what I see when I look at you — what my parents will see?"

She swallowed hard. "What?"

Baritone dropping even lower, he announced, "A powerful witch who belongs to *me.*"

Petra could hardly speak around the lump in her throat. "I wouldn't be here if it weren't for you."

"That's not true. You're a survivor, Petra. My survivor."

She shook her head, more out of a lack of response than a true wish to deny it.

Smoothing his palms over her shoulders and down to band his fingers around her arms, he met her gaze in the mirror. Standing together like this, he looked every inch the malicious force of nature he could be. That didn't bother her as much as the fact she looked... *right* there, too, standing in the circle of his arms.

"When I look at you," he murmured, "I see a powerful, beautiful witch with a cunt that tastes like honey and magic that can burn a man alive in seconds. I see what I almost lost. I see *you,* Petra."

A shiver ran down her spine when he leaned over just enough to whisper in her ear, "Now let's have supper, baby."

It was another shock, one of many to come, for Petra to discover that Silas's parents weren't both demons.

She felt foolish the moment she stepped into the kitchen, where a slim, graying man in a plain button down was setting a tray of perfectly square slices of cornbread on the table. He wore slightly over-sized wire-rimmed glasses and had a dense mat of freckles across his forehead, the tops of his cheeks, and the bridge of his nose. Beneath the freckles, his skin was deeply tanned.

There were no horns, no amber-on-black eyes. In fact, his eyes were a warm brown that crinkled at the corners when he looked up from his task to offer them a smile.

"Look who's up on her feet already," he praised, straightening to put his hands on his hips. His accent was faint, giving the impression that he'd acquired it late in life, but still very present. He turned his head a bit to address the woman who stood a little ways behind him at the stove, ladling chili into shallow earthenware bowls.

She turned, bowl and ladle in hand. A wide grin showed off laugh lines and pearly fangs — a smile that looked remarkably like Silas's. "Oh, look at that! Si, get her a seat. She looks fit to faint."

He was already guiding her, rather forcefully, into a wooden chair. Petra sank into it heavily. She was unaccountably nervous. Not even the tantalizing smell of a perfectly seasoned and spicy chili with a side of sweet cornbread could make her stomach unclench as she took in the scene with wide eyes.

Silas's mother was a whole head taller than his father. Her shoulders were broad, her limbs long and graceful. Her hair was a graying auburn pulled into a loose braid behind black horns that curled into tight spirals. She was pale and boasted prominent, rosy cheeks. When she went to set the bowls on the placemats around the table, she made time to lean over and press a kiss to the crown of her mate's head.

Petra felt like she was caught in another dream state. The tableau was too bizarre for her to make sense of. Not only was Silas's father not a demon, but his parents seemed...

Nice.

It set her teeth on edge. In her experience, very few people were truly *nice*. It seemed patently outrageous that Silas's parents, of all people, would be in that number, too.

Chapter Thirty-Four

"Mama, Dad," Silas announced, standing behind her and settling his hands on her shoulders in an unmistakably proprietary gesture, "this is Petra. She's mine." He paused there, letting that flat, no-nonsense declaration land, with considerable weight, at their feet.

Petra wanted to sink into the floor and become one with the worms when his parents shared a quick glance but said nothing.

Giving her shoulders a squeeze, he continued, "Baby, this is Scott and Connie Cuttcombe. You can call them whatever you want."

That final instruction rang oddly in her ears, but Petra stopped herself from giving Silas a baffled look. *Why would I call them anything but mister and missus Cuttcombe?*

Settling into the seat across from her, Scott reached out to shake her hand. The sleeve of his shirt pulled back a bit, revealing a slowly swirling cuff of shadow around his wrist — very much like the one that clung to her throat.

"Since last night didn't count... It's a pleasure to really meet you, Petra," Scott said when she forced herself to shake his hand. His smile was crooked. A gentler version of the smirk Silas so often flashed her way. "I'm sorry it isn't under better circumstances."

"You saw me last night?" Petra wasn't sure why that disquieted her, other than the fact that she had no memory of it and was struggling to keep up with all the new information pounding her from all sides. Silas had mentioned his father a few times now, but there was just too much for her to take in all at once for her to really figure out where he fit into everything.

Silas sat in the chair beside her and, sensing her unease, placed a heavy hand on her knee beneath the table. He didn't even look at her as he began to load up her bowl of chili with a dizzying number of toppings, then slathered a brick-sized piece of cornbread with what looked like honey butter. Even so, that seemingly unconscious touch went a long way to easing the tension in her abdomen.

Releasing her hand, Scott pushed up his glasses and replied, "You two came straight to our house last night, just past three. Not the first time Si has come home unexpectedly needing healing, of course, so I always keep my clinic prepared. Lucky thing, too. You were in a bad way last night."

Petra sounded dazed to her own ears when she said, "You're a healer?"

"He is," Connie replied, chest puffing a bit with pride as she joined them at the table. "A talented one, too. He's the best healer in the entire county."

"It helps that there aren't that many of us in the Neutral Zone," he quipped. "After the war, there were basically three healers left."

Connie cast her mate a dark look Petra recognized as belonging to Silas as well. "You hush. It's not that and you know it."

Struggling to control her expression, Petra dropped her gaze to her steaming bowl. *Silas's dad is a healer?*

Silas, the monster in the night, famous throughout the UTA for his brutality and willingness to take on any job for the right price, was the son of a *healer*. A being who, as the saying went, was beloved everywhere except a cemetery. A being sworn to protect the sanctity of life. A *healer*.

Petra hadn't grown up with healers in the children's home, but she'd met quite a few in her work. Of course, she was also friends — as much as one could be when she lied through her teeth every day — with the most famous healer in the world, Margot Goode. The sovereign's consort lived up to every stereotype Petra had ever heard about healers, which was mainly that they were absolutely impossible to hate.

She felt like she was missing something. A piece of the puzzle that would make all of this strangeness make sense. Without it, Petra felt like she just kept walking into one funhouse mirror after another. Everything was distorted and unsettling and not as she expected it to be.

Shaking off his mate's loving rebuke with a smile, Scott asked, "How're you feeling?"

Like I'm the insane one, actually. "Fine," she croaked. Grimacing, she reached for her glass of water and took a large gulp. When her throat didn't threaten to squeeze her words out all wrong, she tried again. "Thank you for healing me. If there's anything I can do to repay you—"

Two appalled noises, one high and one low, came from the other side of the table. Scott rushed to cut her off. "Don't think of it. I won't accept anything. Good gravy, you're part of this—"

Silas's low drawl interjected before Scott could finish the sentence. "Petra, you don't owe anyone anything because there's no fuckin' way I was letting you die. I would have dragged you from the underworld myself if you tried it."

His father gave Silas a paternal look. "Watch it, buddy. Grim's always listening."

"Grim can suck my c—"

"Silas Augustus Cuttcombe, *language,*" his mother chided.

That was so singularly absurd that Petra actually choked on her laughter. Some of the tension broke.

Silas eventually eased his grip on her leg, but only after she managed to get a few bites of chili down. Conversation wasn't exactly smooth, but it wasn't horrible, either. Silas's parents seemed to be making a huge effort to be both welcoming and also not too pushy with her, which she appreciated, since she still felt like she was walking through some bizarre, upside down reality.

Silas was mostly quiet, his focus split between the meal and the occasional possessive touches he gave her beneath the table. Watching him eat spoonfuls of homemade chili while his mother peppered him with updates on a laundry list of cousins was a bit like seeing a tiger pretending to be a house cat. There he was, an apex predator, content to sit at the table and pretend like he cared that Janie had another baby while he was away, isn't that nice, and your Papaw will want a visit soon, so don't you forget.

Petra thought they asked polite questions about her, too, but her head was too full to really remember them after the fact. It was muscle memory at this point, anyway, the stories she told when people asked her about her family, her career.

"My parents passed away when I was young." How young? She never said. Most people were too uncomfortable to ask for details.

"I joined the Temple when I was a teenager." Everyone assumed she must have joined immediately after the death of her parents.

"Yes, being High Priestess is stressful, but there are good parts, too." Platitudes usually followed that one, with plenty of *oh I can only imagine*'s and *I could never*'s.

Though she couldn't really recall the specifics of what they asked, Petra did feel like they were dancing around something. Several times one or both of them would begin to say something, but stop themselves or be cut off by Silas. Petra couldn't quite connect the threads, but assumed whatever it was had to do with the fact that they probably knew she was involved in something unsavory. They might've known she'd killed a man, depending on what Silas had shared.

Even if they didn't, it was odd that they never brought up *why* she'd been shot, or why Silas brought her to them for healing rather than to a clinic.

Her suspicions were roused when, after his parents finished their bowls, they stood up and began to clean, their body language speaking of some increasing urgency to leave.

"I made you a big pot of chili," Connie said, speaking softly to Silas as he joined her at the sink. "And there's heaps of meals in there for you both. Half the clan dropped things off, since you haven't had time to stock up for— Anyway, you should be all set for a few weeks. If you need anything at all, give me a call and I'll have your Dad drop it off at the door so you aren't disturbed. The rest of the clan knows not to come 'round."

Petra glanced at the silver pot on the cooker and did a double take. It was *huge*.

Just how long did they think she was going to stay? *Does it even matter?* Silas could keep her prisoner and it wouldn't make a difference. She was a fugitive. It wasn't like she had anywhere safe to go, anyway.

Petra rubbed her eyes. Her head felt heavy, too crammed with every question and unknown for her neck to support it anymore.

Connie paused. Then, in a tone Petra couldn't pin down, she asked, "Is Tal around, honey?"

Silas took a scrub brush to his bowl. "He knows to stay away for a while."

A thread of feeling Petra could actually identify entered Connie's voice: *nervousness.* "Oh, good. Of course. Of course he knows."

Tal? Petra's head really did begin to pound then. *Too much. There's just too much.* She barely knew where she was, she had no idea what she was going to do, and now nothing about Silas or what she assumed of his life made a damn lick of sense.

She wanted to hide somewhere for a while, some place cool and dark and quiet, and curl up into a tight little ball until the world stopped spinning.

A gentle hand touched her shoulder. "Are you okay?"

Petra forced her head back up and summoned a smile. "Still recovering, I think. I probably didn't sleep as much as I should have."

Scott's lips thinned. He shot a quick look at his son and mate speaking quietly as they packed up the leftover chili, the lines on his freckled brow deepening. Holding out his hand, he asked, "Can I take a quick look?"

She wasn't sure why she hesitated to put her hand in his. Scott was a healer and he'd almost certainly saved her life. There was no harm in letting him check her over. And yet something drew her eyes to Silas.

He'd stopped what he was doing and peered over his shoulder. Their eyes met. For a split second, she wondered if she'd sought him out because she worried he'd attack another man for touching her, but dismissed the thought as soon as it manifested.

When he gave her a small, encouraging nod, Petra realized she'd been looking to him for reassurance.

He's safe, Silas seemed to tell her. *I'm here.*

A tight ball of fear unwound in her chest, allowing her to once more reach out for Scott. A handshake was one thing, but the idea of letting a man weave his magic *inside* her made her skin crawl. The memories of what Antonin wanted to do to her, how he'd planned to force her into compliance, made her heart beat erratically.

But Scott was not Antonin. His magic wasn't searing. His expression was kind and patient. When he used his abilities, a warm rush swept through her. It was a bit like walking into a cozy house after a long day out in the cold.

His inspection only lasted a minute, at most, and when he pulled away, Scott gave her a reassuring smile. "You're healing up great."

Petra nearly sagged in her seat. "Thank you. Really."

"It's what we do," he replied. "You're my son's— You're important to him. And even if you weren't, I swore an oath to heal the sick and injured. So don't you worry about it."

She could only nod.

"It's important that you rest as much as you can this week," he instructed her, using the gentle but utterly implacable voice all healers seemed to possess. "I can't stress that enough, Petra. Your wound is healed, but your body was severely weakened in the process. You need nutrients, sleep, and fluids."

His gaze momentarily dropped to her neck. A confusing protective impulse brought Petra's fingers up to touch the shadows there.

Yanking his attention back to her face, he continued, "This is damn bad timing, I tell you what. This time of year is hard on all of us even when we weren't recently shot with molten plasma, let alone when you're newly—"

"I'm not gonna hurt her."

Silas's energy was a dark, angry buzz along her spine. Petra looked up to find him standing just behind her. Despite the fact that he had locked eyes with his father, who seemed like a soft soul, Silas was once again a predator defending his territory.

Tiger's back, she thought inanely. A shiver rippled down her spine.

"Never said you would, son." Scott's expression didn't change. He wore a look of paternal concern when he faced off with the glowering demon at her back. "But demons can lose their heads sometimes, especially when it's so fresh. It's important to remember that she's breakable. She needs some recovery time. That's all."

"Scott." Connie's tone wasn't quite sharp, but it definitely conveyed the message that she thought he ought to stop while he was ahead.

Glancing between them all, Petra got the sense that they were all having two conversations: one she barely understood and another she didn't even *hear.*

Silas slipped a hand under her tangled hair. His palm was warm and a little rough on her nape, the calluses there catching the fine hairs in a way that made a different kind of shudder run through her.

Speaking in that dark, drawling way he did when he was really beginning to get annoyed, Silas told his father, "I'm not gonna hurt her. Not now, not a week from now, not a century from now. She's mine."

Petra wasn't entirely certain where the notion came from, but she was suddenly certain that if Silas hadn't been speaking to his father, he would have added something along the lines of, *"Are we fuckin' clear?"*

He hadn't exactly been polite otherwise, but compared to how he spoke to just about everyone else, it was downright respectful.

Connie rounded the table. "Of course she's safe with you, honey," she said, a little too quickly, as she looped her arm through her mate's. "You know we just want what's best for you — and Petra, of course." She flashed a slightly too-bright smile. "We don't mean to be a bother about it, you know. This is just new and— and unexpected. A happy surprise."

When Silas didn't relax, Petra had to step in, understanding of the multi-layered conversation be damned. "You're not being a bother." She cast Silas a reproachful look. "I really appreciate your concern. It's... Well, it's nice."

"We take care of our own," Connie told her, like it was a fact of life that the sky was blue, Blight was lurking in the dark, and Petra was, apparently, *one of their own*. For a split second, Connie's gaze lowered, her attention unconsciously fixed on Petra's throat, before she hastily redirected her attention to her mate. "Well, this has been such nice supper, but we should get along. I've got an early shift tomorrow. Si, honey, if y'need anything at all, you pick up that phone, all right?"

"Yes, ma'am," he replied, eyes glittering with something dangerous but restrained. "Thank you for supper."

Apparently unbothered by the oddly tense exchange, Scott took a step closer to give his son a wallop on his shoulder. "Make sure she takes those supplements. And if there's any pain at all, you know I'm here to help at any time."

That seemed to ease a little bit of Silas's hostility, but it was a barely discernible change. "Thank you, sir. I will."

His parents exchanged one last charged glance before they hustled out of the kitchen. Petra watched them go. When the sound of a distant door opening and closing reached her, she swung her gaze around slowly, giving herself ample time to formulate her question.

"Silas," she murmured, "what the fuck was that?"

Chapter Thirty-Five

It was really starting to annoy him that no one except Petra seemed to believe he wouldn't hurt his mate.

It didn't usually bother him that his clan danced around him, always expecting a bomb to go off whenever he walked into a room. He knew he'd earned it. No matter how hard his parents tried, they never could get him to see people the way they did, or feel compassion like everyone else. Eventually, after a few visits with deeply concerned therapists and countless trips to Papaw's house for stern scoldings, they learned there was no fixing whatever was broken.

Silas understood that he was lucky. His family could have treated him like an outcast or been outright scared of him. Instead, they went out of their way to include him in things, to remind him that he was a part of the clan without expecting him to *be* one of them. Whenever he was home, someone wrangled him into babysitting. His matriarch asked for help in her garden. His cousins expected him at cookouts, naming parties, mating celebrations.

If they were more cautious with him, a little more watchful than they were with other clanmates, he couldn't say he blamed them. He would be, too. After all, it wasn't normal to talk to wraiths, let alone have them talk back.

Historically, the Cuttcombe clan never stood with both feet on the side of the law, but Silas took it to extremes even his most wily ancestors hadn't — and the family knew it. But clan loyalty went deeper than tree roots. So while he made the clan nervous, his place amongst them was fixed, unshakable.

But this was different.

This was *Petra*.

Something about the suggestion that he didn't know how to be a good mate, that he wouldn't take care of her, made him want to start ripping at the walls. Probably because they were right.

Silas had to consciously unlock the muscles of his jaw before he could reply to Petra with a question of his own. "Are you afraid of me?"

She gave him a narrow-eyed look. "No. Not anymore."

Her answer settled in him, slow and steady, until its weight sank into the pit of his stomach.

Feeling marginally calmer — a relative thing, considering he'd felt like he was coming out of his skin — he shoved aside the visceral offense he'd taken to his father's concern.

"You're mine," he reminded her, just to make sure that fact was burned into her brain. "You're safe. Don't ever think you're not safe with me, because you are. If anyone tries to hurt you again, I'll shove a knife into their spinal cord and twist until they dance for you. Clear?"

Petra's lips popped open with surprise. "That... is a bit much."

It didn't feel like a bit much. It felt perfectly proportional to the roar of terror that still filled his ears. It didn't matter that they'd sat down and had a nice supper together. It didn't matter that he'd watched his own father stitch her side back together, cell by cell, as the sun rose slowly over the ridge. It didn't matter that the warmth of her nape was under his palm.

He was afraid.

I almost lost her.

A swell of nausea tried to force its way up his throat, but Silas swallowed it back down. *I won't lose her. Ever.*

Petra's expression softened with wonder. "You're upset. You're *really* upset."

"I don't like that people think I'm going to hurt you," he snapped. "I won't. Why would I? That'd make as much sense as me chopping off my right hand."

"Because of the bond?" She gave him a searching look. "That's what all this is about. Right?"

It was a novel thing for him to experience a series of contrasting impulses. Normally, he did whatever came to mind first, consequences be damned, but now he felt torn in several different directions.

On one hand, he wanted to say it had nothing to do with her bond and everything to do with how much he needed her. On the other, that brought up the memory of the damn marriage certificate, and his suspicions about what Vanderpoel wanted from her, so he did *very much* want her bond.

But it was no longer about his promise to Tal. Sometime between seeing her in that community garden and being fileted by the sound of her sobbing as she thanked him for coming for her in that damn belltower, everything came into sharper focus.

Petra was not just a means to an end. She was his — now and always.

He knew he needed to explain that, but his mind was scattered, his body ruled by a combination of exhaustion and surging hormones. He teetered on the edge of his rut. A new mating right before the season began would have been bad enough, but the danger to her life had ratcheted up the pressure.

It bore down on him like a screaming m-lev, threatening to flatten them both — and he was the only one who could see it coming.

"Silas?" Petra stood up from her chair and laid a cool hand

against his brow. "You look like you're going to be sick. Are you okay?"

She let out a squeak when he snatched her to him. He buried his face in her hair, smelled himself and his shampoo and *her*. His heart rate slowed. "I don't want to talk right now," he mumbled.

He'd never really needed comforting before, so it was an exquisite surprise when Petra's arms curled around his neck in a warm embrace.

"How long has it been since *you* rested?"

"Dunno."

"Did you actually sleep at all yesterday?"

He shook his head. Even after he came down from the adrenaline and Petra was safely tucked into his bed, her side once more all smooth, tanned skin, he'd been a wreck. He lay wrapped around her for hours as he listened to her breathe and his parents coming in and out with supplies.

Even knowing that his home was warded to the teeth, he hadn't been able to rest. What if she stopped breathing? What if he slept so deeply that he missed her calling out for help? What if he failed her again?

What if what if what if—

It wasn't the first time that he'd gone days without rest, but this time he felt ground down to a pulp. Exhaustion made his limbs heavy, but he tried hard not to put too much weight on her.

"None of this can't wait until tomorrow morning," Petra announced. "We're both dead on our feet. Let's just— let's just go to bed."

He scowled. "Don't say dead."

"Too tired to stand, then."

His witch was right. He'd been beaten to within an inch of his life and felt less bruised.

Back in their bedroom, he stripped out of his clothes and collapsed on the bed, his head turning to watch Petra scuttle about on her little feet. First she folded her clothing, then placed the pile on top of his dresser. She didn't have another nightgown with her — an oversight he didn't regret — so she shamelessly dug around in his drawers until she found an old t-shirt to replace it.

He didn't have the strength to argue with her about the benefits of sleeping nude. It was all he could do to watch her body move under his shirt as she extinguished the lights and padded back to what was now her side of the bed.

The lingering cloud of terror faded just a bit. *She's here,* he thought, almost a snarl of defiance in the face of the universe. *She's here and she's alive and she's mine forever.*

Shadows crept across the blankets as she slid beneath them, instinctively covering her so she wouldn't be so vulnerable in her sleep. Petra didn't complain. Instead, she let out a soft sigh as she settled on her side facing him. They were only a handful of inches apart, their breaths mingling, and it was her who threw an arm across the divide.

In a small, tired voice she said, "Life feels really overwhelming right now."

"It does."

"I bet this was way more than you bargained for when you offered me the deal, huh?"

A ragged laugh escaped him. "I knew you'd be entertaining, but no. I thought you just wanted to blackmail a rival or something. Easy-peasy."

He looped his arm around her waist to drag her closer, until their bodies were pressed together from chest to knee. His cock was hard, pressed between them and flushed with his impending rut, but neither of them made a move to do more. The demand for sex was a cacophony in his mind, but his need for *her* was louder.

He wasn't sure where the question came from or why it mattered, but he found himself asking, "Do you regret asking me for help?"

Petra was quiet for a beat. At length, she answered, "No, I don't think I do. Not yet, anyway."

Something about that stung him. "Giving me time to fuck it

up?" His response came out far more bitter than he expected, and he instantly regretted it when Petra flinched.

"I don't know what tomorrow looks like, Silas."

Scrunching his nose, he muttered, "You're right. I know."

"Can I ask you something personal?"

Silas nearly quipped that she could ask him for his liver and he'd give it to her, but he'd already messed up once, so he simply nodded.

Petra's eyes were big and nighttime blue in her face when she asked, "It matters to you what I think of you, doesn't it?"

He stiffened. "What are you talking about?"

"I mean like what happened tonight with your dad, and just now. It hurts your feelings when I or someone you... value thinks the worst of you."

"Since when do I have feelings?" He didn't enjoy the conversation anymore. Silas opened his mouth to tell her he was done talking for the night when Petra stretched her neck to press a featherlight kiss to his lips. The muscles of his abdomen tensed and his mind blanked. He lay there, stiff but docile under her ministrations.

"I think you do," she whispered, lips stroking his with a tenderness that was both gentle and explosive. "I think you want me to trust you, to think the best of you, to feel safe with you. I think it bothers you when someone whose opinion matters to you assumes the worst — because that hurts."

Silas fisted his hand in her hair, not to hold her in place, but to anchor himself. He felt like he was being pushed out into some dark ocean. Their connection was the only thing keeping him from being swept out into the unknown.

"You're mine," was all he could think to say. Even those familiar words came out like gravel.

Petra nodded, but it seemed like it was more for herself than in response to him. "It's okay, demon. I think I'm beginning to understand."

Are you? Because I don't understand anything anymore.

She let out a soft sigh and settled her head back on her pillow. Closing her eyes, she drew the tips of her fingers up and down his back in a soothing, ticklish caress. An uncontrollable rumble erupted from his chest.

Her lips quivered with a satisfied smile.

He was almost too hungry for the sight of her face to close his eyes, but eventually the rhythmic touches, her body heat, and the perfect scent of her in his bed made his lids too heavy to keep open.

In the hazy place between much needed slumber and wakefulness, he thought he heard her whisper, "You're safe with me, too, you know."

Chapter Thirty-Six

The next day came both too soon and too late.

Silas lifted his lip in a snarl at the sunlight that slipped through the cracks of his curtains. The rest of the house was more or less sun-proofed for Tal, but his bedroom wasn't a space his brother needed to go, so he regrettably hadn't installed blackout curtains.

He bitterly regretted it as the late-morning sun of a hot June day threatened to bake the side of his face.

Silas curled tight around the bundle of fragrant warmth in his arms, his head ducking to get out of the path of the light. But it wasn't the only thing that disturbed his peace.

The bundle was talking.

Soft fingers stroked his arms, nails scratching lightly against the hair there, as a lulling voice murmured, *"...light is the path that guides, the warmth that holds, the magic that binds. Glory's light can pierce every darkness, within and without, for all days begin again with a sunrise."*

"You're in a demon's den," he muttered. "If you're going to wake me up with a prayer, at least make it one for the right god."

The rhythm of her strokes didn't falter. Her voice was soft

when she argued, "You're half demon, half witch. That means you belong to Glory, too."

A deep, gravelly growl shook his chest. Something about the way she phrased that made the animal in him buck and snarl. He belonged to one woman and one woman only, not some sanctimonious, flighty goddess who didn't have the decency to respect matehood.

Silas had her flipped onto her back and beneath him in a heartbeat. Her hair sprayed across the pillows, sparking gold wherever the sun was lucky enough to touch it, and her cheeks were pink with sleep. There were still dark smudges under her eyes and something about her seemed a touch too gaunt, but even so, she looked remarkably healthy for a woman who'd been on the brink of death a day ago.

In fact, she looked remarkably relaxed as she lay beneath him. Suspiciously so.

Silas braced his weight on his palms and leaned in close, examining her with narrowed eyes. "What is this?"

"What?" she asked, brow arching.

"Why are you looking at me like that?"

"Like what?"

"Like..." He searched for a word to describe the faint curl of her lips and the softness in her normally guarded eyes. The woman he'd come to know was all sass and layers of protective masks. This new creature was disarming and strange. He sounded nonplussed to his own ears when he said, "You look like you're happy to see me."

"That can happen when you *are* happy to see someone in the morning, yeah." Petra's tone was dry, but not unkind. "Why wouldn't I be, Silas?"

"No one's ever been before."

Her sharp inhalation was loud in the lull between bird calls. "That can't be true. Your parents—"

"Are usually too relieved to see I still have a head on my shoulders and I'm not locked up in a sigil-lined cell to be really *happy.*"

He crowded her until their noses nearly touched. "No one is *happy* to see me. So what are you hiding?"

Petra went quiet. A peculiar expression pinched her features. Slowly, she said, "That's the saddest thing I've ever heard."

"Are you going to tell me or not?"

He knew that he was being hard on her. Even after a good night's sleep, he was high-strung and temperamental. All he wanted to do was gorge himself on her, to eat her up in tiny bites until she screamed that she was his and she'd never, ever leave him.

It sparked a deep fear in him when he didn't immediately understand her motives. Surely that canny mind was working, planning, hiding something from him. There were still so many unknowns about his mate, huge gaps in his understanding of her. Those gaps became wide spaces where anxiety could flourish.

Petra breathed deeply. He expected her to lash out at him as she had in the past, but she didn't. Instead, she grabbed one of his hands and forced him to redistribute his weight as she laid it flat on the soft flesh above her heart. It beat slow and steady under his palm.

"Silas, I want to make a deal with you."

The muscles along his spine locked, one by one. *Here it comes.* "What do you want?"

"It's not about something I want," she replied, calm in the face of his snarling. "This is for you. I want to make a deal with you so you always know I'm being honest. I think you have trouble reading people. This way you can know for sure that I'm telling the truth — as long as you trust me."

A little of the starch left his spine. The animal in him paced, uneasy but desperate, as he tried to read her expression and failed. "Explain."

"I can't promise I'll always say everything I'm thinking right away, or that I won't hide things. I've lived both a very bad and very good life, Silas, and that's made me into a liar even when I don't want to be." Her hands tightened around his wrist. "But I think we can both use a— a code for when we need the truth from each other. If you promise to not abuse it, then whenever you put your hand on my heart, I'll be honest with you. No exceptions. If you do the same..."

It took him a moment to grasp what she was offering him.

If he agreed to reciprocate, if he could trust her, then she would give him the key to all those shadowy parts of her he was so desperate to see.

All he had to do was rein in his natural urge to ruthlessly exploit it. *Easy.*

"Deal." He didn't waste a moment. Keeping his palm pressed against her chest, he demanded, "What are you hiding?"

A bubble of laughter escaped the plush cushion of her mouth. "Nothing," she answered, heartbeat still steady under his palm. "Seriously, Silas, I have nothing to hide anymore. I'm not planning anything. My life is over. I have nothing— no *one* else. I woke up and I just..." The blue of her eyes, aquamarine in the late morning light, glittered with something warm and vital to his continued existence. "I was just happy to be alive and with you. I feel safe when you hold me. I can't tell you how much that means to me."

Silas didn't like being humbled. It happened rarely enough that it typically wasn't an issue for him, but there was apparently no avoiding it with Petra. While her heart beat an easy rhythm, *his* had begun to pound. Blood rushed in his ears. His stomach went tight and twisty.

"Honest?" he rasped, suddenly back to being a boy again, when he tried so hard to make sense of a world of emotion and connection that seemed forever out of reach.

Petra didn't give him an odd or impatient look. She simply nodded once, her gaze locked with his, and answered, "Honest."

His first impulse was to immediately demand all the other answers he craved. A heady sense of power threatened to overtake him, bigger and more intoxicating than what he felt when he had her on her knees or screaming for him on a sacred altar.

This was a different sort of power, and though his natural

inclination was to exploit it without mercy, some deeper instinct stayed his hand.

You'll get what you want, that instinct promised. *This is the start. Ruin it and you'll never get everything you need from her.*

His second impulse was, of course, to spread her legs and drive himself so deeply into her cunt she would feel him all the way in her ribs, but that, too, was dangerous. For one thing, he was absolutely certain that any sexual contact between them now would set off his rut like lighting the fuse on a stick of dynamite. For another, he couldn't get his father's warning out of his head.

I already failed her once. I can't do it again. I can't hurt her.

Not like that, anyway. There were good hurts and bad hurts. The only kind he could stomach giving to Petra were the sort that would make her go all wet and soft for him.

Not used to restraining himself, Silas bit back a curse and dropped his head to bury his face against her throat. His hand ventured down for a harsh, proprietary squeeze of her heavy breast, but it was a small concession to the monster of his lust.

"You're happy?" he demanded, pressing his face into the bit of his soul she wore around her graceful throat. That piece, just like the rest of him, belonged to her now.

"With my life? No." A soft hand threaded through his hair before finding its place around the curve of one horn. Her voice took on a wry note when she added, "But with you? I know I must have lost my mind because... yeah, I think I am."

It was by an unspoken agreement that they didn't speak about anything of importance for the rest of the morning. Having her all to himself, healthy and curiously happy, helped settle his hormones into a temporary lull, allowing him to think clearly for a while as they huddled under the sheets.

Once hunger drove them out of bed, they quietly worked side by side in the kitchen to assemble breakfast. Silas knew that Petra had questions, especially when she eyed the refrigerator newly filled with mismatched containers of meals ready to carry them through the next few weeks. But she didn't remark on it. Instead, she found the cheese in the crisper and quietly shut the door.

Simply having her there, standing beside him dressed in nothing more than his old t-shirt and a pair of his socks that were so big on her they had to be folded at mid-calf, filled him with an intense wave of satisfaction.

He made coffee and toast — the bread courtesy of his younger cousin Shelley, no doubt, who owned the bakery in town — while Petra scrambled eggs with butter in a pan. She warned, "I'm not a very good cook. Never really had the chance to learn, but I can do scrambled eggs."

"Most of my childhood punishments involved being banished to Papaw's kitchen," he told her, "so I can handle the cooking."

It satisfied something else in him, too, to know he'd be feeding her. What normally was significant for clan life — sharing meals — was given even more importance knowing that something in Petra's past made her sensitive about food. He didn't understand how to connect with her emotionally and he was probably going to be a shit mate, but he could at least always make sure she was fed well.

As they worked around the kitchen and enjoyed their meal, they spoke sporadically about nothing. Petra asked him about his house — *previously belonged to his great-grandfather* — and about how many people were in his clan — *a lot* — as well as how much time he spent there — *not much.*

He asked about what kind of houses she liked, since he had many and could change them to suit her with a snap of his fingers. Her answer was, of course, another mystery. "I've never lived in a house, so I'm not sure. This one seems really nice, though. I like being in the woods. I don't think I could live somewhere like this full-time, but it's definitely nice."

It took a monumental movement of will to keep himself from

digging. *Never lived in a house?* Those blank years before her initiation into the Temple mocked him once again.

But Petra seemed so at ease as she sat across from him, the too-wide collar of his t-shirt sagging over one shoulder and her blonde hair pulled up into a messy bun. His mate had never looked less like a priestess. While he loved the glamorous side of her, he found this new woman infinitely more captivating.

No one, as far as he was aware, had ever been completely at ease with him before. And yet everything in Petra's body language spoke of a trust he didn't feel he'd earned.

He was loath to break the spell that the morning had cast over them, but there was so much they had to talk about and increasingly little time in which to do it. She needed to know what it meant to be a demon's mate before his rut really hit, and he needed to begin sifting through the absurd mass of data he'd stolen from Vanderpoel to determine *exactly* who he needed to kill to keep her safe.

Normally that would have titillated him, but now... Now all he wanted to do was watch her butter her toast with that incongruously focused expression and try to breathe around the thing that expanded in his chest whenever she glanced up at him with a small smile.

But eventually, she finished her toast. Their mugs were drained of coffee. Afternoon crept in, and so did the summer heat.

Petra drew her legs up until her feet balanced on the edge of her seat. Looking deceptively calm, she said, "So... I killed someone."

It was no use debating the point, though he felt like there was some wiggle room there. She *believed* she'd killed someone and to an outsider, all evidence would suggest that she had. Like any criminal, Silas knew the truth was a relative, malleable thing.

"*We* killed him," he answered, watching her closely.

She played with a short lock of hair by her ear, her eyes

lowered to stare at the remains of their breakfast. "Did you get anything from Antonin's suite?"

He snorted. "Yes."

She seemed to be trying to get her thoughts in order rather than working through all the information, so he wasn't surprised when she just nodded. "Did you try to lock me in the closet?"

Silas leaned back in his chair. The old wood, sawed and lathed and assembled by his great-granddad at least two hundred and fifty years prior, groaned under his weight. *Damn Tal.* Silas hadn't been in the headspace to ask why he failed to secure Petra like he'd promised, but now that he thought about it, it explained why the wraith had so happily kept his distance.

He wasn't just respecting Silas's privacy. He was avoiding an ass-whooping.

"Are you going to be mad at me if I say yes?"

Petra narrowed her eyes. "Are you going to lie to me if *I* say yes?"

"No," he answered. After a moment of hesitation, he amended, *"Probably* not."

"Then answer the question."

It was on the tip of his tongue to ask who else would have used shadows to seal her into a closet, but Silas took one look at the glint in her eyes and backed down. He liked fighting with her, but he didn't want her to be *angry* with him — a distinction he'd never made in his life but one which now seemed essential to maintaining his equilibrium.

"I didn't want you to meet with Vanderpoel. You were supposed to stay in the closet until I'd handled him for you." The experience of explaining himself was deeply unnatural, but he pushed through it because it was Petra, and she was his, which meant she was basically an extension of himself. "I planned to get your information, kill him, and then leave with you through the secret door."

"That's why you packed my things."

"Yes. I figured things would be hot for a while and you were set to leave for your sabbatical, so..." He shrugged. The fact that he would have needed to abscond with her anyway for his rut was another compelling reason, but that wasn't why she asked, so he left that bit out.

Petra breathed deeply through her nose before she replied, "You were trying to keep me safe."

"Yes?" Silas wasn't certain why that came out like a question.

She said nothing. Uncurling from her seat, Petra padded around the kitchen table, her socked feet tapping out a pleasant beat, until she stood over him. Silas turned automatically. He was like a tiny astronomical body pulled into her orbit. Where she went, he did, too. Silas wondered if he'd spend the rest of his life circling her. He hoped so.

Soft hands curled around the base of his horns. She used her grip to gently tilt his head back. His cock stirred at her nearness, the way she held him, the lush scent of her. The thought of her taking control of him, using his horns to guide him between her thighs, was extremely compelling.

Fuck. I can't wait to own her — mind, magic, and perfect cunt.

Petra looked down her nose at him. Speaking in a deceptively gentle voice, she said, "Thank you for trying to keep me safe, demon. That was a good impulse. However..." She leaned in close. "If you ever try that shit again, I'll poison you."

If he hadn't been hard before, he was after *that*.

Silas let out a low groan. He couldn't stop himself from pawing at her, his hands shaping to fit the curve of her waist and the perfect slope of her ass. "You know I love it when you're scary, baby."

He loved it when she was icy cold. He loved it when she was soft. He loved it when she was submissive. He loved it when she was a whirlwind of rage and sass and magic. He loved all the different versions of Petra. Within her there was an ever-twisting kaleidoscope. Every time he looked at her, he found something new to dazzle him.

Petra didn't scold him for his reaction. Instead, her expression softened with exasperated amusement. Dropping her head to press a hard, too-brief kiss to his lips, she said, "I don't know what I'm going to do now, but going forward, let's be scary together, okay? Let's work as a team, not against each other."

"Making sure you're not going to get murdered isn't working against you," he protested.

She had the gall to pinch the short, pointed tip of his ear. Silas made an outraged sound more for her benefit than out of any real offense. "You know what I mean."

Whether she knew it or not, Petra was asking him to act like a mate. Silas had seen many good matings and many bad ones, both at home and in his line of work, so he understood the principles of a solid relationship in the way one might understand the recipe for baking a good loaf of bread without ever having made one.

You put honesty, compassion, attraction, independence, and a dash of reliance in a bowl. Knead. Let it rise. Bake for an hour at 350 or until your relationship is perfectly golden brown.

Relationships, like baking or sigilwork, could all be broken down into easily understood parts. All he had to do was follow the directions.

It didn't sound too hard, except for the fact honesty was a flexible thing in his mind, compassion wasn't something he'd been born with, his attraction to her was borderline pathological, he despised the idea of her being independent from him, and he still struggled to grapple with the fact that he was totally and completely reliant on her.

Fuck.

Petra put her hand over his heart.

Something in him went taut when she looked at him like that, like she was silently praying for him to not let her down. "Right now, you're all I have in this world. I want to be able to trust you implicitly. I think you want that, too. But that won't work if I worry you'll go behind my back to do what *you* think is right at any moment. Can you promise me you'll try, Silas?"

"I'm going to protect you," he said, caught between instinct and an existential sort of confusion. He needed to please her, but he also needed to guard her. When those impulses clashed, he was left unsettled, rudderless, and angry at the thing in him that couldn't make up its damn mind.

With more patience than he probably deserved, Petra explained, "I'm not asking you to stop protecting me. I'm asking you to talk to me. To work with me so we can protect *each other.*"

That taut feeling only grew. He fisted the material of his shirt where it fell over her hips and bit out, "I'm not a good man, Petra. I'll never be good. You can't change me. Everyone's tried and failed. I'm a monster. Always will be."

"Demon." The hand not covering his heart found its way under his chin. Petra tilted his head up a bit more, forcing him to look her square in the face when she explained, "I'm not asking you to change. I'm asking you to be *my* monster."

Chapter Thirty-Seven

"Silas, if you're leading me into a torture dungeon, please just say so. I won't be mad, I promise." Petra's grip on his hand tightened as he led her down a flight of rickety, old, hand-hewn stairs.

"I don't have a dungeon," he replied, matter-of-fact.

"Then why do you have so many high-tech locks on the door of this basement?"

"It's a root cellar, actually. Or it was before I expanded it."

He descended ahead of her. As he crossed the halfway point of the stairs, lights came on. Trying to reassure her in his own twisted, Silas-y way, he said, "I don't have the patience for torture. It's messy, loud, and unreliable. Any answers I can get from torture aren't going to be better than what I can get through blackmail or, when I have to, a bolt to the knee."

It said a lot about her that his easy explanation actually made her feel better. She wished she could say that it was because he was being frank with her, but the more honest answer was that she would always be a criminal's daughter, and it was better for her to know exactly what kind of violence she was dealing with than something unknown.

As Max used to say, *"A man who shows you who he is will*

always be more trustworthy than the man who hides himself, even when what you're shown is ugly."

Just to be sure, though, she asked, "Do you *like* killing people? Causing pain?"

"Nah," he answered, easy as you please. "I don't feel much of anything when I do it. Worried the shit out of the clan for a while, but I guess they decided that was better than me liking it."

All things are relative, she thought. Silas probably had no idea how lucky he was to have a family who accepted him, more or less, for who he was. The world was lucky, too.

Gods only know what he might've become if he'd been left to his own devices.

It was an odd thing, realizing that she was coming to know Silas so well. Some essential facet of who he was had clicked into place the previous night, when she discovered he could be wounded and didn't even know it.

Now she felt like she was picking up a foreign language, her understanding snowballing until she could actually understand him — mostly.

It was ironic that at the moment when the world made the least amount of sense to her, she finally understood Silas.

She knew she was pushing him when she asked him to talk to her, but she didn't expect him to stand up from his chair, grab her hand, and lead her to a glamoured door with more locks on it than Rasmus's sex dungeon.

Not that she knew Rasmus had one of those, of course, but one could only assume.

She winced at the thought, recalling what she'd given the were in exchange for the meeting with Silas. At the time she hadn't felt any remorse throwing him some information about the woman he'd been hunting, but now that she was tied to her own undomesticated man, she felt a little chagrined.

Good luck, Healer Mason. You're going to need it.

Petra braced herself as they descended. There were walls on either side of the steps, clearly newer than the steps themselves, and what could only be described as a vault door at the bottom. She waited on the second to last step as Silas paused at the door. He waved a hand.

Magic rippled with a nauseating lurch. She had to brace herself against a wall to stop from swaying.

Silas glanced over his shoulder and used their linked hands to gently pull her away from the wall. "Shoulda warned you. When I took over the house, it needed a lot of work. It was basically left to rot after the war. Meant I could build the wards and sigilwork right into the beams and foundation. In the areas I really want to keep people out, it's a bit stronger than you're probably used to."

In other words, the reason the house nearly hummed with his magic was because it was built *into* the house itself. She'd only felt wards that strong once before, when she got a vanishingly rare invitation to have tea with the extremely busy new Sovereign's Consort.

The hallway that led to the private floor of Solbourne Tower was guarded by a mesh of wards painted onto the ceiling — in blood.

"Did you use sacrifices?" she croaked, not entirely sure she wanted to know.

Silas entered an extremely complex coded pattern of dots and triangles into a sleek glass panel to one side of the door. After a moment, the device he always wore on his wrist beeped. That beep was echoed by the panel. The door unlatched with a hydraulic hiss.

"I don't need sacrifices or blood to make my sigils stick," he answered, a touch waspish. She'd pricked his professional pride, apparently. "Only the unskilled need a crutch like that."

Her necklace felt a little heavier than it had a moment ago. It occurred to her once again that a man like Silas shouldn't have any use for her magic. She was all raw power, sure, but *this...* The hair on her arms lifted in a wave as she followed him through the door.

Cold, smooth tile met the bare soles of her feet. Lights, taste-fully set into the ceiling all around the perimeter of the room, lit the sprawling open space without casting an antiseptic glow over everything.

The room was split into four rough quadrants: One side of the square room was dedicated to a massive wall of computer servers. A desk was set up in front of it, decked out with a single massive, curved screen that nearly spanned its length. Another wall and the space before it was dedicated to what looked like a cross between a workshop and a high-tech, glass-enclosed cleanroom.

Another corner was all movable wire racks holding just about every sort of gadget, metal pipe, wire, and tool known to man or god. Finally, on the far side from where they stood, was a huge stainless steel work table covered in what could only be described as metal body parts.

He was right. It wasn't a dungeon.

It was a lab.

"It might surprise you to learn that I consider my criminal career to be my day job," he explained as he pulled her toward the wall of servers and its single, sparsely decorated desk. Petra's attention refused to settle in one place, which explained why it took her so long to notice the line of red leather trunks arranged on the floor there.

"I like making money and I like doing things I shouldn't. That runs in the family. Anti-authoritarianism is baked into my clan's DNA, so I think someone like me was always bound to come 'round sooner or later. Crime filled both my need for money and kept me entertained. It's never been the *goal*, though."

She was almost too afraid to ask, but there wasn't really a choice. "What's your goal, Silas?"

They stopped by the desk. Somehow alerted to his proximity, the massive, curved screen came to life. A ribbon of changing color undulated across its transparent surface.

Silas waved his hand in front of the screen. A wild array of windows replaced the colorful ribbon: cascading lines of code, math equations, several download progress windows, and sprays of organic-looking sigils that moved on their own. They separated and recombined to some end she couldn't even begin to guess.

He squinted at the download progress, grunted to himself, and then turned back to her. "I'm a sigilhacker first," he finally answered. "I've been doing it since I was old enough to draw sigils in the dirt. I started with mastering wards, then I moved to combining magic with computers. But this shit is expensive, so I needed a quick way to make cash." He shrugged. "Blackmail, murder, and mayhem is fun and pays well."

Maybe a dungeon would have been better. Then she would have known what to expect, at least.

Petra watched the sigils curl and expand, split and reform, and felt a little bit like she was dealing with a complete unknown. Not because she was surprised he was a master sigilworker — Shade was famous for his wards as well as the price he demanded for them — but this was something so far above what she knew that it evoked a sense of vertigo.

Because Petra was no expert, but she knew her way around a sigil or two. She was rusty, of course, after so many years of not needing to use that knowledge, but she *knew* the standard western sigil alphabet.

The sigils scrawling across his screen like infinitely multiplying fractals weren't that.

Their shapes were foreign, jagged. When she looked at them, a tremor erupted from an atavistic place in her brain, a warning to stay still, to not look too closely at a thing that was beyond what her mind could safely comprehend.

This was not the work of a man who tinkered. This was something much, much more powerful.

The cool, filtered air of the lab brushed her suddenly clammy skin. Pieces came together. She glanced around the workshop area, took in the metal parts. She thought of his terrifying skill. She remembered their negotiation in her office, when he made his demands.

He wanted access to the m-generator.

He needs my bond.

She watched those sigils move until her eyes blurred and they became insects skittering across the screen, threatening to burst out and spray across the floor.

He needs power.

So many pieces. So many new connections. She could almost hear them clicking together in her mind. It was the sound of a gun being disassembled, cleaned, and put back together again — the music she used to go to sleep to whenever her father was home.

Petra's fingers went limp in his hold. "What are you making?"

Silas watched her closely, but it was impossible to say whether he picked up on her distress or not. "I could make almost anything with the right amount of time, equipment, and power," he answered. "And I have."

Petra could feel the skin around her eyes and mouth going tight as the first sparks of panic made it through her shock. "But you have a *goal*. You have a plan. All of this has been for something. You need *me* for something. Tell me what it is."

The only thing she could equate her sudden, acute dread to was what it might feel like to walk into a friend's house to discover they spent all their spare time learning how to make poison. It was like opening up their kitchen cabinets, their dressers, and their linen closets to discover that every single one of them was full of deadly chemicals.

No, it didn't necessarily *mean* they were planning on killing scores of people, but they could. They had the stuff for it. The know-how. The opportunity.

It was one thing to sit down and tinker with sigils, to even be a genius with them. People and governments did it all the time. The gods knew what went on in the shady R&D labs of the EVP and other territories. She imagined it was a bit like this.

However, this was *Silas,* the terrifying free agent criminal known as Shade, and there was a reason behind everything he did.

The possibilities were as endless as they were nauseating. Was he making weapons? Bombs? Something powerful enough to destabilize an entire territory, if not the UTA as a whole? If so, was he acting on his own or was he doing it for someone, some*thing,* else? The territories had been at peace for only a little over a century. It would take so little to destabilize that — money, an opportunity, and fire power. All things that could be manufactured with relative ease, given just a dash of luck.

And if one territory fell...

Gods, it'd be war all over again.

"Bodies."

Petra fought to get enough air in her lungs to ask, "What?"

Using her limp hand to drag her to his chest, he repeated, "Bodies. That's what I'm making. That's what I need power for. *Bodies.*"

She had to brace her hands on his chest to steady herself. "For — Bodies for who? For *what?*"

"I made a promise to a friend," he answered, molten eyes so intense his gaze threatened to burn her. "I've only made two real promises in my life, Petra. First to him, and then to you. You asked me to be honest with you, so this is it. This is what I do, and this is how far I'll go for the people who belong to me."

Her dread turned into cold, sickly anger. "That doesn't explain shit and you know it."

His lips quirked. Gods, even now she loved the way that little smirk highlighted the beauty mark above his lip.

"I've adapted and improved experimental m-droid technology to make mechanical bodies for wraiths. The only part I'm missing is enough power to bind them to the machinery. A fuckin' shitload of raw, unfiltered magical power. The kind of power only a gloriana has."

Wraiths? Petra mouthed the word, but it didn't make any more sense than when he said it.

Wraiths were an urban legend. They were the boogeymen in the dark parents used to keep their children from wandering the house past bedtime. They were the stars of ghost stories told around bonfires and the harbingers of doom in tales of the gods.

They were *myth*. And even if they weren't, nothing else about what he said made any damn sense.

Well, almost nothing.

She understood the part about needing magic. She understood that part very, very well.

"You need me, my bond, to make... bodies. For wraiths."

"Yes." He beamed at her with the full force of his wolfish delight. Heavy hands settled on her hips and drew her in a little closer, until she was forced to tilt her head back to keep his face in her eyeline. "You get it."

I don't, no. But she also didn't feel like he was lying, either, which meant that he was being deadly earnest or he was very, very insane.

Probably both.

"It's not bombs." She had to say it aloud to confirm it, or else she'd never get it out of her head. "Guns?"

"No bombs and no guns," he assured her.

"I don't like guns. I don't want you to make them." It felt like a stupid thing to say — what control did she have over him or what he did? — but the words came out in a rush anyway.

Silas's mouth creased in a deep frown. "You were shot. Of course you don't like guns. They're on my shit list right now, too. I always carry one, but I don't like using it. My claws are more reliable."

She shook her head. Right. She'd almost forgotten that she was shot. Was that her brain trying to protect her from something traumatic, or was that a sign that she was finally losing it?

The world just kept spinning and spinning. Every time it felt like she might have her feet under her again, there it went. She was tired of it. So tired. "No. I mean, yes, but also no. I really don't like guns, Silas. My dad ran weapons and it got him and my mom killed. I can't stay here if you—"

"I don't make any fuckin' guns and I'm sure as shit not gonna start *now*," he snapped.

Startled by his harsh tone, Petra looked away. She cursed the way her eyes prickled with reflexive tears. Silas had been far crueler to her than this in the past, but something about this moment felt particularly cutting. Like she'd exposed her soft underbelly to him and he'd barely given it a glance. Guns were a tender spot he had no way of seeing, and with her nerves strung as taut as they were, his dismissive tone hit her harder than was probably fair.

Buck up, buttercup, she silently urged herself. *This isn't a normal relationship. You can't be this sensitive.*

They'd had their tender moments, but she had to remember that Silas wasn't a normal man. She wasn't his girlfriend. For a moment there, when she first saw the shadow around her neck, she thought maybe... But no, she wasn't anything but a means to an end, really. One she firmly believed he'd developed some form of affection for, but a means to an end nonetheless.

Silas blanched. "Are you *crying?* Stop that. I said I don't do guns. I don't make them and I don't sell them. And I don't like it when you cry, so *stop."*

Petra took several steadying breaths and tried to reorient herself now that her initial panic had begun to recede.

Okay, so he's a mad genius making robot bodies for ghosts. Okay. Okay. I can deal with that.

It was better than someone making bombs in their basement by a mile. Weirder? Sure, but she could handle weird. She wasn't exactly normal or well-adjusted herself.

But would I leave if he was making weapons?

Petra dropped her gaze to Silas's bare chest and the cheap gold necklace that hung in the divot between his pecs. Her eyes moved from one pale scar to another, like she might find the answer to that heavy question somewhere in their grisly constellations.

No.

She couldn't picture herself leaving him. Even knowing he needed her for something potentially nefarious, she couldn't. It wasn't just because he was her only friend in the world at the moment — what a deeply troubling thought that was — but because she just... couldn't.

Didn't want to. Wouldn't.

Silas could be cruel, but he was hers. He was essential to her wellbeing now, like a new, more potent oxygen. If he disappeared now, she'd slowly suffocate.

Because she was starting to understand him, and she knew he understood her. He understood her right away. He saw past the masks, the desperation, the fear. He saw every fucked up inch of her and he asked for more.

Whether he truly cared about her or not, whether he wanted to use her or not, they were connected by more than a bargain. They *knew* each other.

Oh Glory, save me. I think I'm falling in love with Silas.

Chapter Thirty-Eight

She swayed into him, unconsciously expecting him to hold her steady when her legs failed. Strong arms looped around her waist as he braced his legs a little farther apart.

"Petra." He said her name with such a peculiar inflection that she really couldn't tell if it was a growl or a whine.

"I'm fine," she rasped. She took a moment to scrub her eyes against her shoulder. "I'm fine. This just really— It caught me off-guard, but I'm good now. No guns, no bombs. Just... bodies. Okay. Yeah."

He looked at her like *she* was the crazy one. Maybe she was. Sure, she'd put herself in some bad spots since her uncle died, but letting herself fall in love with *Shade,* the monster under the bed of the UTA's criminal underground, was probably the most outrageous thing she could have done.

Can a man like him even love someone? The thought was a shot of ice water in her veins.

She knew he could care. She felt it. But could he *love?* What would her life be like if he simply wasn't capable of it?

"No guns, no bombs," he repeated, eyeing her like she was the unpredictable one. "Are you really okay? Because I've got other shit to tell you, but if you're gonna cry again I'll..." His brows drew together as he apparently struggled to find the right words. "I don't know what I'll do, but I'll make you stop."

Petra's chest went all achingly, pleasantly tight. "Tears are natural, Silas. I've been through a lot recently. That means I might just start crying sometimes, especially if you use that tone with me. You're going to have to get used to it."

"No, I won't." Every line of his expression went razor-sharp. "I don't like it when you cry. I don't want it. How do I stop it? Do you need me to say sorry for my tone? I'm sorry. I won't do that again. Did that work?"

"Typically, the answer to not making someone cry is... make the person happy? Be nice, maybe?" Even as she said it, Petra thought it sounded trite — especially in light of her own feelings. Falling in love with a man who didn't even understand that tears were normal didn't exactly bode well for her future happiness.

Silas didn't mock her, though. Instead, he seemed deadly serious when he replied, "I can make you happy."

Petra's tongue tied itself into a knot. All she could manage was a strange, noncommittal sound.

Something dark lurked in Silas's eyes. In an instant, Petra was back in The Broken Tooth what felt like a lifetime ago, squaring off with a predator who looked like he was weighing the benefits of eating her now or later.

"You don't think I can." He sounded very calm. It was an unsettling contrast to the look in his eyes.

"I think that... this thing between us is very new and volatile," she managed to say.

"New and volatile." Silas said it so silkily, so softly, that it actually alarmed her.

It turned out she was right to be worried, because not a moment later he picked her up, swung her around, and deposited her on the edge of his desk.

Wedging himself between her legs, he planted both palms on

either side of her hips and leaned in until their noses bumped. Petra nearly went cross-eyed in an attempt to maintain eye contact.

"Listen up," he growled, silky drawl ground down into pure grit. "You and me— we've got some shit to get straight, right here and right now."

"Silas, I didn't mean—"

"No, you said your bit earlier and now I'm gonna say mine." Petra's mouth shut with an audible *clack*. "You say you want us to be a team, but for that to work, you need to understand something: you're *mine*. You've been mine. You'll always be mine. I'm obsessed with you. If you don't like that, if you're not happy, then I'll fix it. I can fix anything. I can *give* you anything and I can be the monster you need me to be."

He nearly vibrated with tension when he continued, "I'm showing all this to you, telling you everything, because this is it for me. You're mine. I'm yours."

No way. A nervous, fluttering sort of certainty began to rise in her, but Petra couldn't stop herself from whispering, "What are you saying, Silas?"

"I'm saying you've got to come to grips with this," he answered, each word a dark, dangerous thing, "because we've got about a week before my rut hits, there are a lot of people who need killin', and you're my fuckin' mate. I'm *never* letting you go."

Even with her gnawing suspicions about his erratic, possessive behavior, the weirdness with his parents, and the shadow, she supposed it should have been a shock. It should have thrown her into another fit. It should have made the walls close in around her as yet another thing outside her control sent the world into an even faster spin.

But it didn't.

For the first time in years, everything went still.

"...I'm your mate?"

"Yes."

Silas showed her his teeth. One hand circled her throat. The shadows that clung there came alive in a way she couldn't really understand. It was almost as if they were responding to that proprietary touch, reinforcing the claim. Petra recalled the shadows around Scott's wrist and the way both of Silas's parents hadn't been able to stop looking at her throat.

Oh.

Her life had become so complicated and dangerous that it was an immense relief to be given the answers to a puzzle without pain, sweat, or tears. Every other problem was too big to be handled, but *this...* This she could make sense of.

It might've horrified a normal witch to discover she was mated to an unstable half-demon who liked to make money by murder, but compared to her other issues, it seemed delightfully mundane. Normal, even.

Unexpected matings happened every day. She'd blessed enough unions to know it better than most. There was an entire entertainment industry devoted to telling fantastical and tragic stories about mismatched or starcrossed matings. Dragons and orcs were notorious for that sort of thing, what with their predisposition for near-instant infatuation and kidnapping.

Witches rarely stumbled into matings with one another, but the gods knew she wouldn't be the first to find herself bound to another by fate rather than choice. As far as she knew, demons didn't get much of a say in their mates, so it really was just that — fate.

Petra let out a shaky breath. She'd suspected it, but hearing it confirmed made her wonder, *Glory, what in the world are you doing?*

"I'm your mate," she said again, more for herself than for him. She scanned his tense features, memorized the placement of his beauty mark, the exact color of his eyes. "What does that mean?"

Before the vexed expression on his face could turn into a full-on tantrum, she quickly amended, "For *you*, Silas. What does that mean for you? How is this going to work?"

He stuck his chin out at a stubborn angle. Petra touched it, cradled the angle of his jaw in her palm, and assured him, "It's okay to not have the answers right now. It's just a question, demon, not a demand."

"I thought you'd be angry," he admitted, a touch suspiciously.

"About being your mate?"

"Yeah."

"Anger was never on the table." Petra rubbed his cheek with the pad of her thumb, her chest squeezing again. He tilted his head into her hand. "I can't even say I'm surprised. I'm just... I think this is one of those things that I'm going to have to sit with before it really sinks in. But *angry?* No, Silas. Why did you think that?"

"Because you're stuck with me as your mate," he explained with heartbreaking frankness. "No one wants that."

Petra sucked in a sharp breath through her nose. It was a surreal thing, experiencing the sudden and unreasonable urge to protect someone as terrifying as Silas.

"Did it ever occur to you that maybe you're stuck with me, too? I'm not exactly a catch."

Silas's eyes glittered underneath the fans of his lashes. "Liar. Other people want you. Or did, anyway."

"What are you talking about?"

Nodding toward the neatly lined up row of red leather cases, he said, "I took those from Vanderpoel. You know what I found in one of them?"

Petra's attention immediately snapped to the cases. Her heart lurched. She'd glimpsed one of Antonin's entourage carrying something red, but she'd been too distracted by the Protector to pay much attention at the time and assumed it was just more of his endless train of luggage.

"What's in those?"

"Lots of things," he answered in an ominous, measured way. "Files on just about everyone in the Temple. Passports. Offshore accounts. Blackmail. Medical records." He paused. A muscle in his cheek spasmed. "A marriage license. With your name on it."

Petra's skin crawled. It wasn't out of fear of Silas discovering what Antonin wanted from her, but from the memory of the way the Protector had spoken to her, how certain he'd been that he'd be having sex with her after dessert.

And then there was the image permanently seared into her mind's eye: Antonin pointing the gun at Silas's head, his finger on the trigger.

He's dead, she reminded herself as she tried to breathe past the echo of terror. *He's dead and he can't ever touch you or someone you love again. Silas is safe. He's okay. Antonin can't hurt him now.*

Swallowing around the lump in her throat, Petra closed her eyes and explained, "When Antonin visited the first time... just before he left, he said he'd decided I was going to be his wife. It wasn't even a proposal. It was a— an order. He said he wanted to *join forces.* He said he needed a good woman by his side and an heir as soon as possible."

Both the shadows and Silas's hand on her throat tightened. Not enough to cut off her air, but enough to remind her they were there. As if she could forget. Rather than alarming her, the reminder helped her relax a little as she continued to explain, "He said he'd give me a few weeks to get used to the idea while he wrapped up a big project."

Petra found herself leaning forward, until her forehead rested against the smooth skin stretched over his pec. Her voice got smaller, exhausted by the memory of the marathon she'd been running for so long. "I never said yes. I never said no, either. I knew I couldn't. I'd tried every other avenue of getting to the truth and failed. I needed *him.* So I knew I couldn't throw out the opportunity, even if it meant... I don't know. When it came down to it, I wasn't able to even pretend to give him what he wanted."

Silas's hand slid around to cradle the back of her head. His voice was a deep rumble from his chest when he confirmed, "He wanted your bond, too."

"Yes."

There was a long, tense silence. Petra waited for the shoe to drop, for him to accuse her of playing him. He'd be right. She had played him. Never in her wildest imaginings did she ever think she'd actually be standing there, committed to spending the rest of her life with *him*.

But she was glad it had worked out that way. No matter what came next, Petra couldn't regret any of it.

At length, he asked, "When you went up to the belltower, what did you think was going to happen?"

"I thought you would do what I couldn't."

"And if everything had gone right, if I'd gotten away without you, what was your plan? What did you think he would do if he suspected you were behind it? What did you think he'd do if you rejected him?"

Something in Silas's voice made her freeze. Petra tried to choose her words carefully, but there was no blunting the edge of her honest answer. "I figured that whatever happened to me didn't matter as much as the truth."

She didn't need to spell it out for him. Silas was too smart for that.

An ugly feeling twisted up her insides when he pulled away from her. When she opened her eyes, she was disturbed to find his expressive face had gone preternaturally blank. A stranger looked at her with Silas's eyes.

There was nothing there. No familiar, infuriating grin or boyish confusion. No rebuke or snarl. She sensed a great, scorching wave of something behind that blank mask, but she couldn't *see* it.

He was angry with her. Really, truly angry in a way he hadn't been before.

That mattered. It mattered more than she could have ever anticipated. Petra's voice shook when she began to apologize, "Silas, I'm—"

A hard, cruel mouth came down on hers. It was a mean kiss,

all unyielding lips, teeth, and thrusting tongue. It wasn't loving, but Petra clung to him anyway. She'd seen the vulnerable, confused part of him, understood that he'd given her his trust, and it ate at her that she'd betrayed that. A part of her wanted him to punish her for it, just so she wouldn't feel the ugly guilt anymore.

It didn't matter that what she'd done was justified, nor that she had no way of knowing he'd become someone so important to her so quickly. It didn't even matter that her guilt lived comfortably alongside her lack of regret, the knowledge that she'd do it again if she had to.

What mattered was *him*.

Her monster in the dark, the terrifying Shade could be hurt. It was a horrible thing to know she'd been the one to do it.

When he broke the kiss, Petra chased him, her nails sinking into his chest as she leaned forward, seeking that essential connection. But Silas was grim-faced, his shoulders stiff with tension. Shut off.

He set her back and then stepped away.

His intonation was flat when he said, "Look through the boxes. I'm going to start getting the information from his computers decrypted. Hopefully you'll find what you need."

He turned to walk away. Those long legs carried him across the room so quickly, she barely had time to hop off the desk. "Silas, wait! Where are you going?"

His head turned to pin her with a glare so hot, so raw, that she recoiled from it instinctively. "Petra, if I don't leave this room right now, I'm going to end up bending you over a workbench — after I give you the face fucking of your *life* for the shit you just told me. Be fuckin' grateful I'm giving you a reprieve. Go through all the shit in the boxes while you have the chance and then make peace with the fact that I'm never gonna leave you alone again."

Words escaped her. She watched in stunned silence as Silas's head swiveled back around. The muscles of his back stretched and bunched as he stalked out of the lab and disappeared up the stairs.

His harsh declaration rang in her ears, almost painful in its impact. *I'm never gonna leave you alone again.*

She gripped the edge of a workbench, her shoulders rounding with the force of her relief. She couldn't say it, but the scared little voice in the back of her mind dared to whisper, *Thank you, gods, for sending me the mate I need.*

Chapter Thirty-Nine

He gave her until supper.

It nearly killed him to do it, but he did. Flushed with hormones and the instinct to guard his new mate, it was a special kind of torture to keep a whole house between them, but he knew it was necessary.

He was too angry to be trusted with her. It wasn't because he would ever intentionally hurt her, but because he worried he wouldn't be able to control his other impulses. Not just the rut, but the driving need to make her his mate in all ways.

He'd claimed her, but he didn't *have* her. He didn't have her secrets. He barely had her trust. And now he knew that all along, she'd never intended to give him her bond.

That alone didn't bother him, really. In fact, he was actually a little proud of her for double crossing him like that. He adored the conniving part of her. In her place, he would have done the same.

What made him want to rip the walls down was the reasoning behind it. She didn't double cross him with a grand plan to somehow wiggle out of their deal — a doomed prospect, but a commendable one. No, she'd agreed to giving him her bond because she believed either Vanderpoel would take it before he could, or she'd be dead.

He could hear it in her voice, see it in her expression. Even if she never said it aloud, a large part of Petra hadn't believed that she would make it out of that belltower alive.

That really, *really* pissed him off.

It was misery knowing that something essential to him existed inside her now — a soft, squishy, vulnerable thing he couldn't live without. She held it in her powerful hands without even realizing it was there. If something were to happen to her, that essential part of him would die, too.

His mother would say that seeing Petra shot had put the fear of the gods in him. But he didn't fear the gods. Before Petra, he'd never feared anything at all. Now he feared losing his mate before he ever got the chance to have her. He feared losing her in the same way a normal man might agonize over his own death.

No punishment from the gods could be worse than that.

Now that he knew how vulnerable he was, it made him go more than a little bat-shit to think she'd consigned herself to death all along.

Back in the lab, Silas had been about two seconds and one bad thought away from laying her down on his desk, thrusting his cock in to the hilt, and making her swear that she'd never, ever scare him like that again. He wanted to punish her, to make a point, and demand an endless string of promises to soothe that awful, nauseating terror that made a permanent home for itself inside him.

He didn't like being scared and he refused to feel it again. If that meant he had to fuck her hard and fast and mean until she learned her lesson, then he'd do it. But that was the rut and the bastard in him speaking. The logical part of him — and the new, uncertain mate — managed, by the skin of their teeth, to be just a bit louder than his base impulses.

She was recovering. She needed time. If he punished her like he wanted to, he'd tip over into his rut and she wasn't ready for that. He'd fail her again, and he'd hurt her, and she'd leave him because that would be the right thing for any sane person to do.

So he fled, for both their sakes.

But that was then. Now, he watched her like a hungry animal from across the table, a heated casserole set between them. She'd put on some comfortable clothes and pulled her hair up since he last saw her. He'd heard her, though, moving around quietly, doing gods-knew-what with those boxes.

He'd posted up in the living room all day with his tablet and tried to lose himself in decrypting the data he'd stolen, but he'd only been partially successful in keeping his mind occupied and wholly unsuccessful in making any headway. Turns out Vanderpoel wasn't quite as self-assured as he first appeared. The data was locked behind an impressive, multi-layered encryption that, even after the discovery of a backdoor vulnerability, would take his automated systems weeks to crack.

Luckily they had the time to spare. Now that the man was dead, what was the rush? Silas intended to take his time with his witch, who everyone believed was on sabbatical anyway. Even if she wanted to, it was too dangerous for her to return to San Francisco. Laying low was the only option for her — and a boon for him.

Petra looked nervous. That normally would have pleased him because he liked seeing her off-kilter, her masks discarded. Tonight he found it grating.

There were dark circles under her eyes. Her cheeks looked too thin. Even her hair had lost a bit of its luster.

This was not his little goddess. This was a woman who'd been pushed to her limit, and instead of turning to him for support, she fidgeted with her fork and refused to make eye contact with him.

Wrong, his instincts berated him. *You've done something wrong.*

Beginning with their doomed creator, Blight, demons were

unerringly devoted mates. They were supposed to be trustworthy and loyal. They were supposed to know how to *care.*

He didn't know how to do any of that. All he understood was cause and effect, reward and punishment. Stick and carrot. Those techniques had gotten him everywhere in life, but they were almost useless in a successful mating. A part of him wished Tal was around to tell him how to act. Tal wasn't normal either, but he'd been around so long, seen so much, that he'd know what to do.

When Silas was a child, Tal taught him how to navigate a world that rarely made any sense to him. He was the only one who seemed to really speak Silas's language.

As far as Tal was aware, he'd never been a mate in his previous life, but Silas knew he wanted to be one with a frankly unhealthy desperation. It was about eighty percent of the reason his brother wanted a body. Surely, after watching and learning for so long, he'd know what to do and could tell Silas how to fix this.

Unfortunately, the thought of his brother entering Silas's den *now,* just before the rut, made him flex his claws beneath the table.

It didn't matter that Tal was, for all intents and purposes, a ghost and therefore unable to compete for Silas's mate. He couldn't stomach having him or anyone else near her, in their den, during such a vulnerable time.

Tal understood that, of course. He'd taken off as soon as they made it to Silas's parents' house. While he was certain Tal was avoiding a blistering tirade over his failure to keep Petra in the closet, Silas would bet the house that the bulk of the reason he hadn't darkened their door was a respect for the new boundaries that had been drawn.

None of that helped Silas as he glared at his mate from across the table.

He decided he wasn't going to be angry at her anymore. Being angry apparently meant not hearing her voice, and that was more of a punishment for him than her. Not to mention that he discovered he didn't *like* being mad at her, even when he knew he had the right to be.

Being happy with her, entertained by her, lusting after her — those were all far more pleasurable ways to spend his time.

"Did you find what you wanted in the boxes?"

She rubbed the edge of her thumb nail into a groove in the table. Her eyes were down, attention fixed on the food she moved around her plate. "Yes and no. There's hundreds of files in them. I went through the ones he had on me and Max, but I didn't find anything incriminating — other than the fact that he'd connected us through that stupid post office box. Everything is— It's too much. Some of the photos, the records... I could barely stomach peeking at them. And then there's the *scale* of it all. I have no idea where to start. Max refused to tell me anything, so I'm stumbling blindly through hundreds of years of some of the saddest, most vile secrets I can imagine."

She sounded downtrodden. *Damn.*

Silas shifted in his seat and just barely stopped himself from rubbing his horn. "What did you expect? That he'd keep all his grand plans in *paper* files?"

He hadn't meant for that to come out as harsh as it did. Apparently his tone hadn't gotten the memo about letting his anger go. Petra's flinch was a splash of acid on the new, tender part of him.

Her fingers tightened around her fork as she drew her elbow in toward her side, unconsciously making herself smaller. Silas hated that. She wasn't supposed to be small. She was powerful and beautiful and fearless and canny. The fact that *he'd* made her shrink away like that was... bad.

Silas prided himself on being able to fix anything — cars, wards, guns, microchips, *anything.* It was disorienting in the extreme to realize he had no idea how to fix *this,* the most important and complex thing he'd ever held in his hands. Their relationship felt so delicate. One wrong move and he'd crush it.

What would Tal do? Silas tried to conjure the wraith's voice in his mind, to imagine what he might say in this situation.

Trying hard to soften his tone, he told her, "I didn't get a good look at everything before shit hit the fan, but it seemed to me like he's been keeping those files for a century at least. My guess is he just didn't go through the hassle of digitizing them like the rest of his more recent files."

She still didn't look up at him. "My file was printed."

"And it looked like he had it tucked away in his briefcase for ease of access. Who knows? Maybe he was too old to figure out how to easily access shit on his phone. Or maybe he just liked to look at your picture." Silas scowled at her plate. She hadn't eaten a bite, which was unlike her. "I stole a metric shit-ton of data from his computers, as well as several encrypted hard drives. I think you'll have better luck finding whatever he's been up to once I've decrypted them. It's gonna take a while, though."

"Right. Okay."

They lapsed into silence again. He normally liked quiet, but this was a kind of silence he'd never heard before. It was the loudest fucking thing on the planet.

Where was his little goddess? Where was the woman who'd thrown a punch at his head the second she was able to?

Longing for that car ride to his cabin struck him hard. He didn't realize at the time how happy it made him to sit with her, needling her, as she secretly enjoyed the food he'd gotten her. The car was dark and close — the opposite of the airy kitchen and the stupid table that separated them.

Fuck this.

Silas dropped his fork onto his plate and pushed away from the table. Petra jumped. He could feel her gaze tracking him as he stalked out of the room.

When he returned a few minutes later, he found the table cleared and the casserole put away. She was scrubbing her plate in the sink with quick and jerky movements, her back to him. Her shoulders looked like they'd been hoisted up by her ears with rope.

He hovered in the doorway, afraid that if he stepped into the kitchen again, he'd abandon his plans and just throw her over his shoulder. The idea had appeal, except for the fact that he'd almost certainly vault up the stairs and end up throwing her into their bed.

Rest. Recovery. Then *rut.*

"Petra." She froze mid-scrub. "There's snacks in the cabinets. Grab as much as you can and meet me in the living room."

He didn't stay to see what she'd do. If she didn't join him, then he'd figure out something else, but he had a feeling she'd do it, if only because his witch was nosy by nature. No one who went digging for the truth with as much dogged intensity as she did lacked a keen sense of curiosity.

So he waited, listening to the sounds from the kitchen, and held his breath. There was a pause, then the gurgle of the sink draining. A splash of water from the spout was followed by the clink of dishware being set in the drying rack.

Then, slowly, feet padded over the floor. It filled him with immense satisfaction to know that under those perfect toes were slate tiles whose undersides were carved with his own sigilwork. Nearly every part of the house was saturated in his magic. She lived in an invisible fortress, protected from everything short of a nuclear bomb.

His pleasure and anticipation increased when she began to open up cabinets. He silently thanked his parents for the grocery run they'd done for him. Still listening, Silas peeled himself away from his hiding spot just out of view of the kitchen doorway and silently crept toward the living room.

He snagged a bottle of his family's whiskey from the antique cart by the door before he recalled she didn't drink hard liquor. He traded it out for red wine. Dropping to his knees, he crawled one-handed into the blanket fort he'd thrown together.

Anticipation was a feeling he knew well, but he experienced a new shade of it as he waited for Petra to make her way to him. His leg bounced. His muscles were tense, jittery. The urge to rub a horn was constant. Silas plucked the cork from the wine with a claw and found himself taking a deep pull just so he had something to do.

The sound of fabric rustling, feet on hardwood, and the crinkle of wrappers was both sweet relief and a shot of adrenaline to his system.

She paused outside the makeshift tent. He could see her toes under the flap of the entrance. Otherwise she was just a silhouette, backlit by the single lamp he'd kept on. Warm light filtered through the blanket, just enough for her to see by when she entered, but still dim enough for him to recreate that soft closeness he craved.

It took a lot of willpower to restrain himself from snapping a hand around her ankle and dragging her inside.

His patience was rewarded when she knelt and nudged the flap aside.

Petra's expression was wide-eyed when she whispered, "What is this?"

"Get in." He leaned over to take some of the food from her arms, allowing her to crawl in.

She settled into the cushions he'd arrayed on the floor a bit like she was expecting a trap to spring. "Silas, what's going on?"

"I hated sitting at the table," he explained, setting the food around them. He wanted to pull her into his lap, but the skittish look in her eyes warned him against that, so he contented himself with being so very close to her in the semi-dark. Her rich scent of sunshine and incense immediately perfumed the air inside, mixing with his own musk. A tight knot between his shoulders began to unwind.

Much better.

"Why did you hate the table?"

"Because you were too far away." He snagged a bag of chips

and tore it open. "And you weren't eating anything. I thought maybe this would be better for both of us."

He offered her the bag. When she continued to stare at him with those wide eyes, he shook it a little, tempting her with greasy, salty potatoes. "Go on. You need to eat, baby."

Her lips trembled. "You're... you're not mad at me?"

"Not anymore." Silas frowned. He glanced at the bag in his hand. "D'you not want chips?"

He nearly dropped the bag when Petra flung herself at him. Her arms coiled around his neck as she half-crawled, half-leapt into his lap. "What is this?" he demanded, reflexively wrapping an arm around her waist. "What's happening?"

She pressed her face into his hair and clung as tight as a barnacle to him. "I'm really sorry. I'm really, really sorry I lied to you."

"Sorry?" It took him a second to figure out what she was talking about, let alone process the fact that she was apologizing. To *him*. He wasn't sure anyone had ever done that before. Not for anything that mattered, anyway.

Silas set the chips aside as he tried to arch his neck to get a look at her face. It wasn't easy when she was stuck to him like that. Not that he was complaining. Having her skin to skin again after so many hours apart was paradise.

Still, he wanted to look into her face when he asked, "You think I was pissed because you *lied?*"

Petra nodded. Despite his best efforts, her face remained hidden.

Silas gave up trying to catch her gaze. Instead, he leaned forward a bit until he was stooped over her, his arms looped around her back. This way it felt a bit like he was hiding her, gathering her close enough that she might be able to just burrow inside him, where he could keep her to himself forever.

Shadows crept around her legs, holding her in all the places his arms couldn't, when he explained, "Baby, I don't give a fuck that you played me. If you didn't try *something*, I would've been disappointed, frankly. What pissed me off was the fact that you didn't seem to care that you could have died. That's not fuckin' allowed."

"I cared," she whispered into his skin. "It just... it just seemed like the trade I was going to have to make. And it's not like I had anything to lose."

Pissed all over again, he snapped, "Fuck that! You're the High Priestess of San Francisco. You're Petra *motherfucking* Zaskodna. What do you *mean* you don't have anything to lose?"

She seemed awfully small and breakable in his arms. He loved and hated that. Having her vulnerability in his hands was a heady, powerful thing, but seeing her *diminished* was sour. Ugly.

He'd experienced her small and soft before, but not like this. He wanted that other version back. He wanted the Petra who could be vulnerable with him but still fearless, confident, and powerful even when she submitted to him.

"I'm a fraud, Silas," she answered. "I lied to become High Priestess. I'm nothing and no one. My entire family is dead. I don't have a coven. I'm just an orphan from the streets of Los Angeles playing dress-up and hoping I don't get caught. And now — now I'm even less than that."

"So?"

"So?" Petra finally pulled back enough to give him an incredulous look. That was better than tears. He loathed her tears.

"So what?" he repeated impatiently. "So you're no one. I'm no one. So you lied. I lie every day. So your family is dead and you don't have a coven to back you up. Take my clan. I've got more than enough family to spare." Silas skimmed her cheek with his lips until he found her ear. "You're a survivor. You're San Francisco's High Priestess. You got justice for someone you loved. You're ruthless and intelligent and ballsy. Best of all, you're *mine.*"

Petra tilted her head, putting them cheek to cheek. Her chest brushed his when she breathed deeply. "How is it that you can make me feel so powerful, demon?"

"Because I'm the only person lucky enough to see all of you," he replied. "That means I can tell you how it really is, even when you might not want me to. You can't hide from me."

He could feel the curve of her smile. "Are you sure you don't just enjoy giving me shit?"

"Can't it be both?"

Petra's arms uncoiled from around his neck. Before he could inform her that he had no intention of letting her go, she cupped his cheeks and pressed a series of soft, whispery kisses to his lips. His chest went tight with each one, making it hard to breathe.

Maybe he was dying. It felt like it. Not that he cared.

"You *are* a little shit," she murmured, "you're definitely a bad person, and I'm pretty sure you're crazy, but I think I adore you, Silas. I really do."

The tightness made it difficult to speak, but he managed to inform her, "I'm going to make you happy. Then you'll like me even more and never want to leave."

"You keep saying that." She snagged one of his hands and, after a brief struggle to unlock his arm from its place around her waist, brought it up to her heart. Petra gave him such a look that Silas went from *"maybe I'm dying"* to *"maybe I've already died"* in a heartbeat.

"Demon, I don't want to leave you. I don't plan to leave you. In fact, there isn't even the smallest part of me that wishes I was anywhere else." She paused, lips quirking. "Now, pass me the chips, please."

CHAPTER FORTY

HE'D NEVER HAD A FAVORITE SOUND BEFORE, BUT Petra's laughter was without a doubt the best thing he'd ever heard.

No one had ever found him funny. People tended to be too afraid of him for that, or else he ruined what might have been a light moment by saying something that normal people found disturbing.

Silas knew that he hadn't really changed since he met Petra. He was the same as he always was, except now there was a new place inside him, carved by Petra's soft hands to fit her and her alone.

He still said the wrong thing. He still lacked that fundamental thing that made a person *normal*.

But Petra said she adored him, and that changed how he *felt*.

She lounged in the blanket fort with him for hours, passing snacks back and forth to replace the dinner they'd abandoned. Whenever he said something he knew logically was inappropriate, she didn't balk. Petra rolled her eyes, maybe released a scandalized snort. If he was really lucky, she laughed.

As the night wore on and they couldn't stomach more chips or candy, they lay there in the darkness facing one another. She was loose-limbed and soft. Her breath smelled very faintly like wine and sugar. Her hands rested lightly on his chest, the pads of her fingers tickling the base of his throat. They were unnaturally warm and glowed just enough for his demon eyes to catch.

Silas understood passion. Lust.

Tenderness was new.

He found himself gorging on it, on this precious, astonishing softness she showed him. His hands roamed greedily over her side, her hip, her back. Despite his nearly constantly hard cock, it wasn't a lustful touch necessarily, but a craving to feel every part of her at once. His shadows wove around her in a living blanket, similarly unable to pick a favorite part to settle on, and whenever they brushed her hands, she'd smile and spread her fingers encouragingly.

They'd been talking for long enough that their voices had begun to roughen, but he couldn't get enough of her husky voice. It didn't matter what she was talking about. If it was feasible, he would have demanded she never stop talking.

Eventually, as the mood deepened into something nuanced and sweet as molasses, Silas found himself unable to hold back his curiosity any longer. "Why do you really hide food?"

Petra's eyes were closed. She didn't open them when she answered, "I told you it's a sad story."

He figured as much. A part of him truly didn't want to know, only because it would drive him nuts that he couldn't go back and fix it for her. But the bigger part of him, the one that contained the pathological curiosity, had to fill in all those blank spaces in Petra's past so he could understand her *now.*

"Tell me," he urged, rubbing the side of his thumb over her spine.

She took a moment to adjust the position of her head on a pillow, bringing it just a little closer to his. Her fingers slid under the collar of his t-shirt. He suspected she sought his touch for comfort.

How novel.

"You know about my family already. My mom and her brothers moved to Los Angeles just after the war ended. They mainly moved guns and alcohol. Small-time stuff that got bigger over time."

Petra rubbed his skin in a back and forth motion. Her eyes stayed closed, but he could see them flickering beneath her eyelids, as if she were watching the events of her life playing across the pink insides.

"My family was always poor and arrant. No magic, no connections except for the ones we'd made ourselves. When the gun business really took off with all the leftovers from the war, we were doing better than we ever had. My mom met my dad through a friend of a friend and when he proved himself to my uncle, he joined the business. Then I was born. And not long after that, Mad Thad restructured the territory."

Ice tipped into his veins. He was only a decade older than Petra and grew up in rural Appalachia, so he wasn't exactly tuned into major political movements in the 1970's, but he knew the broad strokes. Enough to understand where the story went off the rails, at least.

"The EVP was a mess at that time," she explained, not quite bitterly but not unaffected, either. "Black markets were everywhere. The infrastructure was destroyed by the war. People like my dad and uncles were flooding the market with new, more dangerous weapons that went mysteriously missing from every army in the UTA. That's how my uncle met Rasmus, as well as a lot of other unsavory types. There wasn't enough food for normal people. The elves were in a silent civil war. Los Angeles was a cesspool of desperate people looking for work, food, or guns. For the people my family knew, it was usually all three."

His home hadn't fared much better, but the chaos hadn't been as centralized. Mostly that was because dragons had razed nearly every major population center in the Neutral Zone at least once during the one hundred year war that altered every aspect of life in the UTA. There were simply fewer places for chaos to cluster.

Petra took a deep breath before she continued, "Sometimes we were poor, but mostly things were pretty good for the criminals in my family — until Mad Thad decided enough was enough and ordered the major elvish families to get a handle on their territories or he'd take it from them. Suddenly there was law and order. Curfews. Raids. Overnight, easy money became gang wars in the streets as people fought to hold onto what they had.

"My uncles died one by one. I could see Max withering away from grief as the violence just kept going on and on. He tried to convince my parents to get out while they could, but they didn't have anything else to fall back on. They spent all their money on alcohol and had no skills, no training for anything like normal life." She shook her head a little, as if she had to dislodge something from within her mind.

Silas pulled her closer and, swinging one thigh over her hip, pressed her face into the hollow of his throat. His heart pounded as he imagined all the things she wasn't telling him. The shock of swinging back and forth between prosperity and poverty. The neglect she must have suffered from parents who were so wrapped up in themselves. The fear of living in a city on the brink of violence every day.

And we haven't even gotten to the bad parts yet. Cold sweat broke out across the back of his neck.

Petra's voice went soft and small when she said, "Max was shot and I guess he finally had enough. One day, my uncle just disappeared. Everyone said he'd died from the shot. I was heartbroken. My parents loved me, but he was the only one who ever seemed to *care.*"

Silas bit his tongue hard enough to taste blood. It was clear even to someone like him that Petra was an utterly devoted niece and had viewed the dead priest as a father, but that didn't color how *Silas* saw him.

The man known as Maximilian Dooraker had abandoned

Petra. Instead of whisking her away from a situation with no happy endings, he let her think he was dead.

If you were here, old man, I'd break every one of your fingers one by one. Snap, snap, snap. And when he was done, he'd push Dooraker to his knees and make him recount every sin against Petra until his throat was too raw to speak.

And then Silas would take his head, too.

His mate's soft voice broke through the haze of rage that had overtaken him. "I was ten when my parents were shot in a deal gone bad. My dad used me as a runner sometimes. I didn't see it, but I was hiding close by when— when it happened. When I finally worked up the courage to come out of my hiding spot, I found them face-down in the street."

The breath exploded out of him. "What did you do?"

Petra's fingers twisted in his shirt when she murmured, "I don't like to talk about this part."

His skin crawled at the implication in that quiet statement. What could be worse than what she'd already recounted?

"You don't have to," he said, trying to remind himself that if he squeezed her any harder, she wouldn't be able to breathe.

"No, I want you to know. No one else does."

"Did your uncle?"

There was a long, tense pause. "Max struggled with a lot of what he'd done. I think he spent most of his time in service to the Temple asking the gods for forgiveness. But... but he didn't like to talk about it. He never asked me for details. Once he found me, that was it. All better. Whenever I mentioned something, he'd go all white and— I always got the feeling that if I told him everything that had happened after my parents' death, he would've never recovered."

He took back the fantasy of breaking Maximilian's fingers. *I'd shatter his fuckin' spine, vertebrae by vertebrae.*

"The short version of the story is that I had nowhere to go and no one to trust, so I lived on the streets for a year," she told him, speaking quickly like she needed to get the words out as fast as possible. "I was used to not getting regular meals by then, but obviously it got way worse when I was sleeping in alleys. I had to hoard any kind of scraps I found, since I never knew when I'd find more or if they'd get stolen by someone bigger than me."

Early in his career, Silas had once botched a job so bad that he ended up strapped to a chair as a big, ugly vampire pulled his claws out one by one. Hearing that she'd been a homeless little girl fighting to survive on food she found in trash cans was worse. Much worse.

"I ended up getting caught by Patrol," she admitted. "I was terrified of them, but the elves were shockingly nice to me. I didn't know at the time that they've got crazy childcare instincts, but even if I had, I probably would have been terrified anyway. My dad taught me that Patrol meant trouble.

"They gave me new clothes, lots of food, and a bed to sleep in at the station. A nice elvish lady even washed and braided my hair for me as she asked me all kinds of questions I couldn't answer. Where were my parents? How long had I been lost? Did I have any relatives?"

She laughed a sad, watery little laugh. Not the kind he loved. This one broke his heart. "I spent my whole life believing that the elves were the enemy. They were the ones who had ruined my family. They were the scary predators who would eat me if I stepped out of line. But by the time they found a place for me in a magically gifted children's home, I was desperate to stay with them."

His stomach sank. *Children's home?*

Of course the elves couldn't keep her. It wasn't until basically yesterday that they'd even begun to publicly take non-elves as mates. Fostering a non-elvish child would have been culturally taboo and also legally dubious at best.

But in the years since the last one closed down, the children's homes that had sprung up across the UTA to care for the generation of orphans left by the war had become synonymous with neglect.

"Why couldn't they find you a foster home?" There was a desperate edge to his voice, as if he hoped her answer could somehow change the facts of the past.

Petra sighed. "The thought is that children should be placed with families that can understand them — dragons to dragons, elves to elves, witches to witches. There've been too many catastrophic accidents and misunderstandings to place a witch of my power into, say, an arrant family, despite the fact that I came from one. What if I had behavioral issues? What if I couldn't control my abilities? Someone could get seriously hurt.

"But this wasn't the Coven Collective, Silas. Even if they did find a witch family to send me to, everyone was fighting to survive. No one could take on one more mouth to feed. When they couldn't find a witch family to foster me, I was sent to a private facility that specialized in magical children."

"Tell me it wasn't bad." He whispered the words into her hair. He demanded it. *Tell me something good happened to you. Please.*

Petra's silence was its own answer long before she finally replied, "It could have been worse."

Fuck.

"Mostly we were forgotten about, which, looking back, was probably a blessing in disguise. Mostly that meant we didn't get fed and violence broke out, but it also meant that children weren't being outright abused." She shrugged. "I know that's a messed up thing to say, but it's the truth. I've heard horror stories about what went on in other children's homes. My experience was bad, but not *that* bad."

Yes, he could understand that. All things were relative. That didn't make it right, and it didn't lessen his rage, but he understood it. "How long were you there?"

"Four years."

The blanks filled in. Suddenly everything that had so baffled him about Petra's mysterious past came into focus. His stomach turned.

She hid food because, for at least five of her most formative years but probably more, she'd had to carefully hoard every single calorie she could. She hid her past because it was full of blood and crime and the failures of the state. She hated guns because they'd been the cause, directly and indirectly, of her family's demise. She was so fiercely loyal to a dead man because he was all she had. She lied and masked herself because it was the only way she knew how to survive a world that had brutalized her at nearly every turn.

He remembered the candies he'd stolen from her, and then he remembered how she'd offered him a bit of her protein bar. He remembered, imagining a little girl huddling in an alley, and all he wanted to do was rip his hair out by the roots.

When he didn't say anything — *couldn't* — Petra wryly noted, "I told you it's a sad story."

"I need to know it got better," he grated. "I need to— I need you to be okay."

He knew intellectually it was wrong to allow her to soothe him when she was the one so obviously in need of comfort, but he was too selfish to push her away when she made soft nonsense sounds and stroked his chest.

"I'm okay," she whispered. "The children's home was shut down. Max found me because he had contacts watching for my name in the foster system for years. He got me out and gave me a new life."

"In the Temple?" Silas couldn't help the loathing that slipped into his voice.

"It was my choice. He gave me three options: I could live with a foster family he chose in the Collective, I could join the Temple as an initiate, or he could leave his work to live with me."

A more generous man would have given Dooraker points for offering to leave his vocation for his orphaned niece, but Silas had never been called generous in his life. The fact that he didn't abandon his post immediately upon learning that Petra might be out there on her own was damning.

His clan wouldn't have slept. They wouldn't have eaten. If one of their children was orphaned, lost in a city and thrown into the system, they would have ripped through the streets in a shadow-cloaked mob until they got her back. And if it was *his* daughter... Silas would have done far worse.

He'd never before considered himself particularly lucky to have his clan. They were a fixture in his life in the same way that his house was. He liked it. He made sure it didn't get run down. He came back to it a few times a year, and he knew it'd be there waiting for him whenever he finished whatever it was that had occupied him.

But now, holding his mate close, he discovered a keen appreciation for the gift that he'd been given — and the one he could now offer her.

"Why did you choose the Temple?"

"A couple reasons." The tension gradually began to flow out of her body, once more leaving her relaxed and soft in his arms. "Most of those boil down to the fact that Max had just been appointed High Priest and that I had no future. My education was laughable. The idea of trying to enter the school system and catch up at fifteen was terrifying. I knew that I'd get a similar education as an initiate, but in a much more private environment. The final reason was because..."

Her voice went so quiet he had to strain to hear her. "When I was sleeping in the gaps between fences and under porches, praying that no one would find me while I snatched an hour of sleep, I swear I felt Glory with me." Her breath hitched, forcing her to pause.

"It can get so cold at night, Silas, even in LA. There were a few times when I thought for sure I was going to die. I was so miserable and afraid that I didn't care. But then I'd feel— there would be this warmth, this touch to my face like my mom used to do when I got sick, and suddenly I was okay. I could rest."

Even he knew better than to argue about the many causes one could point to for her experience that had nothing to do with a goddess. Hypothermia was a tricky bitch who liked to disguise cold for heat whenever it struck her, for one, and for another,

Petra was a young witch coming into her power. There was every chance that her abilities kicked in when she went into survival mode, heating her from within.

And he couldn't help but think about what a goddess of sunlight might be doing in the shadows, comforting lost little girls. She wasn't known for her love of darkness, nor her gentleness.

That seemed an awful lot like something a wraith might do.

None of that mattered, though, because taking it away from Petra served no purpose. If she wanted to believe that Glory kept her alive in the darkest moments of her life, then so be it.

What mattered now was his absolute and unwavering certainty that Petra would never need to rely on faith to see her through darkness again. Now, and perhaps for far longer than she realized, the darkness was her protector.

"You know, I feel a little bad," she admitted, sounding chagrined. "One of the reasons I was so shocked when I met your parents was because— Well, I didn't expect you to come from such a normal family. I thought maybe you'd have a story a bit like mine."

It was hard to set aside the storm that raged in him. He wanted so badly to rain an unholy cataclysm on all the things that had hurt his mate when he wasn't looking. He wanted to burn houses and break bones and systematically ruin the lives of every single person who'd failed her.

But he couldn't. Not yet, anyway.

So he forced himself to reply, "You're not the first to wonder about that, I reckon. A number of therapists asked me questions about my home life when my parents weren't in the room. I think folks want to believe that evil has a root in tragedy and misfortune only. They want to be able to easily explain why someone can be what I am. It gives them false hope that maybe they can stop it from happening again."

He hitched her a little closer, until he was nearly sprawled on top of her. Petra didn't complain. She let out a content sigh and rubbed the inside of his calf with her toes.

"Truth is," he whispered, "sometimes we're just born a little wrong and a lot evil."

"You don't think that amoral people can be made?"

"Sure I do, but the difference is that most folks aren't made that way from scratch. Circumstance isn't the only thing that makes the man. Evil, *real* evil, comes from a sterile place in the mind. It can't be tampered with or planted there. It just is." And, considering who he was and what he'd seen in his life, Silas counted himself as an authority on the subject. "People like me... we can't be normal. We can't be taught to care like you care. Doesn't matter how much love we're given or how hard a clan tries."

Petra's volume didn't rise, but there was steel in her voice all the same when she declared, "I don't believe that. Not about you, at least."

"Baby," he said, as gently as he was capable of, "you can't fix me. It won't work."

"Did I say I wanted to?" Petra wiggled until there was enough room to glare at him. Her eyes were slightly unfocused, so he doubted she could really see him, but he felt that glare all the way down to his toes anyway. "Other people have tried to change you, Silas, but you'll never hear that from me. I like you how you are, as fucked up as that might be. What I'm saying is that you're wrong about your ability to care."

He shook his head. "Petra, it's not—"

Doing a truly impressive impression of a demon, she growled, "No, you listen to me. I want you to tell me to my face that you don't care about me. Go on. Do it."

Silas reared his head back to give an incredulous look. His stomach turned. "No."

"Why not?"

"Because— because I don't want to."

"You don't want to or you can't?" Before he could figure out the answer himself, she arched her neck to deliver a swift, brutal kiss. Speaking into his mouth, she hissed, "You care about me. You can deny it until you're ready, but it's the truth. If you didn't, we wouldn't be here. I wouldn't be alive. You wouldn't be holding me like you're afraid I'll disappear. You just wouldn't."

"What if I can't ever give you more than this?" He didn't even realize the fear existed, deep and thorny inside of him, until the words left his mouth. *What if I'm a bad mate? What if I hurt you?*

They shared breath, their world so small and dark and perfect in that tiny blanket fort. Their bodies were a tangle and their words were harsh but soft, like bristles of velvet brushed the wrong way.

Petra's lips softened, but her ferocity didn't. "Then I'll take everything else you have to give me."

CHAPTER FORTY-ONE

PETRA SAT AT SILAS'S FEET IN THE LIVING ROOM. Arrayed around her were the trunks he'd stolen, some of them opened and others not. She felt slimy pawing through them, seeing all the names of people whose lives had been held in the palm of Antonin's hand. Originally she'd set up in the middle of the floor, but when Silas sat down to work on the decryption on the couch, she'd inched her way over until she leaned against his leg.

Things had been bizarrely peaceful since their talk in the blanket fort the previous night. Petra knew it was a peace that wouldn't last, and not just because his rut brewed like a storm on the horizon. Her problems didn't disappear just because they were tucked away in the wilderness somewhere. But when she was with him, she felt like her feet were on solid ground for the first time in years. The world might continue to spin around her, but when Silas held her, she wouldn't spin with it.

Not when she was his mate, and not when he fisted his hand around her ponytail and tilted her head back like that.

She blinked up at him, lust curling in her belly at the light sting in her scalp. He watched her from under heavy lids, his tablet loosely held in his other hand, and murmured, "I fuckin' love it when you look up at me like that."

"Like what?"

His grip tightened, forcing the arch of her neck into a sharper angle. "When you're at my feet and you look up at me like you'd let me do anything to you."

"I like how you look at me, too," she admitted.

"Yeah? Tell me how I look at you."

"Like you want to eat me."

A low rumbling sound erupted from his chest — not quite a growl and not quite a purr, but something in the middle. "You have no idea how much I want to eat you, baby."

Her heart thumped unevenly in her chest. Speaking with more bravado than she felt, she challenged, "Why don't you?"

Silas set his tablet aside and leaned over her. The hand not tangled in her ponytail cupped the side of her head as he skimmed his lips over hers. "Because, little goddess," he whispered, "if I get another taste of that pretty pussy, it'll send me straight into rut. And then I'll fuck you until you beg me to let you rest."

She hardly breathed. Heat flashed over her skin as her magic bubbled inside of her, mixing with lust to make a potent cocktail of power and desire. A keen longing made her want to provoke him, to make his filthy promises a reality.

There'd been so much relief in giving him power over her. Everything went soft and out of focus when he used her, moved her, fucked her mouth until she gagged. Petra had only gotten to experience that freedom so briefly in the cathedral. She wanted that peace back with a sudden, piercing ache.

"Will you?"

His tongue snaked out to taste her bottom lip. "Will I what?"

"Will you let me rest if I beg you?"

His lips curved against hers. "No, baby. I won't. Do you like that?"

"Yes," she breathed.

"Such a good girl." Silas stroked his hand down her throat,

then down under the collar of the shirt she'd borrowed from him. He cupped her breast. Teasing her hardened nipple with his callused thumb, he asked, "Do you like it when I have the power? When I tell you no?"

Petra's bare toes curled. "Yeah."

"My powerful little goddess needs me," he murmured, teasing her with the tip of his tongue and those gentle touches. "You need me to make you feel small and safe. You need me to tell you what to do. You need me to make you come."

None of those things were questions, so she didn't bother denying it. He knew it was true no matter what she might have said. Still, she couldn't help but poke at him just a little bit.

Slowly moving her head back and forth, stroking her mouth against his, she gave into the urge to tease him just a little. "I could make myself come." *But I prefer when you do it.*

In an instant, his delicate touches to her nipple turned into a cruel pinch. Petra gasped, back arching, as a bolt of heat arrowed down her spine to settle between her thighs.

Silas's soft croon didn't change, but she felt the tension in his body and the corresponding tightening of the shadows around her throat when he replied, "You touch that pussy without my permission, little goddess, and I'll introduce you to my belt."

Good gods. Her heartbeat pounded between her thighs as she squirmed there at his feet. She'd never had any inclination toward letting a partner discipline her, but if it was Silas...

Her head filled with a pleasant sort of static and her spine lost its tension as she leaned into him. It wasn't the idea of punishment that made her go soft and wet, but the understanding that Silas had the power to do it if he wanted to. He could take whatever he wanted. Give whatever he wanted.

But he wouldn't hurt her. At least, not in any way she wouldn't end up liking.

Her trust in him was, much to her astonishment, complete.

"Do you like the sound of that, baby?" Silas sucked in a deep, deep breath. When he released it, that rumble in his chest turned into a purr. "Yeah, you do. You're dripping for me right now. What a perfect mate I have."

Her heart skipped a beat. It was one thing to know she was his mate, but to hear him say it aloud with so much desire in his voice was quite another. Reaching up to feather her fingertips over his curls, she whispered, "Is this how it's going to be with us?"

"Do you want it to be?"

Petra's instinct was to say yes immediately, but she stopped herself. This thing, *them*, deserved more thought than that.

Slowly, she asked her own question, "If I didn't, could you live with that?"

Would you still want me?

The hand on her breast moved upward to cover the spot over her heart. "You know the day we made our deal? You were looking at me like you wanted to rip my head off with your bare hands and I thought, *I don't care if I never get to fuck her. She's mine.*"

He pulled back enough to look her in the eye when he continued, "I like dominating you. If I could shrink you down and lock you away inside of me, I'd do it. But if that's not what you need, what'll make you happy, then I don't give a fuck. I'm not giving you up, so you better tell me how to do this right."

"I don't want you to humiliate me or anything like that," she said, forcing the words out through a tight throat. It was weird to have to talk about these things, but freeing in its own way. "But the rest— I like it. It makes me feel..." *Like I'm taken care of. Like I can relax for a second.* "Steady. It makes me feel steady."

As much as she wanted him to move his hands elsewhere, Silas returned to stroking her throat. The look in his eyes was warm with approval. "I'd never humiliate you. You giving me this power is heady as fuck. You trusting me is a gift no one else has ever or will ever give me. I'm not going to blow that by pretending you're not worth a thousand of me. So no degradation, no humiliation. Just control. I won't give you an inch of space, baby, because that's what you need."

Petra searched his expression. "And what about your rut?"

The muscles around his jaw tensed. He took a second to breathe before he answered, "The only reason I'm holding off is because you need to recover. If it weren't for you almost dying, I'd have my cock in you right now."

"I'm pretty sure I can handle sex." And gods, she *wanted* to. Not only because it was what her body craved, but because she desperately wanted to ignore reality and everything in the horrible red trunks for a little while longer.

Silas gave her a narrow-eyed look. "I said no. Not because I'm some fuckin' saint, but because it's not just sex. The rut lasts weeks and is brutal even when it's normal. This one won't be normal."

"Why?"

"Because you're my mate," he answered, as if she could have forgotten, "and all my instincts are telling me to spread you out, fill you up, and breed you so nothing and no one will ever take you away from me. I'm gonna stake my claim, baby."

Petra's brain briefly fizzled out at the thought of children. Talk of breeding was all fun and games when she didn't have a future, but now everything was different. The high of knowing she might actually be able to do that was immediately followed by a crash and a thousand questions. Now she was a murderer, she had no idea what kind of father Silas would be, and she wasn't even certain what her next few days looked like, let alone *years*.

Trying to stave off a panic spiral, Petra took a deep breath and told him, "Um, I've got an implant." Something she'd been smart enough to get in a private clinic a few months before the Protector showed up on the cathedral's doorstep. Even so, it was a minor miracle Antonin hadn't found out.

Or perhaps he had, but he was so arrogant he assumed she'd had it removed in the time between their meetings. Her stomach soured at the thought.

"And I'm on the shot," he replied, unfazed. "I want to knock you up, Petra, but I'm not gonna share you with a kid for a long fuckin' time. Doesn't mean I won't talk about it though."

She couldn't tell if she was relieved or disappointed. The idea of getting pregnant when everything in her life was on fire was horrifying, but since she'd resigned herself to never getting the chance to choose that path...

Yes, it was possible to feel both emotions in equal measure.

She let out a shaky exhale. *Kids with Silas? Gods help me. Now that's going to be a mess.*

Shaking her head, she asked, "So I guess that means no sex until my days of rest are up?"

"That's exactly what it means."

The aggrieved look on his face would have been comical if she wasn't at that moment sitting in a pair of soaked panties. It would take so little to get her off. Petra cast him a look from under her lashes.

Not having sex was annoying, but there was plenty they could do that skirted the line, wasn't there?

As if sensing the direction of her thoughts, Silas tugged on her ponytail and growled, "Nope. If I so much as get a whiff of an orgasm from you, Petra, I'm gonna lose my mind. We're not doing shit, and you're not touching that cunt. Got it?"

She made a face. "Your rules suck."

"But you're gonna follow them, or you'll give me an excuse to deny more orgasms. Push hard enough and you'll get the belt, too."

He released her ponytail, allowing her head to return to its proper angle. Stroking her hair, he said, "Now do you want me to work on decrypting the asshole's data, or do you want me to keep talking about what I'll do if you earn a punishment?"

If he kept up with his filthy promises, she was pretty certain she'd do something that would end up with her meeting the belt. Since she wasn't actually excited by the idea of punishment or pain, Petra sighed and leaned heavily into his legs.

Eyeing the trunks in front of her, she muttered, "How can one man have all this? Not just the files, but all that data, too. How do you even amass that amount of information?"

Silas lazily tied the end of her ponytail around his hand again, but this time he didn't pull. He held it like a loose leash as he picked up his tablet with his other hand. "That's easy: you don't do this on your own."

"I mean, I knew the Ardeo still existed. It's an open secret among the higher-ups, but..." Petra swallowed. "I've been so focused on Antonin for so long that I honestly didn't think it would be this big. How many people are involved in this?"

"Men like him tend to be tyrants. They don't like to share power, even if that power is something they got handed to them by someone else. My guess is that Antonin was the heart and soul of the operation, but that operation had to be approved by someone at some point. Someone more powerful than even him — at least to start."

Her stomach turned. "The High Gloriae."

"It makes sense. Who else would benefit from having this much power?"

Petra almost wished Antonin was still alive. Silas said he didn't rely on torture to get information, but it probably would have made sorting through the mess at least a little easier if they knew what direction to look in.

"The High Gloriae certainly benefit from having all *this*," she agreed, gesturing to the trunk closest to her. "Blackmail means people don't leave the Temple, and it means connections, money, properties. That all makes sense to me."

It was also textbook extortion. Having leverage was the oldest trick in the book. Governments and religious orders had been doing it since time immemorial, and criminal organizations were only half a step behind them.

The Temple was one of the largest private landowners in the UTA. While they didn't officially wield political power anymore, they didn't need to. Glory was the most widely worshipped goddess in the world. The High Gloriae used their influence over their sea of worshippers every day, not to mention the thousands of acolytes under their banner.

Add in the blackmail and the money donated every year that mysteriously vanished into thin air...

Something niggled at the back of her brain, something she *knew* but couldn't fully articulate to herself. *What do they want? What do they not already have?*

The dread that something was wrong — seriously, profoundly wrong — hadn't ever really gone away, but now it took on the weight of a bowling ball in her gut.

"Max wouldn't have confronted Antonin over this," she said, speaking the words slowly as she teased the thread of thought loose. "We all know that something like this is going on in the Temple. You whisper something and it'll be heard. You snitch on someone and it'll get you moved up. You have a skeleton in your closet and it'll be found."

Silas played with the end of her ponytail and muttered, "Sounds like a syndicate."

"It is. At least, once you get into the depths of the organization. Day to day, most of the work done is good, genuine service, but the moment you dig into who holds the power..." Petra dragged the heavy trunk closer, a deep frown curving her lips. "Max knew that. I'm pretty sure that's why he joined in the first place."

"Must have felt familiar."

"It did. For me, at least." Flipping the gold latch on the trunk, she popped open the lid and was only a little surprised to see an odd assortment of ancient-looking files and gold bars inside. *No wonder this one felt heavier than the others.*

She curled her lip in disgust. Petra was born into the criminal world, so she knew how stupid it was to have something like this carted with him everywhere he went. But Antonin was no better than a common criminal kingpin, and they tended to get dumber the more powerful they became. Arrogant, too.

No criminal who actually cared about being caught would keep their safety net with them in the form of gold bars. Not only was it insecure, but it was also flashy. Abnormal. One look inside the trunk and any average person would think, *"Huh, I thought only gangsters had stuff like this."*

She didn't doubt that he had untold wealth squirreled away, but the fact that he kept some with him like *that* said an enormous amount about his ego. *And also explains why he was so put out by my lack of jewelry, I guess.*

"What I don't get, though, is what scared Max so badly," she continued. "Not even knowing that Antonin had all of *this* would have made him blink. Max ran his own organization. He knows— *knew* the score. So for him to risk confronting Antonin, a man he knew was a threat for decades... There had to be something else."

"Maybe he killed someone Max cared about?"

"Maybe." But Petra hadn't heard anything about a disappearance prior to Max's death, and while he was an outwardly charismatic man, his only real connection was the one they'd shared. Things had been a little strained between them since Max unexpectedly took the position at St. Emaine's and left her behind, though, so there were almost certainly things she'd missed. She wanted to believe that if he'd had a partner, he would have told her, but there was clearly a lot he'd never seen fit to tell her. What was one more secret?

"When was the last time you talked to him?"

The familiar ache of grief tightened her chest. "I don't know for sure how close it was to his death, but my guess is just before he confronted Antonin. Maybe hours. I don't know."

Silas's palm smoothed over the nape of her neck and settled there, heavy and warm. "What did he say to you?"

"Nothing helpful. He was panicked and refused to tell me any details. Only that something was really wrong and—" Petra shook her head, trying to dislodge the memory of that final, awful phone call.

"And what, baby?"

"And he told me to leave the Temple."

Silas's grip tightened. Urging her to turn her head with a press of his thumb, he asked, "Why didn't you? You had the money to go off and live a good life. Why'd you stay when he told you to go?"

He looked like he was bracing for some sanctimonious answer, but that wasn't what Petra gave him. "I was angry," she answered, shrugging stiffly. "I'd been angry at him for years. Ever since he left and didn't take me with him. And then he calls and says I need to go? That the life I'd built meant nothing and I was supposed to just drop everything when he wouldn't explain what was going on? I was so damn angry, Silas. Scared and confused and concerned for him and *pissed off.*"

He tilted his head to one side, examining her like he did sometimes — as if she was a squirming amoeba under a microscope. A week ago it would have unsettled her, but now she saw it for what it really was: Silas doing his damnedest to understand her.

"Do you regret it?"

"Being angry at him?"

He nodded.

"Yes and no. Yes, because I obviously wish I could have had the perfect last conversation with him. I wish I could have known what he was up against and begged him to run *with* me." She had to swallow hard before she could continue, but when she did, her voice came out harsh, full of all the hurt she'd kept to herself for so long. "But also no, because he left. I know it's selfish to care so much about that when he felt he was on some moral mission, but it hurt me so badly that I don't give a shit. After everything, he left me all over again."

And then the bastard up and died. That was the permanent sort of leaving that made her want to howl with rage at the injustice of it all.

She loved her uncle with every ounce of her soul, but that didn't mean she forgave him. The first time he abandoned her, she understood it. He assumed she'd be taken care of by her parents. He didn't know what would happen. He was grieving and lost and searching for peace. She understood that unique sort of desperation better than anyone.

But the second time? No, there was no forgiveness for that. Not when she never would have done the same to him. Not when she was *still* fighting for him even after everything, and not when she finally understood what it was like to have someone who would never, ever leave her.

Silas's thumb curved over her jaw to brush her bottom lip. Something dark and full of promise glowed in his lambent eyes. "Good girl."

CHAPTER FORTY-TWO

"Eat."

Petra looked up from the trunk in time to see Silas place a loaded plate beside her thigh. A can of soda, icy cold and dripping with condensation, landed beside it. Her stomach lurched in that pleasant-awful way it did whenever Silas did something sweet. He was so gruff about. So uncertain. It was like he was trying on a new outfit and trying to cover up how self-conscious he was by being stand-offish and hoping no one noticed.

Adorable.

"Did you make me a sandwich?"

"You need to eat." Silas dropped onto his ass next to her, carelessly shoving trunks out of his way to make room. He'd been in and out of the living room all day, his energy a living, restless thing, but he came back to check on her every half hour or so.

Of course, he didn't *say* it was to check on her, but she knew. She felt his need and his concern, clumsy though it was, in every possessive touch of her hair and quick, harsh kiss.

"I can't eat that whole thing," she protested, eyeing the comically overstuffed sandwich dubiously. He'd paired it with a mound of her preferred chips, too. Her stomach lurched again.

The demon can be sweet, and I might be the only person in the world who knows that. Talk about privileged information.

"How about we share?"

Silas gave her another one of his scorching looks, but Petra had to glance away. She was still getting used to that sensation of acute exposure she got whenever he looked at her like he *knew*.

He knew it all. He wanted it all. It was heady and more than a little terrifying.

"I'll take half, but you eat the chips." He accepted the plate when she passed it to him, then settled it on the thick muscle of his thigh.

Worried she'd lose her nerve, Petra leaned over quickly to press a kiss to his cheek. "Thank you for taking care of me," she whispered.

He skimmed his hand over the cage of her ribs before settling it on her hip. Giving it a possessive squeeze, he replied, "Demons are supposed to be good mates. I don't know what I'm doing, though, so you're going to have to tell me when I do it right or fuck it up."

He hadn't said it in any sort of bashful, soft way. There was no vulnerability in his tone. If anything, he said it harshly, like he was annoyed he was expected to care about silly stuff like looking after a mate. But Petra saw him as clearly as he saw her.

"You're doing good so far." She pulled back with a smile. *Gods, this man is a mess. Good thing I am, too, or we'd really be screwed.*

"Tal normally tells me if I'm being a shithead or not," he muttered, nudging the food in her direction. "But he's not allowed near the house, so you gotta do it."

Plucking a chip off the plate, she asked, "Who's Tal?"

Silas had given her the basic, bare-bones rundown of his massive clan, but so far he'd only given her a handful of names. That was likely because he knew she'd never be able to remember more than that, especially when she had no faces to connect them to. She knew his matriarch, his parents, his uncle, and a smattering of cousins. The only reason she knew that much was because he'd explained to her that his family kept their town locked down tight with regular security checks and perimeter patrols.

His uncle ran the successful whiskey business that employed almost the entire family, but historically they hadn't always been on the right side of the law — and they protected what was theirs. So, in Silas's words, she didn't need to lose a wink of sleep over whether the Ardeo would track her there, because the Cuttcombe clan took their "shoot first" policy as more of a family motto.

Petra assumed Tal was another member of the clan, and though she was interested in learning about Silas's family, she didn't think too much of her question. Reaching for another chip with one hand while simultaneously digging around in the trunk with another, she pulled out an old, hand-sewn leather book.

As she opened it up to a random, yellowed page covered in columns of numbers — *measurements?* — Silas answered, "Tal is my brother. He's a wraith."

Petra nearly choked on her chip. Attention snapping to the demon lounging beside her, she wheezed, "You have a brother?" Then, half a second later, "What do you mean he's a *wraith?*"

"Tal isn't technically my brother," Silas amended. "He's my only friend."

"And he's... a wraith." Her mind worked hard to make sense of that even as she connected the dots to what he'd shown her the previous day. "You're building *him* a body?"

Silas picked up his half of the monstrous sandwich and took an obscenely large bite. He nodded as he chewed, looking completely at ease.

Very aware of Silas's vulnerabilities, even if *he* wasn't, Petra took a deep breath and turned her upper body to face him. She couldn't just demand answers or call him crazy. There had to be something more going on, and she could at least let him explain himself before she started worrying about him seeing boogeymen.

"Demon," she began, very gently, "I'd appreciate it if you explained exactly what all of that means, because up until yesterday, I thought the consensus was that wraiths were about as real as ghosts."

"People believe in ghosts," he challenged, lips curling in a shadow of his mocking grin, "and people believe in gods. Wraiths are more real than either of those."

"Maybe," she begrudgingly allowed, "but I don't claim to be best friends with Glory."

"Wraiths are real. The reason there are stories about them is because everyone has probably seen one. They just can't make themselves known to most people. As far as I know, only a few demons in a generation can communicate with them. My family history says I'm the first."

The shadows around her throat shifted, swirling and caressing until they draped over her shoulders and chest. All around the room, dark corners moved ever-so-slightly, responding to Silas's call as he leaned in close to whisper, "Demon lore says that wraiths are the severed shadows of the dead."

Petra tried very hard not to let her skepticism show. "So... ghosts?"

Does Silas talk to ghosts, or does he just have a very persistent imaginary friend? I'm not sure which possibility worries me more.

"Not quite." Apparently fed up with her disregard for his ridiculously sized sandwich, he picked it up off the plate and forced her to take it. Raising his eyebrows, he made it clear that he wouldn't be explaining more until she took a bite.

Petra rolled her eyes, mostly so he wouldn't pay too much attention to the warm flush that overtook her when he took care of her like that. She was pretty sure it didn't work, though. The smug look on his face only got more pronounced when she nibbled on the sandwich, then came back for a much bigger bite.

Grinning, Silas continued, "Obviously, there hasn't been a lot of study into this. One reason is that demons don't like to talk about it with outsiders, and another is that the scientific establishment lacks imagination." His upper lip curled. Petra could only guess what kind of science *he* would do with an unlimited budget and resources.

"I'll remind you that the establishment didn't even accept how elementals are made until relatively recently, despite eyewitness reports that go back thousands of years. The same is true with wraiths. Almost everyone I've ever met has a story about seeing something move in the shadows."

"Brains see things that aren't there all the time." The gods knew she'd conjured her fair share of boogeymen when she slept in alleys. Darkness, exhaustion, paranoia — all of it played a part in seeing things. She still felt it sometimes when she was alone. There was something about the darkness that could so easily make one feel *watched*.

"Or maybe that's an easy explanation," Silas countered. "I'm not saying every shape in the dark is a wraith, but I'm also not saying *none* of them are. Most places I go, I find at least one."

A cold feeling swept down her spine and turned the delicious sandwich to ash on her tongue. It wasn't fear exactly, but the disconcerting, full-body realization that maybe her world wasn't what she thought it was.

"What are you talking about? There are— There's an entire population of *people* just out of sight at any given time? You can't be serious."

"Yes and no." Silas reached over her to snag the soda. Popping the tab with a claw, he took a long draw before passing it to her. "Most wraiths are sorta... unformed. Tal says it takes thousands of years for one to mature into real sentience. When I was a kid, he compared a demon's shadows to a seed. When a demon dies, the seed is planted in the darkness and grows slowly over time until it's something new." He shrugged. "And some don't grow at all."

When Petra continued to stare at him, her limp hands barely holding onto her sandwich and the soda, Silas continued, "My working theory is that they have a lot in common with elementals and likely spawn at around the same rate. They start out as sparks of sentience in the atmosphere that come together, pooling magic, until there's enough to make an m-storm. That blast of energy creates their bodies. Unlike elementals, though, wraiths never get that final explosive push. They're conscious, they have wills, identities, desires, but no physical form. They're stuck."

She didn't think Silas was lying to her, and she didn't believe he was off his rocker — in this instance, at least — but that didn't mean it was any easier to accept what he was saying. Because if that was true, then...

An entire population has been left to languish in the dark. Alone.

She didn't want to believe that, but why would Silas lie about *this* of all things? Her stomach turned. "So, Tal was... a person? Before he became a wraith, I mean."

"He was. His memory of his life is better than most, apparently, but it's spotty. There are key facts and things, some impressions, but that's it. Most of what he knows is from lurking in corners for thousands of years. He likes to watch people."

Petra finally gave up and put what remained of her sandwich back on the plate. She really tried to remain calm, to not show how unsettled she was, but it was impossible when her voice came out so high. "And how did you two meet?"

"I liked to hide in dark spaces a lot as a kid," Silas explained. "When I was three, I found out that one of those spaces was already occupied."

"And this millennia old wraith became your friend?"

"At first I think he thought of himself as more of a babysitter, actually. I was a crybaby with no friends. He said he felt bad, so he stuck around."

Crybaby? Petra could only imagine what childhood must have been like for a boy like him, someone so different from his peers. His family loved and supported him, but it had to have been hard, even for someone as emotionally stunted as Silas.

Heart aching for the little boy who liked to hide, she prompted, "Then..."

Silas tilted his head one way, then the other. "Then I think we both realized it was nice having someone around to talk to. My parents didn't know what to make of him at first, but my matriarch said that we must be shadow-siblings. So everyone calls him my brother now."

Oh, my poor demon.

He said it so simply, without bitterness or sorrow, but Petra knew what he wasn't saying. She couldn't imagine it was easy for Silas to grow up in a big, bustling clan full of normal people, no matter how much they loved him. Tal, whoever and whatever he was, became Silas's friend because he had no one else.

Taking a deep breath, Petra tried to let go of whatever skepticism lingered inside. Whatever was going on, she felt in her bones that Silas was telling the truth. Maybe that truth wasn't real. Maybe he was wrong. It didn't matter.

What mattered was the fact that Silas believed it, and that belief was strong enough that he'd been willing to do just about anything to fulfill a promise he'd made to his only friend — including binding himself to a woman he didn't even know.

"So..." She summoned a small smile. "When do I get to meet him?"

Silas's dark brows arched. "Technically speaking, you already have."

"What? When?"

"He kept an eye on you when I went up to Seattle." A dark look descended on his features. It was all storm clouds and narrowed eyes when he growled, "And he was in charge of keeping you safe while I took care of Vanderpoel."

Comprehension dawned. So did outrage. "The *closet!*"

Muttering to himself, Silas said, "Gonna kick his ass the second he has one." Then, speaking to her, he begrudgingly added, "Wraiths are sensitive to light. It's basically the one thing that can hurt them. Neither of us thought of that when we made the plan to restrain you. I figured since I'd held you with shadows, it wouldn't be an issue. I should have known better. Still fuckin' pissed at him, though."

Petra covered her eyes with one hand. *I cannot believe this.*

Hadn't she felt like she was going crazy while Silas was away? She thought it was the stress, but now she wondered if there really had been shadows moving out of the corner of her eye. Watching her. Reporting back to Silas.

Locking me in a fucking closet.

Shooting back a bracing sip of ice cold cola, Petra hissed as the bubbles seared a path down her esophagus. "I want to meet him," she announced, coughing a little. "I need to know that this is all—"

"I haven't lied to you," Silas protested, holding out his hand for the soda.

She passed him the can. "I didn't say you did. But I need to meet him anyway. My brain can't just accept all this in theory. And if he's your brother, then I really, *really* need to meet him. I can't meet your parents and not your only brother, Silas. It's just not done."

Swallowing, he muttered, "Well, he's not allowed near the house, so we'll have to go outside. And you won't be able to hear anything he says. You might not even be able to see him. So really, it's pointless and you should just stay in the den."

"Why isn't he allowed near the house?"

He set the can on the floor with a little more force than was really necessary. "Because I just found my mate, rut's breathing down my neck, and I don't want another man within ten feet of you until you're fucked so good, you can't remember what it's like to walk straight."

I can't say Silas minces words with me.

"Right, well." She cleared her throat. "Outside it is."

CHAPTER FORTY-THREE

"YOU'RE NOT GOING TO BE ABLE TO HEAR ANYTHING HE says," Silas warned her. He could feel a tic developing in the muscles of his jaw as he fought to stop grinding his teeth.

He'd always intended to properly introduce Tal and Petra, but that didn't mean he was happy about it.

"But I'll know he's there," Petra stubbornly insisted. "Right?"

"Right."

"How do you know he'll be there? Can you reach him somehow?"

Silas loved that his witch had regained a bit of her energy, that spark of something that had so drawn him to her in the first place, but he selfishly wanted all of her attention on him, not *Tal*.

He would do unspeakable things for his brother, but sharing his mate's attention? It was untenable.

But he fought the urge to drag her back into the house. He bit back the growl that rumbled in his chest at the thought of her being so close to an unmated man — mostly incorporeal as he might have been. He didn't do it out of his affection for Tal or even the understanding that Petra getting on board with the plan to give Tal his body back would make everything much smoother.

No, he did it because Petra asked him to.

Soft shit, he silently griped as he expertly picked his way down a nearly invisible deer track behind his house.

He didn't hate doing things for her. In fact, he was surprised to find a deep, foreign sense of satisfaction whenever he did the right thing to make her happy. But that didn't mean it wasn't a little galling.

Silas tightened his grip on Petra's hand, pulling her along after him through the underbrush. The air was muggy and only the faintest traces of a hot pink sunset lingered in the navy blue sky they could barely make out through the gaps in the forest canopy.

"Tal will be there," he finally answered as he swept a branch aside and held it until Petra was safely out of swiping range. "He hangs out in this area a lot when we aren't together. He'll definitely hear us coming."

Tal did like to drift in the ether and pop out in odd places, mostly to watch people, but they hadn't been apart for more than a few weeks at a time since Silas was a toddler. He highly doubted his brother would leave the area now, of all times. Not when everything was such a mess.

"Okay, but where exactly are we— Oh."

They came to a stop at the edge of a small clearing. The underbrush wasn't quite so thick, mostly because a ring of large old growth trees blocked out too much light for the weaker plants to grow. Off to one side, a trickle of a creek wound in a serpentine scrawl. On the opposite end, in the deepest shadows of the biggest tree, was an old, rundown fort.

Clearing his throat, Silas explained, "If you keep following this track, you'll eventually hit my parents' house. As a kid I'd come down here to mess around without getting in trouble."

He'd never been able to play with his cousins. Not for long, anyway. He always ended up doing something that made someone cry or run to his parents to complain. Sometimes he had fun, but mostly he ended up frustrated, unable to understand why his cousins were so sensitive.

So he'd spent his childhood alone, tromping through the deep wilderness, his canvas pack stuffed with books and tools he'd pilfered from various family members. Tal liked to come with him, but only when Silas ventured out after sunset or on particularly gloomy days with little sun.

The fort was initially built as Silas's own little workshop, full of odds and ends of machinery and books on sigilwork he stole, but at some point Tal had taken a liking to it, since he could hide out there during the day, so it became his, too.

He wasn't sure what Petra could see in the rapidly gathering darkness, but he could make out the painstakingly carved piece of plywood he'd nailed over the lopsided doorway.

Tal's Place

Silas could feel the shadows around him seething with life. It was all familiar on an elemental level — the taste of the air, the scents of the forest, the magic that clung to the darkness between leaf and root. He wasn't sentimental, but he liked how he felt whenever he returned to this particular spot.

There was something different about bringing Petra, though. When he looked at her, glowing faintly, dressed mostly in his clothing, free of makeup and all the masks she'd been forced to wear, he felt... centered. Like something that had been missing was returned to its rightful place in the very heart of him and the forest both.

Unable to resist, Silas reeled her into his chest and tilted her head up for a punishing kiss. "You look so pretty in the dark," he rasped. Petra made a soft sound in the back of her throat, but before she could say anything, he ordered, "Now stay here."

Petra's eyes, closed for their kiss, popped open. "Wait, where are you going?" Her fingers curled into the well-washed fabric of his t-shirt like she had any hope of holding him there if he wanted to be free.

Fuck, I like that. His cock, on a hair trigger these days, jerked with interest at the thought of her clinging to him.

"What?" he teased, prying her hands off just so he could feel her reach for him again. "Afraid I'm going to leave you in the dark woods all by yourself, little goddess?"

"A little, yeah. I've never been in a forest before." She tried for a smile, but it came out so weak that she let it fall almost immediately. "I'm a city girl, remember?"

He expected her to tease him, maybe to threaten to run away. Her simple honesty was disarming. Scowling, he cupped the front of her throat and felt her pulse throb under the shadows there. "Well, stop worrying, city girl. I'm not gonna leave you. The only time I'll let you leave my side in these woods is when I wanna chase you down for a fuck in the dirt. Understand?"

He loved the way her skin glowed, but he *really* loved watching her eyes dilate like that. Leaning down for one more kiss, he whispered, "My naughty little goddess. I knew you'd like the sound of that."

He tore himself away from her before he lost the fraying edge of his willpower. Blood rushed in his ears, thick with hormones and the need to claim, but he forced himself back a step. Then another.

It was a good thing that Petra held very still, her eyes locked on him and her swollen lips slightly parted. If she'd so much as twitched or glanced to the side, his instincts would have seen it as a sign that she intended to run. If she gave him an excuse to chase her down again...

Silas cursed and spun around. The memory of tearing out of her pathetic little shower to hunt her down in the cathedral's sanctuary felt like it came from another life. He was desperate for another taste of it. Her.

Mood souring with every inch of distance he put between them, Silas stomped across the clearing. He swiveled his head once to skewer her with a look. She'd crossed her arms but otherwise remained exactly where he'd left her. That small act of trust eased some of his frustration. *Such a good girl.*

He couldn't wait until he could properly reward her.

Having no doubt that Tal was around but wisely keeping his

distance until called, Silas gave the flimsy sign above the entrance a tap with his knuckles, waited a moment, and then bent nearly in half to fit through the doorway.

The inside was quite spacious for a child and a wraith, but for a fully grown half demon, it wasn't exactly a comfortable fit.

Despite the ache in his back, Silas took a moment to glance around and take stock of the fort. It'd been years since he'd bothered to check on it, but his childhood fishing gear remained propped against one wall. The books were gone, but the crude shelves held other things he'd filched for Tal over the years: a bronze spy glass from a rich fuck's desk, an expired packet of shredded gum no one made anymore, and a bottle of his family's most expensive whiskey.

A pair of tiny boots with holes in the rubber soles were carefully aligned by the door, and on the far end of the room a cork board one of his uncles threw out dominated the wall. On it were pinned hundreds of scraps of paper so fully covered in chicken scratch sigilwork and a child's blueprints for mechanical bodies that the paper could barely be distinguished. Moisture had ruined much of the notes, but Tal refused to let Silas take it down.

He was sentimental about it all, though Silas himself cringed at the sight of such poor work.

Annoyed as ever at the sight of it and already itching to get back to his mate, Silas glared at the darkest corner of the fort. Tal's presence was muted. If he could have compared it to something, Silas would have said that it was a bit like someone standing in the corner, stock still, and praying they wouldn't be noticed.

"My mate wants to see you," he growled.

There was a long moment of stillness before the shadows began to cautiously unfurl. When Tal spoke, his voice was pained. *Is that really a good idea right now?*

"No, it's not. This is already driving me crazy. But she asked for it, so she gets it." Silas jerked his thumb over his shoulder. "She stays where she is, you stay by the door here. If you move any closer, I'm going to double the ass-kicking you've got coming for letting her get fuckin' shot."

Tal didn't argue. They both understood that it wasn't really his fault. But the fact was that Tal had been entrusted with the sacred duty of protecting Silas's mate — even if she hadn't been at the time — and he failed. There were consequences for that sort of thing. There had to be, or else they'd never be able to move past shit and let mistakes go.

She really wants to see me? Tal's form resolved a little more. To Silas's trained eye, he was clearly visible, but he wondered if Petra was going to have trouble making sense of the shadowed mass.

Wanting to be done with this already, Silas answered, "She asked, didn't she?"

But she won't be able to hear me.

"I'll translate."

It wasn't like it would be the first time. His clan knew all about Tal. They weren't necessarily comfortable around the wraith, seeing as he was technically dead, but there had been a handful of times where Silas acted as Tal's voice for them.

Okay.

But Tal didn't move. He remained there in the corner, his shadows ebbing and flowing in a way Silas recognized as unease. Already at the limit of his patience, he snapped, "Are you gonna come outside or not?"

Honestly? I'm nervous.

"Why? You've already met her." Several times. One of which involved seeing what the bolt gun did to her insides.

Tal's tone took on a familiar note of exasperation when he replied, *She's your mate, Si. It's a big deal.*

"It's not like it was a surprise to you."

So? It still matters.

Silas had half expected Tal to say something smug about being right, but the wraith hadn't said a word about his warnings. That uncomfortable squirming sensation took up root in his chest again, but he had no hope of pinpointing where it came from.

I want to make a good impression, but I can't because I'm... this. It's frustrating.

"You can't make a worse first impression than me," he pointed out.

You've got me there.

"She's waiting," Silas prodded, growing increasingly antsy.

I know. I'm sorry. I'm just— Tal cut himself off, then, in a resigned tone, explained, *I think I'm jealous of you, Si, and I don't want her first impression of me to be this.*

"I'd be jealous of me, too." He bared his fangs. "But you'll have to kill me if you want her."

I don't want Petra, Tal firmly replied. *But I want what you have. I'd do anything to get it. Horrible, evil things — and I wouldn't think twice about it. I don't want her to see that, or to only know me as a monster in the dark. I want... I just* want.

It wasn't a big surprise to him. He and Tal had always shared the ugliest parts of themselves with one another, and usually those parts lined up neat and tidy. The difference between them was that Tal felt shame. Silas could never manage that bit.

Distinctly uncomfortable, as he always was when Tal got sentimental, Silas rolled his eyes and quipped, "Well, it's a good thing for both of us that Petra *likes* monsters."

"Silas?" His mate's voice, a little high pitched, made all his muscles tense. Silas was already backing out of the fort before he'd even made the choice to do so.

"C'mon, asshole," he muttered, ducking to make sure his horns didn't catch on the ceiling. In a louder voice, he called out, "You're fine, baby. I'm coming out now."

The breath squeezed out of his lungs when he backed out of the doorway and turned around to find her standing where he'd left her, all alone and glowing in the full darkness that had fallen.

A look of profound relief crossed her features. She lifted a foot like she intended to hustle across the clearing, and he immediately tensed. Not only did he not want her too close to Tal, but there were loads of rocks and random machinery parts scattered around, hidden by vines and moss. If she tripped and hurt herself, he was pretty sure he'd lose his mind.

Heartbeat accelerating, Silas held up a hand. It was deeply gratifying to see her halt immediately.

They had a long way to go, but that sign of trust was *everything.*

His voice came out a little hoarse when he ordered, "You keep your pretty ass there. I'm coming to you."

Petra sucked her bottom lip between her teeth, but she nodded.

A dizzying swell of pleasure expanded in his chest. "That's my girl," he rumbled, lengthening his stride.

CHAPTER FORTY-FOUR

PETRA TRACKED SILAS'S FORM IN THE DARKNESS, BUT IT wasn't easy. Even in his more human shape, he seemed to blend in with the shadows naturally, like they couldn't help but cling to him. Her heart thumped unevenly in her chest. *He's coming. You're fine.*

She wouldn't say she was scared of the dark, but she wasn't exactly comfortable in it, either. So many of her worst memories involved being alone in the dark — listening to her parents stumbling into their apartment in the dead of night, drunk and fighting, sleeping wedged against a trash can in a dark alley, and being locked in a dank cupboard in the children's home as punishment for not making her bed.

Petra was a luminist. It seemed pretty reasonable for her to not enjoy the dark even before she began to associate it with danger and neglect.

But it was only when Silas left her there in the clearing that she realized she didn't fear it. Not when he was with her, at least. She hadn't even flinched when he took her hand and guided her into the woods.

Because he was Silas, and if he wanted to hurt her, he'd say so.

She trusted that. She trusted him. When they walked hand in hand in the dark, she believed he knew the way.

That didn't mean she felt at ease in the woods, though, and it certainly didn't rule out the fact that Silas liked to screw with her. She trusted he wouldn't cause her any damage, but lead her into the woods to freak her out a little? Yeah, that sounded like something he'd do.

But she could make out the twin discs of molten bronze that were his eyes. She could just make out the curl of his horns. She could sense him there, moving closer to her at a swift clip, even if she couldn't hear his footsteps in the underbrush like she should've.

And then he was back, warm hands cupping the sides of her face. Silas hunched his shoulders a little and pressed their lips together. It wasn't really a kiss at first. He held very still and took a handful of deep breaths, like he just wanted to feel her there and share a breath.

Petra grabbed the fabric of his shirt above his lean hips and scrunched it. Stretching onto her tiptoes, she pressed a little closer, deepening the kiss until he responded with a low groan.

His tongue snaked inside her mouth to curl possessively around hers. Petra sighed as she tasted him, let him have his way with her. Her mind went so pleasantly fuzzy whenever he touched her. Everything seemed bright and soft and warm. His clean thyme and musk scent filled her nose. Her magic, hot and unpredictable, surged inside her to press against her skin, begging for something she was beginning to understand

The kiss deepened, growing messy, more intense, a moment before Silas threaded his claws into her hair to jerk her head back. "Fuck," he grunted. His fangs scraped her jaw, the curve of her cheek. It felt like a reprimand.

"The fact that you glow brighter when I kiss you makes me fuckin' crazy."

Petra forced her eyes open and discovered that she could make out Silas's face a little better. Not just because he was close enough to share her breath, but because he was right. "I didn't know I did that."

An unsettling gleam entered Silas's eyes. "What? That never happened with anyone else?"

Even if it had, she wasn't sure it would have been the smart move to tell him so. Silas didn't seem like the kind of man who would take hearing about her past sexual partners very well.

"No," she answered, wary of what that answer would do to his ego but figuring it was the safer of the two options. "I always give off a little light, but normally I only really glow when I feel... strongly about something." Historically, that strong feeling was anger.

She could make it happen consciously, too, but typically she tried her best to suppress any accidental glowing — mostly because it could lead to some serious damage to those around her if it got out of hand. Being a gloriana came with many gifts, but there were an equal amount of dangers.

Silas gave her one of his knife smiles, but this time it didn't send a shiver of dread down her spine. "You feel strongly about me, baby?"

After lying about everything for so long, it was a forbidden sort of thrill to answer, "Yes."

His sharp inhale was loud even over the chorus of bugs all around them. In a low, low voice, he promised, "Little goddess, I'm gonna fuck you *so* good."

"Promises, promises," she muttered.

There was something about the way his eyes crinkled that took her breath away. "Don't you worry. I keep my promises. I'll even keep them when you don't want me to."

"Why would I not want you to keep a promise?"

Silas leaned in close to whisper, "Just you wait."

Not wanting to give him the satisfaction of asking what he meant, since she *knew* it was a trap, she asked, "Was he not there?"

Silas untangled his fingers from her hair. They skimmed her cheeks and down her neck, eliciting a shiver, before they settled on the curve of her waist. Half-turning, he pointed toward the ramshackle fort. "He's right there."

Petra squinted into the darkness. At first she didn't see much of anything. The glow of sunset was far behind them, and the moonlight struggled to break through the dense canopy over their heads. Not to mention the fact that her eyes were just never very good in the dark.

"I don't see any—" The words died on her tongue when a shadow passed in front of the little wooden sign above the door. She couldn't quite make out the letters, but she knew they were there. That meant she noticed when they suddenly *weren't*.

Petra sucked in a sharp breath as she made sense of what she was seeing. If she didn't know to look for something, she probably wouldn't have noticed the deeper darkness that pooled in one place. It was like the impression of a person — a cutout in the fabric of the night.

The more she stared, the more she could make out: The suggestion of great height, impossibly wide shoulders, something that might have been horns, and, if she squinted... the after-image of glowing eyes.

An electric current of fear passed over her body, raising just about every hair on her person. Just as fast, Petra's stomach dropped somewhere around her knees. "Holy fuck."

Silas's lips twitched. "Told you."

She barely heard him. A part of her was still convinced she was hallucinating, the animal part of her brain seeing predators in the darkness, but even that slim doubt was destroyed when Tal *moved*.

He'd only drifted about a foot away from the door when Silas snapped, "No, you stay there. Don't move a damn inch."

Petra slapped his stomach with the back of her hand reflexively. "That's not nice."

"You two keep pushing me and we're gonna have even less *nice* on our hands," he growled, dragging her into his side until she was all but smashed under his arm.

Tal stopped his approach and instead made a motion that might have been a wave. Maybe. She was pretty sure.

Wraiths are real. Petra tried to take a deep breath, but it wasn't easy. *Good gods, wraiths are real.*

She was a devout priestess. She put her life in Glory's hands and prayed for guidance not only for herself, but for the world. That meant she accepted, even *hoped,* that there were a great many unknown wonders left to be discovered in the world. But it was one thing to hope those unknowns existed and quite another to come face to face with one.

Speaking through his teeth just a little, Silas told her, "Tal wants you to know that he's happy he finally gets to meet you. He wishes he could say so himself."

She blinked rapidly and tried to get her bearings back. "I'm... I'm glad to meet you, too." Casting Silas a dark look, she added, "And *not* in a closet this time."

Silas rolled his eyes. After a beat, he said, "He says he's sorry he scared you, but he's not sorry he did it. Also, he wants you to know that you *pack quite the fucking punch.*"

That startled a laugh out of her. "If it makes you feel any better, I definitely thought you were Silas."

She had no idea what Tal replied, but it was enough to make Silas growl, "Okay, I think you two are chummy enough. You've met, Petra knows you're real, and now we're done."

Wrapping an arm around her middle, he began to haul her backward, but Petra dug her heels into the dirt. "Wait, that was like two seconds! I have questions!" *Dozens and dozens of them.*

"You'll just have to save them for when he can answer himself."

Petra's mind went blank as she took in what exactly that meant. *He needs my bond to give Tal his life back.*

She'd known since the beginning that Silas wanted her bond for very non-sentimental reasons, but now that she understood exactly why, and who would be affected if she refused...

Petra could barely make out Tal's wave goodbye as Silas pulled her back toward the deer track.

After everything that happened with Antonin and then the shock of finding out she was Silas's mate, Petra hadn't had a lot of time to analyze her feelings about holding up her end of the deal. She still didn't.

All she knew was that they'd just gotten more complicated.

Silas had left a light on in the living room. Not because he needed one, but he'd noticed Petra liked to always have at least one light on. He noticed everything about her. Discovering new facets of her, no matter how mundane they might be, was his new favorite pastime.

He watched her toe off her shoes and then pad over to the couch, her lithe legs weaving around the scattered trunks on the floor. Her expression wasn't upset, exactly, but thoughtful in a way that raised his hackles.

Leaning his shoulder against the door jamb, he demanded, "Tell me what you're thinking."

Petra didn't look at him as she sat on the cushions and drew her legs up. Her brows were furrowed, the skin between them grooved deeply. "It's a lot to process."

"How so?"

"I... I just can't believe that there's been people all around us for probably ever and we've all just— just dismissed them as a myth." She shook her head. "I know it doesn't make any sense, but I feel guilty. Like I've been ignoring people who needed help."

"Guilty?" Silas made a face. "Like one in a million demons can communicate with wraiths, and it's been kept hush-hush for ages because no one wants to be the one to say they talk to dead people. Even if you'd known wraiths were real, you wouldn't have been able to talk to them."

"But I could acknowledge them. I leave offerings for gods who might not even be paying attention. Why couldn't I dignify a wraith with a *hello?*" she argued, pulling her knees tighter to her chest. "I could have done something or— It just feels wrong. I know what it's like to fall through the cracks, Silas. To have people just walk on by you and pretend you don't exist, like you're nothing just because you're on the street or in the shadows or... I can't imagine feeling that way for gods know how long."

"If anyone should feel bad, it's demons. We could have forced the world to see them, but we didn't. That's not just because people don't want to believe there are monsters in the dark, Petra. It's because a lot of demons would have a very serious problem with what I'm trying to do."

"Why?" She finally looked at him, and when their eyes met, he saw anger in the cornflower blue.

He shrugged. "Because I'm basically resurrecting the dead. That tends to upset people."

"But they're not dead," she snapped, like he was arguing with her. "And it's not like worse things haven't been done before."

Silas tipped his head in a nod. "Agreed. That's why I say *fuck 'em.*"

He'd hoped to see the lines between her brows relax, but they only seemed to get deeper. Petra pursed her lips and reached for the old leather book she'd left out on the armrest of the couch. It was the one he recognized from the trunk with the ridiculous gold bars in it.

Watching her crack open the book with quick, agitated movements, Silas pulled away from the door jamb. The fluttering sound of her flipping through pages filled the silence as he crossed the room to make them a couple of drinks. *Gods know I need one.*

He didn't get far before instinct screamed at him to stop.

Silas froze mid-step, his head whipping toward Petra before the gasp had even left her lips.

"Ah!" She all but threw the book onto the floor as she reared back into the couch. In the span of a blink, she went sickly pale.

Silas lunged for her. "What? What's wrong?"

Her cheeks were cold and clammy under his palms, and her lips trembled when she rasped, "We need to— I need to call Rasmus. Right now, Silas."

What the fuck?

Before he could unleash the possessive beast that roared in his mind, Petra pointed one shaky finger at the book on the floor. "We *need* to call him. That's— That's…"

Confused and worried enough to give him a stomach ache, Silas released her just long enough to swoop the book off the floor. It'd fallen open, creasing the ancient spine and allowing him to turn it over to see what exactly had so rattled his mate.

His gaze fell to the yellowed page. There, scrawled in ink that had gone rusty brown over the years, was a familiar name.

Patient #43: Rasmus Jebediah Adams - wolf shifter, aged 17, infected.

CHAPTER FORTY-FIVE

Silas's face was pale, his knuckles bleached white with the force of his grip on the steering wheel. His eyelids were narrowed as he glared through the tinted windshield of his car and out into the tiny, deserted parking lot attached to the roadside diner.

All around them, sloping fields of verdant grass stretched into a sea of green. They were only about forty minutes from Silas's home, but the change of scenery was stark.

Petra understood that this was costing him. Guilt crawled under her skin whenever she spied the sheen of sweat on the back of his neck or caught the cagey way he scanned his surroundings, like he expected someone to jump out from the drainage ditch on the side of the road and snatch her from the car.

She didn't want to ask him to do this, but whenever she thought of that journal, it felt like a thousand tiny pins pricked her all at once.

Just about everyone knew the story of how weres came to be, but that was history. Normal people had been used as experiments in the darkest days of the Great War. They were intentionally infected with a previously deadly virus by an amoral scientist and, at least at first, sent to the battlefield to act as tireless, brutal soldiers. But weres couldn't be controlled, and when the war eventually ended, they had nowhere to go in a world that ostracized them. Infections soared. Most of the weres she'd known, like Rasmus, ended up in the criminal underbelly of the UTA when there was nothing else for them.

While she'd known weres her whole life, it wasn't a story she'd ever dreamed of having a connection to, let alone holding a critical piece of it in her *hand.*

And never in her wildest imaginings did she think that Rasmus might be one of those original experiments. Her stomach curdled at the thought.

Petra hadn't known what she held at first. Her reaction to seeing his name on that yellowed page was visceral and immediate. Instinct screamed that it was *wrong,* and when she and Silas sat down to really figure out what they had, that feeling had only gotten worse.

There were conspiracy theories galore about who funded the infamous Dr. Wyeth's research. Dozens of inquiries had been done over the years, some more politically motivated than others, but no one had ever been able to definitively say who'd done it. The name she'd heard from most weres was Queen Sigrid Seagrim, though evidence on that was, as far as Petra knew, scarce.

While she couldn't say she was particularly well versed in were history, Petra knew for a fact that she'd never, ever heard anyone even suggest that the Temple might be involved.

That horrible pins and needles feeling rushed back, making her skin pebble. It was before her time, and she couldn't say she was particularly good friends with Rasmus, and yet a sickly swell of guilt rose ever-higher in her stomach.

Was that what you found, Max? she couldn't help but wonder. *Did you know?*

Petra felt unclean just holding the thing in her hands. Within its smoky, aged pages were records of unspeakable abuse — not only to "patients" like Rasmus, but to Dr. Wyeth's own daughter, Josephine. There were so many horrifying secrets in those trunks, but this existed in a class all its own. It wasn't just blackmail or personal secrets stowed away for another time. It was a record of a world-changing crime, and it was up to *her* to figure out what to do with it.

Yes, it had been long before her time, but she was a High Priestess of Glory's Temple. It was her responsibility to bring the truth to light.

Giving it to Rasmus was the only thing that felt right. Silas didn't get it, but she didn't expect him to. Her gut told her that it had to go to him. It was *his* name she saw first, and it was *his* story.

And despite his displeasure, his instincts, and his general disregard for things like guilt or morality or "doing the right thing," Silas was helping her put the truth into Rasmus's hands.

She touched Silas's thigh. The thick muscle beneath her palm was rigid with tension.

"Thank you, demon," she murmured, stroking him like she would a big cat threatening to pounce. A little bit of the guilt released when she touched him, and knowing that soon they'd make things right in some small way brought even more relief.

Silas grunted. The bridge of his nose wrinkled when he flashed his fangs at a distant passing truck. "This is a fuckin' terrible idea."

And yet you did it anyway, she thought, chest tightening with a great swell of warmth. Petra was beginning to suspect that Silas would do just about anything she asked of him, which was... heady. Never, not once in all her long, miserable life, had someone been so completely on her side.

It wasn't the time, but she couldn't stop herself from leaning over the center console to press a tender kiss to the base of one curled horn. "I adore you, demon," she whispered there.

"Why?" He sounded suspicious, but that didn't stop him from tangling his claws in a lock of her hair. He stroked it between his thumb and forefinger almost absentmindedly, like he needed to soothe himself.

Petra's lips traced a path from his brow to the corner of his tightly compressed mouth. "Because you have my back no matter how stupid my plan is, and even though you don't care about this at all, you respect that it's important to me."

"A good mate would've told you no," he gritted out.

"A good mate wouldn't have asked you to do this right now, either," she countered. "See? We're equal."

"Petra—"

Oh, she knew she was *really* in trouble when he said her real name. Hoping to distract him as well as ease some of the tension that radiated from him like an electrical storm, her fingers crept up his thigh, following the inner seam of his well-worn jeans.

He stiffened. A low rumble vibrated the air in the car.

"Little goddess," he growled, snaring her wrist just as she reached the button, "what do you think you're doing?"

Petra rubbed her lips back and forth against the corner of his mouth as her free hand snaked around the back of his neck to tease the curls at his nape. "What does it look like I'm doing?"

"Angling for a punishment."

She smiled. Despite every grim reality weighing the air down, desire thrummed between her thighs. It was impossible not to feel it when he spoke to her in that dangerous, raspy drawl, and when her magic lurched toward him, burning just beneath her skin, she was utterly helpless against the tide of need that swept away her good sense.

"Let me help you relax a little, demon," she whispered, her voice husky with want. His grip was like steel around her wrist, but he hadn't pulled her away. She could still brush the rigid outline of his cock where it was probably being squeezed to death against his thigh.

"Look at that — it's another terrible idea." His fingers flexed on her wrist, but he still didn't pull her away. "You know how dangerous it is to send me into rut when we're away from the den *and* you're asking me to expose you to another man?"

"I promised to stay in the car," she pointed out. "And did it occur to you that maybe you might feel *better* if we took the edge off a little?"

He snorted. "I don't think that's how my hormones work."

"You said that if you touch *me*, it'll send you into rut," she pressed. "But you won't be touching me. I'll be touching you to show you how much I appreciate you, and it'll be a little stress relief before Rasmus gets here."

Silas turned his head just enough to pin her with a narrow-eyed look. "And if it triggers my rut?"

Her toes curled within the confines of her shoes. "Then you give the journal to Rasmus as quickly as possible and we haul ass back to the house."

She could see the war happening in his eyes. Her chest tightened just a little bit more. For all that Silas thought he was incapable of caring for her as he should, he unknowingly proved himself wrong at every turn. If he didn't care, he wouldn't have said yes to this meeting, and he certainly wouldn't have bothered to keep his hands off of her while she healed.

She couldn't say how much she appreciated that, but Petra was acutely aware of the fact that she hadn't done a whole lot of caring for him. Before Antonin's grisly death, she hadn't allowed herself to become invested in him. Now, despite all the uncertainty they faced, she *could*.

She wanted to.

And that started with seeing to his needs.

"I'm healed, Silas," she assured him, stroking the back of his neck. Even those muscles were tense. "It's okay. Stop torturing yourself. Once this is done, let's go home and stop fighting it."

"We'll be going at it for weeks," he warned her, all the smoothness scraped from his drawl. "What about the trunks? All of Vanderpoel's shit? Don't you want more time to—"

"Antonin's dead. He can wait."

Silas's expression remained tight, but his grip on her wrist slackened. Petra's lips curled into a soft smile as she began to work on popping the button through the loop. She knew she had to be fast, since they were rapidly approaching the meeting time, but she relished the way he watched her, how he let her take control for just a moment.

His eyes went heavy-lidded when she eased his zipper down. "I love touching you," she whispered against his lips. Her fingers slipped beneath the waistband of his briefs. A hiss escaped from between his teeth when she closed her fingers around the hot bar of his cock.

"I love this perfect cock." She dipped her tongue past the seam of his lips, tasting him, before she playfully retreated. The bridge of his nose wrinkled again when he bared his fangs and lunged for her.

Before he could make contact, she tightened her fingers in the soft chestnut curls that draped over the nape of his neck, forcing him to stop short. Silas's expression contorted with disbelief.

"Are you trying to dominate me?" he demanded, baffled.

Petra glided her palm up his shaft, barely touching it, until she found the slick, ruddy head. It was already wet, and when she gave it a small squeeze, another trickle of lubrication pooled in the juncture between her thumb and pointer finger. *Demons,* she thought, intensely appreciative, *are definitely built a little different.*

"No," she answered him. "I'm just making sure we don't get carried away. I'm taking care of you, demon."

Silas scowled. If it weren't for the way his hips tilted into her hand, she would have thought he barely noticed how she'd begun to stroke his cock, slow and steady. "I want to kiss you."

"You can always kiss me." Petra was a little surprised to realize she meant it. She'd never been particularly physically affectionate — no doubt a result of her dysfunctional childhood — but when it came to Silas, she couldn't get enough. She was always chasing that warm, fuzzy feeling of relief his touch brought.

Leaning in close again, she pressed soft, hungry kisses to his waiting mouth. He made rough growly noises at her whenever she stopped him from going deeper, but he didn't force the issue, either. They both knew he could've and she wouldn't have complained. Not really.

But he let her have her way, and that heady feeling of power returned with a vengeance. For all that Silas loved to dominate her, he was right. All the power was truly in her hands. If she wanted to use him, to lavish him with attention for a change, all she had to do was say so.

Whispering between luscious kisses, she said, "You're mine."

"Yes," he hissed, rocking his hips in time with her steady strokes. Wet sounds filled the car with every rhythmic pull. She'd have to sanitize her hand — and probably other things — after this was done, but she couldn't have cared less.

Silas's deep chest expanded with every panting breath. One hand curled into her hair, but he didn't use it to control her like he normally did. He simply held on as his eyes squeezed shut.

Petra watched him in awe, greedy for the flush that rose in his pale cheeks, the shine on his parted lips, and the furrow of his brow. She tightened her grip and watched as the sensation rippled through his expression, tensing it in a way that almost looked like pain.

"Let go, demon." Aware that they were running out of time, she picked up her pace. Peppering his cheeks, eyes, and lips with soft kisses, she crooned, "You're mine and I love taking care of you. I love doing this for you. Let me take a little bit of the ache for you."

His head dropped to her shoulder with a low, pained groan. "Fuck," he rasped into her neck. "Why does this feel like I'm the one being punished?"

"Because you like being in control? Letting that go must be hard."

"It's not about control. It's about *owning* you."

Petra twisted her wrist on the upstroke and paused, gripping the head of his cock in a tight, possessive hold. "You think I would do this for a man who didn't own me?" Pressing her cheek into the curve of his horn, she admitted, "Nothing makes sense to me anymore, Silas. The world just keeps— it all seems so fucked up and surreal and like it keeps slipping out from under my feet. But not you. Not this. You're the *only* thing in my life that feels like it's exactly as it should be."

Max was dead, she'd killed a man, wraiths were real, and now she had a horrifying piece of history sitting in her lap, waiting to rip open untold wounds.

But Silas was *right*. How she felt when they were together was *right*. How they fit like two fucked up puzzle pieces was *right*.

The parts of him that had scared her seemed so small and unimportant under the light of what she now knew — that Silas was a monster who would die for her, who accepted her for whoever she chose to be, and who belonged to her now.

He panted into the juncture of her neck and shoulder, damp-ening her skin with his breath. He blazed with heat under her slick palm. Her arm was beginning to cramp a little and the angle she had to contort herself into wasn't ideal for her lower back, but she didn't mind. Especially when he began to thrust his hips in earnest, like he just couldn't help but seek more, to shuttle his cock through the mess coating her hand.

"Yes, yes, yes," he chanted, barely audible.

Combing her fingers through his curls, she murmured, "Come for me, sweetheart."

He sucked in a deep breath and appeared to hold it. His hips jerked. A moment before he came, Silas let loose a terrifying snarl and clamped his fangs onto the meat of her shoulder.

He bit down hard — not enough to break the skin but certainly enough to bruise — as his release coated her hand and wrist. She carefully angled her palm, trying to catch the worst of the mess and save his jeans, as she whispered soft things into his ear.

Has anyone ever been truly soft with you?

She struggled to imagine he would ever allow it from a sexual partner. He was too wild, too inexperienced with emotion. No doubt any display of true affection, were they ever offered, would have confused and annoyed him.

The fact that he let her do it was extraordinary.

Petra wanted to laugh at herself, at how ridiculous it was to feel the prickle of tears behind her eyelids while she gently cradled a half demon's cock in her release-soaked hand.

It was just a handjob, but it wasn't. Not really. In that moment, with his fangs digging into her skin and his big body hunched over hers, she felt closer to him than she had with anyone. Ever.

Silas released her shoulder with a grunt. Nuzzling the throbbing pulse just beneath her jaw, he muttered, *"Sweetheart?"*

A bubble of laughter escaped her. Gently putting him to rights, she pulled her sticky hand back to her side of the car. "Can't you be my sweetheart?"

"I've never been sweet a day in my life." He sounded deeply disgruntled, but also sated, which was a good sign. Petra didn't know too much about ruts, but she suspected that if he'd been tipped into his like he feared, he wouldn't have sounded so sleepy.

"Oh, I don't know." She played with one of his curls, admiring the glossy brown color and the way it sprang back when she released it. Memories of their time in the blanket fort made her stomach flutter. "I think you're pretty sweet to me. In your own way."

Silas turned his head to peer at her, assessing her as always. "In a way that makes you happy?"

I'll make you happy, he'd said. *Then you'll never want to leave me.*

Petra's voice came out hoarse with emotion when she answered, "Yeah, sweetheart. In a way that makes me very happy."

CHAPTER FORTY-SIX

THE ONLY THING THAT MADE SEEING RASMUS'S SMUG face within a hundred yards of his mate bearable was the knowledge that she sat in the car smelling like sex and sticky with his come.

Personally, he didn't see the point of any of this.

Even if he hadn't been more territorial than normal, he wouldn't have understood Petra's reasoning for this song and dance. Silas didn't understand why Petra didn't simply keep the stupid journal. After all, it was always good to have blackmail in your pocket — especially if it was on unpredictable bastards like Rasmus Adams. Or if she didn't want to keep it, then they could damn well *send* it to him. He was feral, but Silas was pretty sure the man had a mailbox.

But Petra insisted on being certain he received it, and when she wanted something, she got it.

So even though it went against every instinct he possessed, Silas met the were in the parking lot of Maple's Diner. The journal was tucked into a brown paper bag, tightly sealed with a piece of tape. Petra treated the thing like contraband, which he supposed it was, in a sense.

His mate had spent most of the last day and a half participating in a mostly one-sided debate over whether they should hand it over to Rasmus or the authorities. He really didn't care which she chose, as both options were equally bland, but he did offer his opinion that giving it to Rasmus might earn them a favor in the future. It wasn't as good as blackmail, but it was something.

Petra didn't love that suggestion, but she didn't say it was a bad idea, either. While he suspected most of her reasoning for deciding to hand it over was sentimental — seeing as they were something approaching *friends,* apparently — he wanted to believe she saw his point, too. His witch had a soft heart, but she could be ruthless. It was one of the many things he loved about her.

Rasmus climbed out of his sleek silver car and rested a hand on the roof, his suspicious, mismatched eyes fixed on Silas. He was dressed in dark slacks and a pale blue button down, and his tattoos peeked out from above the collar and from where he'd rolled up the sleeves. His hair, messy on top and beginning to gray on the sides, looked like he'd been running his fingers through it.

Before Rasmus could take a step in Silas's direction, he snapped, "Stay there."

"Why?"

"Because my mate's in the car, asshole."

And since the man apparently had a death wish, his gaze slid over Silas's shoulder to peer at the tinted windshield. Even though Silas knew he could only see the vague shape of Petra, he stepped into Rasmus's eyeline anyway, his shadows rippling across his body in a blatant threat.

"Eyes off if you wanna keep them."

Rasmus made a sucking sound with his teeth. It puckered his scarred lips in a funny way.

The war and a hard life had done a number on him. Silas imagined that at some point Rasmus had been blown up and put together just a little bit wrong, but he'd heard people still thought the man was handsome. He didn't get it, but his tastes ran blonde, buxom, and able to burn his nuts off when the mood struck, so he wasn't the best judge.

"You gonna tell me why I had to drag my ass across the continent or what?" Rasmus asked, one scarred eyebrow cocked.

Rolling his shoulders to ease some of the tension knotting his muscles, Silas strode over to Rasmus's car. The were watched him closely. His eyes had a wild gleam to them, something dark and animalistic, but that wasn't new. Rasmus always looked like he was half a step away from letting the beast explode from within. He claimed it was part of his charm.

"Here," Silas grunted, shoving the package into Rasmus's chest with more force than necessary. To his credit, the man didn't stumble.

Wisely, he also didn't reach for it. "What's this?"

"We came across some information. This is a bit you're gonna wanna see." Considering the amount of raw, encrypted data his systems were still trying to process, qualifying what they'd uncovered as "some" was probably the understatement of the century. Rasmus didn't need to know that, though.

His explanation didn't put the were at ease. Instead, he wisely appeared to grow even more suspicious. "And you just want to give it to me? For free?"

Silas shoved the package into his chest again, but this time he let go of it, forcing Rasmus to catch it before it fell to the gritty asphalt.

"*I'm* not giving you shit. My mate is."

Holding the package in one hand like it might explode at any moment, Rasmus dared to glance toward the car again. "The only reason I bothered to come here is to see if she's alive. Is she doing all right?"

"Fine."

"Really? Because last time I saw her, she had a hole in her side."

Silas's shadows rippled, itching to act on the surge of aggression that coursed through him, but he got a handle on them just in time. He had no particular fondness for Rasmus, and Silas hated that he'd seen Petra when she was at her most vulnerable, but killing him served no real purpose.

Maybe that wouldn't have stopped him before, but it did now. Because now he had a mate to think about. Petra asked him not to hurt Rasmus and so he wouldn't.

Even if he *really* wanted to.

"She's healed," he bit out, forcing his shadows to settle at his feet, where they began to writhe in the darkness below Rasmus's vehicle. The urge to slash his tires was a visceral one.

She's healed, he silently repeated, reassuring himself. *She's healed and she's mine and no one can take her from me.*

And when they got back to his den, he'd finally, *finally* seal that claim.

Rasmus shook his head, his expression troubled. "Look, I certainly can't say shit about mismatched pairings, but you and Pet? Are you *sure?* I want to talk to her, just to see for myself that you haven't fucked with her head or something. She deserves better than you, Shade."

Silas couldn't deny it. He still felt her fingers gently combing through his hair, still heard the sweet nothings she whispered in his ear. He couldn't stop thinking of her quiet certainty that he *cared.*

Petra Zaskodna was a woman of masks, but those masks hid an exquisitely fragile heart. She cared about her people. She was loyal to a fault. She believed in justice, however it might be delivered.

She was good — and that was why she needed someone very, very bad.

No one else could give her what she needed to thrive. He might be a bad mate who couldn't love her in the way he should, but he'd tear the world down to the studs for her.

And he'd *never* leave her.

"I don't give a fuck," he replied, aggression steadily rising like steam within a kettle. "She's my mate. She's happy and she's healthy and she's safe. That's all you or anyone else needs to know."

Rasmus's lips pressed thin. "I want to see her."

"Sounds like you want to die, too."

"She's my friend, Shade, and I'm the one who made the colossal mistake of connecting you two. I need to see that she's okay after *you* got her shot."

"The fact that you're her friend is the only reason you're *here,*" he snarled. His blood felt too hot, his skin too tight. The glare of the sun was searing on the crown of his head and in his eyes.

Fuck this and fuck the sun. We should be in my den.

On the brink of losing control, Silas sought out the bit of himself tied around Petra's neck. The phantom touch of her — the beat of her pulse, the salt of her skin, the hot bite of her magic — soothed the sharpest edge of his rage. For a moment, anyway.

"She's the one who wanted to give you that. She's the one who demanded we meet. You think I'd do this? You think I'd do you a *favor?*"

A keen-eyed animal peered out of Rasmus's mismatched eyes. "What favor are you doing for me, exactly?"

What little patience Silas possessed was rapidly evaporating. "You know what I could be doing right now instead of this? My *mate.* Just look in the fuckin' bag so we can go."

In a headspace not clouded by hormones, Silas would've appreciated the caution with which Rasmus peeled the tape off the package and pulled the edges of the bag apart. After all, there were many ways one could kill a man. Hiding some nasty sigilwork or even some good old fashioned poison in a package wasn't the worst thing Silas had ever done, and they both knew it.

Rasmus was no saint. He'd had an illustrious career as a jack of all trades criminal before he settled down with the San Francisco were pack and took up the job as their enforcer and most recently as the owner of The Broken Tooth. There wasn't much work for weres in the grim days after the war, so it wasn't an uncommon story. The ones who learned to control their beasts tended to band together to share resources. Many of those packs inevitably turned to crime when every other door was shut in their faces. Some were better at it than others, and a select few, like the man standing before Silas, were very, very good.

Like him, Rasmus had killed men in underhanded ways. Many of them.

His skepticism was warranted, as was his clear reluctance to peer into the bag. Silas wouldn't have done it. But he could feel his rut rising in him, putting pressure on all the soft, logical parts that might have found some humor in the situation, if not an overabundance of patience.

He wanted to *leave*.

It didn't make a damn lick of difference to him what happened with Rasmus and the journal. He didn't care about the man, nor weres in general.

And yet, somehow through the cloud of hormones and impatience, a bit of... something managed to get through when Silas watched the man's face go sickly gray.

Rasmus stared into the bag for several seconds before he reached inside to retrieve the old, smoke-scented doctor's journal. His eyes went wide and glassy, his lips colorless. All the life in him appeared to simply shut down.

"Where did you find this?"

"On a dead man."

Rasmus didn't open it. He didn't appear to need to. His fingers gripped the aged leather cover so hard the pads went white. "Who."

It wasn't a question. It was barely even a word. The single syllable was garbled, choked out like a reflex.

Silas didn't want to give him anything, especially any information tied to Petra. Everything about her was on lockdown — particularly her involvement in the death of the Protector of the Gloriae.

But Silas fought to claw back some of his usual cool rationality. He needed to see this moment as he would have a month ago, when everything was different. *What can I get from this?*

He'd never considered allies before. After all, he'd only ever needed Tal. Everyone else who might have been useful to him could either be bought or blackmailed into giving him what he wanted. Silas had viewed the gift of the journal as a sort of bribery for a future favor, but when he watched Rasmus's features tremble, threatening the infamous and horrifying transformation into his were form, he realized that there might be something else gained.

"His name was Antonin Vanderpoel," he begrudgingly revealed. "He was Protector of the Gloriae and the leader of the Ardeo."

"The *Ardeo?*" Rasmus took half a step back, his expression contorting with disbelief. "The Temple hasn't had a military since—"

"Apparently they survived. Or someone has gone to great lengths to remake it."

"Fuck." Rasmus braced his free hand on the roof of his car. His other hand hung stiffly by his side, the journal pressed against his thigh like he wanted to keep it out of sight. If Silas thought he was pale before, it was nothing compared to the sickly pallor that passed over him then.

Almost speaking to himself, the were muttered, "Soldiers. He was trying to make soldiers. Just never found out why."

"Who?"

"Dr. Wyeth." Rasmus's forehead beaded with sweat. He squeezed his eyes shut. "Josephine said it was— She warned me. She was always trying to warn me. I thought it was the Queen. We *all* thought it was the Queen."

Silas could barely follow the thread of what Rasmus was trying to tell him, but there was only one queen in the UTA. The orcish queen of the Orclind was a formidable, ruthless woman, and he had no doubt that she *could* have been responsible, but... "That was never proven, and Queen Sigrid denies it."

"That's where most of us were shipped. Not all, but most," Rasmus replied, brows bunching as if in pain. Silas got the impression that he'd momentarily forgotten who he was talking to. "The Orclind was being hammered on both sides and they'd started running out of soldiers. None of it made any sense, but it was the only theory that had legs. It never occurred to me that they might have been testing soldiers for another player altogether and— and hiding it behind selling us as mercenaries."

The hair on the back of Silas's neck prickled. Voice dropping, he muttered, "I think the Temple has had grand ambitions for a very long time."

"How do you know?" Rasmus opened his eyes and pinned Silas with a glassy look. "How do you know he didn't just— just stumble on the journal? Or buy it?"

They were valid questions. If Vanderpoel was in the blackmail business, as he very much was, then it made sense that much of his information would be bought secondhand. It wasn't outrageous to think he might have had no direct involvement in the scheme to weaponize weres.

"Dr. Wyeth wasn't discreet." Silas gestured to the journal in Rasmus's white-knuckled grip. "There's more than just medical notes in there. There's records of payments, summaries of meetings, complaints about his benefactors. He basically plastered the Temple's name all over it."

Which explained why Antonin kept it. Whether he had a direct connection with Dr. Wyeth or not, it made sense to keep an ace in his pocket. Hiding it saved the Temple from international outrage and prosecution, but if he'd ever needed to leverage something against the organization as a whole... *Yeah, evidence of a war crime would do it.*

Rasmus swiped his hand over his clammy face. "The Temple was building an army. Why?" He paused, eyes darting like he might find the answers out in the grass somewhere.

Silas's mind churned through everything he knew, everything he'd seen and heard in the last few years.

There was nothing concrete, no one thing he could pin his suspicions on, but his gut warned him that he'd been closer to the Ardeo's web than he realized long before he ever set his sights on Petra.

"No organization that has the means and the wherewithal to *make* soldiers stops on its own," Silas replied. "It just changes tactics. I haven't figured out what they're after, but I will."

Rasmus's gaze sharpened as the shock began to wear off. "Is this what Pet needed your help with?"

"No." He scowled. "Not directly. She had no idea what she was stepping into. And stop fuckin' calling her that."

A shadow of a smile came and went across the were's scarred mouth. "How'd she get shot? I figured it was your fuck-up, but..."

It was *my fuck-up.* But Silas still answered, "Vanderpoel."

"When she asked me to set up the meeting between you two, I asked her why. Figured I could probably talk her out of it if I knew. But she said she needed information on someone, and he was dangerous enough that she didn't want me or the pack involved. Must've been him, huh?" Rasmus straightened up a bit, his shoulders no longer bunched up around his ears. "The sabbatical excuse is good for a few months, Shade, but if this is as bad as it looks—"

"I know."

He wasn't naive enough to think the Ardeo died with Vanderpoel, nor that he could hide Petra away forever. Willingly, anyway. The shock of killing Vanderpoel would wear off eventually and she'd want to return to the world, maybe even to her position as High Priestess. The clock was ticking before they were either found or she got it into her head to do something reckless.

Silas had no intention of failing her again, so that meant he had to figure this out before either of those things happened.

He'd put the entire Temple on notice, and he wouldn't sleep until he'd rooted out every threat to his mate. If that meant he had to burn the entire institution down, then so be it.

Pushing himself slightly away from the car, Rasmus asked, "What do you want in exchange for this?"

"My mate wanted it to be a gift."

"Great, but that's not how this works."

Silas fought the urge to turn his head to check on Petra. He'd been gone from her side for too long. His skin was beginning to feel too tight again, his clothes scratchy and stifling.

"You're right," he bit out. "I want you to be my eyes and ears in San Francisco. At least until we get back. I want to know if someone so much as whispers her name. And be on standby if I need something in the next few weeks."

"What are you planning?"

Silas was already turning away, his long strides carrying him swiftly back to Petra, when he replied, "What would *you* do if a shady secret organization tried to kill your mate?"

Rasmus answered matter-of-factly, "Destroy 'em."

Silas lifted a hand over his shoulder and flicked his pointer finger. *Got it in one, asshole.*

Rasmus barked his name, but Silas didn't stop walking. He could make out the shape of Petra nearly pressing her nose against the windshield. Now that he'd sighted her, only an m-lev train could have knocked him off course.

His heart thumped in his ears as a rush of anticipation moved in a prickling wave over every inch of his flesh. *It's time,* the animal in him howled. *It's finally time.*

"Shade! What am I supposed to do with the journal?"

"Whatever the fuck you want," he growled, yanking open the driver's side door with a little too much force.

The scent of his mate and his own musky release wafted over him, more intoxicating than any drug. Rationality wavered.

Gogogogethomegrabherlickhercuntuntilshebegsgo—

Silas bit his cheek hard, fighting back against the animal that threatened to make it impossible for him to drive. Any interest he might have had in Rasmus was blown away like smoke in the wind.

Climbing into the car, Silas didn't spare a thought for the way the man continued to stand there in the parking lot, staring at the journal in his hand like he couldn't decide if he should throw it into the drainage ditch or not. He didn't care what Rasmus chose to do with the journal.

Only one thing mattered, and she needed to be in his den.

Now.

CHAPTER FORTY-SEVEN

NEITHER OF THEM SPOKE. THE AIR WAS TOO THICK FOR speech, and there was little to talk about, anyway.

Silas drove with a proprietary hand on Petra's thigh the entire ride back to the house. Touching her was the only thing keeping him tethered to some semblance of sanity. If he stopped, he worried he'd snap.

Despite the cool air blowing from the vents, sweat slid down the back of his neck in thin rivulets. His jaw ached from clenching it so hard. Every few seconds he'd stroke his palm up and down her supple thigh, too greedy to stop himself.

C'mon, he silently commanded himself. *Don't fuck this up. Just make it back to the den in one piece.*

Fear gripped his throat and squeezed. It battled with raw lust scorching a path through his body and the overwhelming urge to claim her, wholly and completely.

He'd let her down once and nearly lost her because of it. His rut was an inevitability — and hopefully a pleasurable one — but he couldn't allow it to hurt her. *He* couldn't hurt her. Not by becoming distracted and steering the car into a ditch, and not by getting too caught up in the moment, either.

It was still too soon. His father said he needed to give her a week. Silas *tried*. He would have continued to try, if Petra didn't make her wishes clear.

But he was tormented by the thought of causing her any harm. For as impulsive as he was, Silas didn't just lose control. Even during his past ruts, he'd always maintained a clear head. It was something he'd partly attributed to being only half demon. He acted rationally, always in his best interest, and didn't care who he hurt in the process. Now he understood that it wasn't his nature or his genetics that had spared him the worst of the rut. It was missing *her*.

His hand shook on her thigh. Beneath his palm he felt the plushness of her flesh, the slight give of her muscle, and the brittle bar of her bone. She was so fragile. All it would take was one thoughtless move, a rough touch, and she'd shatter.

An electric jolt ran up his arm when Petra laid her hand over his. She didn't turn to look at him. Her gaze remained fixed on the sight of the house's driveway when she simply informed him, "I trust you, Silas."

You shouldn't, he should've said. *That's stupid.*

But he didn't say that because in his heart he'd always be selfish and mean and desperate for her.

He'd take whatever she gave him, whether it was good for her or not, because he was too damn hungry for her to resist.

Parking in front of the familiar white-washed face of the house, Silas let out a long, shuddering breath. It took immense effort to remove his hand from her thigh, and if he'd dared to look at her, he was certain he wouldn't have been able to do it.

Unfolding himself from the car felt wrong. His nerves were shot, each one vibrating with need, and his shadows writhed in and out of him, pulsing across his flesh in time with his accelerated heartbeat. For want of something to do, his shaking hand anxiously rubbed a horn.

The air was heavy with the scent of green things, dusty earth, and the peculiar note that summer sun imbued. Normally he liked it, but at that moment all he wanted to do was chase it away with the scent of his mate — Petra's delicious blend of salt and arousal and incense.

"Demon? Aren't you coming inside?"

His gaze darted to where Petra stood on the porch. She watched him from the shade, one elegant hand on the doorknob. Her expression was tender, like she *knew*.

"Your necklace," he grated, stuck there by the car.

Her brows furrowed. She lifted a hand to touch the heavy gold charm that hung between her breasts. "What about it?"

"There's more." Gods, talking was so hard. Words fragmented on his tongue, and the shards scattered before he could reassemble them.

"More... what?"

He had to close his eyes, blocking out the sight of her, before he could force out, "Glamour. Protection. Location. I built them in."

He needed to rework some of it, obviously, since the ward to keep people who meant her harm triggered both too late and not powerful enough. Vanderpoel should have never been able to aim the gun at her, let alone shoot. Clearly Silas had been too cautious with his sigilwork.

But that wasn't the only protective ward he'd put into it — and the other one he knew for certain wouldn't fail.

Petra's worried gaze searched his expression. "Why are you telling me this?"

"Because." He rubbed his horn again and felt the slight ridges that marked his growth, as well as the tiny imperfection there at the base, hidden by his hair. "If I get out of control, if you get scared, you need to use it."

He opened his eyes just in time to see a look of profound unease ripple across her face. "What are you saying, Silas?"

"There's a sigil there on the back, the one in the center circle. It's for me."

"For you?"

He gestured to his head. "I branded it into my horn as a fail-safe. If you ever— if something happened, I wanted you to have the option to take me out."

At the time, he hadn't been entirely sure why he'd done it, only that it felt right. Part of chasing Petra was about knowing she had all the power and chose to give it to him — it always had been. The concept that she'd had a kill switch at her disposal, that at any moment she could have taken him out, but she had *no idea* thrilled him. It was another part of their game.

So he'd burned the sigil into his horn. What was the harm? If he regretted it, all he had to do was buff it out. Besides, he hadn't even been sure he'd ever tell her what that sigil did. It was his exciting little secret, and if it remained only that, then that pleasure was perfectly acceptable.

"All you have to do is activate it," he continued, chest tightening. "Just activate it and run."

I'll find you. I'll always find you.

But he could give her time. He could give her the power to knock him on his ass if he lost his mind. He could give her the power of choice. Always.

Because she'd never really had that, and if he couldn't give her the love and care she deserved from a good mate, then at least he could give her this.

Petra stared at him, her lips parted and her skin ashen. "Would it *kill* you?"

He shook his head. "No. Just knock me out."

"Why would you give me this? You'd never hurt me. There's no need—"

"I'd never *intentionally* hurt you," he corrected, harsher than he intended. "But what if I fuck it up? What if the rut's too much and I stop listening to you? Tal warned me that I might lose my mind, but I didn't listen. I didn't want to. I thought I could handle it and nothing would be different. Now, I— You can't let me do that, Petra. You just fuckin' can't. I won't let you."

If I hurt you, I'd break.

The truth of that thought rang high and clear in his mind. He treasured her trust in him above all things — even himself. If he were to break that trust... Silas couldn't claim to have spent a lot of time being self-critical, let alone considering the concept of guilt, but he could now see how it might destroy a man.

He'd once thought it might be enough just to have her. What did it matter if she hated or feared him? As long as she belonged to him, he'd be satisfied.

But he saw now how that would be like choosing to drink from a poisoned well for the rest of his life. He couldn't live without her, so he would keep coming back, he'd keep sipping to quench his never-ending thirst, but it'd kill him eventually.

Silas didn't want to die a slow, painful death in the shadows of her heart. He'd do anything to bask in her light. He *needed* her love. He would never be satisfied with anything less than that.

And if that meant going through the agony of rut without his mate to protect her from harm? So be it.

"Silas, I..." Petra trailed off, her voice fading into the summer breeze and tittering birdsong. She didn't say anything more for a long stretch, but when she did, her voice was firm. "I can defend myself."

Holding her stare, he bluntly demanded, "Would you burn me alive?"

Petra held his stare for a long moment before cutting her gaze away, like she couldn't take it anymore. Her lips trembled. "No," she croaked.

"Why?"

"You know why."

He was stuck in her orbit. It was all he could do to stand there for as long as he had, resisting her pull, but it was a fundamental law of the universe that eventually he'd give in.

Silas didn't register the distance even as he crossed it. He didn't feel the gravel under his boots or the warm air ruffling his curls. He didn't hear the creak of the old, sun-baked porch under his weight as he climbed the steps.

He stooped to press his forehead against hers and watched her eyes flutter shut. Pressing his hand over her thundering heart, he demanded, "Why?"

"Because you're mine," she whispered. "I can't hurt you, either."

A harsh breath exploded out of him. Silas cupped the sides of her jaw. Nudging her forehead more firmly with his own, like he might be able to meld them together if he just pressed hard enough, he grated, "That's why you've got to do it. I need to know that you're safe — even from me. Especially from me."

"I *am* safe with you," she argued, softer, a little pained.

"Yes." He smoothed his thumbs over the silken rises of her cheeks, savoring her. "And if that ever changes, you put me down."

When she remained stubbornly silent, he whispered, "You have a piece of my soul wrapped around your throat and my whole rotten heart in your hand. You have no idea how vulnerable you've made me. Promise me, Petra. Promise me you won't let me hurt you. Protect me from that."

If he'd ever needed real proof that Petra Zaskodna was a good person, too good for him by far, this was it. She would never take advantage of the power he'd given her. She would never sell him out or give it to someone else. She was his, just as much as he was hers. She'd protect him — even from himself.

And that's why he knew she'd say yes, even if she hated the idea as much as he would in her place.

"Okay," she breathed, nodding as much as their position would allow. "Okay."

Silas closed his eyes. Relief lifted the weight of the worry that had plagued him, the certainty that everyone was right to believe he'd hurt his mate at the first opportunity.

Knowing she wouldn't let that happen...

He could finally let go.

Chapter Forty-Eight

Silas shuddered. His fingers speared into her silken hair. The animal in him howled for her, ravenous for the way she bent her neck so sweetly for him. It marveled at their luck. How could they have gotten such an exquisite creature in their grasp, willing and submissive?

Silas rubbed his lips over her brow, down over the bridge of her nose, until he finally reached her mouth. Pressing the words into her lips, he snarled, "You're *my* mate."

"Yes," she breathed.

"You're gonna do as I say."

"Yes."

"You're gonna let me use you however I want, as many times as I want, until I'm satisfied."

Her breaths escaped in quick little pants. He loved feeling them, tasting her in the tiny amount of air that separated their mouths. "Gods, *yes.*"

"Careful, little goddess," he warned, backing her slowly toward the front door. "I might never be satisfied."

Gods bless her, Petra had already begun to work on the button of his jeans. His mate was truly a gift.

"Poor me," she sassed, even as her back hit the door. "A hot demon is about to fuck me so good and so hard and for so long that I forget my own last name. However will I survive—"

"Shut up," he huffed, pushing the door open with one hand. His other fisted the hair at the nape of her neck, holding her in place as he drove his mouth down on hers.

Petra made a hungry sound in the back of her throat. Her fingers worked at his fly as she stumbled backward into the entryway. Floorboards creaked as they tripped over one another and shuffled their way inside. Their tongues tangled in a slick dance, sending the roar of lust in his blood to new heights.

Silas couldn't get enough of her taste. The scent of her clouded his already scattered mind. His world was nothing but the feel of her skin and the way she clung to him, desperate for his kiss.

His shadows undulated across the floor, slamming the door shut behind them, and crawled up his body. The feeling of tightness, of not fitting in his skin, got worse and worse and worse until— *snap.*

The man he was, the person he tried to be for her, disappeared. In his place was a demon ready to claim his mate once and for all.

Sheathed in shadow, his body became bigger, his proportions just a little wrong. His horns lengthened into jagged points and his claws extended, easily allowing him to tear through Petra's clothing. Shadows snaked down her legs, pulling off everything he couldn't reach, leaving her completely nude.

She made a soft, squeaky noise of surprise, but she didn't smell like fear when he growled, long and low, at the sight of his shadows circling her throat — the only bit of coverage he'd allowed her now.

Petra pawed at him, her deft fingers turned clumsy as she fought to touch him while his shadows worked all over her body, getting in her way. She didn't stand a chance against them, though. They roped around her wrists and forearms, binding them together, and whirled her around to face the wall. Silas nudged her legs apart with his foot and dragged his shadowed hands down her flanks, admiring her tanned flesh.

Grabbing her hips, he forced her to stick her ass out for him. Keeping her balance meant bracing her bound forearms against the wall and lowering her head until the cascade of her blonde hair nearly touched the wooden floorboards.

Already he could scent her arousal in the air. Her skin was hot to the touch. When he dragged his palms down over the globes of her ass, Petra's back arched in an elegant bow, pushing herself into his hands.

"This is mine," he rumbled, stooping to rake his fangs over her shoulder. Red streaks bloomed in their wake. "This body is mine. This wet cunt is mine."

He slid his right hand down over her hip and across her trembling abdomen to cup her greedily between her thighs. Petra's hips rolled in a short burst, a reflex to his rough handling, but she didn't move to get away. Her stance widened, deepening the angle of her arched back and putting her dripping cunt more firmly in the palm of his hand.

"Yes," she moaned.

He could barely hear anything over the sound of his pounding heart, but that soft, needy word hit him like a punch to the gut.

Grinding his trapped cock into her ass, Silas twisted his left hand into her hair, forcing her head up so he could rasp in her ear, "You're lucky I've got the shot, little goddess, or else you'd be bred by the end of this."

The fingers of his other hand slid through her slippery flesh, never settling but simply luxuriating in the sensation of her arousal dripping over his skin.

"Is that what you want?" He gave her clitoris a quick pinch, just to watch her lithe body jerk. "You want me to breed you? Fill you up and make you mine, inside and out? I'll keep you impaled on my demon cock until you're bred, baby."

"I—"

His shadows crawled up her neck to cover her mouth. They slid between her lips and over her tongue, stuffing her mouth full and keeping her jaw locked at the same time. "Ah, sweet little goddess," he purred, "I don't actually need your answer. Just this cunt dripping over my hand. It tells me everything I need to know."

Petra's nails dug into the wallpaper hard enough to bleach her nail beds white, but when he turned her head to look into her eyes, they were half-lidded and glazed with desire. Above the writhing shadows covering her mouth, her cheeks were a deep pink.

Petra didn't balk at the sight of the monster looming over her, and when he finally speared his fingers into the hot well of her cunt, she moaned long and sweet and just for him.

His thoughts were hazy. Words were scattered, torn in a dozen different directions as his impulses gained more control over him. Silas pumped his fingers into her mindlessly, ruthlessly, as his shadows tongued her clitoris and the beaded nipples that crowned her heavy breasts. When Petra began to squirm, threatening to reflexively close her thighs as her orgasm neared, he didn't think twice about snaring her legs, too, forcing her to keep herself open for his pleasure. Gorgeous, sloppy sounds filled the entryway as she gushed over his fingers.

Silas untangled his fingers from her hair only so he could tear at his clothing, finishing the job she'd started even as drove his fingers into her again and again. Needing more, always more, his shadows expanded inside her and undulated around his fingers.

She shrieked behind the shadows sealing her mouth shut. The afternoon light streaming in from the small frosted glass window above the door glittered in the sweat that dewed on her lithe back. Her hips jerked erratically as her orgasm tightened her muscles around his fingers. Wet sounds and the scent of her desire filled the air and made him lose what little grasp on sanity he still possessed.

As soon as his cock, swollen and dripping, sprang free from

the confines of his shredded briefs, Silas jerked his hand free from her grasping cunt. His world was shrouded, his vision limited to the sight of her bent before him, her pink flesh ripe and ready for him. There were no thoughts in his mind when he drove himself into her in one merciless thrust — only pure satisfaction and a total, all-encompassing sense of triumph.

He rocked his hips mindlessly, luxuriating the wet glide, the heat of her all around him, and the unique feel of *her*. Like he expected, she was almost uncomfortably hot. His cock felt a bit like it was being branded, but he couldn't get enough of it. Her.

Planting a hand on the wall over her head, Silas gripped her throat at the base with his other one and used it to sway her forward and back in short, jerky bursts to match his frantic thrusts. Petra made desperate mewling sounds behind the shadows. Every time he sheathed himself, her channel gripped him hard, like it wanted to lock him there, and every time he pulled back, it was like gliding through liquid fire.

He didn't realize he was talking until the sound of his own voice penetrated the fog of rut.

"...should make you run," he growled, forcing the words out between harsh exhales. "Make you run and run and run just so I can hunt you down. Teach you that you'll never get away. You'll never be free of me. I'll chase you and fuck you in the dirt and you'll *like* it, little goddess."

Petra nodded helplessly, her shining hair swaying with the movement of their bodies, and began to match his rhythm in earnest. Her necklace swayed, too. It was a delicate gold pendulum between her breasts, marking every stroke of his cock into her lush cunt.

The necklace should've been a symbol of her devotion to a goddess, but it wasn't. He'd crafted it by hand. He'd chosen the finest gold and imbued it with his own magic, his own sigils. He'd put it around her neck and given her the power to make or break him at a moment's notice.

When she accepted that necklace and gave him hers in

exchange, she'd accepted his claim — and he'd never, ever let her forget it.

Needing to hear it from her mouth, too, Silas pulled the shadows away from her lips and demanded, *"Say it."*

"I like it," she choked out, blindly reaching back with her bound hands to grip his horns. "I *love* it. Please, please—"

Prying her fingers from his horns, he flattened her palms against the wall and held them there, forcing her back into a supplicant's pose. She shone with a faint internal light in the dim entryway. That precious light, the one thing all demons secretly craved, made his shadows that much hungrier to eat her up.

They crawled all over her body, threads connecting and splitting and forming to her contours. He could taste the salt of her sweat, the sweetness of her cunt. He could feel the pounding of her heart. In that moment, she was nearly swallowed up by him, impaled by him, owned by him in every way. If he could've, he would have forced himself into her pores and the space between her neurons.

He wanted to be everywhere, in everything, because she was already everywhere, in everything inside *him.*

"I want to touch you," she begged, clawing at the wallpaper. *"Please,* Silas."

Giving her ass a harsh swat, he snapped, "No."

Petra yelped. Every muscle in her body went tight below him, clenching him hard enough to make him hiss. When the shock wore off, she rasped a curse and rolled her hips erratically, like she couldn't help herself.

A weak chorus of *please please please* began, but he didn't give in. He was driven by the need to mark, to claim, and that left no room for softness. It was his job to claim her and give her the dominance she so obviously craved. Petra didn't make the rules here. She couldn't make demands. She was at his mercy.

She *wanted* to be at his mercy, no matter how she might beg or plead. His mate blossomed under his control. Her masks fell off. What was left was pure Petra, the very essence of who she was, and he'd hold onto that with everything he had.

So he kept her hands pinned to the wall, he drove himself into the hilt again and again, and he rolled her tight little clitoris between his fingers ruthlessly, forcing short, brutal orgasms that never really ended.

Each one forced his own pleasure higher. His shadows grew even more restless, his form more monstrous. Hungry for her in all ways, they sheathed his cock, thickening it until her body resisted the expansion. Rather than dulling his sensations, it increased them tenfold, allowing him to experience fucking her in every possible way.

Yesyesyesyesyes, the animal in him chanted, egging him on. Pleasure was a constant thrum in his veins. Pressure built at the base of his spine but it went beyond the need to release. It was the sense that once he did, it would only be the beginning.

This moment was the flame racing up the fuse, not the bomb.

Petra made inhuman noises, cursed, locked her muscles, and clawed at the walls, but she could do no more than that. All he allowed her was to stand there and take whatever he gave her.

"Too— *much,*" she wheezed, channel fluttering around him in a desperate attempt to accommodate his new girth. "Too— too—"

"What was that?" Silas rubbed his face into her hair, scenting his mate as he slowed his thrusts to a deceptively gentle pace. There was no mercy in it. If she was struggling to take him, going slower would only heighten the discomfort, not alleviate it. She'd feel every inch of him sliding in and out, bit by bit, and when the crown of his cock once more notched at her entrance, it would feel that much bigger, the discomfort even more acute.

Petra made a high-pitched keening sound. "It's— You're too *big.*"

Using his shadows to keep her arms in place, he fisted her hair in both of his hands and pulled her head back so he could admire her. Petra's cheeks were ruddy, her skin sheened with sweat, and her eyes squeezed shut. Every time he stroked her g-spot with the underside of his cock, she twitched like he'd shocked her.

"I'm too big for you?" He *tsked*. "That's too bad, little goddess, because I haven't even filled you up yet. Now look at me."

Silas tightened his fingers in her hair, demanding her obedience. Her eyes popped open at the bite of pain. "Good girl," he praised, admiring the gleam of tears in her blue eyes. "You can take it. You can take anything. You're my *mate.*"

Petra made a valiant effort to focus on him as he continued to force himself deeper, harder. She appeared terrifically vulnerable as she searched for approval in his monstrous face. It was the hottest fucking thing he'd ever seen.

Silas didn't speed up, but he increased his force until each stroke pushed her up against the wall. The longer he kept it up, the more tension bled from her, allowing him to comfortably pound into her pliant body.

"So good," he growled. He watched her lips, swollen and red from being bitten, part with a needy, animalistic moan. "See? You love being stretched. Glory's pretty favorite was meant to take demon cock. You were built for this, baby."

Petra groaned and nodded helplessly. Her body began to shake beneath his. Each tremor was punctuated with a desperate, whisper-soft, "Silas, Silas, *Silas.*"

"I know what you need. I always know." He pressed his lips to her sweaty cheek and raggedly demanded, "Tell me to fill you up. Beg me."

"Fill— me. *Please!*"

Silas let loose a guttural growl. His shadows slid away from her arms, allowing them to fall limp by her sides. She slapped weakly at the wall in an attempt to support herself as he slipped his arms beneath hers and curled his hands over her shoulders, anchoring her back to his front. Their bodies slid against one another, slick with sweat and arousal, but his grip was firm.

He pistoned his hips, increasing his speed as instinct drowned out everything else. He barely noticed when Petra covered his hands with her own or when she dropped her head back against his chest. The sound of her voice reached him, euphoric and desperate and raw, but her words were beyond him. Sense was, too.

There was nothing more than their bodies connecting over and over, that pressure low in his gut, and the need to mark, to *claim*—

He came with a silent snarl.

His shadows lashed across the ground, across his mate, their tendrils viciously stroking her inside and out until she screamed, her channel shuddering around him as he pumped his release into her in long, hot ropes.

It was messy. He couldn't stop thrusting and he couldn't stop orgasming, either. Seed gushed from where they were joined, mixing with her arousal. It splattered on the old polished wood of the entryway floor between her spread legs.

His mind was little more than a stream of sensation and instinct, pleasure and satisfaction. His instincts didn't care that there was no chance of pregnancy, that she belonged to him whether he fucked her raw or not, whether they fucked at *all*.

The rut only cared about breeding, about marking.

Petra had his shadows around her throat, his heart in her hands, and now she had his seed in her, too.

And that was just the start.

Chapter Forty-Nine

They made it up the stairs. She didn't know when, let alone how.

All Petra knew was the twitching of her muscles and the exquisite soreness between her legs and the monster who laid her down on the bed, spread her thighs, and slid inside her like he belonged there.

He was a horrific sight to behold. Wreathed in shadow, he was little more than a hulking mass of muscle with a crown of twisted horns. His eyes were the only discernible feature in the blank mask of his face. They were two glowing disks of bronze in an oval of nothingness, like one of those moretta masks she'd heard people wore to masquerades. Sometimes, she caught the faint impression of a jagged, animalistic mouth, but it was a fleeting thing.

Mostly she saw it when a great, serpentine tongue slipped out to lick their release from her abused cunt — and then force another orgasm while he was at it. Sometimes it came out when he wished to drive it down her throat, or, if he was giving her a break, to lick a trail down her spine that inevitably ended between her thighs.

If he wasn't impaling her on his cock, he had his head buried there. He was utterly insatiable, and after a while she stopped trying to keep track of silly things like time, meals, sleep, or how often he demanded she give him another orgasm. Her sense of self and her place in the wider world became distorted as she was pushed far past her limits and sleep became a luxury.

She didn't have the instincts driving her to forget about anything other than sex, but she didn't need to when Silas demanded she give him everything anyway. Nothing else existed except him, which was probably exactly what he was going for.

Petra thought she understood the basics of the rut, and she supposed she *had,* but living through it was another matter altogether.

Silas didn't stop. He didn't flag. He didn't need breaks or time to recuperate.

It was endless.

Petra knew she must have slept. She had vague memories of waking up to him nipping her breasts or dragging her to the edge of the bed so he could push her knees up to her ears and fuck her standing. She supposed she ate and drank. Water was forced down her throat, but not as often as his cock was. Food must have happened, too, but the impressions of meals were dominated by his orders to sit on his cock while he fed her, bite by bite, from one hand as he lazily guided her up and down with the other on her hip.

There were impressions of showers, but even those memories were dominated by the eye-watering stretch of his shadow-sheathed cock. Time, memory, any perception of the outside world — none of it mattered. Silas didn't *let* it matter. He dominated her body and her mind until she existed solely to receive pleasure.

And there was so very much of it to receive.

Petra drank her fill of it and yet there was always more. Silas had a thousand hands and tongues and cocks at his disposal. He could fuck her in any way that pleased him and he did so relentlessly. Some part of her was always full of him or his shadows, and she never got completely clean of his release, no matter how many showers they might've taken.

He controlled her even when he allowed her the freedom to touch him, or to guide him using his horns. Always, she understood that he was the predator and she was his plaything. If he gave her power, it was because it pleased him to do so, and he would take it away just as quickly as he gave it if she disobeyed an order.

Petra had never felt so free in her life.

In Silas's bedroom, there was no Temple. No murder. No Ardeo. No red boxes or doctor's journal or mysterious plots.

There was just him and them and the raw, perfect sort of sense they made when they came together.

She had no idea how many days had passed, but when she pried her eyes open one morning to find Silas passed out beside her, his human face squashed into a pillow, she got the sense that it'd been a good long while since that first brutal fuck in the entryway.

Petra squinted at the narrow beam of sunlight that streaked across the bed. It bisected the powerful form of Silas's back, bathing a razor-thin strip of his pale skin in golden light. The rest of the room was cast in deep violet shadows. She wasn't sure what exactly had changed, but the sense of urgency that had driven them had finally dissipated.

Peering groggily at the blanket Silas had apparently thrown over the curtain rod — gods only knew when he'd done that — she took stock of her body. Petra immediately winced.

A quick inspection revealed that her hair was a dry rat's nest, her body was covered in a mosaic of lovebites and shallow bruises, and her muscles felt like each individual strand had been plucked. To top it all off, her stomach let out a low, demanding growl.

No wonder injured people are warned off of doing this, she thought, flinching when she inadvertently rubbed her thighs together. *I'm surprised anyone survives the rut!*

Biting back a groan, Petra summoned the will to sit up. Slowly. *Very* slowly.

She glanced over at Silas expectantly, primed to feel a heavy hand closing around her wrist or his shadows locked around her waist, pinning her in place, but he was undisturbed. Her stomach fluttered at the sight of him finally at ease.

She couldn't recall any clear memories of him sleeping. He *must* have, but probably a lot less than her. If she felt like roadkill, then she wouldn't have been surprised if Silas slept for three days straight.

Not wanting to rouse him from his much needed slumber but unable to help herself, Petra ignored the soreness of her abdominal muscles to lean over and press a soft kiss to his temple. *My demon,* she thought, brushing his curls aside to inspect the tiny brand at the base of his horn.

He'd pushed her to her limits again and again. He'd caused her pain, denied her pleasure, bent her into impossible shapes, stretched her cunt until she was pretty sure she'd never walk right again, but never, not once, had she felt threatened. Even when she'd been at her most desperate, she was acutely aware of the fact that she could end it at any time, with just a simple touch to her necklace. But she hadn't.

Petra trusted him even when he was at his wildest and he hadn't let her down. Everything they'd done, all those limits they'd pushed, were things she'd never regret. In fact, she was eager to repeat most of them.

After some recovery time.

Extracting herself from the bed in a long series of tiny movements, Petra managed to hobble to the bathroom. Every step tightened the band of shadow around her throat. It wasn't enough to cut off her air, but a gentle, proprietary squeeze — like even in sleep Silas wanted to remind her who she belonged to.

And, perhaps, to not wander too far away.

After taking care of business and partially unsnarling her hair — a nearly hopeless endeavor — she donned one of his t-shirts and tip-toed around the room, cleaning up the clothing, food containers, pillows, and blankets strewn across the floor. That done, she adjusted the blanket over the window to completely block out the sun and left her mate to sleep.

Creeping down the stairs as quietly as she could, Petra wandered into the kitchen and discovered a disaster zone.

She stood in the doorway for a long while, blinking the grit from her eyes as she took in the state of the place. Since she had no memories of leaving the bedroom, it must have been Silas who destroyed it. There were containers open everywhere. Packaged food was torn open and left all over the kitchen table, counters, and even the floor. Empty jugs of electrolyte beverage were everywhere, like he'd chugged them and then thrown them aside.

"Good gods." Laughter bubbled up. Petra rubbed her watering eyes, her shoulders shaking, and imagined Silas careening into the kitchen between bouts of raw, borderline violent and depraved sex to guzzle hydration.

Living through a rut and now seeing the reality of its toll in the kitchen left her marveling at how demons got anything done at all.

Yes, other beings experienced mating frenzies — orcs and shifters and even weres, she was pretty sure — but the rut was unlike anything she could've imagined. There was sex. There was even wild, out of control, uninhibited fucking. And then there was the *rut*.

No wonder Silas passed out, she thought, picking a path around wrappers and jugs and tupperware lids he'd tossed hither and yon. *Next time we should have a couple IV drips ready.*

Shaking her head, Petra found some cheese to nibble on before she set about putting the kitchen to rights. The soreness and sharp stinging between her thighs was bad, but it felt good to be moving around again, so she did her best to ignore it. Taking a dose of painkillers she found in a first aid kit below the kitchen sink helped, too.

She didn't possess an abundance of energy, so she didn't try to do more than a cursory cleaning before she threw together a hasty breakfast. Scrambled eggs, left-over seasoned potatoes, cheese, and hot sauce went into three breakfast burritos she piled on a plate. Hooking her fingers through the handle of the only full jug of electrolyte drink left, she carefully balanced her load as she walked back up the stairs.

Nudging the bedroom door open with her bare toes, she found Silas in the same position she'd left him, except he'd moved a few inches to the left to press his face into her pillow. It was a little too dark inside for her to eat comfortably, so she chose to keep the bedroom door open, allowing a little bit of ambient light from the hallway inside. Of course, it also helped air the room out — something it desperately needed.

She didn't want to wake him, but after seeing the state of the kitchen, she was certain he hadn't eaten a full meal in too long. The thought of him being hungry made her skin go clammy.

Huh. That's new.

She'd been scarred by food insecurity for her entire adult life, so her anxieties in themselves weren't novel. They were simply a part of her, like bumps in a road frequently traveled.

It was rare that her issues surprised her. Of course she hated the thought of anyone going hungry, knowing what torture it was, but she'd never felt the same uneasiness she experienced when her caches went low for another person before. She'd certainly never broken into a cold sweat over her uncle missing a meal.

But Silas was her mate, and she supposed that made everything different. He'd taken care of her even when he was out of his mind. Now it was her turn.

Petra sat on the edge of the bed and deposited the plate and jug down on the bedside table. Attention snared by the supplement bottles there, she was surprised to find them nearly empty.

Petra had to curl her fingers into the sheets to keep from reaching for him. *Even when he was out of his mind, he remembered to give me my supplements.*

And he had the audacity to say he'd never been sweet a day in his life. She shook her head at the thought.

A quick look inside the drawers confirmed her suspicion that they'd blown through most of the stash he'd put there, too. That eased her mind a little. Clearly he *did* eat. Probably not enough to sustain his thick slabs of muscle, but she knew from experience that something was always better than nothing.

Leaning down to comb her fingers through his messy curls, Petra murmured, "Sweetheart."

The muscles of his shoulders bunched and released, but he otherwise remained blissfully unaware of her. A smile tugged at her mouth. Petra ran her fingertips over the dull point of his ear and was delighted to find it was ever-so-slightly fuzzy.

"Sweetheart, you need to eat," she crooned, watching what she could make out of his expression twitch in response to her ticklish caress. When he still didn't open his eyes, she blew a soft breath against the shell of his ear. "C'mon, demon. Wake up and eat your breakfast before it gets cold."

Silas shifted his weight beneath her. At last, he mumbled into the pillow, "Y'made breakfast?" He turned his head just enough to allow one lambent eye to peer at her.

"I figured you'd be hungry." Petra stroked the curls away from his eye. "I made breakfast burritos. It's nothing fancy, but—"

One heavy arm wrapped loosely around her waist. Silas pressed his face into her thigh and let out a long sigh. His shadows slithered around her legs, but even they didn't seem as demanding as usual.

"Y'okay?"

Petra patted the top of his head. "Yeah, I'm okay. Worn out and sore, but otherwise perfectly fine. You gonna sit up to eat?"

He grunted, but otherwise remained pressed against her side.

"C'mon," she cajoled. "It makes me anxious knowing you're probably starving right now. Please eat."

Silas's arm flexed around her waist. Suddenly wide awake, his head reared back to fix her with a grumpy look. His cheeks were gaunt and the skin below his eyes was a deep lavender, but even when he was clearly exhausted, he managed an impressively fearsome glower.

"Stop that," he hoarsely commanded.

"Stop what?"

"Worrying." His nose wrinkled. "I don't like it."

Repressing a smile, Petra gently suggested, "Well, maybe if you ate a little something..."

Scowling, Silas levered himself into a sitting position and demanded, "Give me the food."

Scooting back against the headboard, Petra reached for the plate but was stopped by Silas grabbing her around the waist again. Before she could protest, he'd arranged them so she was between his legs, her back pressed to his chest and his arms draped over her thighs. The position brought back flashes of decadent memories from the rut and made her tighten her thighs reflexively as a pulse of desire made it through her exhaustion.

The heavy weight of Silas's head rested on top of hers, like he was just too tired to keep it up for long. The reminder of how tired *he* was helped banish some of her ill-advised lust.

"Poor demon." Petra carefully leaned to the side and snagged the plate. Settling it into her lap, she urged him to take one of the burritos. "Just a snack and then you can go back to sleep. You really tuckered yourself out, huh?"

He grunted again, but she was pleased when he took the food and began to quietly chew behind her. After a moment, he mumbled, "D'you make enough for you?"

"One of these is mine, yeah."

"Good." Apparently already finished with his first, he snatched another burrito off the plate.

Petra relaxed into him as she ate her own meal. Her eyelids grew heavy at the now familiar motion of his breathing, the scent of him, the way he mindlessly nuzzled her neck every few minutes.

When she finished her food, Silas moved the plate back onto the table and took an impressively long pull from the jug. He offered her the jug, but it was too heavy for her to drink without spilling everywhere, so he had to help her.

Done for now, he set it aside and slumped back against the headboard, his arms loosely wrapped around her middle. His head drooped low, until the fall of his curls brushed her shoulder. Just when she thought he might've fallen asleep, he muttered, "You fed me."

Petra pressed her cheek to his. "You're my mate."

The cool tip of his nose kissed the shoulder that his too-big shirt exposed. "Didn't scare you off, huh?"

"Nope."

"Didn't hurt you?"

She couldn't be entirely sure, but she thought he held his breath as he waited for her answer.

"No, you didn't." Petra stroked the contours of his corded forearms, memorizing their topography. "I liked it."

Gently lifting his arms — something he probably wouldn't have let her do if he weren't so exhausted — Petra turned around to straddle his waist. Silas watched her, his eyes glowing faintly in the soft darkness of the bedroom, as she cupped his lean cheeks.

"Is it always going to be like that?" she asked.

"Pretty much." He tilted his head into her right hand. "If we don't have kids, it'll be every year."

She sucked in a deep breath, very aware that they weren't just talking about the rut. They were talking about the future. About what their lives would look like.

It was an alien thing for her, the idea that she had a future to think about, let alone a life that stretched beyond a few months and a few fervent desires.

A part of her shied away from it. After all, who said she had a real future? She was technically a fugitive. It was only a matter of time before someone suspected her for Antonin's disappearance, if they didn't already. Nothing was certain about her life.

And yet she was certain about him.

Petra exhaled slowly. "That doesn't sound too bad."

"You're mine forever," he warned her, expression utterly devoid of softness.

"I think I can handle that, too," she whispered.

Silas's hands traveled up her back. They spanned both sides of her ribcage when he said, "Good. Now make me yours."

It didn't take a genius to understand what he was commanding her to do.

Petra touched their foreheads together and closed her eyes as a bolt of longing, so powerful it nearly stole her breath, hit her. "It'll knock you out."

"Don't give a fuck." He tightened his hold on her, plastering them together. She could feel him hardening against the apex of her thighs. Her body, trained to respond to him at a moment's notice, came alive again when he rucked up her borrowed shirt and yanked it over her head.

Her breath quickened when he rocked her back and forth, building the sweet ache until she could feel the wet glide of her arousal between them.

She reached down to guide him inside her. There was more than a twinge of discomfort when he buried himself deep, but she didn't care. This wasn't about chasing an orgasm or satisfying some primal urge. It was about closeness. She wanted to crawl into his skin and live there. She wanted him more than she'd ever wanted anything.

And because she was selfish and greedy and refused to care what anyone else thought, Petra wrapped her fingers around the base of his horns and told him, "I want to be married."

Silas huffed. His cheeks were flushed and his eyes glittered with some indefinable, dark feeling as he guided her hips up and down. "Done. After."

"I want kids."

"How many?"

"Three."

"Two."

"Two and we get a dog. I've always wanted a dog."

"Two and it's a guard dog."

Petra used her grip on him as leverage to grind down. It was a beautiful sight, the way his eyebrows bunched when the pleasure was a bit too much. The rut was incredible, but she'd missed his expressive human face. "Deal."

Like they wanted to reward her, a tendril of shadow slithered over her thigh to lap at her clitoris, making her hips jolt. Silas gripped the back of her neck with one hand to angle her head up for a messy, demanding kiss. "Deal, baby. Now *do it.*"

Like he commanded her magic *and* her body, a scorching rush of magic prickled her skin, begging to be released. His shadows rubbed her mercilessly, expanding that great internal pressure, as he dragged her up and down his cock.

Silas didn't blink. He didn't make a sound. He held her stare rigidly, daring her to defy him as he pushed them toward an explosive finish.

Never one to shrink from a challenge, Petra met him stroke for stroke, stare for stare, and when the sharp drop of her orgasm loomed before her, she wrenched his head back by the horns and hissed against his lips, "I want you. I trust you. I love you, demon."

Her magic bloomed like a supernova between them, arching out in great lashes of energy and light from the burning core of her soul. It arrowed into him with enough force to knock his back against the headboard. His rhythm stuttered, his hips jackknifing upward as he came with a grunt.

She wasn't sure what was her orgasm and what was the bond, but it didn't really matter either way. For what felt like a lifetime she was blinded by magic and euphoria. She could taste it on her tongue, metallic like blood, and feel him there — not just the shadow around her neck or where their bodies were joined, but *him,* the roaring too-much, too-powerful presence of Silas inside all the dark parts of her she'd always tried to hide.

Everywhere that'd been empty was filled. Everywhere that was dark was alive. All of it, all of her, belonged to him.

And now he belonged to her, too.

Silas stared up at her with wide eyes for the span of a heartbeat before he abruptly leaned forward to drop her back onto the mattress. Thrusting savagely between her thighs, he grated, "Yes, yes, *yes.*"

Petra dug her nails into his scalp and held on as they both chased the waves of their orgasm, sharpened to the finest, most exquisite edge by the new bond that sang between them.

Finally, when they could do no more, Silas gripped her shoulders and rolled them onto their sides. His eyelids drooped even as he hitched her thigh over his hip and ground his half-hard cock into the wet, sticky mess they'd made between her legs. "I won't let you regret it," he promised, speech slurring.

Petra's world began to narrow even as her magic continued to expand, to burrow deeper and deeper into him. "I know," she whispered, stroking his sweaty hair away from his brow. She moved to kiss him on instinct as the rest of her began to shut down. "I wouldn't have anyone else, demon."

Silas's grip slackened. His restless hips stilled. A moment before the bond claimed him completely, he muttered, "Good girl." As soon as the final syllable stumbled past his lips, he went limp.

Her magic made a current between them, an elemental cycle of push and pull and rejuvenation. She shuddered under the onslaught as the bond scorched a path between them.

The bond was a link that could never be broken. It could never be tampered with. Only death could separate them, and even then, Petra had her doubts.

Blackness, familiar and comforting in its wildness, beckoned. She didn't fight it. With her mate's arms around her, there was nothing for her to fear.

Chapter Fifty

Silas woke to his mate sprawled on top of him, his head throbbing like someone had taken an ax between his horns, and blanketed in a contentment he hadn't felt in his entire existence.

They were also laying the wrong way on the bed.

He breathed deep, taking in the lingering scent of sex in the air and the perfume of his mate's skin. Magic was a tinny note at the tail-end of each breath. It tasted like blood and sunshine on his tongue. Like *her*.

Bonding with Petra was a bit like being struck by lightning, he discovered. Her power had blinded him as it coursed through his veins, leaving tracks of pure fire in its wake. When it was over, he was left remade, transformed like ordinary sand to crystalline glass.

He'd always possessed magic, but this was different. What was once a spark was now a roaring furnace inside him.

Staring at the ceiling and listening to her even breathing, it occurred to him that he could do anything with it. With his expert control, he could bend any sigils to suit his will. His options were limitless and his hunger for discovery immense. Nothing could stand in his way now.

But as he sifted his claws through his mate's long blonde hair and stared at the dark ceiling, there was a curious lack of desire to do more than that.

He felt no urge to run to his lab. He considered his many, many schematics and the ideas he'd been forced to set aside due to lack of power but felt no enthusiasm to revisit them. He didn't feel the victorious rush he often did when he got what he wanted from someone who'd initially refused him.

Silas felt... good. Satisfied. Like he'd been hungry for something his whole life and finally, finally had his fill.

It was an odd thing to feel no itch, no need to find the next rush. Silas's lips twisted into a wry smile. *There's no rush that compares to my witch. If I'd known what a thrill it'd be to have her... Well, Petra's lucky I found her when I did.*

He figured he'd always be drawn to creation, to puzzle-solving and tinkering, but he couldn't imagine running off to take outright illegal jobs now. Not because he'd discovered a sense of morality between Petra's perfect thighs, but because it just didn't interest him anymore. The risk of getting caught or putting his mate in danger wasn't worth it.

She didn't know it yet, but his services had become exclusive to her and her alone.

He was her one-demon army and he wouldn't rest until every one of her enemies was dead.

"What are you thinking about?" Petra's groggy voice drew his attention back where it belonged — her.

"Destroying the Temple for you," he answered, rubbing a strand of her hair between his fingers. He loved her hair. It was captured sunlight — like her magic, like how she made him feel, like *her*.

"Okay, I think the bond hangover is scrambling my brain. What'd you say?"

Silas frowned and switched to gently massaging her forehead. "I'm going to destroy the Temple for you."

Petra sounded adorably confused when she grunted, "Huh?"

"Because they're a threat to you," he explained, amused by her sleepy befuddlement. He loved this new version of her: well-fucked, safe, and drowsy.

When Petra continued to stare at him, he went on, "We've been in here for almost..." He finally thought to check his watch. "...two weeks. My programs should have cracked the encryption on the files by now. It'll be a bitch to figure out where to start going through all the data, but as soon as I don't feel like I was hit by a truck, I'm going to track down everyone involved with Vanderpoel. Then I'll kill them."

"But what if that's the entire Gloriae?"

"Might be," he replied, recalling Rasmus's mutterings about soldiers. "Antonin probably acted relatively independently, and I can't rule out that he didn't have leverage over the High Gloriae, but I think it's more likely that whatever he was up to, it was being done with the permission of the Temple's ruling body."

Maybe not all of them. Maybe not even most of them. But enough. *Someone* gave that man the power and money to do what he'd done. *Someone* set everything in motion, and Silas had a gut feeling it wasn't Antonin. Tyrants couldn't exist without enablers, and *they* tended to be far more dangerous.

A tyrant couldn't resist making himself known, but an enabler was a snake in the grass, hidden and waiting for an opportunity to strike.

"Silas, you can't kill the Gloriae," Petra protested.

"We'll see," he replied, giving her an indulgent smile. Not wanting to make her headache worse, he changed the subject. "Weres— when were they made?"

Giving him an odd, sleepy look, she replied, "I— I don't know. Near the end of the war, I think? What does that have to do—"

"How old was Antonin?"

"I don't know." She paused. Her brow furrowed. "Not too old. If he was involved with that, it had to have been when he was pretty young."

"The resources and the planning something like that would have taken wouldn't have come from a man at the start of his career."

He was willing to admit that Antonin was smart, but *making* one's own army was very rarely the first step a young man took to taking power. Even if he was fabulously wealthy, even if he was ambitious, that kind of plan didn't come from nothing.

Petra rubbed her forehead. "I want everyone to be held accountable for their actions — for the weres and Max and *everything* — but I don't necessarily want everyone *dead*. That's not always real justice, Silas. A lot of the time people need to live to get what they deserve."

"What do you want to do with the Temple, then? Do you want to be the new High Gloriae? Do you still want to be High Priestess? Tell me." He couldn't let threats to her survive, but he'd make sure she got what she wanted, even if it didn't look quite like she imagined.

Petra opened her mouth, but it was a long time before words came out. "I... I don't know."

"Your assistant said that no one would accept you with a demon for a mate." He didn't care what anyone thought, and he found the taboo nature of their union pretty damn enticing, but that didn't mean he was ignorant to what it would cost Petra. People would have a problem with Glory's own flesh, her representative on Earth, being mated to a demon.

It didn't matter that he was only half, and it didn't matter that Glory and Blight were once mated themselves. There was no hiding it when his shadow would remain around her throat for the rest of her days.

And certainly not after she carved the marriage sigils into their brows.

She would be seen as inviting Blight — his cursed gaze, his disease, his creeping darkness — into Glory's sacred house whether Silas stood by her side or not. If she wanted to remain High Priestess, he'd silence every critic and force worshippers into the pews at gunpoint, but somehow he doubted she'd be in favor of that.

Petra shook her head. "It doesn't matter what I want. I can't go back there."

He scowled. "Of course you can. I'll take care of everything."

"You can't un-murder a man, demon."

"No, but I can make sure no one asks any questions. You'd be surprised how many people get away with murder, you know." Skimming his palms up her arms, he urged her, "Stop thinking about what you *can't* do. Think about what you *want*. I told you I'd make you happy and that I'd give you everything you ask for. So tell me what that is and I'll do it."

Her eyes darted, clearly searching for something in his expression. "What about what *you* want?"

"I have everything I want." He gave her arms a small, possessive squeeze. "My mate in my bed. That's it."

She cocked her head to one side. The small movement sent her hair slithering over his naked chest with a ticklish caress. "What about Tal? The wraiths?"

"Tal will get his body as soon as we get back to San Francisco," he explained, thinking of the empty shell waiting in his lab. He wished he'd thought to bring it, but those last few days in the city had been too chaotic, and he hadn't wanted to risk something happening to the delicate internal machinery in transit. "And the other wraiths will just have to wait until I can sneak into Solbourne Tower to get a peek at that generator."

Petra looked away, her expression troubled, when she said, "I wish I'd known about them before. I would have been able to ask Margot, but now..."

"Now, you've just gotta tell me what you want and I'll make it happen. Do you want to be High Priestess again, or do you want to be Petra? Just Petra."

Everything hinged on her answer. No matter what, he'd destroy the people connected to Vanderpoel and the Ardeo, but the rest was up to her.

Petra laid her head back down on his chest. She tucked her arms in close, folding herself into a small bundle there in the circle of his arms. She belonged there, nestled between his lungs, far more than his heart did.

"I don't know what I want," she admitted in a small, hushed voice. "Or maybe I do. I guess... I know I don't want anything to happen to my people at St. Emaine's. I know I don't want to go to jail for murder. I know I want to still be friends with Margot. Better friends, even. I..."

She trailed off, but Silas didn't push her. He was content to wait for her as he stroked the bumps of her spine.

"You know, four years ago I was totally happy with what I was doing. I know I wasn't very high up in the hierarchy, but I liked teaching. I was content to live a little, safe life all by myself. Now I can't imagine going back to that."

"Four years is a long time to work at something," he replied, thinking of all her mad plans and her hunt for justice. "And living like you did for that long will change a person."

He wondered if he would have been as drawn to that version of Petra — the school teacher, the devoted niece, the quiet priestess content with her work. He thought so. Silas was drawn to every facet of her and suspected that wouldn't have changed no matter when they met. However, he doubted *that* Petra would have ever given him the time of day, so he was glad their paths crossed when they did. It saved him the hassle of kidnapping her, probably.

He liked his fierce, canny priestess. He found the sharp edges of her beautiful. *This* Petra was a perfect match for him.

She let out a soft sigh. "Yeah. Four years is—" Petra cut herself off. She went stiff under his hands.

Alarms ringing in his mind, he bit out, "What? What's wrong?"

Petra lifted her head, but she didn't look at him. Her gaze wandered sightlessly as she propped herself up. "Four years."

"...Yes? That's how long you've been High Priestess."

Petra sat up completely. He followed her up, despite the fact that his body protested every tiny movement. The rut hit him hard, and the bond had taken what little strength he'd had left, but he ignored his discomfort in favor of peering into his mate's pinched expression. She looked like she was trying to solve an invisible puzzle and failing.

"Petra, what's happening? What are you doing?"

Without looking at him, she grasped his forearm and held tight. "Four years ago. What happened four years ago?"

He really wished he had some psychic abilities. That way he could have rifled around in her mind to see what on Earth she was trying to put together. "You decided to find out what happened to Max."

"Yes, but before that?"

"Max died."

Petra nodded, but her eyes had squeezed shut. "Uh-huh. What else?"

"I don't know. He caught Antonin with his hand in the cookie jar?"

"Max refused to tell me what he'd found. I asked Antonin to tell me why he killed Max, but he wouldn't say. Not until we were bonded." Petra didn't seem to notice the way a growl rumbled out of Silas's chest. "But—"

"It had to have been something he uncovered around that time."

"I assumed it was blackmail," she muttered. "Everyone knew the rumors. I thought maybe Max found out he was abusing his power, using the blackmail to do awful things. I mean, for *Max* to think it was bad enough— It had to have been really, really bad. Something awful happening within the Temple, like when the scandal broke about the orphan indoctrination in 1930 and half the High Gloriae stepped down. Then I thought maybe it was the stuff with the weres. Except that's not urgent. Not something that he would recklessly run into without a plan."

Petra finally opened her eyes. There was so much dread in

them when she asked, "What happened the summer Max was murdered?"

The hair stood up on the back of his neck. His shadows began to ripple with agitation and the need to protect her from an unseen threat when he demanded, "What do you mean? What else would it have been?"

"What happened four years ago?"

"I don't *know.*" And it was really starting to annoy him that he didn't.

Her nails bit into the flesh of his arm when she rasped, "What event would have even brought him to St. Emaine's in the summer of 2044? Not Max's appointment as High Priest. He'd been there for years and St. Emaine's was considered extremely stable. No money problems, no bad acolytes, no scandals. The Protector would have had no reason to go, and if there was an internal issue — something or someone worth dragging the Ardeo in — I would have heard rumors about it by now."

"So it was something *outside* the Temple." Silas's mind raced.

Soldiers, Rasmus had said. *They wanted to make soldiers.*

Why would an organization need soldiers like werewolves? Why did *anyone* want an army?

Speaking slowly, like she didn't want to say the words, she asked again, "What happened, Silas?"

"Delilah Solbourne abdicated," he answered slowly. "And everyone thought the EVP was about to tear itself apart."

Why did anyone want an army? To take something they wanted, usually a territory.

When was the best time to take a territory? During a war. Civil wars were preferable, as a fractured society was easier pickings than one united by a common cause.

But no war had come to pass. Theodore Solbourne managed to calm the territory down and hold his seat. His marriage to Margot Goode had significantly strengthened his position less than a year later. Whatever opportunity Antonin might have seen in the power exchange hadn't manifested.

But it could've.

With a few hundred brainwashed Ardeo soldiers in Solbourne Tower, the wealth and religious sway of the Temple, as well as the potent blackmail Antonin had on the leaders of the UTA...

Successful coups happened with far less.

Gray-faced, Petra asked, "Max was invited to the ceremony as a gesture of good will. I remember because that's what I called to ask him about that last time we talked."

"What did he say about it?"

"Nothing. He refused to talk about it. About anything. He was terrified. So upset it was hard to understand him. He just told me he'd learned something about the Protector and he planned to confront him. It never occurred to me that the events might be related."

She swallowed hard. "If that's what brought him to San Francisco in the first place... What brought him back?"

CHAPTER FIFTY-ONE

PETRA WANTED TO APPRECIATE THE SPECTACLE OF Silas working in his element, but she couldn't focus on anything other than keeping her breathing level.

She didn't want to be right. She wanted Silas to find more illicit personal information, not any evidence of a plot. She *needed* to be wrong.

But the knot of anxiety in her stomach wouldn't budge. It was the same feeling she'd gotten the day her parents were killed. It was that gut instinct that told her to hide mere moments before the shooting started.

There were so many reasons she could be wrong, though. Really, what evidence did she have? Nothing but her gut and suspicious timing.

Petra gripped the arm rests of the chair Silas had pulled over to his desk for her. It was extremely late. Her body was exhausted from the long rut and the witchbond, but she was too wired to care, let alone sleep.

She tracked the data streaming across the wide, curved computer screen, but she couldn't make any sense of it. He'd been quiet for a while as his long, clawed fingers flew over the buttons projected onto the desk.

The urge to ask Silas how things were going was a visceral one, but she bit her tongue.

They'd only been down in the lab for half an hour, she reminded herself. It hadn't been the eternity that it felt like. But every minute seemed to stretch into hours, and every tap of his fingers jolted her nerves until her whole body was wound as tight as a spring.

While she waited, Petra scrubbed through every interaction she'd ever had with Antonin and everything she'd learned over her years as High Priestess. She tried to peel away her past interpretations, to really *see* what was going on beyond what she assumed at the time. Mostly she hoped to dissuade herself from her hunch, but it didn't work.

She'd been focused on what Antonin did to Max for so long. It never occurred to her that Max might simply have been a tiny diversion in a much larger, more sinister plan. That *she* might've been an even smaller piece.

Her skin crawled. Why did she think everything began and ended with Max?

This wasn't the streets of Los Angeles or the dingy halls of the children's home. Antonin was no petty criminal and Max hadn't inadvertently walked into a turf war. This was so, so much bigger than anything she'd known before. Why couldn't she have seen it?

She was friends with the *sovereign's consort*. Petra was the spiritual leader of one of the most powerful cities on the continent. She had conned her way into the highest tiers of an organization that controlled vast land, wealth, and influence.

It was an oversight to think that Max would've confronted Antonin for anything less than something earth-shattering. It was an even bigger one to think Antonin *wouldn't* be up to something a lot grander than blackmail and extortion.

After all, he was already wealthy. He held untold amounts of influence. She'd taken his desire for her and an heir at face value, but a man like that had to have higher ambitions than simply standing in the shadows of the High Gloriae.

Why did he need an heir? Petra rubbed her temples, desperate to ease the dull pounding in her skull. *What was the project he said he was in town for?*

The more she thought about it, the more tense she became. Her nails dug into the armrests of her chair until the beds blanched white. *What was he doing?*

She wanted to believe that whatever it was, it had to be over now that he was dead. He couldn't harm anyone now. But she couldn't stop thinking about the empty-eyed soldiers of the Ardeo, about where his aid Nicolas had gone, that friend he mentioned when she refused Antonin's advances—

The low buzz of Silas's watch vibrating on his wrist nearly made her jump out of her skin.

He cast her a concerned look and settled his hand on her thigh. Lips turning down into an even deeper scowl, he told her, "Rasmus is calling."

"Answer it." Petra practically crawled into his lap to reach for his left arm. "How do I answer it?"

She'd known Rasmus long enough to understand that if he called, it was for a good reason. If he called *Silas,* it had to be for a *very* good reason.

"I have to program your biometrics in," he replied, pointing to the screen. "Remind me to do that after we're done with this."

She didn't have time to savor the burst of warmth that came with that easy acceptance into every aspect of his life, let alone his easy confidence that soon this would all be over. Maybe later she would, but not now, when she felt like someone had hooked up a generator to her nerves and cranked it up to the highest setting.

Silas tapped the screen, answering the call. "What did you hear?" he grunted, eyes already back on his computer screen.

Rasmus had a deep, raspy voice. Even coming through the tiny speakers in the watch, it made an impact when he announced, "You can't come back to the city."

Silas's fingers paused their rapid movement. "Why?"

Her heart jumped into her throat when Rasmus answered, "I

just mediated a little get together between a certain spymaster and the McCorrans. You remember the bounty put out for Dr. Atria Le Roy and Ruby Goode?"

"What bounty?" Petra reached for Silas's arm again. Speaking directly into the digital watch face, she pressed, "There was a *bounty* on Atria?"

They hadn't met yet, but Petra knew Margot was good friends with one half of the duo famous for their breakthrough with the m-generator. The other half, Ruby Goode, was her cousin — who had been mysteriously absent from the m-generator's presentation. Her absence had sparked a tsunami of rumors, but Petra had been too caught up in her plans to pay attention to any of them. She was pretty sure she'd remember talk of a bounty, though.

"Pet?" Rasmus sounded surprised, but his tone immediately shifted to gruff concern when he growled, "You all right? Shade wouldn't let me see you. If you need help, say the word."

"I'm fine. Just—"

"I told you to stop calling her that. Do it one more time and I'm taking a finger," Silas warned. "You know what? Actually I'm taking all of them."

Petra lightly swatted her mate's arm. "Who cares about that? Rasmus, I'm *fine.* Explain what's going on. Why can't we come back to San Francisco?"

"A couple months ago, someone put out an anonymous bounty for Ruby Goode and Atria Le Roy. Now we know it was probably to get their hands on the generator shit, which is worth more money than you or I could ever imagine, but at the time it seemed fishy. Some anonymous entity offering a comically huge amount of money for two random scientists? Please. If it wasn't a trap, then it was bound to start a war between the shits dumb enough to all go after it at once. Anyone with sense ignored it, thinking it was either a scam or not worth the trouble, but obviously there are people without any fucking brains in their heads."

Silas bit out, "Who?"

"A rogue group of gargoyles split off from the McCorran clan. Kaz took them out."

Kaz? Petra summoned the name out from a deep place in her memory. An outrageously handsome orcish face came with it.

Looking at Silas expectantly, she asked, "Isn't Kaz a captain of a Patrol unit?" She'd only met him briefly once, but she'd noted his rank because she thought it was pretty strange that the sovereign would give an orc such a powerful position in his military.

"That's his official title, yeah," Silas answered, like he knew the man well. "But his real job is intelligence. He's in charge of security for the entire territory."

Huh. It wasn't the time to ask, but she was suddenly extremely curious about how an orc came to be the eyes and ears of the sovereign himself.

Shaking her head, she pressed on. "What does any of that have to do with us?"

"The McCorrans came to settle up with Kaz. They didn't give their permission to accept the bounty and didn't want any retribution for the attempted kidnapping on elvish land — or from him personally. To square things up, they gave Kaz information on whoever put their men onto the job."

A heavy stone of dread dropped into the pit of her stomach. *Oh, Glory, no.*

Silas met her gaze when he slowly asked, "And who was that?"

"Don't know," Rasmus answered, "but their last known location before they started their hunt for the witch was St. Emaine's."

Petra closed her eyes. "When?"

"Sometime in early May, maybe late April. Dunno."

"I'm wrapping up a project," Antonin told her the night he turned up at the cathedral out of the blue. *"Just thought I'd stop in and finally behold Glory's rising star for myself while I had the chance."*

"Demon," she whispered. "The first visit. When he made the

proposal. He showed up out of nowhere and only stayed for a night. It fits."

He squeezed her thigh. In a deep, threatening voice, he asked Rasmus, "What does that have to do with Petra?"

"She suddenly went on sabbatical and disappeared off the face of the Earth right before a major festival, Shade. It doesn't take a genius to see what Kaz might get when he puts those two things together. If I didn't know better, even I would be suspicious."

There was a long, tense pause before Silas's sharp smile unspooled across his face. It was the smile that promised pain, and even now it sent a shiver of unease down her spine. "Kaz is hunting for my mate. That's a bad choice."

"He thinks Petra is involved with *his* mate's attempted kidnapping, Shade," Rasmus explained, like he could see the violence brewing in Silas as clearly as Petra could.

An electric sensation zipped across their bond, one that raised all the fine hairs on her body. It was like the magic that filtered through him had taken on Silas's unique flavor — and his rage.

"No," she muttered, covering the hand on her thigh with her own. "You can't kill him. Calm down."

"Aren't you and Kaz friends?" Rasmus asked. His skeptical tone belied how much stock he put in the idea. "Get in contact and tell him Petra had nothing to do with it. If you clear her name, she can come back to the city."

Silas's upper lip peeled back from his fangs. Before he could argue the point, Petra reminded him, "We have bigger fish to fry. It lines up with my timeline, which means that he must've wanted the m-generator. If we can prove that—"

Rasmus cleared his throat. "Who wanted the m-generator? Was it Vanderpoel?"

"None of your damn business, nosy wolf," Silas growled. Flicking the watch's screen, he ended the call.

Petra barely noticed. Her heartbeat was a frantic rhythm in her ears when she asked, "What could Antonin have done with that kind of technology?"

Silas's lips pressed into a hard line. He was quiet for a moment. Those clawed hands found their way back to the projected keyboard, but this time they moved even faster than before, inputting code so quickly she could barely keep up.

A window popped onto the screen. It was normal-looking, as far as she could tell. Just a square with two input fields: one for a username and another for a passcode.

Her heart sank, but she didn't have time to ask if there was a way around having a passcode. Silas pasted a long string of symbols into both fields and hit enter.

Sitting back in his chair, he stared hard at the sea of neatly organized files that filled his screen. "He could do just about anything, but my best guess is weapons."

Petra swallowed hard. It did little to quell the bile that scaled the fleshy walls of her throat. "They're building a prototype in the Tower."

"That's why I rolled into town, too."

"But that won't be ready for months," she reasoned, trying hard to find some way to make it better, a little less terrifying. "Even if he still thought he could get it, why would he come back to San Francisco so urgently?"

"Maybe he didn't want to wait." Silas dragged his gaze away from the screen to pin her with a dark look. "Maybe he saw a different opportunity."

"How do we find out what that was?"

"Whatever he had planned, it took coordination. You can't do that without a paper trail." He gestured toward the computer screen. "It's in here, baby. We just have to look."

She couldn't seem to catch her breath. Her voice came out whispery with panic when she asked, "What do we do if it's bad, Silas? Really bad."

It'd been one thing to hand over evidence that Antonin was behind Max's murder to a journalist, but if the truth was as big as it appeared to be, then things were a lot more complicated — and infinitely more dangerous.

Silas didn't appear panicked. He was deadly calm when he answered, "That's up to you."

"Me?" she squeaked, appalled.

He nodded. "If what we find puts you in danger, then I'll take care of it. If it doesn't... Then it's up to you."

Petra's stomach turned. "What if I make the wrong choice?"

Silas shrugged. "You won't. Now tell me where to start looking."

She turned her gaze to the screen. He'd told her how much data there was. She tried to imagine just how much information that had to be, the countless secrets and plans that lay innocently behind pixels and files labeled in mundane, boring ways.

Where did one even begin to find the truth when there was so much? *The same place I did.*

Taking a deep breath, she said, "Start with Max."

CHAPTER FIFTY-TWO

SILAS COULDN'T SAY HE WAS SURPRISED BY WHAT THEY found. In many ways, he and Vanderpoel had always been after the same things. They both wanted Petra — not just for *her,* but for her bond and her access to the m-generator — and between them, they didn't have a drop of morality to spare.

He didn't have any particular feelings about it one way or the other. A different man might have felt guilt or disgust knowing he had so much in common with someone like Vanderpoel, but Silas wasn't the type.

If anything, he was relieved. Once he understood exactly who he was dealing with, it was easy for him to trace a logical path through the ocean of information at his fingertips.

If I wanted to take over a territory, what would I do?

He'd wait for the right opportunity. A moment of profound destabilization in the center of power, perhaps, or when a new leader was at their weakest. Should that chance slip past him, then he'd find a way to make a new one.

If that plan was discovered, he'd take out the threat.

Even before he found the order to dispose of Dooraker's body in a neatly organized file of communications between Vanderpoel and several members of his private army, Silas knew exactly what had happened.

Vanderpoel and whoever he worked with saw Delilah Solbourne's abdication as a chance. Somehow, Dooraker discovered whatever they'd planned — an assassination, most likely — and threatened to bring it to light.

It all made sense. If the Gloriae, or just a few fanatics in their ranks, had it in their heads to rebuild the empire they'd lost, the EVP was the perfect place to start. If violence had followed the abdication, the ruling families would've torn the government apart. The citizenry would've panicked, afraid of another era of bloodshed like the one brought by Mad Thad. If a powerful, trusted entity stepped in to bring peace, the populace would've flocked to them before they risked putting their lives in the hands of the elves again.

But if that window of opportunity closed, if rumors began to swirl about an incredibly powerful new technology, one that could provide limitless energy...

All Vanderpoel had to do was position himself to be in the right place at the right time with the necessary manpower. Marrying Petra, San Francisco's beloved priestess, would've given him credibility with the people. Most likely he would've put her center stage and acted as an older, stabilizing partner. Having a child on the way would've sealed the deal, giving him an heir and casting him as a family man. Nothing distracted an impressionable public desperate for distraction quite like a baby.

And even if all of that failed, Petra herself was the perfect connection to the Solbournes and the Tower itself. Antonin could've easily used her to get direct access to the m-generator first, then used the technology to get everything else he wanted quickly thereafter. Silas had planned to use her for the very same reason.

It was all there, laid out before them in coded messages, invoices, and no-frills commands shared on private encrypted servers.

The order to dispose of Dooraker's body was there in black and white, alongside an invoice for his cremation and a flowery but vague press release about his tragic heart attack. Following the time stamps, he discovered messages between Vanderpoel and someone labeled simply as Red. A series of messages laid out their plan to replace Dooraker with a more "easily influenced" High Priest. Many more detailed their surprise as Petra was put forward by Theodore Solbourne as his choice to be St. Emaine's High Priestess.

"Do you know who Red is?" he asked.

Petra, white as a sheet, answered, "No, but that— that note there? That's all information that would've been given to the High Gloriae directly. No one else." She didn't seem surprised, but maybe the deluge of information had simply numbed her. "Antonin said he had a friend in United Washington who would get me to agree to bond with him. Do you think..."

"Are there any High Gloriae members there?"

"I don't know. They're secretive about their personal lives. All I really know about them is that they meet up every year for Temple business and make decrees on the—" Petra cut herself off abruptly. Slapping a hand on his thigh, she rushed out, "Demon, check the solstice."

"What?"

"June twentieth." She pointed a shaking finger at the monitor. "Look for anything mentioning June twentieth."

"Of this year?"

"Yes."

He nodded. His fingers flew across the familiar, smooth surface of his desk. It was hard not to look at her, to check that she was holding up okay. Petra needed him to be sharp. Never in his life could he have imagined a world where having access to so many secrets wouldn't interest him nearly as much as a woman, but this was his mate, and nothing about her was ordinary. He suspected she'd outshine anyone and everything for the rest of his life.

Silas sat back in his seat, his lips flattening into a hard line as he watched an unsettling number of hits pop up on the screen. Instead of analyzing every document himself, his gaze slid to Petra.

She'd braced her palms on the desk and leaned forward to peer at the screen. The light from the monitor cast her jewel tones into sickly pastels, highlighting the look that grew ever-bleaker in her eyes.

"He said he planned to stick around for several weeks," she murmured, almost to herself. "He'd be in San Francisco for as long as it took. I thought he meant bonding and knocking me up. I never considered it would be for *this.*"

"He definitely meant knocking you up," Silas bit out. His headache got a little worse every time he imagined Vanderpoel putting his hands on Petra. It became *distinctly* uncomfortable when he thought of his mate carrying Vanderpoel's spawn, too.

I wish I could kill him again.

Silas hadn't even thought of getting Petra pregnant when he made his plans. He'd fully intended to set her aside as soon as Tal had a body and they had access to the m-generator. But he had no plans to take over a territory. If he *had,* knocking up Petra would've been at the top of his list.

While he still had no interest in taking over a territory, he did discover a previously untapped well of desire to see her tied to him in every possible way. After he handled everything, he decided, they'd discuss moving up the timeline on those two kids.

Forcing himself to focus on something other than breeding his mate, Silas thought, *An m-generator-turned-super-weapon. A new witchbond. A small army. A wife beloved by the whole territory and a baby on the way...*

Vanderpoel could've taken the EVP with barely any effort at all.

"Yes, but that's not *all* he meant," Petra argued. "Silas, the thing that brought him to San Francisco— It wasn't just the m-generator. It was an *event*. Look at that order there. He planned to have his soldiers in the cathedral on the one day a year that... Good gods."

He arched a brow. "What day?"

"The solstice," she breathed. "The biggest festival of the year. The one that brings Margot and Theodore to the Temple *every* year without fail. They always make a speech and give an offering. Always."

It was no wonder he didn't realize what the date meant. Demons weren't exactly known for celebrating the day dedicated to Glory. The solstice was celebrated in small ways, usually with a picnic and bonfires, but elsewhere it was a grand event with complicated ceremonies, feasting, and fireworks.

Silas drummed his claws on the desk. "If he wanted to plan a successful coup, his best opportunity to take out the Solbournes would be when they're in the cathedral, surrounded by the soldiers no one even knows he has. But he'd still have to think about the Tower. That's the seat of power, with or without the sovereign inside."

"The solstice is tomorrow." She paused, checked the time and date on the monitor, and blanched. "Gods, not even tomorrow. It's in a few *hours*. Everyone will be out in the streets or visiting family. The Tower will be a ghost town." Petra found his hand and gripped it hard. Her breathing went quick and shallow. "Silas, we left his soldiers in the cathedral. I thought they might just leave to hunt me, but if they're taking orders from someone else, too, they might still be there. Oh, gods, the *staff*. What's been happening to the staff?"

A look of stark horror drained all the life from her face. "Margot and the sovereign might be walking into an execution."

Silas wished he could tell her no. He wanted to be able to reassure her, inept as he might be at it, but he couldn't. He stared at the screen, his gaze bouncing from one incriminating document to another. There weren't many messages between Antonin and

Red. Silas suspected they did most of their communication in person, which was smart, or on another server he didn't have access to.

But what he *did* have was enough.

A message from Red asked, *Do you have enough soldiers? We're spread thin, but I can send a few more. Don't want you to miss your chance to put a crown on your queen's head.*

And below that, Vanderpoel's answer: *The elf has the rest handled. You have fun.*

He stared hard at the message. Fingers moving unconsciously over the projected keyboard, he did another shallow search for the word *elf.*

Hundreds of results sprang up, so he sorted them by most recent. Eying an order to funnel money to an elf in Las Vegas for *"the retrieval"*, he asked, "Which elvish family hates the Solbournes the most?"

Petra shook her head. "I don't know. Several of them had issues with Theodore taking over for his sister, and Mad Thad did so much damage to everyone... But I thought things settled after he lifted the ban on taking mates and married Margot. I was at the Summit when it was announced. Most of the crowd was ecstatic, and I always got the impression that he was popular."

"In my experience, the more popular a ruler, the more determined their enemies are." Pulling up yet another window, he searched for anything else on the dates of the most relevant messages. Amongst all the useless hits, an m-jet manifest came up.

"Who's in Las Vegas?" Petra whispered.

Silas sat back in his chair and let out a long sigh. "The Luz family."

He wasn't sure how it was possible, but Petra managed to go even whiter. "Don't they have a lot of money?"

"Yes," he answered, claws drumming on the desktop. "Elio Luz owns most of Las Vegas and he's a mean, petty sonofabitch. His son is worse."

"How so?"

"He's *smart.*"

"Do you think they'd help Antonin?"

Silas pursed his lips as he considered the possibility. He'd never bothered working with Elio because he seemed like too much of a pain in the ass. His son Epifanio had never reached out to Silas for a job, mostly because he was very smart and even more paranoid. Despite never working for them, Silas heard enough to make an educated guess.

"Epifanio? No," he finally answered. "He's too smart and he's been planning on deposing his father for too long to blow everything up with a half-baked coup. His dad, on the other hand... Yeah, I can see him doing it. I doubt his people couldn't get free access to the m-generator, but they could get into the Tower. With enough firepower, that'd be enough."

Silas hated to do it, but he had to explain the reality of what they were dealing with. Placing a hand on her knee, he said, "Listen, baby. I know you think you have friends in the Tower, but that ends right now. If you see one traitor, that means there are a dozen more just out of sight. We don't know who Elio or Vanderpoel or Red might've slipped into the inner circle, the staff, the guards. *No one* can be trusted."

Petra looked like she was going to be sick. If it had been all Vanderpoel, he might've been able to ease some of her worries, but with an unknown player and an unseen snake in Theodore Solbourne's court, he couldn't lie and say that the threat died along with the man.

While it was *possible* that Vanderpoel's death might've derailed any plans, Silas doubted it. There were too many players, too many moves already made. If the Ardeo soldiers were still in the cathedral, then there wouldn't be any real reason to call it off. It seemed likely that Red was calling the shots now. If their plot hinged on taking the EVP, as it appeared to, then there was a very real possibility that the sovereign couple would walk into St. Emaine's and never leave.

Bracing himself, he asked, "What do you want to do?"

Petra boggled at him. "I want to stop whatever it is that might be happening! We need to tell someone or— or go to Patrol or—"

Silas hooked a finger under her chin and tilted her face up for a brief kiss. Speaking against her lips, he promised, "You got it, baby."

Chapter Fifty-Three

Petra threw her bag at his feet and declared, "You are *not* leaving without me!"

"We're *not* having this conversation," Silas replied, completely unbothered, as he slipped a sheathed knife into his boot.

"You're right. We aren't. Because I'm *coming.*"

"It's cute that you think you're gonna get your way, little goddess, but it isn't fuckin' happening." Silas rose from his crouched position to pat his pockets. "Knives, fake ID, explosives... I'm missing something. Oh, right." He reached for the old, yellowed file he'd taken from one of the red trunks, but Petra snatched it first.

Holding it tight to her chest, she announced, "Silas, you're not leaving without me. Those are *my* people. That's *my* friend. I need to help."

"And you're *my* mate," he argued, brows arching. "What makes you think I would ever let you walk into a situation where you're actively being hunted by two separate groups and we strongly suspect someone will at least attempt a regicide?"

"What makes you think I'll let *you?*" she demanded. "You're my mate, too! We're a team, remember? You are not going into that by yourself. I have every reason to be there. I can *help.*"

Silas's lips turned down in an expression that, on anyone else, might have been a sympathetic frown. On him it was a lot more likely that he was simply trying to figure out the most efficient way to appease her and still get what he wanted.

Before he could argue his side, she charged ahead. "Listen, I'm friends with Margot. I don't care that Kaz is looking for me. She'll hear me out. I know you said it's not safe to contact her secretary, but I can go to her directly if we show up at the Tower. And what if something has happened to my staff, Silas? I've been cozying up with you for weeks thinking that they've just been getting on without me, but what if they're being held hostage or tortured or—"

"Baby," he drawled, stepping around her bag to gently grip her shoulders, "we *are* a team, but you need to understand something: you are irreplaceable. I'll never, *ever* risk you." Those familiar hands, so big and warm, glided up her neck to cup her cheeks. He pressed a featherlight kiss to her lips before murmuring, "You are powerful and capable, little goddess, but I'd rather let this coup happen than put you in harm's way. I'd watch the whole world burn if it meant keeping you safe. I'd even strike the match myself."

Still holding the file with one hand, she gave him a solid thump in the center of his chest with her other. "Don't try to sweet talk me, asshole. You said you wouldn't lock me away again. You tried it once and it didn't work, remember?"

"I didn't promise anything," he replied, unfazed. "All I recall is you saying you'd poison me if I tried it. I'm willing to take the risk if it means I never have to see you hurt again."

The shadows in a dark corner of the living room shivered. Goosebumps rose on Petra's arms as a niggling awareness drew her gaze to the puddle of shadow untouched by the soft glow of the floor lamp.

She still couldn't quite see what Silas did and she couldn't hear what Tal said, but she thought she could sense him there, like someone standing just off to the side, waiting to be acknowledged. The feeling was a visceral one, very different from the indistinct sensation she'd experienced before. Petra had the niggling suspicion that bonding had strengthened her connection to Silas and tied her to his brother, too.

Whatever was said, it clearly didn't go over well with Silas. He dropped his hands to her arms and swung his head around to glare at the dark corner. "You really want to take her side when I already owe you an ass-whooping for the last time?" He paused, apparently listening to the wraith's response, before he demanded, "If it were you, what would *you* do? I don't care how useful she might be. I'm not taking the fuckin' risk."

"How's this for a risk?" Petra pinched Silas's chin. Turning his head back around to face her, she warned, "If you leave without me, Silas Augustus Cuttcombe, so help me Glory, I'm going to find my own way back to San Francisco. I'll hitchhike if I have to."

A thunderous expression darkened his features. His shadows roiled, the threads of darkness writhing across the floor and around her throat like a pissed off rattlesnake. But Petra wasn't scared of him, nor his temper. Giving his jaw a tiny shake, she warned, "You can't keep me here. You can't lock me up. You can't do anything, demon, because you *know* that if you did, it'd hurt me. And I don't care what you believe you're capable of — you love me too fucking much for that. So either I go with you and Tal or I find my own ride. You choose."

Silas abruptly tipped his head to one side to nip the meat of her thumb with his sharp fangs. Yelping more out of surprise than any real pain, Petra withdrew her hand.

"I'm sincerely regretting not having that dungeon," he growled, snatching the file from her.

Her heart leapt. "Are you taking me with you or not?"

Somewhere down the long, tree-shrouded driveway — nowhere close to the house, since Silas said he only allowed clan near his den — a massive burst of magic tore through the air.

Every shelf in the house rattled and all the bottles in the drink cart clinked together before the air settled once more.

Their ride had arrived.

She held her breath as she waited for his response. Petra didn't want to fight him, and she seriously didn't want to have to find her own way across the continent, but she would. For her staff, for her friend, for the Protectorate as a whole, she'd do it. She'd *walk* if she had to.

Petra guessed that Silas must have seen some small sliver of her determination in her expression, because he bit out a curse before he ducked to give her one of his signature punishing kisses.

"I'm absolutely investing in a crop," he hissed against her lips. Her toes curled in her shoes. "You have no fuckin' respect for rules."

Petra patted his chest. "Whatever makes you feel better, sweetheart."

∼

"Shade."

Silas tipped his head in a nod. "Witch."

Adjusting the strap of her bag over his shoulder, Silas pushed her past the heavily glamoured man who waited for them at the end of the gravel driveway. Despite the thick, smoky glamour disguising his features, the witch hadn't bothered trying to hide his tattoos, nor the way he'd dressed to the nines. Sporting a rower's build and a general air of tightly restrained power, whoever it was Silas had wrangled into transporting them to San Francisco was no common gatekeeper for hire.

Wearing what looked like a luxury sweater with neat, slim-fitted slacks and a thin black leather belt, he looked entirely out of place against the wild backdrop of trees and underbrush that nearly consumed the narrow track of the driveway. Something about him seemed vaguely familiar, but no matter how hard she tried, she couldn't place where she might know him from.

If anything about the situation bothered him, however, she couldn't tell. His body language was relaxed and the line of his broad shoulders smooth. He'd tucked his hands in his pockets. She could make out a thick silver watch around his wrist — and more tattoos dotting the backs of his hands.

He was covered with them, and they weren't the decorative kind. They were *sigils*. The closer she peered, the more she could make out.

A sort of recognition rippled through her mind. It was the same kind she felt when she sensed Tal, and perhaps any being related to the shadows that now coiled around her throat.

She knew without needing to look closely that at least some of those sigils were Silas's work. It wasn't just the jagged, distinctive scrawl of them, but a particular hum of energy she recognized instinctively.

Gatekeepers, those few witches powerful enough to tear holes in space, often used sigils to help stabilize their abilities, but she'd never seen so many before. This man's tattoos peeked above the collar of his sweater and ran down the forearms he'd freed from his sleeves.

She couldn't make out his expression or see where his gaze was aimed, but she felt the weight of his attention when he turned it on her. "Nice to see you again, High Priestess. And all in one piece, too."

Petra blinked. "Have we met before?"

"I repaid one of my favors to Shade a few weeks ago," he explained, unruffled by the way Silas bared his fangs at him. "You wouldn't remember, since you were passed out at the time."

Oh. She'd figured an m-gate had been involved in their quick trip across the continent, but Petra hadn't thought too hard about who might have done it. Maybe she hadn't thought to question it because it was *Silas.* He was capable of anything. If he'd revealed some hidden ability to teleport, she wouldn't have been terribly surprised.

"And you're repaying another one by taking us back to San Francisco," Silas growled, "not by chatting up my mate."

The gatekeeper shrugged. "Can you blame me?"

Petra gave him a quelling look. "If you like your head where it's at, I wouldn't antagonize him."

"It's more fun this way," he replied mildly, like he didn't have a single worry in the world. That was remarkable, considering he stood not three feet away from a demon who really wouldn't think anything of killing him.

She was about to tell him how stupid that was, but when her gaze drifted down to the sigils on his neck, Petra stopped herself. A man whose power needed to be contained like *that*... Maybe he really didn't have anything to fear from Silas.

Still not smart, though.

Petra wouldn't put it past her mate to ruin his life in other, more creative ways.

"Open up the fuckin' gate," Silas ordered. He wrapped an arm around her shoulders and dragged her close, until she fit snugly under his arm.

The gatekeeper slowly inclined his head before he pulled his hands from his pockets. "You've gotten a lot more direct since you took a mate, Shade. I like it."

While he readied himself, Petra stretched onto her tiptoes to whisper in Silas's ear, "What about Tal?"

"He travels in his own way," he assured her. "He's probably already there, actually."

Petra figured as much, but it was nice to know. She couldn't speak to Tal — yet — but she felt a deep kinship with him. Not only because he was a fellow lonely soul who fell through the cracks, but because he'd been there for Silas when she couldn't.

Tal was Silas's family just as much as his parents or the rest of his clan was. Maybe even moreso, because he'd made the choice to stick by Silas even when he didn't have to. That meant he was her family now, too, and she intended to take care of him.

Magic began to gather around them. The finest strands of her hair stood up as an electrical charge hummed in her ears. It was like an approaching thunderstorm — all static and ozone and curiously heavy air in her lungs. The tang of metal came with it. The taste of blood dripped down the back of her throat with every breath.

Out of the corner of her eye, she watched the gatekeeper raise his tattooed hands. Light gathered before him, sparking into existence from nothing but the raw, blinding power he carried inside him. Heart lurching in her chest, she asked, "Do you think we can do this?"

Silas gazed at her for a beat. Tracing the line of her jaw with his thumb, he replied, "I think we can do anything, baby."

Chapter Fifty-Four

Petra had never consciously traveled by M-gate before, so feeling like she'd been squeezed through a pinhole and then extruded out the other side took a bit of adjusting to.

As soon as a solid surface reformed under her feet, she was forced to swallow a surge of nausea. Bizarrely, she got the sense that she'd stumbled and also that she hadn't moved at all. Her sense of self became malleable, as did her relationship with her various limbs, bits, and parts.

All she saw was white light, and even though she was pretty sure they'd come with her, she had to consciously check to assure herself that her eyeballs were where they ought to be.

She blinked hard to clear her vision. Real sensation, not just the impression of having been put through a potato ricer, returned to her limbs as she swung her gaze around. Cool air kissed her clammy skin. The ringing bell and rumble of a streetcar were somehow uncanny, like musical notes from another world.

They appeared to be standing in the center of a walled court-yard. Elegant wrought iron light fixtures cast a golden glow over manicured hedges and towering columns of flowering jasmine. It was dark in San Francisco, which was a jarring change from the warm morning light they'd left in Tennessee.

An oddly familiar burbling fountain stood proudly before her, the center of a brick circle. Lights danced alongside a shimmering reflection in the dark water. The gatekeeper stood by the fountain, his left arm lifted to check his watch like everything was normal and he hadn't just torn apart the fabric of space. For him it was, but the lack of ceremony was jarring.

It took her dazed mind a moment to place the lines, shapes, and muted colors that danced across the water's surface. The dark face of the cathedral, recognizable even at night, stretched across the ripples in a broken streak. A jolt of surprise ran through her at the sight.

A warm hand cupped the back of her neck. Silas loomed over her, demon eyes glowing with sinister light, and rumbled, "You okay?"

"I'm fine." *I think.* "Where are we? I thought we were going to your cabin, not across the street from the cathedral."

"This is my house. I don't have a lab in the cabin."

"Your *house?* What..." Petra turned on her heel, searching for a house. What she found was not that.

"It's a little gaudy," the gatekeeper quipped.

Silas glared. "Why are you still here?"

Gaudy wasn't the word she'd use, necessarily, but that didn't mean it wasn't fitting. The building that towered over her in all its three story, neoclassical glory was not a home. It was a *palace.* One she'd seen hundreds, if not thousands of times and admired wistfully in those rare moments when she didn't feel like she was running for her life.

"You own the *Flood mansion?*"

Silas shrugged. "It's a good location."

A garbled noise escaped her throat. It was all she could manage, since words were beyond her. A faint, nearly non-existent memory from months ago of Robert mentioning that the mansion across the street from the cathedral had been sold echoed in her mind. She recalled feeling a silly pang of disappointment at the news.

As if I could've ever afforded a place like that, she'd thought. *Not in this lifetime, and definitely not on a High Priestess's salary.*

She'd never stepped foot in the sprawling courtyard, let alone been inside, but she didn't need to. A glance was enough to determine that it was one of the most beautiful properties in the entire city.

When he said *it's a good location,* he had to mean the fact that it was directly across the street from the entrance to the cathedral. Which meant that he'd probably bought the mansion — the famous, outrageously expensive, historical, two-city-block-spanning home built by a silver baron before the near destruction of San Francisco in 1906 — sometime *before* they met.

When she whirled around again, she took the time to really look at the courtyard and beyond the tall fence. Sure enough, there it was: the cathedral and, more importantly, the clear path she walked every day as she went about her work.

"You've been watching me, haven't you?" she asked, already knowing the answer.

Silas gave her an odd look. "Of course I have."

Pressing a hand to the small of her back, he steered her back around and began to march her toward the front door. She let him lead her, too dazed to do much else, and only shook her head when he called over his shoulder, "Get out of here, witch. And if you tell anyone where we live, I'll kill you and everyone you've ever loved."

"You can try," the gatekeeper replied, as unruffled as ever. "Enjoy the holiday, Shade." A moment later, magic singed down her spine. A soundless explosion blew her hair around her shoulders and then the air cleared.

"Who was that?" she asked, trying to keep up with Silas's long strides.

He grunted. "A client who pays me extremely well to not ask any questions."

"So you don't know his name, but you trusted him enough to get us here?"

Silas shrugged. "He'd be dead without me, so I figured we'd probably be fine."

Petra shook her head. It took a lot of restraint to stop herself from asking more questions. His history with the gatekeeper wasn't important, and she knew that if she kept pushing, he'd only give her answers that spawned more questions.

Even with Silas hustling her along, it felt like it took ages to cross the expansive courtyard. When they reached the stone steps of the ornate entrance, a familiar hum of power sizzled over her skin. Silas's wards, once foreign and uncomfortable when they clung to her skin, now felt as comforting as his touch.

She knew for certain that she was safe within the bounds of Silas's magic, just as she knew that he'd never let anything happen to her when he held her in his arms.

"Tell me you didn't buy this house because of me," she demanded, watching him disarm the security system by the front door.

Silas pushed the door open and ushered her inside the palatial foyer. "I didn't buy this house because of you."

"Are you lying?"

"Yes."

"Silas!"

"What?" He looked around with a deep frown. "Do you not like it? I can get us another one."

Petra boggled at him even as he began to lead her down a dark hallway. "Do I *like* it? Silas, this is a palace! Of course I like it. But it's— it's so *much.*"

Without missing a beat, he replied, "It's exactly what you deserve."

"But—"

He stopped to give her a long, exasperated look. "Baby, I bought this house because I hated letting you out of my sight. If you think it's too big, we'll move. If you don't want to live in San Francisco at all, that's fine, too. I don't care where we live. The only thing that matters to me is you."

And then he kept walking. "Tal!" he called, keying in a code on a panel by a normal-looking door. "Get your ass in the lab!"

Petra stood there in the hall for a moment longer, rooted to the spot.

She wasn't sure why she was so stuck on this. They had much bigger, deadlier concerns. After all, she was now in a city where she was *maybe* a wanted criminal and directly across the street from a cathedral full of very, very deadly men looking to overthrow a government. Possibly. They were pretty sure.

And what they were about to do was perhaps not illegal, but absolutely toeing the ethical line. All things considered, losing her mind over Silas's extravagant house was a little silly. The minutes before dawn were dwindling. They didn't have *time* for her to worry about a house.

Except it wasn't just a house.

It was a home he'd bought specifically so he could be close to her before they'd so much as exchanged a word. She wondered if he even realized what a gift that was for her. Did he understand that if she was allowed to continue her work as High Priestess, she couldn't have picked a better spot to live with him?

It was a far cry from the one bedroom apartment she'd spent most of her childhood in, and it was on a completely different planet than the communal rooms she'd lived in at the children's home. Her accommodations in the Temple had seemed luxurious to her compared to those, but *this...*

There was nothing normal about Silas purchasing a house like this before they'd even met, but Petra had long dispensed with comparing him to any standard. Silas did what he wanted, when he wanted to do it. Usually he did it selfishly, too, and yet somehow he always seemed to do it for her, even if he didn't know it himself.

She placed a shaking hand on the gorgeous vintage wallpaper and released a breath. *Okay. Wow. This is your house now. There'll be time to let that sink in later. We've got shit to do.*

A shiver of awareness passed over her. Out of the corner of her eye, the deep shadows of the hall seemed to undulate. If she squinted, she thought there might have been the shape of a large man. Or maybe not. It was impossible for her to tell what was real and what was her brain filling in the blanks.

What she was certain of, however, was the feeling that came with Tal's presence. It was gentler than the wildness that followed Silas like a thunderstorm, but no less powerful.

Casting the shadows a nervous smile, she dryly noted, "He didn't tell me about the house."

She couldn't hear his response, of course, but she didn't need to when Silas poked his head out the door. "You can shove that up your ass, Tal. Now get in here before I decide actually *giving* you an ass isn't worth the trouble."

Of course, Tal had no eyes with which he could share a look with her, but Petra got the feeling they did so anyway.

She could feel him trailing after her as she stepped into the makeshift lab. It clearly hadn't been designed to be one, but Silas had made it work by setting up large stainless steel work tables, a computer bank, and what looked like a mobile clean room in the corner. It didn't hold a candle to his lab back in Tennessee, but it was still impressive.

What shocked her most, however, was the being laid out on the biggest table in the center of the room.

Petra knew intellectually that it was lifeless, but the closer she drew to it, the more wary she became. It looked like a sleeping giant lay strewn across the table — one hewn in metal and a strange black enamel material she'd never seen before. A cavernous chest piece held pride of place in the center, but it was the head that drew her gaze.

Sleek, black, with an articulated jaw and proud features, it boasted a set of short, spiky horns and an empty, fathomless gaze.

"Is that Tal?" she whispered, almost afraid to wake the giant.

"It will be." Silas drew the seat away from his desk and hunched over the projected keyboard, his focus honed on the windows that popped up on the computer screen.

A lump of emotion formed in her throat. Petra couldn't quite stop herself from glancing at the body as she passed it. When she looked at it, she didn't just see a shell. She saw the years — decades, even — of hard work and care Silas had put into its creation. She saw the love there, even if Silas would never admit to it.

And she saw the longing in those striking lines. The loneliness in the empty sockets of his eyes. The man there, just waiting to *live*.

It was more than just a shell or an experiment. It was the vessel for all Tal's hopes.

"Kaz is going to have a stroke," Silas muttered, sounding far too pleased with himself.

Petra forced herself to focus. Crossing the room, she stood by Silas's hip and picked at her thumbnail nervously. "Call him again."

Silas's fingers didn't pause their rapid movement over the keyboard. "I tried. He's not gonna answer and we're out of time."

"Then we should send a tip to Patrol." If her nerves got any worse, she was pretty sure she'd throw up. "This is really extreme, Silas. What if they find out it's you?"

"Oh, I'll tell him." Silas shot her a cheeky wink. "And technically this counts as telling Patrol, since it'll come with a message."

"But—"

"Baby," he drawled, "do you trust me?"

Petra exhaled slowly in an attempt to get her heart rate under control. "Of course I do."

Without looking, he reached over to pat her ass. "Then you've got to let me work."

She bit her tongue as the images on the screen changed from incomprehensible code to something more recognizable: a map of San Francisco.

"It won't all go down immediately," he explained. "It's a multi-step system with failsafes, so it'll take a while for everything to shut down. Vital services will stay up, but everything else —

private communication and everything not on back-up power —
will shut off for exactly one minute."

"And that'll trigger the security on the Tower?" Margot's face
appeared in her mind, smiling and unaware of what would
happen in a matter of minutes. Petra desperately wanted to call
her and warn her, but the chances of not being taken seriously
was too high. With the suspicion around Atria Le Roy's bounty
clouding things, they couldn't rely on her trusting Petra's word,
and if her call was sent to Margot's secretary instead, then there
was no way of knowing if the elf was in on the coup or not, too.

Silas warned her that the only thing worse than knowing there
were traitors in the Tower was the prospect of accidently alerting
them that their plot had been discovered — and the conspirators'
timeline moving up accordingly.

All they could do was act and hopefully live to beg for forgiveness after the fact.

"Yep," Silas answered, pressing *enter* with a flourish. "The
Tower and all government buildings are designed to go into room
by room lockdown in the event of a potential threat. Helpfully
for us, a suspicious failing of the grid counts. I found the exploit
for it a few years ago and figured it might come in handy, so I
never told Kaz."

"Will it happen while Margot and the sovereign are on their
way to the cathedral? If the grid goes down and an alert goes out,
their guards would take them somewhere safe, right?"

"Only if we get lucky," he replied, pushing away from the
desk. "But I doubt it. Getting through the failsafes takes time,
which we don't have. When do they normally show up for the
ceremony?"

Petra glanced at the time in the corner of the wide screen. Bile
churned in her empty stomach, scouring her insides. "In about
thirty minutes. Forty-five if they're running late."

Silas gave her a long, unhappy look. He didn't need to tell her
that it wasn't enough time. "If you stay here, the wards will keep
you safe, and Tal will be here guarding the computer just in case."

She wasn't built for intrigue, let alone life or death plots. Petra liked the ritual of her life. She enjoyed teaching her initiates, teasing Robert, and giving services. It became very clear to her then that she wanted nothing more than to spend her days running the cathedral and her nights with Silas in his ridiculously expensive house. They had a life to live, babies to make, and a dog to adopt. She didn't want to put herself on the line or save the day.

But there wasn't a chance on Burden's green Earth that she was staying home while Silas did it for her.

"Max died for this," she told him, straightening her spine. "And I didn't come this far to put my mate in danger while I sit here twiddling my thumbs."

Silas sucked in a breath through his teeth. "If I get even a *hint* that you're at risk, I'll do what I have to do to protect you. No warning. No hesitation. No mercy. Understood?"

Petra hooked a hand behind his neck and drew him down for a hard kiss. *Gods, I love this man.* Grabbing one of his hands, she placed it over her heart. "Understood. I'm not asking you to sit around and watch me get hurt again. I still want a wedding, remember?"

He slicked his tongue along the contour of her lower lip before he replied, "And two kids."

Her fingers shook when she smoothed them over his chest. His heart beat steadily under her palms, so unlike her thundering pulse, and knowing that he was mostly calm helped settle the worst of her nerves. Offering him a thin smile, she reminded him, "Don't forget the dog."

CHAPTER FIFTY-FIVE

IT WAS A LOT EASIER BREAKING INTO THE CATHEDRAL than Petra thought it would be, but then again, it wasn't like anyone expected her to return, seeing as it was an objectively stupid thing to do.

Silas kept reminding her of that as they hustled through alleys, tracing a familiar path to the secret entrance to her suite. Despite the pre-dawn hour, the city was already coming alive in ways it normally didn't. Red and gold paper decorated storefronts and banners with Glory's symbol dangled from street lights. A massive flower arrangement nearly eclipsed the grand door of the cathedral, and all throughout the Temple complex, lights were on.

A crowd had already begun to gather in the streets, making the use of her necklace's built-in glamour necessary.

Of all the days to sneak around the cathedral to theoretically stop a coup, the solstice was the worst possible one. By the time the sun touched the horizon, the streets would be overflowing with revelers, vendors selling drinks and sweet treats, and pilgrims making the two hour trek from the cathedral to San Francisco's highest point, Mount Davidson, where they'd dance and sing and eat until sunset.

Normally Petra loved the solstice. It certainly came with its own set of challenges, and was the day when everyone in the cathedral was stretched to their limits, but it was the one day of the year since Max's death when she'd allowed herself to simply enjoy life.

She loved the music that played throughout the city. She loved the sticky, fatty foods served from carts everywhere she turned. She loved how joyously people came into the cathedral, how much love they radiated as they prayed to the goddess.

And she especially loved watching her staff cut loose a little after sundown in the belltower. For one day of the year, she could smile and *mean* it.

But this solstice was different. Everything was different.

She ignored the sting of exhaustion in her eyes and the hunger pangs that came with the scent of cooking things on the breeze. Her body had to carry on with little more than adrenaline.

Silas squeezed in through the secret entrance first, his form fully cloaked in shadow. He gestured for her to wait outside. After a beat, she felt a gentle pulse around her throat and hurried in after him.

With the unassuming access door shut behind her, she whispered, "What if the cameras in the suite are working again?"

Clearly a little offended by the question, he answered, "I left signal jammers around before we got outta Dodge. I also infected their entire server and all connected tech with a virus that bricked the whole system. Unless they shopped around for new tech, we're fine."

She breathed out a short sigh of relief. "Of course you did."

It was so dark in the passageway that she nearly missed it when he stopped. If his shadows hadn't snagged her around the waist in time, she would have smashed her face into his back.

Something tapped the tip of her nose. "Stay."

Petra listened intently as he opened and then shut the secret door into the closet. Her heart raced, but not because he'd left her in the dark. She wasn't scared of that anymore. No, what made her palms sweat was having Silas out of sight, knowing that he could potentially walk into an ambush. There was little doubt he could take care of himself, but he was *hers,* and she hated the idea of not having his back.

Magic surged under her skin, ready to unleash holy calamity on anyone who'd dare touch him. *C'mon,* she urged, rocking from foot to foot as her nerves strung ever-tighter. *Please be okay.*

Luckily she only had a few moments to rile herself up before he threw open the door. "C'mon," he muttered, pushing the coats and her ceremonial gown out of her way.

She emerged into the dark sitting room of her suite and looked around. A wave of disorientation washed over her. It wasn't quite deja vu and it certainly wasn't nostalgia, but some mix of intense emotion that came with returning to a place that had been both prison and refuge.

For three years, the suite had been the only tenuous connection she maintained to Max. She'd imagined him sitting in one of the retro chairs, an ankle propped on his knee as he read the news after dawn service. She could see him pacing, arms tucked behind his back, as he practiced his sermon for the next day. For a while, she thought she could make out traces of his scent in the closet — cheap tobacco and even cheaper cologne.

But as she looked around the darkened room, Petra no longer saw his ghost. She didn't feel his presence. Maybe she never had. Maybe it had always been in her head. Now that she had more to live for, she didn't need to cling to the memory of a dead man to keep herself from drowning.

That wasn't what she wanted to believe, though. Petra chose to think that perhaps her *dyadya* had lingered until he knew she could handle herself, and that the cause he'd died for would continue. She chose to believe that the memory of his spirit that had saturated the air in the suite had at last crossed the river to join Grim in paradise.

Swallowing the lump of joy and grief and fear that clogged her throat, she turned to Silas and said, "I need to talk to Robert. He was going to be my stand-in for the ceremony, so he'll know when

Margot and the sovereign are supposed to arrive. He should know what's been going on since we left, too."

He had to, because there wasn't time to consider what might've happened to him if he wasn't around.

Of course, she knew Margot and Theodore's rough routine and had glanced at the details of this year's ceremony, but Petra also hadn't thought she'd be around to see it. So she'd left the vast majority of the planning and execution to her assistant, who would act as High Priest during her sabbatical — or whatever was to come of her after her meeting with Antonin.

Silas rolled his shoulders and stalked toward her. When he spoke in his shadow form, his voice was much deeper, almost a growl, and it conjured decadent, sweaty memories of the rut. "I need to figure out how many of the soldiers are around, so I'll pick him up on the way back. Go sit on your bed and wait for me."

Petra gave him a funny look. "Why the bed?"

"I warded the floor around it," he explained, like that was totally normal. Cupping her cheeks with hands tipped in jagged claws, he pressed a kiss to her lips that ended in a sharp bite. "Be good, baby. And don't open that door for anyone who isn't me."

"Are you sure you can move around without being seen?" she worried, fingers curling into his shirt.

"I've been doing this a while," he dryly reminded her. "Pretty sure I'll be all right. Who would expect a demon in Glory's Temple, anyway?"

He moved to leave, but Petra hung on for just a moment longer. Trying to summon her courage, she whispered, "Okay. Just... be safe. Please."

"Oh, I'll be very safe," he replied, gently breaking away to stride toward the door. "It's everyone else you should worry about."

⌀

Petra wasn't sure what she was supposed to do while she waited for Silas's return, so she sat on the bed and tried to be as quiet as possible. Time crawled by as she strained to hear any small sound, but there was nothing except the gradually increasing noise of the crowd outside.

Minutes stretched too far as she picked at her blankets. Her mind ran in every direction, working through all the possible ways their plan could go right or horrifically wrong.

She was just contemplating being very *not good* and hunting Silas down when the sound of familiar, rapid footsteps reached her.

Petra shot up from the bed, her heart jammed into her throat, as the door to her suite eased open. Rushing out of the bedroom and into the sitting area, she held her breath as she waited for a sign that it was Silas out there. That sign came not a moment later when the shadows around her throat pulsed twice.

Robert's dear face, pasty except for the blotches of red on his full cheeks, peered out from behind the door. "Your grace?"

Knowing he wouldn't be able to recognize her through the glamour, she whispered, "It's me, Robert."

Gasping, he threw himself inside and nearly slammed the door in Silas's face.

"Watch it," her mate growled, shoving her assistant farther into the room.

Robert hardly seemed to notice. He stumbled toward her, and Petra met him with arms extended. His crimson ceremonial robes fluttered with every hasty step.

"I'm so glad you're okay," he wheezed, gripping her hands, "but what are you *doing* here? It's not safe!"

"Don't worry about that. Tell me what's happened since I've been gone!" She shot Silas a questioning look, hoping he'd give her some good news and they would get to call everything off. "Are Antonin's soldiers still here?"

Silas leaned against the door and crossed his arms. He shook his monstrous head. "They've taken over a wing."

Dread washed over her. Searching Robert's expression, she asked, "What have they done? Did they hurt you? The initiates?"

Shaking his head vigorously, Robert answered, "Nothing! That's the bizarre thing. They haven't done *anything.*"

She hardly had time to feel any relief when the strangeness of his statement immediately put her on edge. "What do you mean?"

"I thought after the Protector, uh, disappeared and you left, they would ransack the place or try to find you or interrogate us or— But no. Nothing happened. They've just acted like nothing's wrong. All they do is watch us and patrol the grounds. I nearly had a heart attack when one of them asked me what time the ceremony would start yesterday. They hadn't said a word for weeks." He leaned in close to whisper, "Your grace, I don't even think they've noticed he's gone."

Uneasiness rolled down her spine. "How is that possible?"

"They're brainwashed, and no one's been around to change their instructions," Silas interjected with a shrug.

She and Robert turned to give him identical horrified looks.

Frowning, Silas waved a hand in front of his eyes. "You didn't notice? There's nothing going on in there. Every soldier I've seen has had the same look, and the one in the bathtub died when whatever it was keeping his brain on a leash hit my wards." He snapped his shadowed fingers. "Went out like that."

A chill ran down her spine. "And you never thought to mention this?"

"Never came up." Silas shrugged. "And I've been... distracted."

Petra opened her mouth to vehemently insist on a later discussion about what information he deemed important to disclose to her, but instead found herself asking, "*Bathtub?*"

Robert waved away her high-pitched question. "I took care of it, your grace. Don't worry."

"Took care of *what?* A body in a bathtub?" Petra covered her eyes. "Good gods, I've got to figure out how to get you a raise."

"The brainwashing makes sense," Robert gravely informed

Silas. "I'd heard rumors about something like that, but I always thought it was a scare tactic used to keep dissenters in line. And there've been stories about luminists being forcefully recruited for years. The more talented, the more likely they were to just disappear one day. The way they've acted, though... It's like they're toy soldiers just waiting for someone to play with them."

"That's exactly what they are," Silas replied, "and they're about to come to life."

Robert squeezed her arm reflexively. "Why? What's happening?"

"We think there might be a plot to depose the elves," she rushed to explain before Silas could say something that would send her assistant into a panic attack. "Something involving the Ardeo, Antonin, and someone else. That's why Antonin wanted to be here, Robert, and that's why he was interested in me."

Cold sweat broke out across her chest at the thought of the Protector having a small army of brainwashed soldiers. *No wonder he was so confident,* she realized. *He didn't have to worry about anyone questioning him or disloyalty. He probably would've turned me into one of them, too.*

Was that what he'd meant by changing her mind? The possibility made her want to kill him all over again. Blackmail, coercion, torture — all awful prospects, but none of it held a candle to stealing a person's *will.* Their mind. Their sense of self.

And Robert was right. Max had always warned her to keep her head down due to those same rumors. Luminists came in many types, but someone like Antonin would no doubt highly prize those who were extremely talented at weaving light into illusions or disappearing from sight altogether. Any number of nefarious things could be done by those hidden in plain sight.

If they didn't want to be part of the Ardeo, then he didn't have to ask twice. He could pluck the best and brightest from the Temple's ranks, add them to his little toy chest, and kill the humanity in them little by little until they were nothing but husks.

Petra was viciously glad the Protector was dead. She almost wished she could kill him again, for the sake of everyone he'd hurt.

"Depose the..." Robert's complexion went from ruddy to green in a heartbeat. "Oh, Glory. One of them asked about the service. I thought it was weird but I didn't— I didn't know. What should we do? We— we need to call someone. Tell them not to come to the dawn service!"

Using her most calming, authoritative voice, she explained, "We can't do that, Robert. We have evidence that something might happen at the Tower, too, and if that's the case, they can't stay there. They could be targets in their own home."

She doubted anyone could break through the blood wards guarding the family suite at the top of the Tower, but if Margot and Theodore were anywhere else... It was just too risky.

Looking like he might actually be sick, Robert asked, "Then what do we do? How do we stop them?"

As usual, her mate was quick with an answer. "I planned on killing them all."

"Silas!"

"What?" He gave her a long-suffering look. "They're all in one wing right now. If I locked the door and started a fire—"

"No."

"If I threw in a grenade—"

"Absolutely not!"

"Baby, if I just killed a *few*—"

Petra sliced her hand through the air. "No, *no*. We are not killing innocent men!"

"Are they innocent if they've done Vanderpoel's bidding for who knows how long?" He lifted his lip in disgust. "They *watched* you, remember?"

"If they were brainwashed, then it wasn't because they wanted to," she argued. "They could be locked inside their own minds right now, Silas, screaming for help. They could be begging us to stop this but completely unable to control their actions. We *can't.*"

"We don't know that all of them are brainwashed. Seems unlikely."

"We don't have time to make that call, and I'm not risking it. We don't play fast and loose with innocent lives, Silas. I don't want any more bloodshed in my damn cathedral." She gave him a hard look. "I'm not budging on this. We aren't killing a dozen men who have no control over their actions. Period."

Robert smoothed hands down his ceremonial robes. In a hoarse voice he asked, "Then what do we do? None of the staff know how to fight, and even if they did, they have *weapons,* your grace."

Petra scraped her hair back from her face and muttered, "No one is fighting. I'm not risking anyone's safety. We just need to knock them out of commission for a while. We have to get them out of the way, like—" She whirled on Robert and demanded, "Where are they now?"

"About to eat breakfast in the guest wing, I think," he answered, brows furrowing.

"Have they gotten their food yet?"

"No? I— I don't think so. The initiates were helping in the kitchen when your demon dragged me down the hall — which was very scary, by the way. Why?"

"Do you know if any of the staff takes sleeping pills? Sedatives of any kind, medicinal, recreational..." She waved her hand in a jerky circle. "Anything."

Comprehension slowly dawned on Robert's face. Near the door, a guffaw erupted from Silas.

"Yes, I do," Robert breathed.

Petra licked her dry lips and ordered, "Get them and deliver them to Yelizaveta. Tell her to give the soldiers one pill each in their food and then lock the door to the wing behind her."

Speaking in a whisper, he asked, "Just one?"

She shared a glance with Silas, who only lifted a shoulder. Attention swinging back to her assistant, she amended, "Best make it one and a half."

Chapter Fifty-Six

IT WAS PURE BAD LUCK THAT THIS YEAR, UNLIKE ALL that'd come before it, the sovereign couple chose to forgo their usual discreet entrance through the back of the cathedral. Normally Petra hosted them for a few minutes in her office. She'd hoped to catch them before they walked out in front of the packed crowd waiting for the solstice service, but Robert informed her that for reasons unknown to him, they would instead enter the cathedral at the start of the ceremony.

It was more bad luck that whenever she glanced at Silas, he shook his head, wordlessly confirming the fact that the grid hadn't gone down yet. She trusted that it *would*, but as the minutes ticked by, it became more and more likely that she would have to intercept Margot and the sovereign herself.

"You're *not* going out there," Silas flatly informed her as she released her glamour.

Already stripping out of her casual clothing fast enough to tear seams, she argued, "It'll be the easiest way to get to them."

"They're expecting Robert to give the service, not you. I'm not putting you up there when we don't know what they had planned. What if they planted a bomb?"

Petra tried to hide a shudder. *I didn't think of a bomb. Why didn't I think of a bomb?*

After all, Margot and Theodore Solbourne's relationship began with the bombing of her healing house. It would've been tragically ironic for their story to begin and end with a bomb. The dirty little secret that the public didn't know, and the main reason she'd been taken into Margot's confidence in the first place, was that the person who'd planted the bomb was Delilah Solbourne herself. The only reason Petra knew *that* was because she happened to be in the room when the truth came out, and she'd been very firmly sworn to secrecy by the sovereign himself.

But knowing how precious Antonin had been about using Glory's iconography to assert his importance, she doubted that he'd blow up her seat of power in the city, especially if he intended to utilize his connection to the Temple to win trust with people.

"If Antonin had planned to be here for this, then a bomb would've been stupid," she replied, fervently hoping she was right. "And if all of his soldiers are knocked out, we shouldn't have a problem. Performing the ceremony will give me a chance to talk to Margot up close."

She could see in his sour expression that he hated the idea, but he also had no good arguments against it. Unzipping the garment bag that held her wildly expensive ceremonial gown, she added, "You'll be there, so I know I'll be safe. You'd never let anything happen to me, right?"

Silas let out a slow exhale through his teeth. "Never."

"See? Everything will be fine."

She'd just shimmied into her ceremonial gown — a weighty confection of crimson velvet, seed pearls, shiny gold thread, and garnets — when Silas allowed Yelizaveta into her bedroom.

After a moment of shocked silence, the pale yellow dragon scurried across the room, a stream of words flying from her lips. Petra could hardly understand half of them. It took a precious minute before she could calm the initiate down enough to ask, "Did you do what Robert told you to?"

Yelizaveta's tail whipped back and forth behind her. "Yes, your grace, but I don't— what if they don't eat their breakfast?"

Petra shot Silas a panicked look. *First a bomb and now this. Why didn't I think of that?*

It was all too stressful. There were too many things that could go wrong. It seemed that every time she thought she knew what to do, there was some new factor added to the equation that she'd never considered.

"If they're real soldiers with strict orders and they eat their meals at the same time every day without fail, then I doubt they'd skip breakfast," Silas assured her.

"See?" Petra forced a smile. "I'm sure it'll work."

Yelizaveta's wide eyes darted between Petra and Silas. Shuffling half a step closer, she whispered, "Why do you have a demon with you? He's *terrifying.*"

Petra could feel Silas's gaze on her as the nervous dragon waited for her answer. Taking a deep breath, she gently clasped Yelizaveta's hands. There was no time to be nervous about how her staff would react to the news or to consider whether she'd still have a future in the Temple after this was all done, but she wasn't about to lie or brush it off.

No matter what happened next and no matter what anyone said, Silas was hers.

"He's my mate," she answered simply. "And once this is all over, we're going to get married."

Yelizaveta's eyes went impossibly wider. Her great, leathery wings mantled with surprise before they settled back against her spine. "You *Chose?*"

Knowing how seriously dragons took mating — or *Choosing* — Petra nodded firmly. "I did."

There was half a beat of stunned silence before she blurted, "Are you going to leave the Temple?"

Releasing Yelizaveta's hands with a small squeeze, Petra admitted, "I honestly don't know what's going to happen, but I'd like to stay."

A friendly chime echoed outside in the hallway. Silas tensed and turned toward the door. Hiking up her skirt, she shoved her feet into her heels and explained, "That's the warning bell. We have five minutes before the ceremony starts. Yelizaveta, I need you to run back to the initiate hall. I want you and all the other initiates to leave the grounds. Kitchen and custodial staff, too. I don't care what they're doing. Get them outside until *I* say it's safe to come back. Okay?"

The young dragon's complexion went ashen. "But your grace, we can't—"

"You can and you will," she interjected. "Above everything else, you keep yourself safe. If you run into any of the Protector's men, you have my permission to roast them and then fly away as fast as you can."

Yelizaveta's voice was barely a whisper when she replied, "This is very scary."

"It is," Petra replied, voice thick, "but that only means it's time to be brave. Never forget that we don't walk alone — and our goddess is not just love and sunshine. She's also scorched earth."

Pressing a kiss to Yelizaveta's clammy cheek, Petra tried not to let the initiate see her uncertainty. She didn't want to see fear in the dragon's eyes. She also didn't want to be right about any of this. A large part of her hoped that they were wrong, and they'd done all this for nothing.

The ceremony would go off without a hitch, there'd be no attack on the Tower, and she'd look like a paranoid fool.

But she didn't think so, and that meant she had to make sure her people got out.

Petra reluctantly released her initiate and hustled across the room. She grabbed Silas's shadowed hand and felt a little bit of her fear release when he immediately tangled their fingers together.

"We'll go out through my office," she explained, reaching for the door.

"Wait!"

They turned their heads to look at Yelizaveta, who'd spread her wings wide with agitation. Looking perfectly aghast, she exclaimed, "Your grace, you can't do the ceremony without your *crown.*"

Before Petra could summon a response or say it really didn't matter, the dragon had already darted into her bedroom to hunt for Glory's Crown, the heavy headdress she was forced to wear for important events.

Silas's lips curled into one of his knife-sharp smiles. "Do I finally get to see you in the sexy crown?"

Giving him a warning look, she primly informed him, "It's *ceremonial.*"

"Ah, baby, you know how much I love *ceremony,*" he replied, conjuring vivid memories of their time on the altar. His hungry gaze slid down her body. Glory wasn't particularly prudish, so most of Petra's ceremonial outfits were composed of plunging necklines and form fitting cut. Despite the stress of the situation, it was something he seemed to appreciate *very* much.

"When this is done, I want you to keep that dress on," he ordered. "I'm fucking you in that."

Face flushing, Petra murmured, "If we get everyone through this alive, I'll wear whatever you want me to."

Silas clicked his tongue. "A dangerous bargain."

Leaning in close, she whispered, "Couldn't be more dangerous than the other one I made with a demon, right?"

A pleased rumble rattled his chest. The shadows around her throat pulsed, and something hot zinged across the electric current of their bond.

Yelizaveta burst from the bedroom waving the gold crown in the air. Rushing over, she shoved it into Petra's hands. "Here!"

"Thank you, Yelizaveta. Now *go.*" She gently pushed her toward the door with one hand. The dragon looked like she desperately wanted to say more, but there was no time. "Remember what I said, okay?"

"Okay," she squeaked, hurrying out of the room.

Petra dared to lean a little bit into the hall to watch her go as she fumbled to get the crown on. Fashioned to look like a blazing sunrise bisected by the horizon, it was a regal but uncomfortably heavy thing she normally spent a long time fussing with in order to get it to sit *just* right.

She was still adjusting it when Silas took her hand and began to lead her to the service corridor that connected the residential buildings to the cathedral proper. He moved at a swift clip, and as they walked, his shadows gathered around around him and along the walls, spiderwebbing out until she doubted any tiny movement would go undiscovered by their seeking tendrils.

The corridor was blessedly deserted, however, and by the time they made it to her office, she was pretty sure she'd gotten the crown on straight.

The rumble of voices, hushed but undeniably excited, made the cathedral's sturdy concrete walls vibrate. The building energy and the urgency of what they had to do hummed in her bones. Her mind went blank. She didn't check her reflection in the mirror by her desk like she normally did before a service. She didn't feel the gauzy material of her veil as she plucked it from the hook on the wall and draped it over her crown and face. She didn't go over what she planned to say. She didn't think of anything except getting through the next few minutes, seconds even, and making it out onto the other side to finally, finally have a future worth fighting for.

Turning to Silas one last time before she pushed the door open, Petra lifted her veil and rose up onto her tiptoes for a hungry, lingering kiss.

"We'll make it," she promised him, steadied by the possessive grip of his hands on her waist and the comforting scent of thyme and musk that she couldn't live without.

Breathing in her ear, Silas gave her his own promise, "I won't let anyone take you from me."

"Good," she whispered back.

Pressing his forehead to her temple, he rasped, "The thing you said earlier. It's true."

"What thing?"

"That I love you too fuckin' much." His breath hitched. "I have to, right? Or this wouldn't feel like I was putting my heart in front of a firing squad. It wouldn't... it wouldn't be this *hard.*"

"You do," she answered, feeling too full and hollowed out all at once. "I know it because I feel the same way."

With one last kiss, she forced herself away. He hovered behind her, ready to slip out into the shadows. She could feel his tension in the air and could only imagine the force of will it took for him to let her do this, let alone the respect he must've had for her to take the risk. If he didn't respect her so much, she had no doubt that she'd be back in another closet, locked away while he dealt with things as he saw fit.

I hold the power, she thought, steeling her spine.

Forcing her hands to stop shaking, Petra opened the door and walked calmly down the short hallway. Her heels clicked a rhythmic beat on the red-brown tile floor.

Click-clack, click-clack. She focused on the sound, on Silas's presence, and touched the shadows around her throat as the low roar of the gathered worshippers grew louder and louder.

A discreet screen obstructed her view out into the belly of the beast, but she knew what she'd find: a thousand people crammed cheek to jowl, laden with offerings for the sacred fire that burned inside Glory's statue, and every last one of them eager to get their eyes on the sovereign couple.

Glory, she prayed, edging out from behind the screen to face the crowd, *please let this work.*

CHAPTER FIFTY-SEVEN

Silas knew he could live for a thousand years and he'd never, ever forget watching Petra ascend the dais. Someday his shadow might live on, separated from his flesh, and even that echo of his soul would remember her.

Crowned in gold, dripping in pearls and red gemstones, and draped in the nearly translucent white fabric of her veil, she appeared utterly ethereal in the dark alcove. Light hadn't yet touched the massive stained glass window behind the altar, leaving her illuminated by hundreds of flickering candles and her own magic. Fragrant smoke curled in the air, softening the edges of her until it appeared as though she emerged from a wispy fog.

Gasps of delight popped like bubbles in the suddenly still, fragrant air of the packed cathedral. Murmurs followed, hushed exclamations of surprise and speculation about Petra's unannounced return, but those soft waves of sound came to an abrupt stop when she took her place before the altar. Haunting music, slow and rich with low notes, flowed from red-robed musicians tucked into the smaller alcoves that lined the sides of the cathedral's main floor.

Silas sat in the front row, his seat stolen from a person who didn't have the guts to deny him when he demanded she move, his unblinking stare fixed on his mate. Although he appeared more human with his shadows forcefully tucked away, he didn't feel it. He hadn't been nervous about much until now. There were no real stakes for him when he didn't give a damn if the entire continent burned, but seeing her up there, exposed to a thousand strangers — any one of them a potential threat — made him want to rip his hair out by the roots.

Acid singed the back of his tongue as he tracked Petra's graceful movements and those of the senior acolytes arrayed around her. They were all swathed in veils and long crimson robes, but none of them matched the sheer resplendence of his mate. He thought he recognized all of them, or at least what he could make out beneath the fabric, but what if one was an impostor hiding a weapon?

Petra wasn't Vanderpoel and Red's target, but that hadn't stopped her from getting shot before.

Planning had never been his forte. He liked the excitement of jumping right into the thick of things with only his brain, his skills, and a goal in mind. Life was more fun when he had no idea if he'd live or die from one moment to the next, and the rewards for his efforts always felt a little bit more satisfying when he managed to come out on top.

But that was yet another thing that had to change. Sitting in the pews, watching Petra stand up there despite everything they knew might happen, made him question every decision he'd made. Allowing her to come, not simply taking care of the soldiers himself, leaving Tal at the house rather than having him do recon in the cathedral — all his choices flashed before his mind's eye as a ripple of excitement passed over the crowd.

There was so much more to think about now, too many precious things at risk, and the only reward he sought for his efforts these days was the life he wanted to build with his mate.

Every head turned around him as all eyes except his own were drawn to the entrance. Silas risked a glance at his watch and bit back a venomous curse. His program was still chipping away at the failsafes. At any moment the grid would go down and his message would be sent to all Patrol units in the greater San Francisco area, but every second that passed was torture.

I should've checked on the soldiers myself. I can't believe I let her go up there. What the fuck am I doing, letting this happen? Silas gripped the polished wood armrest of the pew, ready to say *fuck it* and drag Petra away from the altar, consequences be damned, when everyone around him climbed to their feet.

Not wanting his view of any threats obstructed, he did the same. His attention was caught by the entourage that flowed down the aisle. An almost fearful hush descended on the crowd as the Sovereign's Guard, dressed head to toe in black and their faces obscured by sleek helmets filled with smoky glamours, prowled ahead of the sovereign couple themselves.

They passed him on silent feet, their movements fluid and predatory, as they moved to take their places to the sides of the altar. None of them, as far as he could tell, spared him a glance, and if they were unsettled by Petra's unannounced appearance, it was impossible to tell.

The sovereign couple were a different matter.

Margot Goode, dressed in a white off-the-shoulder gown, wore the serene expression of a seasoned healer. With her pointed chin up and her almost fox-like features set in calm lines, she appeared perfectly relaxed as she held her husband's arm. In her free hand she held a ceremonial bundle of smooth, perfumed branches wrapped in silk cord. Adoring looks followed her every soft step down the aisle.

But for all that her expression remained placid, her lips fixed in a soft half-smile for the fawning crowd of worshippers, her copper-colored eyes were keen. They landed on Petra unerringly. They narrowed, and Silas could practically see the wheels turning in her mind as she tried to puzzle out why his mate would appear without warning.

Theodore Solbourne, on the other hand, was not so discreet.

Blue-skinned, with towering elvish height and radiating dominance, he swept his wife down the aisle at a swift, no nonsense clip. The sovereign's dark gaze swept over Petra and around the altar, his expression openly scrutinizing. His shoulders, made wider by the layers of his elvish suit and formal cape, went tight when he passed Silas's seat.

It was impossible for Theodore to recognize Silas's face. Not even Kaz knew what he looked like, and he deeply enjoyed finding new and creative ways to foil facial recognition technology. He'd never been in the same room as the sovereign before, and even if he had, he wouldn't have done so undisguised.

But for just a moment, the span of a heartbeat, when Theodore Solbourne locked eyes with Silas, it was like he *knew*.

Silas had never been to a solstice ceremony before, but he knew the basics of what was supposed to happen. There'd be talking, some offerings would be made, and songs sung as the sun rose. Then all the worshippers in the cathedral would stream toward the altar to give their own offerings in exchange for blessings. It was like any other dawn service, except everyone was dressed up in their best clothes, important people actually showed up, and there was a real possibility that someone would be assassinated.

When the sovereign couple walked up the short steps to the altar. They stood to one side but on equal footing as Petra. Just as the disk of the sun began to touch the stained glass window, she stepped forward and raised her hands in welcome.

Silas tensed. His skin felt too tight as he fought to restrain his shadows from bursting out and snatching her. Her magic buzzed like a livewire beneath his skin. Restless and paranoid, he swept his gaze from side to side, taking in all the adoring faces peering at her from the pews.

Her greeting carried through the cathedral without any assistance from microphones, amplified by the design of the building, but he barely heard it as his mind buzzed with worry. *She's too exposed,* he thought, sweat gathering under the collar of his shirt. His claws dug into the pew, splintering the wood, and the person closest to him leaned away.

The cathedral was too big. He wondered if the Sovereign's Guard took into account how many places there were to hide — from the columbarium across the main floor to the catwalks overhead and the numerous hideaways where shadows thrived.

Did they only see the crowd as a possible threat? With the way their heads slowly turned left and right but not up, he wouldn't have been surprised. Elves had a way of becoming complacent with their sense of power over their world. They thought because they had diamond claws and sharp noses and all the money they could want that they were invulnerable.

They got *comfortable* with the status quo, and even the best of them tended to think that they were the apex predators in the room. That was why Silas had always found it easy to get the upper hand on elvish targets. Maybe that was what Vanderpoel thought, too.

Or maybe it was because, for the first time in a very long time, the elves really *were* vulnerable.

Watching the way Theodore shifted slightly, putting Margot's much smaller body just a little behind his own, hit Silas as eerily familiar. He recognized the stance, the tightness around the elf's eyes, and the way his hand reached up almost unconsciously to brush the delicate fingers nestled in the curve of his elbow.

The elves had been a monolith for a long time, only making alliances and sharing power amongst themselves after their population nearly collapsed. Now they had prominent, visible weaknesses — the mates they'd begun to change all those rules for. They'd given the rest of the world a glimpse at their soft underbelly, and if Silas cared to take what the elves possessed, he wouldn't have hesitated to go for it.

As the sun cast its rays through the colored glass behind his own mate, Silas didn't breathe, didn't blink. He only saw his own vulnerability standing up there without him, and he realized that whatever Vanderpoel had planned, Theodore Solbourne likely wasn't his main target.

It was the exposed beating heart standing right beside him.

An elf didn't go down easy. There was good reason for their arrogance, after all. A single bolt shot wouldn't do it. One had to get in close and go for the throat or the belly to off them with any sort of efficiency.

Or, according to rapidly multiplying rumors, one simply had to take out their mates. He'd heard that an elf rarely lasted a few months without them, and some refused to wait even that long before joining their mates in the dirt.

And like demons and weres and dragons, an elf was rumored to do anything for their mate — even throw themselves into the line of fire.

Silas was so distracted by the revelation that he nearly missed it when Petra reached up to drape her veil over her crown, revealing her face to the eager crowd. His mind blanked. Silas wasn't sure why he hadn't thought she would show her face for the ceremony, other than perhaps to hide the fact that she hadn't had time to do her hair or makeup like she normally did.

And, he'd supposed, that she'd planned to keep her connection to him a secret.

Not everyone would know what it meant that a band of slowly moving shadow circled her throat, but enough would, and he suspected Robert was right that there would be backlash for it. It only took one person to know the truth for it to ripple out through the assembled crowd, and there had to be far more people than that.

Petra didn't flinch or try to adjust her veil to hide her neck. She didn't bat an eyelash when bursts of murmurs and several gasps erupted from the crowd. With her veil draped behind her, the plunging neckline of her gown hid absolutely nothing. His claim was there for all to see.

A swell of pride made it hard for him to draw breath when she said with perfect calm, "My siblings, welcome to a new day bathed in Glory's light. I'm so... *happy* to be here with you on this day when our goddess blesses us with so much warmth. Truly. I wouldn't be anywhere else."

She angled herself toward the sovereign couple. The elf's eyebrows were nearly in his hairline, and even Margot's serene expression had faltered with surprise. "And I am honored, as always, to be joined by our sovereigns. Their offering will be the first to light the fire as the sun rises."

Going by the deepening crinkle in Margot's brow and increasing volume of the crowd's murmurs, Silas figured this wasn't quite how things normally went. When Petra regally gestured for them to step with her up to the empty-eyed statue of the goddess, the couple did so with slight hesitation.

More whispers filled the air, and the mood shifted as heads came together, speculating about whatever it was she'd changed in the ceremony and the meaning of the thing around her throat. Someone nearby harshly whispered, *"...a demon? You can't be serious!"*

Making a mental note to deal with that person later, Silas leaned forward, his eyes narrowed as he tried to understand what she was doing. As soon as the couple separated to stand on either side of her, their backs to the crowd, he thought, *My clever witch.*

They knelt together on the red brocade cushions laid out before the statue. Only a handful of inches separated their shoulders as Margot slipped her bundle of branches into the opening at Glory's feet. A hush once more fell over the crowd as Petra reached inside. Flames erupted, filling the empty statue with heat and light. Those empty eyes began to glow, and the scent of the perfumed wood turning to sickly sweet smoke drifted over the heads of the worshippers.

Their heads bowed in what looked like prayer, but Silas was watching close enough to not be fooled. He didn't need to hear what Petra was saying, nor feel the rapid fluttering of her pulse beneath his shadow to know exactly what was going on.

She's warning them, he thought, relieved to realize that would likely be the end of the ceremony.

Margot's head turned toward Petra just a little too fast, and not a moment later, Theodore's spine went ramrod straight.

A flicker of movement in the deep shadows between candle sconces caught Silas's eye. *Si,* Tal called, his voice clear and urgent in his Silas's mind. *Get Petra off the dias— now!*

Before Silas could react, there was another flicker in the shadows, but this time there was no recognition, no spark of the magic that connected all demons to the shadows. There was just an odd sort of shimmer, something uncanny like the reflection of a mirror rather than a true image. Silas surged out of his seat, but it was too late.

Everything happened at once.

His watch began to vibrate on his wrist a heartbeat before a wail of sirens cut through the chorus of whispers in the cathedral. They were piercing, and echoed in an odd way that meant it wasn't just one set of alarms going off, but many across the city as it became clear that San Francisco's infrastructure was under attack.

Theodore had surged to his feet just as his guards sprang into action, ready to sweep the couple away from the crowd, when the shimmer in the corner flickered into the vague shape of a red-uniformed man.

Silas moved just as a bolt melted a hole in the great stained glass window behind the altar.

Another shot went wide, striking the front of Glory's statue, and the man disappeared as quickly as he'd flickered into existence. The guards and Theodore lunged for the women, but the sovereign had no way to stop a bolt shot. The way the guards moved defensively told Silas that they hadn't spotted the luminist in the shadows.

The second shot wasn't a good one, either, but plasma didn't need to hit someone directly to kill them — especially when the victim was the waifish sovereign's consort.

Silas's shadows were faster than his legs, and this time they didn't fail him. They spread from Petra's throat to cover her as she tackled Margot to the ground and huddled with her at the base of the statue. One of the guards rushed toward the witches but took a glancing blow to his shoulder and went down. It barely stopped him, however, as he and the sovereign grabbed the women and began to shove them off the dias.

Silas thrust aside panicked worshippers and vaulted over the altar. His transformation was instant. Shadows ripped their way out of him as higher thought slipped away. He only saw the odd, out of place flicker of light in the shadows and the unmistakable curl of smoke from the barrel of a bolt gun.

His mate was safe now. He stood between her and the attacker. Nothing would touch her. The panic behind him, the sovereign, the guards — nothing mattered except his prey.

Tal's shadows coiled around the attackers invisible legs, holding him in place as Silas descended on him like a cataclysm. Another shot went off, eerily echoing the confrontation with Antonin in the belltower. The shot went high and struck the steel rafters. Even though he couldn't see him or smell him through the fog of smoke and incense, Silas's shadows acted as sensory limbs.

There was no hiding from a demon in the dark.

Fueled by the drive to protect his mate, Silas heard nothing but the roar in his ears as he grasped the attacker's arm and twisted. The sound of bones snapping like green twigs didn't reach him, and neither did the clatter of the bolt gun hitting the stone floor of the alcove.

The attacker didn't scream, but his illusion flickered rapidly as he fought to focus through the pain. In the flashes Silas saw of him while he slashed with his claws, he discovered an unremarkable man with vacant eyes. His magic sputtered as he staggered under the onslaught of Silas's attack.

He'd clearly managed to escape being drugged. Some small, logical part of Silas wondered if he'd been staked out in the dark corner the whole time, unmoving, his scent covered by the heavy incense smoke. A luminist skilled at illusion could go entirely unseen, but he appeared to lack any offensive abilities. Being invisible wouldn't save him when his legs were bound with shadow and a demon descended on him.

The attacker slumped to the floor, his glassy eyes rolled back in his head, and Silas knelt behind him, shadowed hands gripping his jaw and the back of his head, ready to twist hard enough to pop the whole thing off his scrawny neck for *daring*—

"Sweetheart, no."

Silas looked up to find Petra knelt before him, her crown and veil discarded. His shadows had mostly retreated back to her neck, but they covered more than usual, as if they weren't about to let her go completely before the job was done.

She was ashen, but her expression was gentle when she fearlessly reached out to touch his monstrous hands. "Easy," she coaxed, petting him. "Easy now, sweetheart. He's out cold. No need to do anything more."

His bloody fingers flexed on the man's slack jaw, itching to twist, twist, *twist.*

Petra shuffled a little closer. Her fingertips skated across his knuckles, mapping them with the utmost care. "I know it's hard, but I need you to let him go."

"Why?" he demanded, staring into her precious, perfect face and seeing exactly what could've happened to her. *Again.*

Petra's gaze bounced around them. Her throat bobbed nervously, and Silas finally bothered to look beyond her, to the ring of black-clad guards who all had their weapons trained on him.

He tensed, lip curling away from his teeth, but Petra moved closer still. She peeled one of his hands off of the attacker's head and placed it over her heart. Blood smeared over the golden skin of her breast when she murmured, "Because you did your job and protected everyone. You don't need to do anything more."

"He would've killed you," he snarled. "That's un-fuckin'-acceptable."

"You're right, but he can't do that anymore, so you've got to hand him over to the guards now." Her heartbeat thundered beneath his hand. Petra paused, lips pursing, before she slowly added, "If you kill him next to my altar, Silas, I'll be *very* unhappy."

Damn.

A jolt of unpleasant feeling ran down his spine to settle in his gut. Logic came back online slowly. Silas glanced around at the guards, then back to his mate, as he considered just doing it. She'd be angry, but she wouldn't leave him. He was sure of that.

But he also realized that the guards saw him as a threat, and they probably wanted the would-be assassin alive. They might even shoot him to ensure that. It was what he would've done, and that meant refusing to give up his kill would once more put Petra in the line of fire.

And it'd make her unhappy. He disliked that most of all.

Shadows slowly retreating back into his body, Silas released the attacker. The man collapsed onto the floor with a wet thud. Blood pooled on the tile and fancy rug from his wounds, and his right arm was twisted in a gruesome angle, but he was breathing.

As soon as Silas let him go, Petra fisted her hands in his shirt and dragged him to her for an almost painfully tight embrace. "Thank you," she whispered into his sweaty neck. "Gods, I love you. Let's never do anything like this again, okay?"

Silas cupped the back of her head and pressed her closer. His gaze caught on a pair of shiny leather shoes and roved upward to find the sovereign staring back at him. His dark elvish eyes were wild.

"Never," Silas promised his mate. Gaze locked with Theodore's, he continued, "The next time someone tries to kill the sovereigns, they can call someone else for help."

Chapter Fifty-Eight

It went against everything in him to play nice, but Petra asked him sweetly, so Silas didn't shove his boot down Theodore Solbourne's throat when he put them under armed guard and transported them across the city for interrogation. He thought he was especially well behaved when he didn't reach for his knife after the sovereign broke up Petra and Margot's long, tight hug and whispered conversation.

"Right now she's a security risk," the sovereign informed his mate as he gently but firmly pulled her away from the embrace.

Margot, pale but otherwise apparently unruffled by the assassination attempt, raised her brows. Silas wasn't particularly surprised by how collected she seemed. In his experience, it took a lot more than a little danger to make a healer lose their cool. His father was the calmest person he'd ever met. What part of that was training and what was natural inclination, Silas would never know.

Margot's red hair had fallen out of its neat twist and there was some blood splatter on her white dress, but her voice was calm when she argued, "She saved our lives today, Theodore, and she's a friend. One of the few I have."

The air grew thick with the scent of ozone and magic as the

sovereign couple stared at one another. They appeared to be having some kind of telepathic conversation, if Silas had to guess, and he was instantly annoyed that he couldn't hear his own mate's thoughts.

It was impossible to know what was said, but after several seconds, Margot turned to give Petra's hands a squeeze. "I need to finish healing Aman," she explained. "We'll talk more when I'm done, okay? Everything is going to be all right."

The air was charged with suspicion as an entire battalion of guards ringed the walls and manned the doors, their gloved hands resting on the hilts of their weapons. Petra kept glancing at them, her wary gaze straying to their guns, but she managed a small smile for the sovereign's consort. "When you're done, I want to tell you everything. All of it."

Margot nodded. "We'll talk over tea." Turning to her husband, she reached up onto her tip-toes to press a kiss to his cheek. "Be nice, please."

Theodore made no promises as he guided his wife out of the room, accompanied by her own personal guards. Silas and Petra were instructed to sit on a low couch in the living room.

The sovereign came to stand before them, his cape and suit jacket discarded. His hard gaze zeroed in on Silas. The lines of his face were severe, and when he spoke, it was in a deep, pissed-off baritone. "Who the fuck are you?"

Silas didn't like his attitude. When he simply crossed his arms and stared at the sovereign, the tension in the room ratcheted up another notch.

Theodore narrowed his eyes and slid his attention to Petra, who sat stiffly beside Silas on the ridiculous velvet couch. Silas hoped they got blood all over it. "What about you, High Priestess? Do you have something to say?"

Silas tilted his head a bit to one side. A smile curved his lips. "Better be polite to my mate, rich boy."

Petra dropped a hand onto his thigh and squeezed hard. No

doubt she would have hissed a warning for him to stop while he was ahead, but Theodore beat her to it. "Watch it, demon."

"Or what?" Silas leaned forward to brace his elbows on his knees. There were tacky patches on his slacks where blood had begun to dry. It was already flaking off his claws and his face, despite Petra's hasty spit shine in the uncomfortable ride over, so he could only imagine what he looked like when he bared all his teeth in an approximation of a grin.

"I don't care what you think of me," he explained to the sovereign in what he considered a very pleasant tone, "but I care *very* much how you treat my mate — without whom, by the way, all you motherfuckers would be dead. I would've let you die and not lost a wink of sleep over it. I still wouldn't. So maybe *you* watch it. And your fuckin' tone."

Theodore put his hands on his hips and declared, "As of right now, you're a terrorist being held under suspicion of attacking the infrastructure of my city and playing a role in the attempted assassination of my *wife*, so if I were you, I wouldn't be so comfortable making threats."

"We are *not* making threats," Petra hastened to interject. She squeezed his thigh again, but Silas refused to be the first one to break eye contact. Sounding both stressed and exasperated, she continued, "Sovereign, please ignore him. He thrives on confrontation. It's basically his favorite pastime."

Appearing like he was rapidly losing whatever patience he'd hung onto, Theodore broke their staring contest to fix Petra with a furious look. "Then *you* explain what the fuck just happened. Last I checked, you were my wife's friend, but from where I'm sitting, it looks like you're an accomplice. You knew this was going to happen. I need to know how. Now."

"It looks bad," Petra agreed, fingers digging into Silas's thigh. "I totally get that, and I have a thousand things I need to explain to you and Margot about what's been going on, but to start, we found evidence that someone within the Temple was planning an attack basically two hours ago. I think. It was a long night and I've kind of lost track of time."

Silas frowned. He'd forgotten how long they'd been up. After the rut and their bonding, she had to be exhausted. He opened his mouth to tell her they didn't need to deal with this and they ought to just leave, but when she caught his eye, she shook her head and gave his thigh a reassuring pat.

"We rushed back to the city as soon as we realized that something might happen at the ceremony." Petra ran a trembling hand through her hair and let out a slow exhale. "I was hoping we were wrong, but we obviously weren't."

Theodore's expression was a stone wall. "And why didn't you get in contact with Patrol? Or try to tell my consort beforehand?"

Swallowing hard, she glanced around the room at the rigid, faceless guards. Her voice dropped to something just above a whisper when she answered, "We thought there might be a traitor inside the Tower and couldn't take the risk when I had no way of speaking to either of you directly. I only had her secretary's number, and what if she was in on it? Gods know something even worse could've happened. There just— there just wasn't time to figure anything else out."

There was a beat of silence. Theodore's expression didn't change one iota as he stared hard at Petra, taking her measure. Then, like the cracking of an ice sheet, something a little more human came through the severity.

Theodore sank stiffly onto the opposite couch. The air shifted. The change was nearly imperceptible, but every guard loosened their stance just enough to not appear as though they were ready to shoot on command.

"Fine. I believe you," he announced, sounding suddenly exhausted. In the span of a blink, he went from a man on the brink of violence to one deeply shaken. His blue skin was chalky and his eyes slightly too wide, like he was going into shock — or might throw up on his tacky carpet.

Theodore fisted his hands between his knees. The line of his shoulders rounded ever-so-slightly when he peered at Petra from beneath his brows. "Tell me what's going on. The whole story."

Sitting up slowly, like she had to will some steel back into her spine, Petra answered, "When we first met, I... Well, I came to San Francisco to solve Maximilian Dooraker's murder. He was my uncle." She blinked hard and something tender in his chest squeezed.

Acting on instinct, Silas wrapped an arm around her shoulders and dragged her into his side. She pressed her hand to his heart. Slowly, the tension in her muscles loosened. "I believed that he was killed when he confronted a man named Antonin Vanderpoel. I didn't know what for or why, but I knew that was what he'd planned the last time I spoke to him. Just before he was announced dead and cremated with no investigation, no ceremony, no... No nothing."

"Antonin Vanderpoel?" Theodore's brow furrowed. "Why do I know that name?"

"He's the Protector of the Gloriae," she answered. "Or he *was.*"

The elf's heavy brows rose. "Was?"

Brushing self-consciously at the bloody handprint on her chest, she answered, "He shot me a few weeks ago. He's dead now."

Theodore's gaze wandered back to Silas, who offered him a glib smile. The sovereign's frown deepened. "Is that why you disappeared?"

"Technically I did announce I was going on sabbatical," she hedged, "but yes. I was injured, so my mate took me somewhere safe to recover. Honestly, I thought that was the end of things. I figured if Antonin was dead, then..." She waved a hand in the air. "But obviously that was naive."

Turning to Silas, she murmured, "Do you have the file on you still?"

After a quick pat of his slacks, he discovered the folded up and slightly blood stained file. Petra passed it to the sovereign, who wrinkled his nose when he gingerly accepted it. "Antonin was in charge of intelligence for the Temple. He collected blackmail on just about everyone you can imagine, and we took almost all of it with us when we left," she explained. "He was also head of the Ardeo, which we believe he and another person were using as their personal army."

Still holding the bedraggled file with the very tips of his claws, Theodore scoffed, "The Ardeo hasn't—"

"Yeah, I thought so, too," Silas interrupted, just for fun. "But you're wrong."

Theodore scowled, but before he could tell Silas to shut his mouth, Petra jumped in to explain, "I don't believe it's what you're thinking, Sovereign. It's not the massive, kitted out army the Temple used to have. It's more like— It's more like a shadow squad."

Every elf in the room tensed. Sitting up straight, Theodore demanded, "Explain."

"I don't mean to offend or bring up bad memories," Petra replied, holding up her hands, "but I'm not being hyperbolic. Your father had his shadow squad, who answered only to him and were used to collect intelligence, silence dissenters, and disappear people. That's the Ardeo we're talking about now. I think it's like your father's shadow squad, but on a much smaller scale. Antonin spent gods know how long using them to amass information and power, and when the time was right, we believe he intended to use his soldiers to stage a coup."

She nodded toward the file in the sovereign's rigid grip. Speaking in a gentler tone, she said, "He even had information on people close to you, Sovereign."

Theodore looked down at the file. His jaw hardened as he slowly peeled apart the wrinkled pages. His lashes obscured his gaze as he took in the contents of the file for several long seconds.

Carefully, he extracted the old black and white photograph of Sophie Goode and her sister from the file and held it to the light. One edge had been slightly stained, but it was otherwise mostly unharmed.

A single guard, utterly indistinguishable from the rest, peeled away from the wall behind the sovereign and bent to whisper something in his ear.

Speaking slowly and with his gaze still on the photograph, Theodore murmured, "Patrol just found a large group of men with weapons in one of the locked areas of the Tower." His eyes flicked upward. There was no softness in them, no mercy, when he finished, "You said there was a traitor working with Antonin. Who?"

"I... We didn't have time to dig more," Petra explained, looking relieved but also a little sick, "but there were mentions of elves and trips to the desert. Las Vegas, too. There was too much information for us to sort through so quickly, but we'll hand it all over to you and your people. Hopefully you can find the truth and you can figure out what to do with all the men roped into the coup."

Silas balked. "We *will?*"

"Yes," Petra replied, giving him a *look,* "because we're the good guys, remember?"

"They have all the soldiers in their custody," he argued, deeply vexed to be giving up the ace in their pocket. "We saved their lives and their territory. I don't see why we can't keep *some* insurance."

Somewhere in the sprawling apartment, a door opened and shut. Silas went on alert, but when none of the elves in the room appeared concerned — or more concerned than they already were — he didn't immediately reach for the knife in his boot.

He almost wished he had when a familiar green face appeared not a moment later.

Kaz, a hulking orc dressed in a beaten leather jacket and shit-kicker boots, came in like a hurricane. Stomping across the room to point a kohl-darkened finger at Silas, he demanded, "Are you fucking kidding me?"

"I tried to call you," Silas replied mildly.

"And when I didn't answer, you knocked out the *electrical grid?*"

Silas shrugged. "At least I left a note, right?"

Though they'd never been in the same room before, Silas didn't need to be familiar with Kaz's expressions specifically to recognize the look of a man who wanted to hit him. It happened frequently enough for him to know it on sight. He did think it was interesting, however, how very similar Kaz and Theodore's particular brand of that look was. If he didn't know better, he might've thought they were related.

"What did the note say?" Petra asked, though she didn't sound particularly eager to hear the answer.

"*Coup incoming. Answer your phone,*" Kaz told her, "signed, *S.*"

Rounding on Silas, Petra muttered, "Seriously? I thought you meant an explanation or a warning, not *that.*" Petra rubbed her eyes, but he could see the corners of her mouth twitching with an irrepressible smile. "You know what? That's my bad. I should've known better. Sorry, everyone."

Squinting at Kaz, Theodore asked, "Do you know this guy?"

Kaz ran his tongue over his teeth and glared at Silas for a moment longer before he answered, "This is Shade."

There was a weighty pause, then, "The *criminal?*"

"Allegedly," Silas clarified, deeply pleased by the renewed attention, "and if I was, I wouldn't be anymore. I happen to be engaged to a High Priestess now."

"That doesn't make you not a criminal," Kaz snapped.

"It does if you can never prove I did anything illegal."

Kaz leaned in close to hiss, "You knocked out our power grid."

"Only for a minute," Silas argued. "And the lockdown probably stopped an invasion of the Tower. So you're *welcome.*"

"What do you want?" Theodore demanded.

Petra frowned. "We don't want anything. We were just—"

"No offense, Priestess, but your mate here said he would've let us all die and not lost any sleep over it. You might not want anything in exchange for this, but forgive me if I don't believe *he* feels the same way."

Silas settled back into the uncomfortably stiff couch cushions with an easy smile. Propping his ankle on his knee, he rubbed soothing circles on the exposed skin of his mate's arm when he answered, "I want three things: first, to be given a full, blanket pardon for any alleged crimes in my past, no matter how heinous, negligent, or malicious they might've been. Second, permanent residency here in the city so I can live with my mate without having to constantly look over my shoulder. And third... a favor."

Both Kaz and Theodore hadn't looked tremendously pleased after his first two requests, but it was the third that really set them to scowling.

"What kind of favor?" Theodore asked, suspicion practically dripping from each word.

Silas offered him a benign smile. "The kind we can talk about later, when my mate has had some rest and a hot meal. She's had a tough day, what with all the saving you and your mate's lives out of the good of her heart."

Petra dipped her chin and muttered under her breath, "Laying it on a little thick, demon."

Across the marble-topped coffee table, the sovereign let out a long, frustrated sigh. "I can grant you the first two, but the third one has to come with conditions. I can't just—"

He was interrupted by the buzz of a cellphone. Kaz cursed and pulled it out of his pocket. His brows dropped into a deep furrow as he read whatever message he'd received.

Theodore opened his mouth, probably to ask what was going on, but Kaz barked, "Teddy, where's Margot?"

Theodore shot to his feet. "She's in the spare bedroom putting Aman's arm back together. What's wrong?"

Kaz looked up from his phone. The grim expression on his already brooding features sent a shiver of unease down Silas's spine. Instincts blaring, he sat up straight and reached for the knife in his boot.

"Because," Kaz answered, "you weren't the only leaders hit today."

EPILOGUE I

"WHAT CAN I DO?" SHE ASKED, ANXIOUS TO HELP.

"Nothing." Silas clicked something into place and then turned to adjust a dial on one of the machines. A pale blue liquid began to flow through clear tubing that snaked beneath the bottom edge of the chest piece. "You've already done everything I needed you to do, baby. Just sit back and watch."

Silas stood hunched over the table, his hands moving quickly doing gods' knew what. He appeared to be securing all Tal's limbs into their proper places, but there were so many tubes and wires and strange fluids pumping through the machines arrayed around the table that she couldn't be sure of anything.

"What if it doesn't work?" It seemed insensitive to ask when Tal was within hearing distance, but Petra had to know.

"Then no harm done. We'll just try again."

Petra picked her way around the tables to perch on a chair identical to the one he had in his lab in Tennessee. "You're sure it won't hurt him?"

"We've tried this several times before and it hasn't," Silas replied, gaze flicking her way. "The worst thing that's ever happened is he had to lay low for a couple weeks and recuperate."

There was a pause, then, begrudgingly, "He says thanks for the concern."

The lights in the lab were dim, so there were too many dark corners for her to guess where he might be. But she'd gotten pretty good at sensing him in the weeks since she and Silas had officially moved into the mansion, so she felt him there.

Speaking to Silas, she said, "Of course I'm concerned. He's your brother. That means he's mine, too."

Silas stilled. He turned his head ever-so-slightly to one side, to a corner of the room that was just a fraction darker than the rest, and murmured, "I know."

Petra strained to make out Tal's form in the shadows but couldn't quite manage it. "What'd he say?"

He cast her a lingering glance over his shoulder. "That we got lucky."

A lump formed in her throat. "Yeah, well, me too."

She'd never had a brother before, but no one had ever said she struggled to adapt to new circumstances. Petra didn't take any kind of family for granted, especially now, after everything. If he was Silas's brother, then he belonged to her, too, and she was nothing if not intensely loyal to her people.

And whether or not he admitted it, Petra knew it was important that his brother got to stand with him at their wedding.

He didn't have very many requests, since demons didn't put much stock in something as ephemeral as vows, but when they discussed eloping, he'd hesitated. Tal really had waited a long time to get his body back, Silas told her, and it seemed a little rude to not invite him to the wedding.

It was so casual, almost flippant, that she was pretty sure he believed he'd gotten away with admitting he *cared.* Of course he hadn't, because Silas was about as subtle as a bull in a china shop. She'd seen right through the act, and moreover, she agreed with him.

They couldn't get married without his brother there to witness it — in the flesh, such as it was.

Her mate's focus was perfect, his every movement fluid and precisely calculated as he buzzed around the table. Magic gradually built in the air as he worked. Petra's breathing deepened, her body falling into a meditative state as Silas channeled more and more of her power into his task.

She watched from under heavy-lidded eyes as he shut off the machines one by one. It was as if the air pressure in the room had increased, which simultaneously made her drowsy and invigorated as the sense that *something* was happening built and built.

Gradually, Silas cleared away everything except for the body on the table. It was whole now, its limbs connected in all the ways they should be, but it was lifeless, limp like the body of a dead giant.

Empty eyes stared at the ceiling, waiting.

The lights began to flicker, first intermittently, then with increasing frequency until, one by one, they began to go out. For just a moment she was taken back to the night she met Silas in The Broken Tooth, when she glimpsed him for the first time in the shadows between flickering lights. She'd been terrified then, but now his appearance in the darkness only filled her with relief.

"Everything is gonna be okay," she whispered to herself and to the men in the room, too, even if they were too distracted to hear it. She *willed* it, and she sent that will outward, into Glory's radiant ear.

When the magic in the air grew almost too thick to breathe comfortably, Silas, wreathed in darkness, circled around the table to stand by the head. He placed his palms down on either side of it and announced, "Let's do this, Tal."

It was too dark to see much of anything besides Silas's pale skin and glowing eyes. Not that it would've helped her understand what was going on any better if she *could* see. He'd given her the basics of how it would work and the warding techniques he'd modified to bind Tal to the biomechanical marvel on the table, but most of it was too high level for her.

For all intents and purposes, he'd explained, it was a real body.

It functioned with an artificial circulatory system, senses, and was, for better and worse, mortal. When Tal bound himself to it, Silas was nearly certain that he would be tying himself to the machine's lifetime. When the magic that powered it at last guttered out, so too would he. After that, they really weren't sure what would happen.

Despite its apparent fragility, Petra was astonished at what her mate had accomplished, and deeply humbled that she'd had some small part in seeing it come to fruition.

Sigils, unseen until that moment, blazed to life all around the table and bathed the body in a kaleidoscope of colors.

She had no doubt that they would have a fight on their hands when the truth of what Tal was came to light. People would be scared. Some would think it was blasphemous, a crime against the gods, necromancy, or a slap in the face of the natural order of things.

But at that moment, when her magic blazed a path from sigils to shadow to body, she *knew* it was a miracle. It was magic that flowed through the grooves and joints of Tal's new form. If there was such a thing as the divine, Petra could find no better proof of it than that.

Glory was the goddess of warmth and magic and sunlight, but she was the goddess of wildfires and wrath and rebirth, too. And when the empty eye sockets began to glow, something passed over the back of her neck — a warm, tender touch from a hand unseen.

There was one last flare, a controlled explosion of magic so intense Petra had to close her eyes and turn her head away instinctively.

Then it was over. Her ears rang. The stench of magic and blood and something like ozone permeated every breath.

When the spots cleared from her vision, Petra turned her head just in time to see Silas stagger away from the table. She rushed to him, heart pounding, and caught his arm before he stumbled into one of the machines. "Are you okay?"

Silas shook his head hard and blinked several times. The expression on his face was slack-jawed with awe. "Holy *shit.*"

Petra's hands fluttered around him uselessly. "Demon, are you okay? What's wrong? Did you get hurt?"

"I'm fine." A laugh exploded out of him. It had an edge to it, the kind of laugh one might let out after being pulled out of the way of a moving vehicle. Focusing on her, he gasped, "Good gods, Petra. Is that what it's like for you all the time?"

"What are you talking about?"

"Like you've got a supernova inside you. Like it could burn you alive."

Petra gave him a questioning look. "Isn't that what everyone's magic feels like?"

Silas stared at her like she'd grown a second head. "Having all that inside of you with nowhere to go— No wonder witches blow up. Using my magic isn't like that. I thought my cells were roasting one by one. I *never* want to try that again. As soon as the m-generator is running, we're calling in that favor."

"Well," she replied, "I don't think *blow up* is really accurate. And you are half demon, so—"

A metallic *clunk* interrupted her. Petra and Silas shared a wide-eyed glance for the span of a heartbeat before they both whirled around to stare at the table.

At some point the lights had come back on. They cast a soft yellow glow over the enormous form sitting up on the table. Two huge hands curled over the edges, one finger at a time, almost like he was practicing his grip.

Tal sat very still. There were no tiny motions that gave the subconscious indication of life — no movement of the chest with each breath, no twitching fingers, no blinking. He simply sat there, eyes blazing with an ever-shifting range of colored light, until he slowly, so very slowly, turned his head to peer at them.

"He—*llo,*" he whispered, synthetic lips forming the word with some difficulty.

Petra could scarcely breathe, but she still somehow whispered, "It worked. It really worked."

Silas shook himself and broke away from her. "Everything normal?" he demanded, voice pitched a little higher than usual, as he came to a stop at Tal's side. Silas's gaze swept over his brother's huge body, assessing his work like he hadn't just completely shattered the wall between life and death. "Can you move everything? How's the temperature?"

He can feel temperature? Petra's mind spun. She knew he'd said something about a synthetic nervous system and skin, but...

"It's... wa-rm," Tal replied. His voice was deep, kind of throaty in a way that reminded her of crooners from the 1950s. She wondered if Silas had made that, too, or if that was something Tal had brought with him. Petra couldn't even begin to guess how that would work.

The wraith slowly moved his hands away from the edges of the table and held them up to his eyes. Flexing his fingers in and out of fists, he added, "Hands work. Toes... also."

"Can you stand?"

"I... don't know."

"Let's find out." Silas held out his hand to his brother. Tal looked at it for a long time before he tentatively raised his own and clasped Silas's forearm.

Petra blinked back a wave of intense emotion as she watched her mate help Tal off the table. He didn't rush him or get impatient when the wraith took a moment to consider every small movement required. And when Tal's huge feet touched the ground, Silas held him steady, his own knees locked to take his brother's weight when at first his knees couldn't hold him.

The white sheet that had covered his groin slid away. Petra was glad neither men paid attention to her when she found herself balking at what was revealed. Hastily averting her gaze, she decided it wasn't appropriate to ask questions like *who decided to make it that big* and *did Silas have to hand-sculpt that?*

Really, she shouldn't have been surprised that he was fully

equipped. Silas told her that Tal wanted a body so badly because he wanted a second chance at finding a mate and having a family, so it stood to reason that he'd want the whole kit and caboodle.

Petra thought she could be forgiven, however, since she never could've expected the caboodle to be the size of a wiffle ball bat.

"How's your balance?" Silas asked, thankfully derailing her train of thought safely away from his brother's genitals.

Tal shifted slightly, testing it, before he answered, "Good."

"Test your resistance." Silas patted his chest. "Push."

He'd seemed large on the table, but standing, Tal was a behemoth. He dwarfed even Silas, who was a large man in his own right. When Tal pressed his palms against Silas's chest and pushed, her mate staggered back sharply before he caught himself. Her mate looked incredibly pleased when he declared, "You almost knocked me flat on my ass!"

Petra had no idea how Silas had managed to make Tal's face so human and inhuman at the same time, but he had. At rest, his features were a little too bold, his glowing eyes uncanny, but when he smiled, it was *real*.

Tal shook out his arms and began to move from foot to foot, obviously testing his limbs. He rolled his shoulders and paced a few steps. Each new movement seemed to bolster his confidence. Every stride was a little more graceful. In a matter of minutes, with a bit more testing and prodding from Silas, Tal moved naturally, with a straight spine and easy balance. Speech came easier, too.

"How do you feel?" Silas asked after about an hour of experimentation.

Tal ran his palms over his short horns and answered, "Good. Very good."

"Do you feel strong? Stable?"

"I feel like I could... take on Tem-pest himself."

Silas uncrossed his arms. A warning bell rang in her mind when he cocked an eyebrow and asked, "You strong enough to take a hit?"

Tal paused for a beat before he gravely answered, "Yes."

Those bells rang even louder. Speaking up for the first time since Tal sat up, Petra asked, "Silas, why are you asking him—"

Before she'd even finished the sentence, Silas's fist shot out to clock Tal clear across his cheek. His head whipped to the side, but he didn't rock backward like a normal person might have. He merely shook his head and lifted a hand to rub his jaw.

Aghast, Petra hurried over to get between them. Pushing on Silas's shoulders, she demanded, "What was *that* for? He's barely been here an hour!" Craning her neck to peek at Tal over her shoulder, she asked, "Are you okay?"

"He knows he earned that," Silas assured her with a roll of his eyes.

"For *what?*"

"For letting you get hurt," Tal answered, like it should have been obvious. He didn't even sound upset that Silas had punched him as hard as he could. And she knew he had, because the knuckles of his right hand were busted and bleeding. "You were my responsibility and I failed. This makes things square."

"He's lucky I don't want to ruin all my hard work," Silas muttered, drawing her closer with a hand on her waist, "or else I'd take a crowbar to one of his new knees."

"*Silas!*"

"What? I'm not gonna."

Petra wiggled out of his hold to stand back a bit, allowing her to glare at them both. "I can't believe I have to say this, but you should not settle scores with your loved ones with violence."

In any other circumstance, it would have been cute how they wore identical expressions of confusion.

"But it's more efficient," Tal argued.

"You literally just got a body back and he welcomed you with a punch to the face," she replied, exasperated.

He nodded. "If I were in his... place, I would have done worse."

Great, she thought, pinching the bridge of her nose, *there are two of them now.*

"Tal, come here."

He stepped closer cautiously, and when she waved him down, he hunched his massive shoulders until they were at eye-level. Ignoring Silas's rumbling growl, she clasped Tal's cool cheeks. The texture and give of his skin was almost normal. There was even a subtle heat to him that felt very human. The only thing that her brain couldn't account for was the layer of metal just beneath the soft flesh, and the smoothness of the skin that was normally broken up by tiny, nearly invisible hairs.

"There's a blessing we give to new babies. Do you know it?" she asked, staring into his glowing eyes. Up close, she was astonished to realize that they gave off a very faint kind of exhaust, like the magic that fueled him burned up the air when it escaped his eye sockets.

Tal gave a tiny nod of his head.

"You're not a baby, but I think it's still appropriate. Since Silas clearly has no idea how to welcome you back to corporeality, I'd like to bless you, if you're comfortable with that."

After a beat, he answered, "I would... be honored. Th-ank you."

Petra touched their foreheads together and closed her eyes. Magic tingled in her palms, warm and gentle, when she whispered, "The world was made in love and so were you. May the first siblings send you down a safe path. May Burden hold you. May Glory warm you. May Blight guide you. May Craft hear you. May Grim have mercy on you."

She pressed a kiss to his brow. "Welcome to the light, brother."

Epilogue II

An excerpt from the article "San Francisco Stands United: Sovereign Couple Attends Unprecedented Wedding Between Hero High Priestess and Demon" written by Elise Sasini for *The San Francisco Light*—

On July 20th, exactly one month to the day from the attempted assassination of Theodore Solbourne and Margot Goode at the solstice service, the sovereign couple returned to the scene of the crime for a much happier occasion: the marriage of High Priestess Petra Zaskodna and a demon named Silas Cuttcombe.

A massive crowd gathered around the perimeter of St. Emaine's as the couple exited their vehicle, heads held high, and entered the cathedral for the first time since that fateful day in June. In the days leading up to the ceremony, which was quietly announced to the public just a week before it was set to take place, there was speculation that the sovereign couple might not attend — and that protesters would.

As the UTA grapples with the events of the solstice, many have rallied around not only the sovereigns, but High Priestess

Zaskodna herself. In front of a packed cathedral, she and her fiancé were witnessed thwarting the assassination. An already beloved figure in the community, Zaskodna's star rose to near sainthood when footage of the event went live across the continent — a much needed ray of light during the dark days that have followed the simultaneous attacks on Sophie Goode and the Shifter Alliance headquarters, the disappearance of Isand Taevas Azdaja, and, tragically, the assassination of Queen Sigrid at her home in Boulder.

As the United Territories was rocked by the attacks perpetrated by a militant group hidden within Glory's Temple, many have come to see Zaskodna's actions as a heroic stand against conspirators within her own organization. While worshippers across the continent have turned their backs on the Temple — at least until the investigation into the conspiracy concludes — St. Emaine's has been packed every dawn and dusk.

The sovereign couple have already awarded her and her fiancé the highest honor for their service, the Sovereign's Hand, as well as announced their support of her maintaining her position as High Priestess of St. Emaine's.

In a statement released to the press a week after the solstice, the sovereign offered his support. "My consort and I owe our lives to High Priestess Zaskodna and her mate, who stood against the established order, followed their instincts, and chose to do the right thing even when it put them in grave danger. While we adjust to this new reality and forge a path through grief and anger, I cannot think of another person I would trust more in the position as San Francisco's High Priestess. She has our full support — and our eternal gratitude."

But not everyone can overlook the other revelation that came on the heels of Zaskodna's heroics. Not even a daring attempt to save the lives of the Elvish Protectorate's leaders can completely turn the heads of those who staunchly object to her relationship with a demon.

Little is known about Silas Cuttcombe besides the fact that he comes from the Cuttcombe clan, famous in certain circles for their small batch whiskey made in Tennessee. The clan turned up in force for the wedding, too, as a long line of vehicles pulled up to the doors of St. Emaine's to deliver a host of rowdy demons of all ages.

Though the calls for her resignation on the grounds of disrespect and even blasphemy were few, they were loud. When the wedding was announced, those calls grew in volume and were accompanied by a widely circulated plan to protest at the event itself.

Understandably, security was tight on the morning of the wedding. Patrol closed off all the roads within two blocks of the cathedral, and no one was allowed on the grounds without explicit permission. Helmeted guards stood in a ring around the cathedral itself, prepared for the worst.

But as noon neared, it became clear to everyone that those who came to show their support vastly outnumbered the protesters, whose signs were all but swallowed by the crush of people eager to catch a glimpse of the couple and their privileged guests.

The sovereigns were the last to arrive. They briefly greeted the crowd from the steps of the cathedral and were met with roaring approval. The city is clearly still riding the wave of relief that came hand in hand with the grim news of the other attacks that put Sophie Goode in critical condition and killed Queen Sigrid — as well as Taevas Azdaja, who many speculate might also be dead, though Draakonriik officials have flatly refused to give up the search for him. The wedding, it seems, became a much needed spot of cheer and camaraderie as the people celebrated in the streets.

The ceremony itself was a much quieter affair.

The Light was given exclusive access to the event, which was held in the main cathedral. Demons, Weres, acolytes, and elves sat in attendance as Zaskodna's second in command performed the ceremony. An unknown being identified only as the groom's brother stood as Cuttcombe's witness. The sovereign's consort, wearing a huge smile on her face, stood as the bride's witness. Margot Goode helped Zaskodna with her veil, and when it came time for the families to exchange gifts, she performed the familial duty with a lavish offering from the Solbourne vault.

Zaskodna wore a simple crimson gown and her groom wore a matching tie with a black on black suit. Cuttcombe, a handsome demon reportedly responsible for the recent anonymous purchase of the Flood mansion, cut an intimidating figure against the backdrop of the damaged stained glass window. The only adornment worn by the High Priestess, whose order is well known for their love of gold and opulence, was a simple gold necklace and the now-famous band of shadow around her throat — the mark of a demon's claim.

The ceremony was short, and the roar of the crowd could be heard through the towering walls of the cathedral throughout it. The couple didn't exchange personal vows, but Zaskodna did perform the branding part of the ritual herself. When the time came, Cuttcombe knelt before her and, to this reporter's discerning eye, didn't appear to blink once through the entire process. He then held the mirror for her when she branded herself between the brows with a traditional marriage sigil.

Family offerings were exchanged before the couple collected their ember from Glory's feet and were blessed by Zaskodna's grinning second in command. The couple then shared an enthusiastic kiss before their assembled loved ones, who cheered riotously in the pews.

Before the party moved to the banquet hall, this reporter was lucky enough to overhear the groom say, "Well, you're *really* never getting rid of me now."

To which High Priestess Zaskodna replied, "Sounds like a good deal to me."

THE END

Also by Abigail Kelly

Find all new releases, bonus chapters, and exclusive content on the Works by Abigail Patreon!

Fragile Beings: A New Protectorate Novella Collection

In the first volume of The New Protectorate Stories...

Fate can't be contained.

#376: A fey Changeling is rescued from captivity by a reluctant demon on a quest to find his fate. Of course Dom expects trouble, but he is

shocked to discover his fate is tied to an imprisoned fey woman. Charlotte's a kicking, spitting, hissing little Changeling — and she's his.

A dragon's kiss burns cold.

Astray: When Paloma Contreras, arrant scientist, accidentally dooms a rogue dragon to death, she'll do anything to save his life. If that means giving up the mountaintop she's called home her entire life, so be it. Too bad Artem Aždaja has no plans to steal her roost. He only wants one thing: *her.*

Desire fogs the mind.

Weathering: Elise Sasini, an intrepid reporter and weather witch, sets out to uncover the story of San Francisco's legendary sentient fog and gets a lot more than she bargained for. The mysterious elemental agrees to tell his story in exchange for a taste of the life — and the woman — he craves.

Three novellas. Three couples. One fractured world. Step into a magical near-future where love builds, breaks, and defies boundaries.

Available in Kindle Unlimited, ebook, and paperback!

EMPIRE: THE NEW PROTECTORATE STORIES: VOLUME TWO

Love blooms in the dark.

After a lifetime of service to the Amauri vampire family, retired assassin Harlan Bounds lives his life exactly as it pleases him – on his private estate, surrounded by beauty, and unbothered by the bloody politics of the criminal underworld he left behind. He doesn't need or want for anything... except, perhaps, the tantalizing witch hired to look after the acclaimed rose garden on his grounds.

Zia North has nursed a crush on the mysterious vampire that is her boss for nearly a year. They've never spoken, and she knows the rules by heart: never stay on Empire Estate's grounds after sundown and never, *ever* bother Mr. Bounds. There's no chance for her to fulfill her sensual fantasies, so what's the harm in indulging a crush that will never see the light of day – or the kiss of darkness?

It's all daydreams until she makes a mistake that finally brings her face to face with the intimidating vampire. Harlan's dark intensity draws her in, and Zia's light sparks a craving that can't be denied. Fantasy clashes with reality when his dangerous past threatens to bite them both, but not even the violent conflicts of the vampire syndicate can sever a bond forged in blood.

Available in Kindle Unlimited, ebook, and paperback!

STRIKE: THE NEW PROTECTORATE STORIES: VOLUME THREE

Passion is electric.

After a millennia of longing, Hele has finally gotten her chance to live. A lightning elemental with a voracious hunger for knowledge and experience, she takes to her new life with a gusto that surprises everyone she meets. After two years of learning how to navigate the world she's been thrust into, Hele is only missing one thing: love. She wants one particular dragon, but when he turns her away, she decides that life is too short to wait.

Vael has been a loyal soldier of the Draakonriik for a century. He's never wanted anything more than to serve his clan and his leader... until the day he snatches a beguiling elemental from the sky. For two torturous years, he's resisted the call of his Chosen, trying to give her a chance to fly before he claims her and hides her away in his nest.

But when Hele decides to set out on a quest to find a mate, that resolution goes up in smoke. His lovely elemental is about to learn a very valuable lesson: a dragon will do *anything* to win his Chosen.

Available in Kindle Unlimited, ebook, and paperback!

VITAL: THE NEW PROTECTORATE STORIES: VOLUME FOUR

There's power in connection.

Josephine Wyeth has only ever known the shadow of war. Sheltered by her father's secretive work, she exists as both prisoner and caretaker as the violence creeps ever-closer. Once powerless, now she is something else: a new being crafted by her father's cruel hands, proof of his genius and threat to all who meet her. She's desperate to escape, but with no friends and the horrors of war lurching toward them all, her future is bleak.

There's no hope — until the day she's thrown in a cell with her father's latest experiment.

Otto Beornson, a fierce shifter from the wilds of the Northern Territories, is the latest in a long line of victims captured from the front and shipped to her father's laboratory. He shouldn't be any different, but when they meet, their fates intertwine in a way no one could have expected. Standing on the brink of an abyss, their blazing connection is a lifeline.

He'll do anything to save her, even if that means giving up his soul. She'll do anything to free him, even if it means becoming the monster her father always hoped she'd be.

Available in Kindle Unlimited, ebook, and paperback!

Glossary

A full character directory and map can be found at Abigailkkelly.com

Places

United Territories and Allies: What we would consider the continental USA. A loose federation of sovereign states established after the Great War. The UTA capital is United Washington, in the Neutral Zone.

The Elvish Protectorate: Also known as the EVP. Stretches from Oregon to New Mexico. Capital city is San Francisco. Led by the elvish sovereign Theodore Thaddeus Solbourne and Margot Goode.

The Coven Collective: Also known as the Collective. Encompasses Washington state. Capital city is Seattle. Led by a large coalition of witch covens, with Sophie Goode acting as their leader.

The Orclind: Encompasses much of the Midwest. Led by the Iron

Chain, a close-knit government made up of orcish clans and Queen Sigrid Seagrim. Capital city is Boulder.

Shifter Alliance: Takes up a section of the midwest and all of the south. (Unfortunately includes Florida.) Run by a very, very loose alliance of shifter packs from three capital cities — Minneapolis, Oklahoma City, and Atlanta. Unofficial leader is Lee Seymour.

The Draakonriik: Also known as the 'Riik. The second smallest territory, it takes up all of the Great Lakes region and stretches to New York. Led by Taevas Aždaja, the *Isand* (ee-zand) of the dragon clans. Pronounced: *dra-kon-reek*

The Neutral Zone: Also known as the New Zone. Technically it is held by a coalition government consisting of representatives from the UTA, but in reality it is run by a syndicate of feuding vampire families. It is a small strip of land squeezed between the Draakonriik and the Shifter Alliance.

GODS

Light & Darkness: The primordial gods who created all the others. Also known as The Lovers and First Union. Both are generally represented as female.

Loft: God of the sky and creator of flying beings. Twin sibling to Tempest. They know no gender. Also known as the Boundless One.

Tempest: God of the ocean and creator of all water beings. Also known as the Hungry God and the god of love.

Burden: God of the Earth, creator of all beings who live within it — most notably the orcs. Husband of Glory.

Glory: Goddess of sunlight, magic, and creator of elves. Worshipped by witches for giving the gift of magic to humanity.

Blight: God of forested places and disease. He works in partnership with his daughter Grim and shares her dominion over demons and all reviled creatures.

Grim: Goddess of death. Known as the Merciful One and the Brilliant Lady. She is widely beloved.

Craft: God of change, newness, and messengers. Creator of humanity and viewed warily by non-worshippers as the Chaos Maker. They change their gender frequently, but generally is referred to using he/him pronouns.

TERMS

Alpha: a broad term used by many communities generally associated with a leader — either of a small family group, a pack, or even a territory.

Anchor: a vampire's mate. Anchors are carefully chosen and usually longterm-to-permanent arrangements, as they take considerable energy to make/become. A vampire must inject their venom into a host many times before their blood chemistry adjusts such that they become unsuitable for consumption by another vampire and their sleep cycle switches to a nocturnal pattern. At this point, they can can also produce/carry to term a vampiric child. Temporary anchors do exist, although they are relatively rare due to the intense withdrawal symptoms associated with ending the regular venom intake.

Arrant: someone born without m-paths, or the ability to channel and use magic.

Burnout: the colloquial name for the degenerative medical condition caused by excessive magic in humans. Over time magic can damage nerves and brain tissue, which will inevitably result in death if not treated with with development of a witchbond.

Change: an elvish term for a sudden shift into adulthood. This is marked by 5-14 days of "madness", usually triggered by some stressful event around the age of 16-18. The elvish body is flushed with hormones to the point where sudden growth, overwhelming hunger, and aggression take over. Viewed as an incredibly vulnerable time, only immediate kin are charged with the care of their loved ones — which includes isolating them, preventing harm to themselves/others, and feeding them. The change marks the second phase of an elf's life, when they are no longer coddled children but young adults who can accept challenges and family responsibilities. Formal adulthood is attained at 30.

Changeling: a term first used to refer to fey children fostered out to non-fey homes, now more widely used to mean any person raised by people who are not the same beings. *Ex:* A dragon couple raising a human child.

Chosen: the formal term for a dragon's mate. The act of finding a mate is called *Choosing,* and is considered sacred.

Consort: an elvish mate. A term used exclusively by elves to refer to someone they are biologically compelled to pair up with. This usually involves intense sexual attraction, but can vary from person to person.

Demon: a being with horns or antlers, pointed ears, and symbiotic shadows. They are generally considered to be some of, if not *the* toughest beings in the world, as their shadows can make them almost indestructible. They are also naturally extremely strong and durable. Demon clans tend to be extremely close-knit, partially due to the fact that the world at large is not wholly accepting of them and their mythological connection to the god Blight. Identifying mating features are utter devotion, heightened protectiveness, and the sharing of shadows. This is when a mate is "given" a piece of the demon's symbiotic shadow, which will then live on that person for the rest of their life.

Dragon: a person with a dual form. In their bipedal form, they have claw-tipped wings, horns, and a tail. In their quadrupedal form, they are roughly the size of a standard SUV and can fly at extremely high altitudes for weeks at a time. They come in a variety of extremely saturated colors that shift with the time of day (light to dark). They breathe cold blue fire and can see the Earth's magnetic field. Identifying mating feature is marked change in behavior, including the overwhelming urge to nest.

Elemental: a being created by a spontaneous magical eruption. They often take on the attributes of whatever weather they happen to be born into, *i.e.* a lightning storm might produce a lightning elemental, or a blizzard might make a snow elemental.

Empath: a person with the ability to feel and manipulate the emotions of others.

Elf: someone born with jewel-toned skin, claws, pointed ears, and four fangs. Very secretive and considered apex predators who require a strict hierarchy to function. Average height of 6-7ft. Identifying mating feature is the retraction of claws.

Fever: shifter mating imperative triggered by the "animal's" choosing of a mate. Marked by a perpetual near-shift — elevated body temperature, increased aggression, build-up of magic, and the compulsion to mark. A shifter displays their readiness to find a mate by creating a den.

Fey: a person with nearly vestigial, insect-like wings, small fangs, and claws. Usually live in large groups. Identifying mating feature is bioluminescence.

Foresight: the ability to see multiple possible futures. The average number is between 2-4, with the likelihood mental instability increasing with each subsequent possible future.

Great War: a conflict between the territories of the North American continent that began in 1817 and ended in 1917 with the signing of the Peace Charter, which established the United Territories and Allies of modern times.

Halfling: the elvish term for an elf with mixed heritage.

Healer: a person who possesses the ability to see into and heal bodies through touch.

Isand: the title of the leader of the Draakonriik. Pronounced *ee-zah-nd*

M- : M- is frequently used as shorthand to denote when something is infused or otherwise combined with a magical element.

Marriage Sigil: a custom symbol branded into the foreheads of spouses (pairs or multiples). Each one is unique and infused with a small amount of magic as a reminder of the power love holds. They are typically sought out by worshippers of Glory — mainly witches and arrants. Elves, though worshippers, don't usually take a marriage sigil when they find their consorts or form a unions with other elves.

Mate: a catchall term for a significant other. Used by many cultures, it has varying degrees of weight. To shifters, orcs, and demons, the word mate is synonymous with family, monogamy, and dependence. It is much more loosely used within arrant society, as well as amongst elves, who generally prefer the term *consort.*

Merfolk: a catch-all term referring to sentient beings who live in the ocean, lakes, or rivers. Due to the nature of the ocean and its inhabitants, classifying all beings individually is almost impossible, so a much broader term is used to refer to both mammalian and non-mammalian beings than would be used for those on land.

Met: acronym for *magically enhanced tech.* A branded home assistant that can do everything your Alexa can, as well as small, low-level magic to help around the house.

Metallurgic Inoculation: a vaccine given to all elves within hours of birth to make them immune to iron poisoning.

M-siphon: a containment device used to imprison a magical being and siphon off their magic. Highly illegal.

R-siphon: also known as *reverse siphon.* New technology that redistributes magic away from the siphon instead of into it.

M-lev: a play on *maglev,* meaning a high speed train that levitates using magnets. In this case, magnets *and* magic.

M-weather: magic weather. Very common, but can result in "clusters" or storms that wreak havoc if not properly contained. In rare circumstances, it can also produce a sapient being known as an *elemental.*

Orc: a person with green, gray, russet, or blue skin, two fangs, and claws. Widely renowned for their strength and beautiful voices.

Identifying mating feature is "the kohl", or altered, dark pigmentation of the hands and feet developed after meeting their mate.

Pixie: a small, winged creature with compound eyes with about the same level of intelligence as a rat. In the wild they live in trees and in burrows, but have adapted to living in walls, pipes, mailboxes, etc.

Pull: elvish mating imperative. A sudden hormonal shift caused by exposure to a compatible partner's pheromones, marked by the retraction of claws and volatile mood shifts. The pull is only "satisfied" when hormone binding occurs — the term for long term exposure to a mate, resulting in permanent biological dependence on their pheromones. This process increases fertility and often results in the conception of multiples. Lack of exposure to a mate can cause severe physical reactions (lack of appetite, muscle pain, headaches, insomnia) as well as the deterioration of mental stability.

Shifter: a person who can shift into an animal form. They can partially shift (changing only parts of their bodies at will) and often take on characteristics of their other half. Famous for their strength and tenacity, as well as their dual-voiced "shifter purr" which many people find deeply attractive. Usually found in packs.

Sigil: a symbol used to channel magic. Western countries use the alchemical alphabet formally codified in the 1800's, though many, many variations are used all over the world.

Sovereign: the title of the ruler of the Elvish Protectorate. It is capitalized when used in place of a name.

Turbo Virgin (c): Theodore Thaddeus Solbourne, Sovereign of the Elvish Protectorate and Head of the Solbourne Family.

Union: an elvish marriage. Usually done for financial, political, or procreational benefit. The parties involved are not fated or biologically compelled to be with one another, and might have many lovers or even a consort outside of their union.

Vampire: a person who drinks blood to survive and cannot go out in sunlight. Vampirism can only be "caught" with the exchange of fresh blood, and as of 2045 is much more widely spread through procreation. Vampires can only breed with their *anchors*. Identifying mating feature is marked change in behavior, including overwhelming desire and need for total isolation.

Ward: a magical barrier with varying levels of protection. A ward can be something as simple as a proximity alert — "someone walked into my garden" — or as complex as full on defense — "someone crossed the threshold and has now burst into flames". The severity of the ward depends on the complexity of the sigils used to create them, and wards can have many layers, each one with a unique purpose. Personal wards can also be used, such as in clothing or embedded into jewelry, though they tend to be expensive and difficult to foolproof.

Were: a person infected with the were virus, a much mutated strain of the vampirism virus, resulting in altered physiology and magical ability. They can be identified by their heterochromia, or different colored eyes. They are the newest magical race and viewed warily by the general public for a variety of earned and unearned reasons. Identifying mating feature is marked change in behavior, including highly increased territorial instinct and the urge to nest. Pronounced *ware.*

Witch: Humans with the ability to use magic, which is passed down genetically. A person needs to be born with m-paths (a unique nervous system) to use it, however, humans were not initially adapted to use magic safely. Geneticists believe they acquired the ability through interbreeding with other beings. This interbreeding resulted in many unique qualities, such as the massive variety of abilities, power levels, and unique skills known to select families. However, it is also responsible for "burnout", which is the degenerative neurological condition a witch with mid-to-high level power will experience if they do not share their magical load with another being via witchbond. Witches are classified from least to most powerful — brightling, brilliant, and gloriana.

Witchbond: a magical bond formed between a witch and another being. Due to the nature of magic and humanity's much more recent adaptation to it, witches of *brilliant* and *gloriana* power must form a bond with another being usually beginning around 150-200 years old. This bond filters magic through the other being, neutralizing its damaging effects and reducing the chances of burnout to almost none. This bond also gives a power boost to the partner. A witchbond is permanent and can only be severed if one of the partners dies, at which point the surviving partner can form a new bond. Though commonly associated with a romantic partner, a witchbond is not inherently romantic and can be shared with a friend, sibling, or (ill-advised) an enemy.

Wraith: sentient shadow beings not dissimilar to elementals. They can affect the world around them in small ways, but can only speak to a very small number of demons. They lack physical forms but those that fully develop have complete sentience, personalities, and desires.

PRONUNCIATION GUIDE FOR NAMES OF IMPORTANT CHARACTERS IN THIS BOOK

Petra Zaskodna: peh-trah zas-code-nah
  Silas Cuttcombe: si-lahs cut-cohm

About the Author

Abigail Kelly is a writer and illustrator of alternate histories, love stories, and women with drive. Her work is heavily influenced by both her modest family roots and her passion for history. Her favorite authors are Shirley Jackson, V. E. Schwab, Ursula K. Le Guin, Kresley Cole, Nalini Singh, and just about anyone who writes about the weird and wonderful.

She lives in San Francisco with her dog, Babs, who remains stubbornly illiterate.

Content warnings

Murder, graphic violence, guns, vomiting, parental death (past), brief mentions of parental alcoholism (past), in-universe religious themes, food insecurity, stalking, audio/visual surveillance, crime, arranged marriage, discussions of pregnancy, childhood homelessness, blackmail, government institutions for children, suggestions of high-functioning antisocial personality disorder, power dynamics, in-universe religious sacrilege, scent marking, possessive kink, loose D/S dynamics, breeding, rut, shadow play, and explicit sexual content.